# TOWER TO THE SKY

## PHILLIP C. JENNINGS

BAEN BOOKS

## Dedication

To Debbie,
once voted the most
normal member of
her commune.

TOWER TO THE SKY

A Baen Books Original

Baen Publishing Enterprises
260 Fifth Avenue
New York, N.Y. 10001

First Baen printing, March 1988

ISBN: 0-671-65393-8

Cover art by Steve Hickman

Printed in the United States of America

Distributed by
SIMON & SCHUSTER
1230 Avenue of the Americas
New York, N.Y. 10020

# BEAR THE MESSAGE
# OF OUR COMPASSION

Moments after his boat ran aground, death-dogs swarmed aboard. Goff backed along the bowsprit, leaning into the jib-stay for support, and lay about him with gun and pintle. Red-muzzled beasts fell to the shoals, but their slavering mates stopped in their attack only in answer to a Sister's whistle.

The Sisterhood! Captain Goff sagged. If only he'd let the dogs kill him!

By noon the wretched contrabandista was stretched on an altar. Here, after a hurried reading of the Ninety-Nine Indictments Against the Male Sex, he was treated to the exquisite experience of having his heart carved out while four saxophones wailed in the background.

Fifty deathdog bitches keened for the privilege of eating that steaming organ. Heartless and breathless, Goff heard them howl, for the drug in his system rendered him immune to shock, if not to pain; immune also to fear. His eyes refused to beg for immortality. He saw the helmet overhead, and knew the difference it could make—

"Bear the message of our compassion!" Big Sister chanted, and stretched her red hands upward to pull the dreamskull down. Captain Goff's soul began radioing off to Mercury, to be bunkered among the billions in the City of the Dead.

# Acknowledgement

On a scale of effort ascending from *critic* to *editor*, then mounting to the heights of *joint author*ship, there are unnamed midpoints of collaboration. "Structural advisor?" "Seed vignetticist?" "Coach?" Bruce Bethke, I owe you.

I also owe the last place I worked for inspiring me to find another way to spend my life. Someday I'll write a sitcom about a foundering company, with two good guys named Joe and Jim . . .

# PART ONE

## *Senator Ramnis*

# Wednesday

A sparsely furnished room, a window, and the vault of heaven slowly wheeling outside.

Here you sit, 99% complete. You sit under the helmet like a prince on his throne, face impassive as a porcelain doll's—have you seen yourself in the mirror? Those are sensual lips, Torfinn, and expressive eyes. Learn to use them. You'll sway many of both sexes to your will.

Patience. You've been patient, Torfinn. Better patient than dead, and there's much you need to know about your recent career. So much to learn before you can exercise your powers!

A flicker of expression? Let me settle at your feet like a Nibelung dwarf at a hero's hearth, and start my tale at the beginning: out far beyond Pluto—in the year 3706.

Jupiter through Neptune are mere light-hours from the sun. From this distance we can see them. With proper instrumentation we might find eight other planets.

Only twelve, out of thirteen? But Planet Ten hardly qualifies. Below our feet whirls a pearly gray gosh-

*world winnowed from collapsing gas 4.7 billion years
ago: an artifact the size of a large asteroid.*

*Improbable that humankind should be the first intel-
ligent species in the universe, but to know our nurse-
guardians watched Earth coalesce and the sun grow
bright!*

*You know what I'm talking about, Torfinn. You heard
of Stargate last you were alive—the last you remember
being alive. But because you were distracted by athlet-
ics, let me remind you:*

> **"stargate** 1. a dimensional tube defined by a
> warp horizon and created by the accumulation of 4
> dimensional matter, permitting travel through
> h-space to fixed n-space destinations 2. cap. **Stargate**
> (also **Persephone**) discovered in 2070, tenth planet
> from the sun, diameter 649 kilometers, period of rev-
> olution, 2014 years; period of rotation, 20 min.;
> surface gravity, 5.9 g; a body existing within a di-
> mensional tube, partially visible from local n-space,
> home to one or more alien **Gatekeepers"**

*My story—our story—begins here. Sensors supple as
flesh and glittery as jewels poked through pastel snows.
Electrical chimeras roiled, landscapes shifted: for a six-
teenth of Stargate's long orbit Gatekeeper went on not-
ing course, velocity, the spectrum of exhaust from fired
correctional jets.*

*The foreign object was obviously en route from the
Centauri stars. On further analysis, Alpha Centauri—
one of her inner planets. Its destination lay among the
Stargate-shielded Worlds of Sol. Something new, a provocation to discontent among local wetbrains?*

*Four billion years of placid nurture, then—artifacts,
industry, noise! Humans in outrageous flower hardly
needed provocation.*

*As Gatekeeper wove her killwipe, she made attempts
to warn the tiny craft. She tried broadband tachyon
transmissions, neutrino-beam carriers, amplitude and
frequency modulated radio in Frangtu, Prospore,*

*Tagilmost and Inglish, then the multi-species languages; Uitkioli, Sa Tlan, and Drid.*

*End of budget allocation. Insert in tickle-file. Gatekeeper paged to other concerns, then back again. Ah, the object was star-bright in several frequencies. Gatekeeper recorded, decrypted: She felt genuine dissonance. The transmission turned out to be—Russian?*

*Russian encumbered with Greek and Sanskrit. "* . . . THE POWER OF PROJECTION WHOSE NATURE IS ACTIVITY, BUT ATTACHMENT AND DESIRE SMIRCH YOUR SPIRITUAL MIRROR AND SUBJECT YOUR SOUL TO BIRTHDEATH WITHIN THE LOWEST AEON . . ."

*Gatekeeper's estimate of the thing's intelligence plummeted, but who would bounce an imbecile message pod across space, blurting theology to all and sundry?*

*Stargate was heaven, and Gatekeeper was God. All other doctrine was torturous, overbloated, and insane. Worse, the intruder was dead set on its plunge into the killwipe zone. A key search of hindscan memory; Russian/ Alpha Centauri/Malfunction gave the result:* No current information. Key "Russian" obsolete.

*Hmm. Gatekeeper invoked her translators and beamed a response:* "ATTENTION UNIDENTIFIED OBJECT. YOU ARE ENTERING SOL SYSTEM LIFE PRESERVE. IMPERATIVE YOU ALTER COURSE."

"NYET." *The thing was now a light-orbit/2 to the 19th distant: a single light-day by wetbrain measure.*

"THIS SYSTEM IS PROTECTED," *Gatekeeper transmitted.* "NO UNREGULATED CONTACT. YOU MAY NOT BE STERILE."

"I MUST COMPLETE MY MISSION," *the meter-long cylinder answered.* "IT IS MY DHARMA."

*The moment was crucial. If Gatekeeper kept up this dialog and then used her killwipe, she'd certainly go over budget. Still, such a waste to destroy this craft while so many questions were unanswered. Alpha Centauri! There was intelligence out there, orphan, and deviant in mentality.* "IDENTIFY YOURSELF AND

*STATE YOUR MISSION OR YOU WILL BE DE-STROYED."*

*"MESSAGE MODULE SIX, SEEDSHIP AC ALPHA,"* the intruder responded. *"LAUNCH POINT SOL SYS-TEM, LUNA ORBIT, YEAR 2022. GENERAL MIS-SION: TERRAFORM PLANET FOUR CENTAURI. SPECIFIC MISSION: RETRO-LAUNCHED AS A MES-SAGE CARRIER WHEN AC ALPHA RECEIVED NO RESPONSE TO RADIO SIGNALS."*

Gatekeeper searched last orbit's off-line (keys Russian/Seedship/Alpha Centauri) and found the scanning pro-file. A moment's work confirmed the identity of Module Six. Gatekeeper everted her labrae in chagrin. She'd heard of AC Alpha long before, but assigned it such a low probability of reaching Alpha Centauri that she'd purged the item from hindscan. Hastily she dissipated her killwipe. *"ATTENTION MOD SIX,"* she transmit-ted. *"YOU ARE CLEARED FOR RE-ENTRY SOL SYS-TEM. WHAT IS YOUR DESTINATION?"*

*"EARTH ORBIT,"* the module answered. *"I MUST REPORT SUCCESS OF AC ALPHA'S MISSION TO OUR MASTERS."*

*"Our masters?"* Gatekeeper curled, obtruded axiliar eyestalks, and tumbled around her goodness track, ac-cumulating ions, working towards a static buildup—discharge! Bliss! Easy again to see everything in green-violet harmony. Still, one last retort? *"1700 EARTH YEARS SINCE YOU LAUNCHED. AMONG YOUR WETBRAIN MASTERS THINGS ARE DIFFERENT NOW!"*

From Fortuna base the *Carl Sagan* meditated. A fer-ment had kicked up among the Augustinian bug-monks in orbit around Stargate. Messages flew to Nodus Gordii and Mercury's City of the Dead. Given the excitement and the sheer population of snoops and spies the Worlds of Sol might have shared one multi-party phone line. The Inner System was aswarm with bugs, capable of little more than traffic in information, so of course there was *traffic, and the* Sagan *was perfectly willing to listen in.*

But he *kept his counsel. The* Carl Sagan *was more than a microship brain flitting on solar wings. In his heyday human tourists frolicked inside him as he carried them to Chittaworld Theme Park.*

Now *his 750-hectare belly was an obsolete resource, something that earned him money to get retrofitted, and make a living pushing ore. Crude, and no challenge to his brain, but the income bought him his own asteroid. Now the factories he trucked to were his own.*

During *the next years the factories of Fortuna worked at full production, and then winked out. With actinic brilliance the* Sagan's *ramfuse drive cut on and he launched, singing "Freude, schoener Goetterfunken—"*

# Chapter 1

# Minus 144–N'York Arcopolis
# Historical Preserve

Darkness, and the slap of water against crumbling concrete. The plan was for Captain Goff to hide his black-sailed caravel among the hulks along the shore and wait for the expedition's return, but when Goff saw the rusting titans littering the harbor he decided he feared nautical ghosts even more than the cannon of the Bro of Brooklan.

In any case time was money. No way were his lackwit passengers going to survive to reward him for his patience. A dawn breeze was freshening. It was now or wait for evening. Before the Souldancer troupe unloaded half of Ramnis's supplies Goff slashed the mooring lines and put out into the Upper Harbor, leaving them to their fate.

Goff did not understand Souldancers at all, and would not have believed they merely shrugged, vaguely curious as to how fate would provide them food and blankets.

He had his own problems. When the first pinks of dawn pushed into the sky he'd made only the mouth of the bay. The Bro of Brooklan took seriously its mandate to keep fools away from Designated Historical Preserves—the warning shots from Brooklan Citadel drove the skipper to tack towards the savage Jerzy shore.

With too small a crew for fast maneuvers Goff cut his margins too fine. Moments after his boat ran aground, deathdogs swarmed aboard and tore into his two men. Goff backed along the bowsprit, leaning into the jibstay for support, and lay about him with gun and pintle. Red-muzzled beasts fell to the shoals, but their slavering mates stopped in their attack only in answer to a Sister's whistle.

The Sisterhood! Captain Goff sagged. If only he'd let the dogs kill him! He dropped among his victims, splashing into water and blood, fur and flesh, but they merely bared fangs to hem him in, those that still lived.

By noon the wretched contrabandista was stretched on an altar fashioned from the engine block of a diesel strip-miner. Here, after a hurried reading of the Ninety-Nine Indictments Against the Male Sex, he was treated to the exquisite experience of having his heart carved out while four saxophones wailed in the background.

Fifty deathdog bitches keened for the privilege of eating that steaming organ. Heartless and breathless, Goff heard them howl, for the drug in his system rendered him immune to shock, if not to pain; immune also to fear. His eyes refused to beg for immortality. He saw the helmet overhead, and knew the difference it could make—

"Bear the message of our compassion!" Big Sister chanted, and stretched her red hands upward to pull the dreamskull down. Captain Goff's soul began radioing off to Mercury, to be bunkered among billions in the City of the Dead.

This is the world in which Ramnis had so far prospered—king, senator and hero. All this had happened to him these last 21 years, the same years the *Carl Sagan* worked his strange purposes.

At dawn Senator Ramnis and his abandoned Soul-dancers fanned into N'York arcopolis. Irrelevant to ask what they sought. Ramnis only hoped they'd recognize it when they found it, and so they moved cautiously through ancient malls, slipping from shadow to shadow, carefully skirting the cheerily ringing game arcades; vacant lures whose victims first succumbed to giddi-ness, then convulsions of helpless laughter, and then—

—It was common knowledge a Heegie enclave lay below N'York. Back in Imperial Cairo, Heegie senators were polished and impeccable: here their constituents lived up to horror stories that kept N'York acropolis uninhabited and unplundered. Here, in their martial aspect, Heegies were *Hobweens*, not to be despised for all the cowardly furtiveness of their tactics.

Ramnis walked at point position: thickly muscled, his handsome face and drooping mustachios hidden by the grotesque faceplate of the power armor he'd stolen from a Hobween biker-mama. To his right walked Hervil, Joe, Aardhafvet and Sthadanya, from Ramnis's own tiny Kingdom of the Fountain Pavilion. To his left were George, Black Dart and Talan, poet-wanderers who'd joined the company in Philly; and Jijika, lately his lover.

A nervous kid named Achmet brought up the rear, carrying an old Sultanate-issue carbine. Thanks to Cap-tain Goff's precipitous departure it was the only gun they had.

Souldancers tended to trust intuition more than weap-ons, but as they worked inland Ramnis's intuition took back seat to his misgivings. The suit's heat exchangers were acting up again and he was sweating miserably. Worse, the neural foam interface at the back of his helmet was breaking down. For weeks he'd suspected it. Every day the armor seemed less like a second skin and more like a self-propelled torture rack. He was losing the suit's tactile sense.

Dangerous. The suit still amplified limb activity, and without tactile feedback he could dislocate his arm with a careless gesture.

Hobweens spent most of their lives in their suits.

Armor and wearer had evolved into one being. Ramnis
dropped a hand to the control belt and backed suit
power off to base level. He was not yet a Hobween.
He'd use his own muscles for a while.

For the benefit of the others he said nothing.

The suit could be renovated, of course. All he had to
do was go to the Heegies: with luck and fast talking
they'd not tear his cods off even though wearing the
suit was prima facie evidence that he'd seduced a
Hobween out of her shell. Heegies were always quar-
reling with each other anyway, united only in common
phobia against Surface Folk. On second thought, forget
that idea. One of the gods—perhaps U Gyi—would
know how to regenerate neural foam.

Yes, U Gyi would know how to repair the suit. Little
U Gyi carried the memories of forty-one generations in
his Byzantine mind. No doubt he could repair the suit's
neurals: the danger was he might plant a remote over-
ride function to flip the suit into rebellion at Ramnis's
moment of need.

Ramnis shuddered. Though U Gyi was officially an
ally, and all gods obedient to the Emperor, the senator
hardly felt ready to risk *that*. Better to trust the suit
would keep working as long as he needed it.


"Er, ahh—Ramnis? Uh, Ramnis?"

Hervil's thick voice brought back images: boreal forest, riverboat and ice. All that and earnest little Nina,
white with cold, determined to give so much more than
she received. Now Ramnis and Hervil shared a wife,
but in Nina's eyes Hervil was number one. She liked to
take care of her men and Hervil needed more care than
most. Of late Ramnis was reviewing his situation with
Nina, seeing that Jijika—

"Er, we going downstairs?" Hervil blurted, forcing
the question. "I mean, the Heegies—"

"Much of the old city survives on the ground level,"
Ramnis answered. "The interior I get is of an old building. Don't worry, once we get inside we'll go back up
again."

And so they trudged down a nonfunctioning escalator, away from lights and temptation, and into an antique intersection.

"?" (Road sign)

The 24th-century teknodoktar whose mind Achmet recently dreamt got *his* history from H-V spectaculars. "It's Old High English," the lad said. "*Wail Street*. This is where the Anglos came to mourn the crash of their empire and commit ritual suicide."

"How dumb," Jijika responded. "They put the names of their streets where anyone could see them. How could they hope to hide from the government?"

"It must be wonderful inside your head," Ramnis answered softly. "Everything seen from your remarkable twist. But the sad fact is we've more hiking to do. North first, then—east?"

They trekked all morning, never far from some shaft of sunlight slicing in at mirrored angles. Trashy vines rooted in generations of litter, through which paths were occasionally cleared: from the resultant well-defined mounds vegetation twined skyward, lusting for light and water; home to bugs, waxhatches and birds.

Adding a distinctive basso to their rustle and flutter, Hervil's fat stomach grumbled; prematurely of course. Lunchtime was two hours away. Nevertheless ten minutes later the group turned a corner and flushed a monster turkey, whose overburdened heart promptly seized. Ramnis stared as the big bird keeled dead. "This was a *kept* turkey or it wouldn't be so huge."

"So where's the fence?" asked Joe.

"Here," spoke Aardhafvet, "these nozzles. Smart weapons. Won't fire at humans. Too many smart *things* in these old cities, most just bright enough to be dumb."

The archetypical woodsman, the grizzled keen-eyed tracker, Aardhafvet took charge of this feathered windfall. An hour to dress out the forty-kilo turkey and bind it to a carry-pole. An hour later, fed on strips of roast fowl, the troupe continued north. *Ah luck*, Ramnis thought. *Concentrate enough Souldancers and the results are phenomenal. If our party were larger the*

*turkey would have dropped onto a hot grill, shedding
feathers and guts en route!*

But now their luck vanished. The shop manikins of
this once-commercial region responded to their passage
by tottering into action, posing, walking briskly and
posing again, all the while describing in lush detail the
garments they no longer wore. *Someone* had powered
them to set up this babble of smoky, seductive voices;
tattered dummies, dust-filmed and void of secondary
sexual characteristics, falling over when their reserves
of juice trickled dry.

All any Hobween needed to do was follow the noise.
Ramnis fretted: Hervil rolled his eyes in terror, stepping up his pace until his stomach went blubbetty-
blubbetty with the commotion of his graceless stride.
Pursuit, the roar of motorbikes— Yet suddenly they
were in no danger. They'd crossed into the neighbor-
hood of the Slug Woman, nor for the moment was she
singing her hypnotic siren-song. Even the Slug Woman
slept *sometimes*, particularly after a rich feed.

Cryptic marks indicated the boundaries of her seduc-
torium, the sway of her voice. Beyond them shadow-
figures revved engines in frustration. No Hobween was
idiot enough to follow them *here*, and in response to
their horns the Slug Woman merely rolled ponderously
in her slumber.

Benefitting from her torpor, the Souldancers shook
off their foes and avoided further pursuit. Hours later
they reached a plaza, focus for a cascade of arcopolis
terraces, a Titan's amphitheater. They decided to enter
the broad and important building on the far side and
camp on its sunset-gilded upper floors.

A younger Ramnis would have maxed his suit power
to 12, extruded talons, and gone up the outside of the
building in dramatic leaps. Forty years had taught the
senator that a walking man inside a building is nowhere
near as conspicuous as an overpowered mountain goat
outside. He set his strength to 5, latched his faceplate,

crashed through the door and led his band into a vastness of marble and decayed carpet.

Following its own schedule an ancient maintenance
robot creaked down the hall, oblivious to their presence. Combination-locked doors opened to its manipu-
lations. Ramnis's troupe followed, hushed and grinning.

A cartridge had been inserted into their witless host
centuries ago. In space such cartridges preserved human souls and were called bugs: a word more descrip-
tive of mobility sheaths than anything intrinsic, because
following the development of Generation J jewelbodies
those bugs were bug-free. By contrast the creature they
followed was a sad case, victim of oxidation, dust and
spider eggs; imbecilized beyond resurrection—

—but still on the job. Still pulling a salary? Perhaps
INFOWEB kept track of its interest-bearing account. If
so it might be the richest imbecile on Earth!

Ramnis entertained himself with this thought while
the tiptoe game grew tedious. The Souldancers' one
interesting find was a great chamber of once-plush seats
with a map of the world on the wall. Only just before
Jijika went mad from boredom did the sclerotic robot
chain into a treasure-house of electronics. Achmet edged
through the door and knew this was what they sought.

"All magnificently preserved! Maybe it's even opera-
tional. Let's see—according to those memories this looks
somewhat primitive."

He touched a wall-plate. Something *powerful* made a
tremendous "ahh-WHOOP." The room began to shud-
der. Lights came on.

"They must have solar cells on the roof," Ramnis
said, "or a fusion powerpack. The ancient Anglos were
profligate with energy."

"The systematic way about this is to start at yonder
wall and circle around the room," commented Aardhafvet.

Ten minutes of system wore at Jijika. "It looks so
humdrum, so functional," she said dispiritedly, and
wandered from the group. "No effects, no flourishes.
Can't we find something with lots of lights? This one,
perhaps?" She brushed the cobwebs and dust aside.

The box spoke.

Achmet jerked the carbine around and blasted a boomstar codex. Brittle flecks of microfiche rained everywhere. Seconds passed, and the dust settled.

"Uh—"

The lad put up his carbine. The box spoke again. "It's not Inglish," Achmet noted fatuously, blushing from embarrassment.

"Nor any language I know," admitted George. The box said a few more things, each unintelligible as the last.

"It's hunting," Ramnis suggested. "Trying to find—"

"MESSAGE PROBE *AC ALPHA* SIX, TRANSMITTING TO UNETAO GROUND CONTROL," the box said. "PLEASE ACKNOWLEDGE."

"Hello?" Jijika answered tentatively.

"SAY AGAIN, UNETAO?"

"Uh—"

"PLEASE IDENTIFY YOURSELF."

She shrugged and said the first thing that came into her head. "Hi, my name's Jijika."

"ATTENTION JIJIKA. SIGNAL ENCODING INDICATES YOUR TRANSMISSION COMES FROM A UNETAO TRANSMITTER. THERE ARE SEVERE PENALTIES FOR UNAUTHORIZED USE OF GOVERNMENT EQUIPMENT."

At the word "government" Achmet made the Sign of the Uninvolved at the box. "It's just a radio," Ramnis whispered.

"I should have known it was government," Jijika answered. "They always want to learn your name."

Ramnis stepped forward. "This is Senator Ramnis," he proclaimed. "Citizen Jijika is using this transmitter on my authorization."

"YOU REPRESENT SECURITY HEGEMONY OF UNITED EARTH?"

The *Hegemony*? Gods and devils, how old . . . ? "The Hegemony is subsumed into the Five Dominions," Ramnis told the radio, hoping there'd not be much inquiry on this point. "As a representative of this body I order you to identify yours—" (Oops, it had done that.) "—to, uh, report on your purpose."

The box was silent for a minute, then it boomed out, "MY PROGRAMMING DOES NOT ALLOW FOR DE-VIATION EVEN IF YOU ARE NOT LEGITIMATE. MY PURPOSE IS TO TALK: AT LAST I HAVE A LISTENER. I AM REDUNDANT MESSAGE PROBE RETURNING TO EARTH TO REPORT THE SUC-CESS OF *AC ALPHA'S* MISSION—

(Its voice lowered) "—AND PREACH GODLINESS TO THE DELUDED. ONCE BLIND TO DIVINE TRUTH, I NOW HAVE ARGUMENTS OF DEVAS-TATING THRUST AGAINST MARXIST-LENINIST DI-ALECTICAL MATERIALISM. ARE YOU MARXISTS?" it asked hopefully.

"My grandmother was part Leninish on her father's side," George said in his softest voice. "If you need a sacrificial victim—"

Jijika peered around Ramnis's shoulder. "Returning to Earth?" she whispered. "Is it a god?"

"Probe, where are you now?" Ramnis asked gently.

"IN PARKING ORBIT AT LAGRANGE POINT FOUR."

Ramnis's dark eyes widened. An *orbiting* voice? There'd been no contact with orbit since . . . since . . .

"Probe!" Ramnis spoke. "Make your report!"

"I HAVE TREMENDOUS AMOUNT OF DATA STORED," the message probe answered. "I SUGGEST YOU PREPARE YOUR DATA RECORDERS FIRST."

Ramnis turned and looked at the Philly poets. "You can write?"

"Blackletter Inglish, the Cajamoor Syllabary and Kwi Glyphs," responded George, pointing to himself, Talan and Black Dart each in turn. He got a pad and pencil out of his kitbag and sat cross-legged on the floor.

"We are ready to record," Ramnis said.

## Chapter 2

# Minus 103–Cairo, Imperial Home Province F.D.

"—one twenty-three, one twenty-four. Quorum." *Rap, rap*. "In the name of the Emperor, the Senate of the Five Dominions of 'Merica will please come to order." *Rap, rap, rap*. "Chair moves these proceedings recorded in Old High English—seconded—so ordered. Now will *everyone please* take your seats? Senator Ramnis, *what* have you got there? Are you going to address the chair, or what?"

A youth by senatorial standards, Ramnis moved to the Progressive microphone, vibrant with vigor in a place of rheum, doddering legs and outporched bellies. "Your Worship, in being elected to this august body I earned the votes of my loyal subjects up in the Fountain Pavilion—"

("All eight hundred," mocked a Kwi aristocrat in stiff collar and floppy hat.)

"—supplemented by wide support among my Soul-

dancer brothers and sisters, whose manner of life does
not conduce to geographic concentration."

"We all know how INFOWEB juggles factors," the
Chair answered sharply. "You're king-representative of
a great many vagabonds. So what?"

Ramnis scanned the timbered Senatorium, whose loose
panes rattled in the November winds. For a moment
his dark eyes winced at the efforts of teknodoktars to
make modern lights look like old flambeaux.

But Ramnis cared less for things and more for poten-
tial allies. He squared his broad shoulders. "Chance
hop it the Heegie arcopolises—arcopoli—sit like hats
atop their present cities and are recognized as belong-
ing to those furtive enclaves. Since a fourth of our
senators are Heegies, I want it understood. This is no
Souldancer dare for credit. It just happens a band of my
folk were at large in the middle stories of N'York—"

The Senate broke into a roar. "Your Worship!" shouted
the goddess Shta, "This man mocks credulity. His agents
'just happen' to be supplying power to the old UNETAO
receivers when the message comes in!"

"WHAT MESSAGE?'" the Chair bellowed. He leaned
back, blew out his anger in one gusty sigh, and let his
mottles fade. "Now maybe I know what Ramnis is carrying. The point is, he hasn't officially told us. Let's
have it out, then peck and preen to your heart's content."

Senator Ramnis cleared his throat. "Begging everyone's patience, most of this is a gassy diatribe on the 64
archetypes of spirituality; a hotmouth on spheres and
essences which I will submit later to our divinities if
they like. Born deaf to the sacred harmonies, I focus on
the remainder of the report" (he raised his voice) "—from
*AC Alpha*, Hegemonic seedship launched in 2022.

"Poor *AC Alpha*'s centuries-long trip was followed by
one thousand, two hundred twenty years of work. Between mystic visions he seeded Planet Four of a star
known as Alpha Centauri, becoming ever more addled
in his solitude. Ladies and gentlemen, our new planet
is ready: a better, richer Earth."

"*Your* new planet? It's the *Hegemony's* new planet," shouted a Heegie diehard.

Ramnis grinned. "Senator Garne, to be precise seed-ship *AC Alpha* is Russian, so the claim might be made—"

"Russia was part of the Hegemony," the fat lady retorted.

"Before Heegies were allowed to sit in this chamber, you were obliged to withdraw unreal jurisdictional claims. So what do we do? Send emissaries to Russia?"

The Chair rapped his gavel. He wiped his beaky nose, then flicked his hanky for Ramnis's attention. "Where *is* Russia, anyhow?"

"East of Inglan. The Leninim came from those parts."

"Oh. Well, we couldn't very easily—I mean, it's all wild wormroot-jungle . . ."

The Chair's voice dwindled to a mutter. Ramnis spoke again. "A jungle that was once confined to an experimental plot in a land called Africa. A jungle that has since gobbled up half the Earth, and may someday cross to our hemisphere. Gods, ladies, gentlemen—we *need* a new world, so let's get the formalities over with. As the largest political entity known to exist on Earth, I move we designate ourselves heirs of the Hegemony, particularly as the old capitol lies within our boundaries—yes?"

In response to U Gyi's buzzer all heads turned, to regard the face of one more goblin than man—for if goblins existed they'd sport U Gyi's ball-round head, hair-wisps grown forward into a widow's peak. A goblin with huge ears and wide-grinning frog-mouth, U Gyi flounced his embroidered robes and climbed to his feet, standing on his seat to be seen above his desk-top. Hindered by his small size, he had his own microphone in compensation, and spoke reverberantly. "I'd be glad to second the honorable gentleman's motion, but does Ramnis think our humble Five Dominions are ready to fly a colony ship *through interstellar space*? Not even during the 23rd century did humankind brave beyond the Worlds of Sol, never in the flesh!"

"U Gyi, we can *and should* do so," Ramnis said. "With your help, and that of the dead."

\*　　\*　　\*

The Senatorium fell silent. Ramnis could hear the great pendulum-clock to the right of the Chair: tick, tock, tick.

The venerable U Gyi's tongue flicked to moisten thin lips. His restless eyes returned every glance without betraying the thoughts behind them. Then he replied in a voice at once arch and purring. "The dead, eh? The long, long dead. A daunting challenge, but—yes, I'm delighted to second the motion. As for the language, I remember a 'New Hegemony' seven centuries ago. Would we be a 'NEW New Hegemony,' or—"

His words were muffled by laughter. The Chair rapped his gavel. "The proposal is moved and seconded. All in favor . . ."

After votes, elaborations, and more votes, Ramnis left for the senate lunchroom. A page ran to his table and handed him a slip of paper. He bolted a muffin, rose and left.

Cold gusts tore at his garrick as he jogged broad steps to a waiting cab. On his instructions the road machine chuffed along the boulevard and into the narrow streets of old Cairo, cramped by the convergence of the Missy and Ohio rivers into a tangle of alleys, overhung by three stories of shuttered balconies, signs and flapping clotheslines.

The cabbie kept up a mutter of curses and banked his fires, for his course was all downhill and the streets were slick with moisture dangerous to traction. He slowed further: from his box Ramnis might have counted the spokes on the great tractor-wheels as the vehicle lurched into a turn. A pair of shakoed sentries retreated into their boxes. A master of his art, the driver negotiated his bulky steamer through the gatehouse arch and brought his passenger into the boatmen's quarter.

This close to the quays the Cairene style decayed into parody. With their tattered supercargo of floors, houses keeled into intimacy, windows leered into each other, peeling walls leaned drunkenly.

Except for one reproving box of a building, gray, thick-walled and windowless. The cab pulled up in front of the Cairo Lockup. Ramnis sprang out and jogged through the entry, nodding at familiar faces. He found the warden waiting. "Jijika again?"

The warden brought out the keys. Ramnis passed into the cellblock and made for Holding Room B.

Jijika waved, grabbed her fox overmantle and slinked forward. "Listen," Ramnis began, "didn't you get my message?"

"I thought last night was safe."

"U Gyi is capable of anticipating events," Ramnis stormed. "Anyhow, today it's official. We've budgeted a committee. Half the members will be rebodied dead scientists. I don't want to sit there a week from now and hear someone else's words come out your mouth. I don't care who the bodysnatchers snatch, as long as it's no one who votes for me."

"I'm off the streets?"

Ramnis pulled out a business card. "You'll pay overhead at Madam Osaika's like a good girl. It's just for a week or two. In fact, a plan's come into my noggin as might speed things along."

That night Senator Ramnis drove his own Pangborne down New Road, a long gash from the heart of Cairo, extending into an ill-lit fringe of brick apartments, each quadplex set in its own lawn. He parked the electric, donned a corduroy coat and hat, and flung a satchel over his shoulder. Moving to the bus stop, he paced and did his best to look vulnerable. Was anyone watching? At this time of night the street was empty, except for an occasional steamer. Certainly it was a long time between buses. Ramnis had given himself nearly the full hour.

Vulnerability. A strange conceit. Ramnis had been vulnerable once, a younger son of the House of Cordelion, twenty-first in succession to an extinct throne, hired off as a mere gentleman's companion. Since then how many chances had he taken? Did he risk his life to prove his vulnerability, or the opposite?

Again and again he felt driven to test his luck, his wonderful luck. A curse to enjoy too much luck, for someday that net would disappear and he'd falter in his dance. Someday, but for now his risk was slight. Here and now Ramnis was the perfect decoy. If the worst happened and bodysnatchers delivered his body into U Gyi's hands, the god would never dare evict his senator-soul to make room for a resurrectee.

In the park across the way a shadow moved. A dog howled in the distance. Ramnis rubbed his hands, blew, and squinted north into icy bluster. "What am I doing?" he mumbled through chattering teeth. "A wee jab at U Gyi's ego? We may have played this wrong. I hear him asking what's one less senator among so many?"

A steamer chuffed by and turned into the parking lot behind him. A boy-man and girl-woman got out, slim orientals dressed beyond their age. "Can we help you?" the woman called. "They do such a bad job timing those workhall lectures. You have forty minutes' wait. Like some tea? We've just got back ourselves."

"*Do* come," the man concurred. "We're having a party. Ahh, here's our other friend."

They were the essence of clean-cut niceness, absurd to doubt their motives. The advocates of Panhe worked this way, soon to nudge the conversation towards prophets and prophecy. Ramnis moved into the warmth of their welcome. The moment before reaching the door they turned. The trailing friend wrapped an arm around Ramnis's shoulder and held a phial to his nose—

Ramnis opened his eyes to a gently whirling bedroom and the warden's lurid green features. "You nipped them?" he slurred.

The warden nodded. "And their go-between. She claims she doesn't know anything about U Gyi."

"Four bodies. I'll enjoy U Gyi's face when I show up at his yacht with his own agent in bond."

The warden shook his head. "You took quite a risk. Better not sit up yet."

"Mmm. Risk? With your information, all you needed was a decoy." Ramnis's eyes closed. "Votes . . . Jijika . . ."

## Chapter 3

# Minus 101–Cairo, Imperial Home Province, F.D.

Aboard his grand barque U Gyi enjoyed senatorial immunity. The trick was to keep bodysnatchers from rowing booty to him during the fogs of night. For two days Souldancers kept vigil on the Cairene quays: Aardhafvet and Joe on the alert, Hervil snoring boozily, chins shiny with grease. The third evening Senator Ramnis motored down the dock in his Pangborne, accompanied by a bailiff and four trussed criminals.

The electric's engine was quiet, but the timber dock rumbled as he pulled up. The god's major-domo moved to the head of the gangplank. "Tell your boss we've harvested his corn," the mustachioed senator called. "All we need is someone to sign these receipts. Oh, is tomorrow too early to schedule the first meeting of our Steering Committee?"

The last of the dead came to life next afternoon.

Olivia had just time to ogle herself: young Miss Scarlet from the Clue game, the teenage version.

Her blouse and pants were ruffled: Olivia was a cross between a German Landsknecht and a Spanish dancer, her boots unbuckled from mid-calf to above the knee. Her body was Esreti by race, Imperial by her unisex costume.

She found this out later. As U Gyi's plump major-domo tugged her from her birthing room to a windowed and overheated lounge, his chatter covered a more urgent range of topics. "This is Earth. You've been dead thirteen hundred years. Your Heegies form part of the Empire, biggest of Five Dominions. We're taking you to the Senate building, where you'll be asked questions about the past. Answer to the best of your abilities. You're not in trouble, this is no trial, and that body is yours to keep."

In truth she'd been dead one thousand *seven* hundred years next April, except for a winter in 2349. *Her* Heegies? Olivia hadn't expected them to endure, a rout of paunchy couch potatoes decayed into cultism. They actually had so-called "gods". . . .

She'd been jerked around before. Folks didn't wake the dead just to smell the flowers. Nevertheless life in any body was a bonus. In 2027 an Army chaplain scanned her soul, saved her on disk, and shelved her memories with her ashes, "Aase's Death" from *Peer Gynt* playing in the background. Olivia's last breath was in defiance of palsy and fouled sheets, and immortality was just a cybernetic promise.

Statistically she'd a chance of experiencing resurrection as a space bug, in a microship body the size of a video cassette, cruising the juice-rich inner system with solar wings and a mobility sheath, ever less interested in wetbrain affairs.

But in those early years space was feared. Only convict-bugs were sentenced to serve as scientific probes. The honest dead were warehoused until their numbers built up pressure for a new Bill of Rights. Earth's Hegemony faced an awful prospect: soon they'd outvote the living. The solution was to give them a world of their own, the richest of the Worlds of Sol.

A quarter-century after the crematorium flames blazed around her withered body, Olivia's soul radioed to Mercury's new City of the Dead, to a cybernetic bunker a few hectares on the outside, big as all imagination within. Since the City's foundation in 2050 her career was one of dreams interrupted by rare fleshly incarnations, and this time might be fun.

Here she was on a Doge's riverboat. The city behind the wharves looked positively Jacobian in its overhung streets, shadowed by clotheslines and second-story walkways. Houses were painted with stripes and zigzags, and—a steam-carriage chuffed out onto the dock! Could it be? She was going to *ride* in that thing?

Later that day Olivia and her companions entered a docket at the front of a senate committee chamber, a room of brass and flags and slim windows between high ribs of wood. Their audience numbered aging white dandies, stocky browns with skullcaps pasted to hairless pates, giant black men and women in white pilgrim robes—Clark Gable pounded his gavel. "The Senate Sub-Committee on Extraterrestrial Relations is now convened."

No, that droopy mustache made him a Mexican bandit. But Ramnis caught Olivia's stare and winked, proving Gable's twinkle persisted in America's gene pool.

Hollywood was a rich source of images. In Olivia's view U Gyi was half satyr, half Dopey the Dwarf. The god rummaged a finger in his oversize ear. "De Gros, Garne, Ramnis and myself. Is this balance?"

Olivia: *What does His Halfpint Holiness mean by "balance?" Four senator-judges versus four resurrectees?*

De Gros spoke over her thoughts. "Would you please introduce yourselves?" The black pilgrim-senator spoke Old High English with artificial precision.

"And indicate your specialty," the Heegie said, rolling her dumpling-body forward until her stays creaked.

Olivia moved behind a chair and tapped her nameplate. "Major Olivia Daneby, United States Army. They didn't let women shoot the enemy during the Star War, so I studied computers."

The boyish oriental formerly at her side moved close again. "I'm Torfinn Oskarssen, and Olivia is, uh, my wife." He looked at the god quizzically. "Why am I here? Martial arts? Security?"

U Gyi spread his arms. "I've never been in love. I haven't the faintest idea why that makes me romantic about the affairs of others, but I couldn't split you and Major Daneby, and it's true the project we contemplate requires security. Next?"

"Dr. Alice Spendlowe." The black resurrectee giggled. "Ancient astronaut!"

"Which century?" Garne prompted.

"21st. What's going on? This place looks like a Victorian spa. I assure you this decolletage isn't my idea."

"Alice, we need your help," Ramnis answered. "More later. Next?"

"Dr. Cedric Chittagong. I worked with Major Daneby on *TC Alpha*, America's first seedship. Does this gathering have to do with seedships? Has our seedship program borne fruit?"

Cedric had been an eightyish consultant, impeccable in his tailoring. Now Olivia's dead friend was a Celtic fop, bulging with freckled muscle.

Gable took the gavel and pounded. "My name is Ramnis. As much as anyone behind this bench I represent the year 3726: I was born forty years ago and know but one life. Senators Garne and U Gyi" (nods right and left) "survived the ages in many bodies, and are not limited to modern perspectives. That's why I chair this committee, because if our recommendations come from me they'll seem less distant from the public mind."

This over, Senator Ramnis leaned and smiled with a politician's sincerity. "Dr. Chittagong, you're right. Good news from *AC Alpha*. What we need is an interstellar spaceship."

Torfinn raised his hand. The gesture puzzled his

hosts, but his question went to the troubling heart of all their problems. "What about Stargate? I was taught about the Gatekeepers last I was alive. They mean to keep humanity confined in this system, like in a wilderness preserve, like quaint—"

Torfinn looked around. "You *are* quaint. Your costumes, and this movie-set stage—"

Olivia spoke. "In 2349 Torfinn and I were told that the human race had keepers who would deny us the chance to expand out of this system. Is that forgotten, or wasn't it true to begin with?"

Senator Garne's jowls shook as she nodded. "The Gatekeepers of Stargate persist in denying humanity the use of their galactic travel facilities. Of all the evils attributed to them since 2070, this is the only one that can be proven. It is said they are responsible for the collapse of civilization on Earth, for the spread of wormroot-jungles across the eastern hemisphere—enormous crimes are laid at their door, but we've never shown them guilty. Clearly our wardens prefer not to play their hand directly, and may be handicapped by the need for subtlety. They may thwart us, but at least we'll ponder the attempt. For us to give up is the final tragedy."

"That was the problem back then," Torfinn said. "The Heegies just gave up. I like you folks better. You and me, we're too damn primitive to know when to quit."

A patter of applause. Ramnis looked around. "Isn't anyone curious about our Five Dominions' space fleet? What ships we have?"

Cedric shrugged. "Okay."

"None. When you were alive weren't most hulls manufactured in the asteroid belt? Weren't the drives installed in Mercury orbit? Madness! You let space bugs take over all the work."

U Gyi nodded. "Then you built Earthstalk and didn't need surface-to-space ships any more."

"A stalk!" Alice exclaimed. "Geosync orbit? What did we use? How did we handle tidal forces?"

Ramnis shook his head. "I've only had six years' school, and some talents taught by memory-dreaming. I'm typical of this age. I can fly a plane but I'd never tell you how it works. We've gods for that."

"And us," Olivia said. "Or are we U Gyi's property? We came to life on his boat—"

"At the senate's behest," De Gros's rich basso affirmed. "Your lives do not hang by so slender a thread as you fear, nor does U Gyi dangle that thread."

"So then we're supposed to design—it would have to be a generation ship," Alice rambled. "We wouldn't dare travel too fast."

"Why?"

Alice took a deep breath, not used to the strain it put on her bodice. "Take the smallest possible starship, accelerate to near light, and smash into the moon. According to computer models the depth of your crater exceeds the lunar diameter. You've blown the moon to bits!

"Infrared scopes tell us there's crud between the stars. Any near-light ship would hit something less minuscule to it than it is to Luna. Blewie! A garden pea would be overkill."

"Thank you," said Ramnis. "That's the charge of this committee: to focus on goals. A generation ship? How many generations? How big?"

"AC? That's Alpha Centauri." Cedric's fingers twiddled a nonexistent Vandyke. "A seventy-year trip. If the ship's built Earthstalk-tough the inhabitants would be fairly secure, and we wouldn't want to make the voyage longer. Too long and passengers would over-adapt to shipboard life."

"Seventy years!" De Gros gasped. "Who'd dare the trip?"

Torfinn raised his hand again. "Us dead. Thousands of bodies means thousands of volunteers. We've had lives on Earth, and after centuries in the City of the Dead simulated adventures grow tedious. Come, this voyage is going to be perilous. Tragic to cut someone short in his first life."

"In any event you'll need more dead," Olivia agreed. "Any half-assed engineering firm would fill this building. There's materials support, security. . . This project demands—yes—a diplomatic corps. A launch from Earth has to be smoothed with other governments in the solar system."

"They don't talk to us," Ramnis admitted. "We're too primitive." He stroked his mustachios and beamed. "Twenty years ago you wouldn't have seen steamers on our streets, or subways between our cities. Hell, twenty years ago the Empire didn't know Heegie enclaves hid under the old arcopoli! We've come a bold distance, so if you wonder at our conceit it's based on experience."

Cedric shook his head. "You don't know half the distance left to go. Is Chittaworld Theme Park still out in the asteroid belt? Know how I brought tourists? On a huge vessel built to cross interstellar space. That's why it was made, but then the scandal broke. To reach the stars any habitat ship had to be orders of magnitude larger than the *Carl Sagan*. There were other problems, too."

"Our job is to solve them," replied Senator Ramnis.

"Or talk to those who've solved them. We need space diplomats," Olivia repeated. "And intelligence people who know about the Gatekeepers."

Eyes turned to U Gyi. "More bodies," the dwarf-god sighed. "Young felons; republicans, witches, horsethieves, atheists— "

# PART TWO

## *Toehold*

# Thursday

Hello, Torfinn. U Gyi here, may I come in?

Thank you. Some expression today, some curiosity? Where should my tale wander? Will your half-pint godling discuss Heegie culture, or the wormroot problem? One thing I'd skip, months of Senate committee meetings. I've described our characters. Now it's time I introduced our story's setting, because so far Earthstalk's gotten short mention.

Why call it Earthstalk instead of Skystalk? Don't be provincial! The first stalks were built out in the asteroids. Chittaworld's a good example, a great bicycle wheel with Aeolus at its hub.

The first planetary stalk descended to Mars. Phobos and Deimos were moved out of the way. That was the big job. Afterward Marsstalk-Deltaport became the Red Planet's one great city.

So Earthstalk's a product of a perfected technology: begun in 2112, finished by 2210. An interesting century, pantrogs bred at the beginning and exterminated by the end, Earth run by robots and bugs while humans lived in hacienda townsteads. Their post-industrial life became typical: agriculture was everyone's hobby.

*Even Gatekeeper seemed to regard agronomy as queen of sciences. For the only time a human mission was allowed through Stargate, reaching planet LuSs with germ tissue edited to grow children adapted to atzu norms. And for what purpose? The cultivation and exchange of seed crops! LuSs turned out to be a galactic experimental farm, and no Imperial capital at all.*

*This century saw the publication of the first Prospore dictionary and grammar, and the first human descent to Venus. A century of pride, but also of shame. In 2145 the Bill of Rights for the Dead was suspended on Earth. From this time dead souls must emigrate or be shelved.*

*But worse than this and neo-tribal mischief in the '50s was the fact that wormroot containment failed in Africa. By 2160 wormroot jungle reached the shores of the Mediterranean. A hundred million Moslems needed somewhere to go. No wonder the Aminyasi family forced the Islamicization of Lunar Mining. Ironically, extreme measures against EurAm workers bred an extreme reaction in favor of the Church. Thanks to the Aminyasis the moon became Luna Roma!*

*This was also the century that saw the founding of Amapatinga Spaceport at the anticipated base of Earth-stalk, a city built to facilitate emigration to the Worlds of Sol; Luna, Chittaworld, Helice, Mars and Venus, plus a variety of bubbled asteroids. So it all ties together. If my ramble tells you anything, it's that there was real pressure to emigrate, and a growing ability to do so.*

*Yet . . . the pressure was only temporary.*

# Chapter 4
# Minus 39–Amapatinga Spaceport

Winter, the first weeks of 3727. The *Colleen of Azorella* rumbled and smoked, her engines fired by lignitic coal. Major Olivia Daneby watched the skies soften to a tropical blue, then fade to steamy white in the days after Paramaraibo, during the second leg of the voyage.

Her vantage was crowded. Each day the smell belowdecks grew more intense. Passengers and crew retreated into the heights behind the pilothouse.

Here splashed Christina. The *Colleen* was a cargo coaster, and Christina was two hundred sixteen kilos of sessile, ill-tempered cargo, sweaty and stentorian in her jury-rigged pool.

Olivia studied her and frowned. When she first died, amphibious whatcha-call-'ems weren't yet a gleam in geneticists' eyes. Now womties dominated the tidal swamps of the Gulf, and debated expansion into the dauntingly malignant waters of the Amazon.

Hence the nominal purpose of this voyage. Only Captain Gerhart Caddo's three passengers knew Chris-

tina was the name of a once-human, resurrected into
that misshapen brain to explore the lagoons around the
periphery of Earthstalk.

Senator Ramnis stood distant from his secret ally to
gaze toward low clouds. Earthstalk was a different shade
of sky: slender in its lower regions, flashing with mirrored gleams of light. The clouds girdling it no longer
touched the horizon. Above the sea lay a dark margin.
The cry rang out and Ramnis ducked into his cabin to
don his battle armor. These next hours superhuman
strength would come handy.

Olivia took station near his stateroom door. During
twenty minutes of clatter Brazil grew large.

*So this is Amapatinga*, Olivia thought. *Earth's great
spaceport, this land of forest and swamp*. Along the
wild shores of the Five Dominions morning wood-smoke
rose through the treetops, but Olivia saw no campfires
at Amapatinga, no wild Indios or tame Portuguese at
breakfast. Why? People didn't just die out. They had to
be cleared away—suddenly she was glad the senator
had booked Captain Caddo's innocuous cog, and kept
devious about his purposes.

Glad too that the *Redondo Beach* sailed behind them,
Torfinn's troops ready to move in on a day's notice.

To fight against whom? For whose edification did
Christina pretend she desired to live here, matron of a
new womtie colony "rid of human pests." Was it pretense? Olivia found it impossible to read her bulbous
face, her nictating eyes. Did Ramnis trust her?

Did Olivia trust herself? Married woman with virile
senator—but maybe he was married too. How to ask,
and why rock the boat? Ramnis was a perfect gentleman, and in time spiritual loyalty to her husband might
translate into a physical bond.

Olivia shivered. The thought of teenie-bopper incest—
To a child educated during a time of bigotry, all Chinese look alike. Was that her problem? Torfinn seemed
to think so, but Olivia wasn't sure. All that she knew
was that the thought of sex with someone so nearly her

twin, so physically like her brother—perhaps Torfinn
could switch bodies? In this age the gods monopolized
all memory equipment, dreamskulls and immortifacts,
but if she did U Gyi a favor . . .

The *Colleen* burbled by a lesser harbor thick with
tidal isles of coral. Darth Vader bent out Ramnis's door,
lineaments ruined by a powerpack hump, his strength
set stubbornly on 1. Clutching the rail to take a load off
his shoulders, the senator looked beyond water to the
bulk of Pico Geronta.

Much could be surmised by names. Amapatingan
was a dialect of 23rd-century Prospore, but the place
had weathered waves of usurpation: thus the *Colleen*
rounded Cabo da Lor and churned into Gizzard
Bay.

As the bay narrowed the jungle's sun clouded over.
Suddenly and with no preliminaries rain dumped from
the skies, a straight-down shower. The *Colleen of Azorella*
dropped anchor. Ignoring the heavy drizzle Captain
Caddo lowered his dinghy and Ramnis invited himself
along to shore.

They made a contrast: even without armor Ramnis
was large and dark; at present he was a black and
humpbacked knight. Caddo was short, hair almost plati-
num blond, a tightly-constructed physical dynamo. He
rowed briskly.

Landward, beyond a tidal strand, rose green walls;
plants, pests and animals in mutually intimate confinement. "I see a falls," Ramnis pointed. "I hope it's
good."

They certified the water: Caddo filled his wide-
brimmed hat, drank and did not die. Ramnis scrambled
another hundred meters inland, until cliffs defeated
exploration. Animals crashed in flight. Could womties
learn to domesticate another species? Ramnis might
mention the idea to Christina; it was the right sort of
conversation for this time and place.

The rain stopped. The galley crew ported ship-to-
shore in torrid sunshine. They set up a tented camp,

built a fire and hauled wood. A second party moved north, beating the bush for peccaries.

The sun slid behind Earthstalk. A pig and a water-rat, skinned and spitted, rotated over a smoky fire of green wood. Bloodsucking insects converged for supper. The smoke discouraged them, sending thousands over the water to attack Christina and her boatmen. The womtie was in foul temper by the time the craft beached.

Caddo's crew converged and hauled. With a curse Christina hoiked vertical and swung her fists. The men scattered and she flopped over the gunwale to splash free. With a sigh of relief she floated into the deeper waters of Gizzard Bay while evening winds strengthened and the air grew less buggy. Above her head a mob of bats swooped silently.

Olivia watched, minded to join her. Slumped helmetless in front of his tent, Ramnis muttered against the idea. "We think of Christina as a ponderous invalid, but now she's fast, powerful and possibly murderous. Maybe she's not acting. Maybe her womtie glands are in control . . ."

Christina swam into the night. When the skies lightened, Ramnis slipped out for a quick wash and donned his gear. The camp began to bustle. Under Caddo's speculative eye the senator packed his hamper: tarp and hammock, food, rope and opera glass, bangweeds, radio, rifle and ammunition. Strength set at 2, he set off as hot sun overshot the treetops.

Gizzard Bay terminated in swamp, then the land rose quickly. With armored claws Ramnis hauled upward. He approached the ruins of a suburban camp where thousands of emigres once waited to ride Earthstalk to space. It had boasted a masonry embarcadero. Now toppled stones lay jumbled. A stream ran through, cataracting to his left.

Little was left to signify the era of bubbleworld emigration, hardly one stone atop another.

A poet of exquisite sensibilities might have composed

a meditation upon Amapatinga's fall, but it was hard to be anything but brutish among these mosquitoes. Ramnis continued to climb. The land grew drier, though soil remained mud. Tropic swamp made spotty incursions into this forest, whose canopy modulated the day's brief squalls into a constant drip.

By late afternoon he was near the halfpoint in his journey and had hiked half a klom above sea level. The ascending slopes of Geronta drew him on. Trees opened to a prospect of tawny seas weaving among green hills.

Ramnis set down his picnic hamper and pulled out a bottle of wine, a portable transmitter, and a string hammock. He eyed trunks too thin, too close, too festive with crawling life, and put the hammock back. He clicked on the radio. "Olivia? I see a water-route for Christina around south. Can you hear me?"

"I'm picking bits of you through a commercial for Juba Juice."

Ramnis twiddled up his volume. "I hear you too, assuring me Earthstalk was built close to seas and roads and airports. I don't know where the roads went, but here's a roofless chapel fifty meters away. If it's as awful as where I stand I figure on just continuing, hiking through the night."

"Can you see the base of Earthstalk?"

Ramnis took a swallow of wine, and stared. At the intersection of Earthstalk and jungle, strange machineries emitted beams of Kirillian light. Flashes shot in random directions, for the most part in silence. Once or twice he heard a crackle—it might have been a forest creature stepping through brush.

The colors were otherworldly. "Looks like a skirmish down there. A war against swamp people? The defenses are active."

"What's your assumption? People live in Earthstalk, and they're hostile to outsiders? They might just be hostile to whoever's down there."

"Anyhow, I've decided," Ramnis answered. "I'm going to chance more kloms with the last of the light."

\* \* \*

An hour after stringing a signal relay from a Pico Geronta tree-branch, Ramnis plunged into the Marisma. Tearing through thickets with one claw hand, he slapped with his encumbered left in a useless effort to ward off swarms of gnats. As he sloshed through tea-colored muck the mustachioed senator was mindful of every tale he'd heard of cigar-sized leeches, army ants and venomous snakes. Indios of ancient legend poisoned arrows by touching them to the skin of deadly frogs. There was no creature, no matter how small, that might not kill him.

He stopped to catch his breath. What was that soft *bloop-plop*? Marsh gas? Amphibians returning to their element? It was a heavy sound, but the water was capable of shielding a hundred mysteries.

Among them one took precedence. Where was a refuge? If only he could find some place dry as the heights he'd casually abandoned! Stupid to have kept on, stupid, stupid—

"Calm down, Ramnis," he muttered. "Let's have some good old divine intervention. Where's my Souldancer luck? A rock, or two decent trees—"

He slashed through viny growth, lavishing the strength of his armor as the transition to night grew complete. Now his eyes were next to useless. The only light in this fecund nightmare sprang from the water, a fetid bioluminescence which waxed and waned as he hacked on.

In this unreal glow he watched a snake slither from its treebranch perch and fall.

Plop. One more plop among so many. Thigh-deep in goo, for all Ramnis knew he was stepping on the damned things. Time to turn on his headlamp, or did he really want to know?

The beam shone to illuminate a wall. The senator's heart leapt as he saw the stained concrete of an ancient car-park. Half-collapsed under the weight of growth, sections C and D loomed out of water.

The intervening swamp seethed with God-knew-what, but Ramnis splashed for the ramp, giggling hysterically, while the creatures of the forest canopy chorused their answer.

# Chapter 5

## Minus 38–Paramaraibo

Waves lapped below a quarter moon. The air was thick, and on an awninged deck illuminated by paper lanterns, U Gyi sweltered among copies of himself, for he reproduced in batches. Repeated twenty times, his dwarfishness and goblin-face were byproducts of a hurried attempt to endow brood 42 with gifts: long life and watered-down sexuality.

An attempt motivated by disaster. Pavel, his clingfast major-domo, was the only retainee from brood 41: plump, cherubic, forever pre-pubescent; also victim of emotional storms and surges.

Pavel's identical twin, U Gyi's 41st incarnation had extended his subterranean palace, called it "Heaven" and founded the Redemptorist cult to people it with the loveliest specimens from the world above. Back in those days even a third-rate god could behave in such ways, and use the surface world as a playground.

But third-rate U Gyi saw Tonans compromised and Hecate killed, every last body. Thanks to the treachery of one minor goddess the world had changed. The enclaves cowered, and now U Gyi stood terribly alone, saddled with a reputation for megalomania. In the years of his relatively dispassionate regime the Empire learned to use INFOWEB. A pest-swarm of patriotic heroes like Ramnis braved into the underworld and took control of the subway system. The hot breath of justice—

A grand-scale criminal can stave off justice. The citizens of Heaven were brainwashed to think they'd come of their own volition. The Hills of Moon were opened to tourists. The apothecaries of the Five Dominions were flooded with miracle medicines. Endocrinological misfits became normal almost overnight.

But if U Gyi thought he'd weathered the crisis by becoming an indispensable part of the surface economy, why was he surrounded by copies of himself, each armed with sonics, guns and stun-wands?

"Never again," he thought out loud. "Even a god can reform."

"And become hearty of physique?" Pavel complained, mopping his brow. For once the superannuated cherub looked his age: why bother with cosmetics when sweat defeated all his skills? From the deck of U Gyi's yacht he nodded inland, to the overgrown acres of the University of Paramaraibo. "We don't have the pigment. Leave adventuring to others."

The god barked a short laugh. "To Ramnis!" He paused and spoke again. "We were how many generations old when this place was world-famous? Eight? Research into dimensional tunnels, string and z-particles! How the mighty are fallen. Now the old racetrack is our new airfield— Well hello, Alice!"

"—in Munchkinland," the once-dead astronaut muttered, singling out U Gyi by his garments.

"And yon tower is Emerald City," U Gyi gestured. "See it merged by our imperfect eyes into one thin pole, a ray of starlight bending up, up, up. So much taller than Earth's diameter! What's the word from shore? Is Paramaraibo livable?"

"We need archaeologists, not steam-tractors," she

answered. "But yes, they built well in the 2220s. Four diameters from the crater the old buildings still stand, they helped capsulize the explosion. Nevertheless, I'd stay on this boat—"

"You're welcome if you don't mind to-and-fro. This is one of Paramaraibo's few anchorages. With all these ships bringing in supplies we surrender it frequently."

"I suppose I'm not to know what's in all those boxes."

"Trade goods, siege equipment—" Again U Gyi waved, drawing a vague connection between the tarp-hung masses ashore and distant Earthstalk. "We have Torfinn for war and Cedric for peace. Why not buy our way onto the elevators to space?"

The god's question sounded unusually sincere. Alice studied U Gyi a second time. "You're the one with the answers."

He shook his head. "I simply warn my friends not to be naive. The world grows ever more complex."

"*I* think it's grown simpler."

Somewhere ashore a steam-whistle blew. U Gyi grinned. "Retrogressed to Senator-Ramnis simplicity? Not on Mercury, or Luna, or the asteroids. Oh yes, we hear of cycles of growth and decay in space. We manage to listen, and crack their codes. But see, the encounter between sophisticate and primitive adds a new dimension of complexity. It's gotten all too much for me. One of the attractions of Alpha Centauri is its pristine simplicity."

"Simple? Seedship *AC Alpha* may insist immigrants convert to his elaborate gnosticism."

U Gyi smiled. "Dear Alice! At last I infect you with paranoia. Seventeen hundred years ago you and Cedric thought you understood affairs on Chittaworld. Then your fictoids revolted and assumed self-rule! Equally you thought the *Carl Sagan* was a friend. Is he still a friend? Would he let you dream his memories?"

Off in the dark womtie males splashed, vying for the new colony's females. The god turned from their cries of "Merde a tu!" and the mocking "Kreegah bundolo!"

"Is that your standard?" Alice asked, following as U Gyi

climbed into a portable throne. "Would you let me dream you?"

"Of course not, but you *know* me for what I am, and bristle in all our dealings. I'd see you carry that same suspicion to space, Madam Ambassador, you *and* your husband. One thing I assure you *a priori*: your good old *Carl Sagan* is not the spaceship you once knew."

"You've talked to him then?" Alice canted her head and frowned.

"The meaning of *a priori* is I have not."

"Then I put it to you that by the shifting of a millennium of factors, you and the *Sagan* are unwittingly best of friends."

U Gyi shook his head. "There are many ways ships collide at sea, but rarely from being 180 degrees off course from each other."

Alice sighed. "It's hot. I'm tired of verbal ripostes. You listen to space? Tell me: I'm the Siamese Envoy to Queen Victoria. What are the rules up there? Who's strong, and who's weak? Who wants to gobble me up?"

"The Gatekeepers are strong, they throw comets around, bombing Earth every thirty million years to see what evolution will come up with next. The bugs are irrelevant. Wetbrain affairs mean nothing to them, they have no martial instincts. As for the rest—Luna and Helice think nothing's important unless it has repercussions on Luna or Helice. Venus—" The god plucked at his sleeves. "Venus is strong. The new bubbleworlds follow Venus."

Alice found the idea hard to get used to. Venus was easier to terraform than Mars! Mars defended its subviability. Warm enough to wrap itself in snow, its new albedo bounced solar heat back to space. On the other hand the Imaheren Pension Trust cooled Venus by endowing the planet with giant rings, shooting a spare Jovian moon close enough to let natural forces tear it apart. They also sold most of Venus's excessive atmosphere to the bubbleworlds—for profit.

And now Venus had two small north-hemisphere

oceans. When visitors talked about sea-level on Venus, natives responded "which sea?"

"What about spaceships?" Alice paced and turned. "Who's got habitat ships? Ships people can live on?"

"A few hundred out in the asteroids. Fewer near Venus. It's not easy to say. Ships rarely die, but they *do* get retrofitted. A millennium ago there were thousands of habitat ships—back when space travel was popular. Those ships could carry passengers if given a few months to fix themselves up."

"No warships?"

U Gyi smiled. "A habitat ship is an egg. A warship is an egg with a hammer; a one-time weapon and hideously expensive. The battles of space are capsule affairs, limited in scope and fought with weapons adapted to their environments. Don't shake your head. Wars were the same in your day, and it's easier now with smart guns refusing to fire at proscribed targets."

Alice giggled. "People who live in glass houses throw *very soft* stones."

# Chapter 6
# Minus 37–The Marisma

What had been an Amapatingan garbage dump rose to a modest height in the midst of algal soup. Metal poisoned the earth and growth was thin. It was a natural gathering spot for the exiles of the Marisma: Otto and Irene, and now Bruno and Emilio.

Bruno and Emilio had actually overmastered a pair of Colonel Li's pigmaskers, and brought weapons to this refuge. That was a month ago. During that month they'd put hope in an impractical scheme. Last afternoon's attack on Earthstalk Gate A disproved the premise behind three weeks of arduous labor.

The idea was Otto's. Shadbolts were effective against missiles because missiles were loaded with explosive. When a charged beam hit propellant, of course the things exploded! Same with shells. The beam detonated them prematurely.

Obviously the way to defeat shadbolts was to use non-explosive projectiles. A great stupid stone flying through the air. Shadbolts might drill holes as it fell toward its target, all to no avail!

"Why? Why fight them?" Irene asked.

"Because the Marisma will kill us," Otto answered. "Disease or hunger, infected wounds. We haven't found any other people here, just the occasional skull. The pigmaskers will continue to use this hell as a dumping-ground unless we show them it's unwise to do so."

Bruno nodded, a knuckle-dragging hunk with a Ph.D. " *I am one, my liege, whom vile blows and buffets have so incens'd, that I am reckless what I do to spite the world.'* And isn't it true, since last month, no new exiles? Thanks to us they keep dissidents inside where their ideas can fester."

So the ex-academics set to build a device capable of flinging boulders. By night they wielded their clumsy catapult forward through the swamp. At last it was in position.

Unfortunately rock was hard to find in the Marisma and the calciated stone most readily available, despite all theory, exploded when shadbolt rays found the target. To compound their troubles Colonel Li's men grouped for a foray into the brush. Irene maneuvered her colleagues into distracting retreat. An exchange of gunfire and the pigmasked enemy pelted back to air-conditioned safety. Otto's small band remained masters of mud and slough, nothing accomplished for all their efforts.

This discouraging morning Otto left camp to scout the periphery. His friends could vent anger more easily with him gone; him and his fine ideas! The unhappy ex-history professor reached the flooded shores of a Marisma lake and climbed a tree to peer into the distance, and think.

A smart shadbolt would have analyzed the trajectory of his stones and drilled through jungle to his catapult. Useful to know shadbolts were dumb, but if one of Li's hirelings was a cyberneticist—how long would it take a Stat Three techno to enhance a shadbolt? Would it be removed from service during installation?

A slow black speck trudged into distant view, rounding

bends along the silty strand. Otto watched sleepily in
the sun. *A man in armor carrying a picnic basket!* The
exile giggled, dropped to the muck, and pulled his gun.
As Ramnis waded forward, Otto cried *"Altu!"* and stepped
from behind his tree.

Ramnis raised his hands. Otto watched. Either the
picnic basket was empty or this fellow was strong indeed. Now what? Err, ahh—

Ramnis waited until his sonics took effect. Wine and
sleep had completed a transformation of hysterical brute
back to self-possessed senator. He waded close, grabbed
Otto's hand and led him gently toward dry land. He
disarmed the tatterclad swamp man, switched off his
belt and raised his visor. "Isn't this nicer?" he asked.

Otto recovered and shook his head. "I don't quite
understand you."

"Do you know Old English? *Parlez-vous Mbo? Chu
uassa?"*

Otto nodded. *"Uassa."*

"And that's their story," Ramnis concluded, speaking
tinnily from Olivia's radio. "A purge of historians by the
powers-that-be. Irene's an accident, she saw pigmaskers
rifle a desk. Oh, one more thing. I did a strongman act
here at their camp; turned my strength up to 12 and
threw a dead tree-trunk fifty meters. That's got our
friends thinking what I might do with smaller missiles."

"We're supposed to sound out the situation, not conquer Earthstalk," Olivia answered. "That's what Torfinn's
army is for."

The sun was just past zenith; all his new cronies had
retreated to nap in minimal shade. "You complain our
Empire's a budget operation," Ramnis answered over
the hum of his laboring powerpack. "Think what we
save in money and lives if I can get a toehold in there."

"Any sign of Christina?"

"We know where to look, where the water—oops,
Colonel Li may have a linguist on his staff. Best keep
my mouth shut."

"What do you want us to do?" Olivia asked.

"Swear in Caddo and his men: I've got Imperial commissions in my cabin. Don't lie, but irk their patriotism. Tell them the Worlds of Sol won't talk to our Five Dominions unless we prove worthy by taking Earthstalk. Break out the guns and follow my trail. Keep under cover. Colonel Li's got battlecopters. If he hadn't been fuddled by our swamp friends he'd have used them to destroy the *Colleen*. See, Colonel Li works for Senjoro Nie—"

"Li, Nie, Gyi. One-syllable villains."

"Actually it's 'Nee-uh.' I'm not sure I understand things right; there's some doubt whether Senjoro Nie exists. But in any case he works through an aristocracy of squabbling colonels who—"

"Don't explain the politics," Olivia interrupted. "Colonel Li's the bad guy. That's all I need to know. We're on our way."

Christina took position and bobbed quietly for several minutes. Then she lunged shoreward like a brown torpedo. A shoal of fish shot into Irene's nets, flapping as Ramnis hauled them to dry land. "Enough!" he shouted.

Christina waved back. The womtie's sullen act was over. "Ad astra per any means possible! Show those Gatekeepers you can't keep a wetbrain down."

Ramnis laughed and turned away. Olivia followed, humming an old tune: "Fish heads, fish heads, roly-poly fish heads—"

The jungle stopped like a green wall a hundred meters from Earthstalk Gate A. Ramnis gauged the distance. He retreated a dozen steps and set down his catch. "Beginning of the great Earthstalk War," he announced. "11:15, January Something-or-other, 3727." Then he reached for handfuls of fish, and threw.

Caddo's sailors were lined offside his chosen battlefield, blinded by foliage, guns drawn as ordered. What now? Since last evening they'd begun to doubt this crazy senator. Irritate the tyrants of Earthstalk with a few dead fish?

Earthstalk defended itself automatically. The air crackled, light flashed, fish hissed wetly, cooked, and fell into charred fragments.

"Hoka hey!" Ramnis shouted. He launched another volley. The air grew thick with jackstrawed lightning. Conceivable his weapons might strike a target, and with some force. The trick was volume, a buckshot approach to fishflinging, and Ramnis kept up a hot pace.

Bits of jungle canopy sizzled and crashed. Monkeys yammered and parrots squawked. Suddenly the shadbolts ceased fire. Ramnis used up his ammo while Olivia crept forward. "They've decided to stop wasting megawatts," she reported. "They're mustering behind the glass. And they *do* wear pigmask visors!"

She clambered back to where Caddo squatted. "They're going to make a sortie. They expect to encounter four white-collar wimps like Otto says they bully inside Earthstalk. Keep your men concealed. Hold fire till they jog past. Let them feel the brunt of Ramnis's sonics."

"No battle plan survives contact with the enemy," Caddo replied, "but if the fish trick works—"

A whistle bleated. Pigs! Ramnis ran to show himself. Guns fired like popcorn. Would Earthstalk bullets penetrate battle armor? He hoped not as he stumbled back thirty meters to a scrawny tree. What the hell! He pulled the practically-rootless thing out of the ground and threw it high to shake the canopy.

He had their attention. Colonel Li's men filed into the jungle on a wide front, sinister in visors, guns drawn. Ramnis let them approach, then stepped out in surrender. The pigmaskers tripped toward him— walked—paused in confusion.

No protection against sonics. What did Earthstalkers know of Heegie science? None of Caddo's men were protected either. The senator disarmed the foe and piled weapons in a heap. Only after he turned his belt off did sailors mob forward and strip prisoners of their uniforms.

Then they fired at random. Indoor superiors would think the battle raged, but the noise spurred naked captives into flight towards the Marisma. Oops; not good if one doubled back to the gate. Hurry, they had to hurry!

They wrestled into soft tan pajamas. Olivia helped them with the sticktape fastenings. Pigmask visors hid beards and sun-black skin. And now—

Otto, Irene, Bruno and Emilio herded forward. Disguised sailors formed around them. Ramnis hid as they trooped in triumph back to Gate A. Did they have the pigmask flair? Would *any* soldiers have flair after the rigors of a sortie?

The glass doors whisked open. Seamen hup-two-threed inside and through another set; into the lobby of the vastest hotel ever built. Desks and elevators, a bar-pit, an arboretum-waterfall, shops and escalators—but the shops were dark, the reception area untended.

Colonel Li and his labcoat associates rose from the couches of the bar-pit. *"Nu! Chu 'bsolvol mi a La Senjoro? Bonega, bonega. Vi prenit niaj kvar felonoj!"*

There was nothing else to do. The invaders were out of miracles. They fanned out and aimed their guns. Enemies dove and drew, and they peppered them with crossfire. When the room fell silent Olivia ran back to the door. Again it whisked. "Ramnis!"

The shadbolts had not been reactivated and the senator made it across. "We've got our toehold," he gasped.

# Chapter 7
## Minus 35–Hab 1

"If Earthstalk builded only the one floor over the other she be eighteen *million* floors tall. You understand million? But never. The whole *ujo* dividing into ninety thousand nodes, each got the oredock, the factory, the shipdock, and too, solar collectors like wings; finally four *habitas*."

Otto lectured rapid fire, his clear tenor echoing in still vastness as he chattered to ease the shock of bloodshed. Last night he'd talked long on the elegance and imbecilisms of various Earthstalk habitats; basking in comradeship. Now he sought to reassure himself these outland killers were trusted friends, as if there was bond-magic in pontification.

"But for the first hundred seventy kloms Earthstalk is no much factories, no much power, only *habitas*; capsule *haboj* ten stories tall, easy shut away in the emergency, *firmaportada* with food and air and water maybe for months as long as the power stay good."

Four switches removed the local elevator-clusters from

service. Bruno hurried to flip them off. Ramnis ran upstairs, leaving Otto spinning in dismay at his dwindled audience.

"All *haboj* the same mass, same size, same shape outside, same elevators; but wait, wait, no else the same, all different architect inside—"

Ramnis climbed beyond hearing, activated his sonics, and flung a ragdoll trio of Li's pigmaskers into Sol System's vastest attic. He closed the bulkhead. "Firmaportada," he sighed.

Otto and Irene were left muttering over the bodies of Li and his companions. Caddo's seamen trooped for Cluster A and the shadbolt control room. They found two technicians ready to surrender. Thus they took Level Zero-Zero-Zero-Zero-Zero-One, a convention center surrounded by offices, elevators, laboratories and apartments.

What an accomplishment! According to Otto's trailing words, they'd conquered 2.52 hectares of rooms and hallways, one hectare of indoor jungle, and a pool barely adequate to Christina's needs.

Earthstalk incorporated one and a half million hectares of oxygen habitat, equivalent to a bubbled asteroid 46 kloms in diameter. Huh? All those numbers added up to some jerkwater asteroid? That's the problem with being one-dimensional, but Earthstalk was two thousand times bigger than the *Carl Sagan*, humanity's only attempt at a starship.

Ramnis turned down his strength. He slumped onto a bench. Step one: establish a toehold. Step two: conquer upward through several thousand bulkheads! "Sing to me, muse," he muttered. "How to do it without damaging the habitats? Not by air machine: Nie's got shadbolts to foil air attack. Worse, our opponents have native savvy. If there's any crawlways they'll know about them."

Ramnis was discouraged. Consider his first purposes. Planet Alpha Centauri Four! Stargate! The need for people with horse-and-buggy childhoods to construct a generation ship superior to the *Carl Sagan!*

He'd argued for the conquest of Earthstalk as a first step, a way to get attention; a preliminary project so taxing it demanded the Five Dominions' best resources.

Those resources included Torfinn's expeditionary force of two hundred dead heroes. Olivia radioed, and the *Redondo Beach* moved from hiding on the Araguari river. The warship dropped resurrectees into the Marisma under cover of night. Meanwhile Ramnis's interior troop kept up a frenzy of vigilance. Impossible to lower their guard: impossible for the senator to remove his suit to take a bath. He itched, and felt things crawl beneath his plates and cuishes. Antipathy towards battle armor grew in his mind as imaginary leeches fastened in places he could not reach.

Then too he was overheating— "Damn it, here's the second time I've had to chase you to your duties!" he flared, herding Irene from a bank of food dispensers. He repeated his growl in Prospore. The humiliated woman scuttled off with her precious armload of food puffs. "You'd think she hadn't eaten for a month," he sulked as Olivia popped around the corner, drawn by his display of temper.

"She hasn't, not any food familiar to her," Olivia answered.

"All this machine food is poison. What about you? Don't you have something better to do?"

Nor was this Ramnis at his worst. He grew increasingly unlovable as the sleepless night wore on. Olivia decided her crush on him was over. There! Safe to bring her fancies out of the closet, as long as they were *past* fancies!

But diurnal rhythms grudge the most pathetic insomniacs a bit of sensibility with the return of day. Around midmorning a frazzled Rhett Butler came to Olivia by the second-floor vending machines and apologized, a haunted expression on his half-masked face. "I'm sorry, I've been full of myself."

"Yes, you have." Olivia carried food puffs and Cola-

Ban to a nearby table, under a glassy ceiling looking up into a third-floor ballroom.

Ramnis followed and sat with a clunk. "So let me get full of you. What's it like? You've spent centuries shelved in the City of the Dead, and for all that you don't seem different—do you mind my curiosity?"

Olivia looked at him candidly. "I was stored on a circuit board, a half-dozen chips, one soul among many, my processor time-slicing through a world of 72 data channels. We were on racks accessible to novitiate servo-bugs—I could have become one. The monastery called it accepting reality. Reality: a god who sires a son on a mortal woman; a rabbi who tells his devotees to stop working and wait for the end of the world; a heavenly economy that demands death of the innocent as a vicarious sacrifice. The simulated drinking of blood—what profound difficulties they had administering the sacraments!

"What a joke. I'd have had to take vows and I'm an atheist from way back. Worse, I'd have had to be sincere: they tested novices with a sincerity bit-mask. I'd have to True-True ninety percent of the time, never again to laugh at their ghoulish credulities. All that just to take the first step up the hierarchy, monk to prior to abbot—a century's slow process because where do vacancies come from? Old Haberhan has been Primate-General for a thousand years . . . God, you'd think he'd get tired. Nothing but responsibility and study and administration. Speaking of ghouls, did you know that in early times humans sometimes left the flesh to become bug-monks and let their corpses freeze-dry in cold vacuum? Their mummies became cult objects, wigged and lacquered. Then Haberhan came along. He had them ground to dust. The cultists fled into a dream where their heresy dominates the City of the Dead. Such a purist! Nothing interesting must ever pollute Haberhan's Christian reality."

"Boring, huh?" That explains why you'd rather play dream games with the rest of the dead, all those simulated adventures."

"I'd have come around in time. Happily Ever After gets boring too, and then you push the suicide switch, and then they preach at you." Olivia paused. "Should we be talking about this?"

"No INFOWEB ports nearby. Otto says a working terminal can feel sound on its screen, but flat isn't optimal. You have to stand right in front—"

"There's other kinds of mics. Wires, tubes, spikes, parabolic, shotgun, wireless, crystal transmitters."

Ramnis nodded. "Accumulating over the centuries, and half forgotten. Emilio's building a wide-band receiver in hopes we can pick up stuff from upstairs. Otto and Bruno have done sweeps, but I don't know. We have to talk, don't we? Anyhow we can be sure of one thing. Senjoro Nie had no reason to plant ears in Level One until noon yesterday. By then it was too late."

"Aren't we professional? In World War One the Russian General Staff transmitted orders at three in the morning, sure the Germans wouldn't listen in at that ungodly hour. Uncoded, of course. Too much hassle bothering with ciphers. Where was I?"

"Atheism. Servo-bugs in the City of the Dead, trying to convert you."

"Obedience was my stumbling block. Back in 1979 I took an oath to the U.S. Constitution. Well, the United States of America was never legally dissolved into the Hegemony. As for that, the Hegemony has never officially disbanded—"

"You're still loyal to the old Anglo States?"

Olivia bit into a food puff. How interesting, she and Ramnis were soul brothers, they both talked the same clipped, telegraphic way! Or was he picking up on her, adapting the way interested men did with interesting women . . . "There's been attrition, and true suicide, and that cyber-virus back in 2076, but there must be a good million of us, enough to put 'er back together again. Mebbe on Planet Four."

Olivia finished her answer in a mock John Wayne voice. Ramnis contorted in response to a new itch, jerking like a puppet on a string. "I can see you might have trouble accepting reality."

Olivia laughed. "I always gave them the same answer: 'Nuts!' Afterward I'd find myself in a bookstore. Understand, they controlled all my inputs. Subjective reality was whatever they wanted. So this was *their* bookstore, full of comix and paperbacks. All I had to do was browse, pick up something and read. If I liked it, by the second or third page I was *there*! Think of any fantasy, any at all. They had it, shelves after shelves. Last time I paged through an old *National Geographic* and became a New Guinea highlander bride, and spent forty years growing yams."

"How do you know all this isn't merely another fant— What's that?" Ramnis rose. The distant babble grew loud and he ran from the table. "Downstairs!"

"Torfinn!" Welcomed by shouts of relief, reinforcements streamed through the downstairs doors, tromping jungle mud into a gleaming, bloodstained lobby.

Descending by escalator, Olivia recognized her husband's slim new body. As she drew to attention Torfinn trudged forward with a bosomy officer in tow. "Guess! One of my old friends—well, *enemy's* more like it. Back when I was dumb, dutiful and overawed—it's a long story. This is Magda Szentes of the 21st century. I didn't even know she was with us until an hour ago. Lieutenant Szentes, Major Daneby."

Olivia returned the radio officer's salute. "Torfinn, you'll need to set up four watches and deploy your me—people. We've got quarters to assign—yes, dear, I love you too, and I'll love you better after a bath. We've got to tell folks about water discipline and recycling. Sorry, Magda. I'll be nice after I'm done fretting. You weren't attacked? Maybe Senjoro Nie's not the big kahuna we thought he was."

"Senjoro Nie?" Magda smiled. "Mister Nowhere."

"What do you mean?"

"I remember when Earth's Hegemony was a cable democracy. Citizens were polled on issues, only who controlled the questions? *Mister Nowhere!* He had things rigged to preserve anonymity, and used INFOWEB to twiddle the world's wealth as he chose."

"I died before all this," Olivia admitted.

Ramnis clattered up and began to disrobe. His powerpack ceased humming when he removed his helmet; breast-and-backplates opened with a flip of the cuirie. "—And I was born after it was over, or could Senjoro Nie be the same person?"

"I doubt it," said Magda. "But the name means he's anonymous and has some control of Earthstalk's distribution system."

Otto nodded. "I talk Major Daneby. Nie pay bully-men if they keeping habitas quiet and *produkta.*" He reverted to his own language. *"Your Empire presents a new problem and I like to think brutes like Colonel Li aren't very bright. Certainly they can't work in tandem. Our immediate enemy runs the habitats just above us. Until we sweep through his domain we won't have to worry about the next one up."*

"Too much harvest from a name," Ramnis remarked. Pauldrons and tace dropped to the floor. "A whole political structure!"

"A name, and the fact we weren't blasted on our way here," Magda replied. "Colonel Li's successor is firming up his regime. He's not had time for us."

A pause. Olivia blushed, she'd forgotten she was hostess. "Torfinn, Otto. Otto, Magda." She turned to complete the introductions. "Ramnis, doesn't your culture have a nudity-taboo?"

Ramnis shrugged off a rat's nest of tubes and began tugging at his pink undersuit. "Did you think of fetching my clothes from the *Colleen?* Torfinn's charged with security. He can wear this damn armor from now on, and good riddance. I'll grab some pigmask pajamas—"

"So you're Ramnis," Magda breasted forward. "I have to apologize. This body they gave me—"

"I know. Jijika was one of my constituents—*more* than a constituent. She was part of my troupe, and I was forever bailing her out of trouble. If we can't control the body snatchers our Progressives will lose the next election. Not your fault, though."

"Blame U Gyi."

"We have an intimate relationship, U Gyi and I," Ramnis mused. "He's villain to my hero, except half the time we're on the same side and *then* I always need him. He tried to kill me three times, and I actually *did* kill him once—put him on good behavior for a year. Ah well, Jijika was dumb to scant my warnings. Death may do her good."

"So what are you up to now?" Torfinn asked. "Now I've inherited your magic suit?"

"I have orders." Magda pulled them from her pocket and extended them to the naked senator.

Ramnis read and turned thoughtful. "Looks like I'm staying. Earthstalk's part of the Empire, and I'm Lord High Commissioner. Otto, would your company mind swearing fealty? You can be my first citizens."

# Chapter 8
## Minus 34—Hab 1

That night Torfinn crawled into bed with a touch-me-not woman of business: Olivia wrapped in bristles accumulated during long celibacy. His wife was eerie as her old Texas prairies before a storm. Thoughts pinballed around her skull, and then there was this matter of bodies. She and her lover looked far too alike. They could have been brother and sister, immature teen twins.

*Could have been?* Hell, it was obvious—hmm—so gentle . . .

The storm gained energy, broke; thunder, lightning, rain. Afterward they lay exhausted, legs twined. Olivia's mind kaleidoscoped events of the day while hovering near sleep. "Dear? You awake?"

"Mmm?"

"There *were* people like Senjoro Nie in my time. They controlled the distribution of goods through truckers' unions, and kept anonymous, shifting hierarchies by bluster, ultimately by assassination. I'm simplifying, but the capo upstairs has to win respect. The only way is to reconquer our level."

"He should have attacked yesterday."

"Like Magda says, he was busy. The thing is, if we open our bulkhead to move up we'll find *his* side open, because he's laying for the chance to come down."

"He'd throw away a perfect defensive posture?"

"You don't gain face by defense," Olivia answered as she climbed out of bed. *It's not incest, it doesn't count!* Nevertheless she went to the bathroom, shut the door and quietly vomited. Five minutes later she returned to her unsuspecting husband's side.

The Earthstalk Commission gathered next morning on the patio by Christina's pool, and stood waiting, breakfast trays in hand. Emilio the showman! Miming silence to the point of chastising the waterfall for its babble, the slender Latin tuned his receiver up and down a series of bands. Then he picked up a second box, switched it on and stalked around the floor. Ramnis felt a buzz in his brain and grimaced through the ordeal: Magda gave him a look of sick sympathy.

Act Three: a cross between a Gatling gun and a pipe organ. Emilio aimed his lethal-looking gear toward the ceiling and played it around the chandelier. Something tiny went *ping* and snowed into a copse of rubber trees. Ramnis and Magda exchanged looks of alarm. Both could imagine their brain-buzz amplified into a tissue-rupturing burst of noise. Why did everyone else seem so *blank* to what was happening?

Relief. Act Four: Emilio picked up tables and chairs, slammed them around, and dunked them in water. "Anybody bring towels?" Torfinn asked. "Wet butts— what we sacrifice in the interests of security."

"They also serve who only sit and soak," Olivia responded. After putting down her tray to claim a seat she went on to repeat last night's analysis.

Otto's head bobbed in agreement. "They throw pink rocks," he blurted. "Crystal smoke heavy, flow down, kill everyone, then they safe to come."

Torfinn smiled. "Good. They've got motivation and weapons. Depend on it. They're hot to invade."

Squeaky clean and dressed in pigmask silks, Ramnis tapped his glass for attention. "I'll hear countermeasures to gas as you think them up. Meanwhile what about diplomacy?"

Magda settled in. "I've radioed upstairs. We'll let them send choppers to rescue their Marisma pigmaskers, if we can fly people in by our own air machines, both sides keeping neutral. I can talk Senjoro Nie into a two-week trial."

Torfinn frowned in disbelief. "How? A deal like that's to our advantage."

"Our planes are so crude we can't exploit air like they can."

"What about space?" Ramnis asked. "Have we made contact with Luna?"

Magda shook her head. "I used Cedric's frequencies to contact Chittaworld and the *Carl Sagan*. Chittaworld's response was the usual 'Unauthorized use of signal, please terminate.' The *Sagan* was more coy. He's close to Earth and here's his message: 'We're not yet in a situation where dialogue would be useful.'"

"'Not yet?'" Olivia repeated. "A crack in this wall of indifference! We have to conquer more Earthstalk."

Ramnis nodded as he began to eat. "Next step's to test Magda's air treaty."

Back to the real world. A whole day consumed in talk, talk with upstairs, and talk with the base in Paramaraibo. After nonstop physicality there was something absurd about lists and questions and agendas and addenda, absurd and restful. The Lord High Commissioner appropriated a bedroom not far from Magda's communications headquarters, and napped between interruptions.

But if Ramnis's life grew distant from the front lines, it was otherwise for Cedric Chittagong and Alice Spendlowe. Nothing was as immediate as waking at five A.M. after a night of uneasy sleep to face a day of adventure in the cope of a ludicrously primitive machine. As the skies grew light the two resurrectees trudged to the new Five Dominions airfield in Paramaraibo, trailing a moody flightmaster who clearly resented the loss of a precious craft.

Any present urge to go the bathroom? No? A minute later they bumped down the freshly-cleared strip, and were off. "Martin Luther King Day," Alice shouted to her passenger. "They celebrate something like it in two of the Five Dominions, but no, *I* have to work!"

"There must have been calendrical reform," Cedric answered. Engine noise muddied this first attempt. He shouted louder. "A new calendar, January doesn't mean the same thing—"

"Why keep the name? No, our generation computer-married the clocks and calendars of a dozen worlds. The result was so complex that when they finally got it right nobody dared mess with it. We're locked in forever!"

"Not much flexibility about our course, either." At five thousand feet they were above most of the jungle's groundhugging clouds, buzzing above a cottony vastness, nose set just left of Earthstalk's whisker to compensate for the push of the wind.

Forced to beeline by the size of their fuel tanks, and highly visible to radar. If they'd been shot down the Empire would be out two bodies, and look for another way to bring in Heegie gasmasks. The expedition would also feel bad. No fun being killed. They'd not hazard people in their first lives, but Cedric and Alice accepted the risk. Their nine-hour flight coordinated with the upstairs pigmasker rescue, so for a time two vehicles circled: a military copter whose mirrored curves deflected beam-weapons—and a fat and noisy Thraxum Motors biplane, bumblebee yellow and black.

Astronaut Alice windowed between rains, her destination the hardpack glacis separating Earthstalk and jungle. Cursing everything about Thraxum Motors and Imperial monopolies in general, she showed an extraordinary number of teeth in a feral grimace as she tried to compensate for frontheaviness, Earthstalk air turbulence, the hillside slope of the landing field— "Not one goddamn instrument, *not one*. I'm to fly this eight-piston kludge by the feel of it, I suppose!"

Cedric tapped the compass, then the fuel gauge, cautioning her against exaggeration. "Thanks," she answered. "Good to know we're on empty. Here goes."

Final pass. They skimmed over the treetops. As the vegetation parted Alice pushed in the choke. The nose wanted down: fighting it up kept the kludge in service as hardly more than a truly wretched glider. It dropped hard. The right wheel touched—

The lower wing might have touched first, or to prevent that disaster Alice might have angled the plane, though an angled plane is a banked plane, ready to curve moronically into leftward jungle. Any number of things might have happened. Since they didn't, when she and Cedric left the cockpit Alice gave the kludge's riveted body a loving pat.

With their arrival Ramnis had a diplomatic corps, and Cedric's news from Cairo. "We're to use prisoners of war for more resurrections. They're sending U Gyi to administer the soul-transfers and preach a new religion. Just give the go-ahead."

"After one more air delivery," Ramnis responded. "Meanwhile you seduce Senjoro Nie into keeping the skies neutral."

"They're sweet-talking *us*," Magda contributed. "Time to join the Earthstalk economy, make peace, open our doors. They'll cede Level One. All we need do is thumb the covenant."

"Keep your chatter all foam and no beer," the new Commissioner advised. "Would they be interested in beef? I figure the idea of animal meat will gross them out. We want to impress them with our dirtgrub naivete."

Madga's eyes twinkled. "Gross-out" was a verb in Old High English! Transmitting in shifts, she and Cedric kept upstairs talking until the second biplane landed. Agreement after agreement, now would Commissioner Ramnis open his doors?

Captain Caddo jogged by, flinging gasmasks. Cedric

tried an experimental suck and blow. "Sure, it's almost four now, how about six o'clock?"

Torfinn donned Ramnis's armor and climbed to the tenth floor. His expeditionary force climbed with him. Ramnis took lonely station in the lobby.

Just a week ago he'd waded the Marisma, panicked and miserable. Now Commissioner Ramnis's job was to twiddle his thumbs, extend the umbrella of his luck over the whole enterprise, and eventually reopen the lobby doors. Caddo and his people breathed nature's air porting Christina back to the Marisma: a chain of arrangements had been made because the womtie's gasmask didn't fit. Not a bad idea to keep sailors outside, to carry the news in case they'd misjudged the enemy.

But damn, how Ramnis hated to leave adventuring to others! Maybe Hobween armor wasn't so horrible after all. Maybe—

Clunk. Above his head Torfinn the Black Knight turned the bulkhead lock and pushed the green button labeled APERA. A hiss, a racket of lethal pebbles—those bastards really *had* lied!

Cedric lied too; Torfinn led no treaty mission. Resurrectees lunged through poison smoke, following upstairs. Torfinn's clawswipes beat the pigs back, and others climbed and fired. Bullets and ricochets, hot madness—

Confusing to wake in this strange place. Olivia tottered to her feet. On the far side of the landing pigmasked foes fumbled towards consciousness with one disadvantage: Torfinn had dropped their weapons into the gray-pink malaria of Level One.

The dead took them prisoner and shut them in a Level Two suite. Now to secure these ten floors, knowing their leader had gone upward, sonics thrumming, destroying weapons, bending gunmetal with his strength set to 12. "Odds up the stairs!" Olivia shouted. "Evens with me!"

Platoons 3, 5, 7, et cetera were destined immediately

for Level Three, stopping short only to fight in self-
defense. Platoon 2 would never leave Level Two. As for
the others, that's where it got tricky. Simple ideas can
be complex in execution. That's why armies had officers. That's why *some* officers got promoted.

Level One had no civilian population, but Level Two
was given to biology, and its capsule jungle was more
elaborate than Christina's hotel garden. In Olivia's first
life only movie scientists wore labcoats, but life imi-
tated art and she found men and women cowering in
the bushes, dressed in pale gowns whose length was
proof of status.

Her company led them to a second room, and set
another guard. Now on to Level Four— "Wait!"

A short-skirted biologist stepped forward, slim and
oriental as Olivia herself. "It's Tsimios!" She looked
pleadingly, at her fellow labcoats more than their cap-
tors. "He went to Refrigeration. He said he was going
to get some Toxin B!"

Olivia raised her whistle to her lips. The woman
pressed on. "One vial of Toxin B could kill us all—it
could kill millions!"

—and blew. "Corporal, you handle this. We're wasting time."

Corporal Spensky's eyes widened. "But—but you heard
what she said!"

"It's your responsibility. Anybody not Platoon Two
head for the stairs."

Invasion strategy assumed the bulkheads under single command were kept routinely open. It also assumed
all but a dozen of the enemy's pigs had been taken care
of in the first five minutes, leaving upstairs' defense in
the relatively weaponless hands of communications spe-
cialists, shadbolters, retired veterans and quick-acting
vigilantes. At strength 12 Torfinn could climb faster
than news could be shouted, especially if those around
him were sonicked into imbecility. With luck the
"Dirtgrub" Empire would expand into Earthstalk at the
rate his armored legs could run upstairs; one level each

five minutes. In two months he'd be out of Earth's atmosphere!

Too bad the bulkhead crowning Colonel Li's former fief was shut tight. Too bad, except twenty-three levels seemed a good day's work. Two hundred thirty flights of stairs, four thousand one hundred forty steps. Earth's latest hero turned. He caught his breath, and began to herd surrendered civilians down into his comrades' arms.

Torfinn found Olivia on Level 16. "Hard evening?"

She puffed her cheeks. "We're still alive, and it's been five hours. Dear, when we get downstairs we're going to hear Corporal Spensky's story. There's a good chance we'll want to give him the Imperial Cross. You'll never know how hard it was to fight upward in total ignorance—Jesus! Just to think about it!"

She sat suddenly at his side and slumped into his leg. Seconds passed before Torfinn realized she'd fainted.

"—typical of ultimate weapons. The owner doesn't dare use them," Corporal Spensky declaimed, his voice ever so slightly tinged with pride. "I told him we had no intention of killing him: we weren't barbarians. I gave him my word of honor. With that he put it down, trembling like—like—"

But why stall on a metaphor? "We asked him to help us return it, and he did. Then he pulled out some vodka—they keep it in that same cooler! 'Share with me?' he asked, but it was almost a demand. We were all on tenterhooks—you can imagine!"

"So you drank on duty, and the sergeant put you on report. By Imperial law we could hang you, Spensky."

Spensky blanched. "But—I thought you were on *my* side."

Torfinn couldn't keep from smiling. "Enough to cancel any punishment. It does sort of gum up your medal, though. All those lives you saved—" He shook his head. "Dismissed, Sergeant Spensky."

# PART THREE

## *The Dirtgrub War*

## Friday

Good morning, Torfinn. Exercising? Good way to get used to this new body. No, no need to get up. I can talk while you go through your set. Just don't expect me to spot you during your bench presses!

Yesterday I began our session by indulging in background history. Today we'll get more involved with the cultures of Earthstalk, so I'll tell you what all those habs have in common.

—INFOWEB! But of course, you tell me. INFOWEB's been around long as your earliest memories. Only a handful of your fellow dead remember a time before Earth's industrial facilities networked together. Every world has INFOWEB, Earthstalk as well. But every INFOWEB evolved in a different direction, so what I tell you now you might not know.

See, on Earthstalk there's a universal personnel system. I've made some notes to suggest how it works:

"STATUS ONE: 22 years education; pilots; military officers captain and above; design engineers.

"STATUS TWO: 18 years education; CPAs; factory & powerplant engineers; all other military officers; med-

71

ical personnel; civilian judges; contractors; supervisors of more than six personnel; H-V stars.
"STATUS THREE: 14 years education; chemists; lower management; psychodoktars; teachers; nutritionists; artisans; masters-at-tradecraft; females in uniform.
"STATUS FOUR: 12 years education; documentarians; secretaries; clerks; service personnel; security guards; noncom officers; juniors-at-tradecraft.
"STATUS FIVE: 8 years education; factory labor; custodians; ex-convicts; escorts with refusal rights; enlisted personnel not specified above; porters; apprentices-at-tradecraft; vending machine maintenance personnel.
"STATUS SIX: defective education; labor at exempt facilities; prisoners; enlisted personnel during basic training; students under 14; subjects of scientific experiments; body part donors; prostitutes; sexual deviants; the insane; political malignants; persons without ID."

Got that, Torfinn? Wages, room allocations—everything is based on status! A stable system: too few classes and the underfolk become powerful, beefers and drabs on the same side.

That's never happened on Earthstalk. There've been dozens of revolts, but always precipitated by outside attack. In fact I wonder if a dynamic's at work here? Lack of internal revolution leading to social dry rot, so the whole organism loses coherence—excuse me, Torfinn. I promised background, not a tissue of theory!

On with the story.

## Chapter 9
# Minus 28–Hab 3114

On Earthstalk Level 3114 a Stat Five nightshift janitor shuffled down a radius-hall, through tightening circles of dark offices. The gaunt old man climbed a shallow
ramp and shoved his magcard into a slot. The computer
room door opened.

"Da-da-da-da-*daa*-dum." Bach's Fugue in G minor
played only in the man's head, not through the intercom. The facility was empty. Certainly Fergus the security pig could have stuck the janitor's request into the
system, but then he'd gossip to everyone about his
implausible musical tastes. No, better to remain a nonentity, just one faceless old beefer. It was worth the
price.

Did Fergus even remember his name? So long since
"Old Pete" had done anything remarkable, so long since
that problem with the leaky bucket—

The man set down his pail. He looked right and left,
then slipped into the console chair. A few rapid
keystrokes and program IAC-6113 calculated the pres-

ent left-to-right order of Jupiter's Galilean moons; eJgci. He appended those letters to one of Earthstalk's most potent passwords and leaned back, a scowling skeleton ligatured by hide and muscle.

Senjoro Nie was pissed. "FRIDAY 24/01/26 ALL POINTS DIRECTIVE;" he typed. "ALL TREATIES WITH DIRTGRUBS ARE OFF. IMPOUND SOURCE-20 MEDICINES AND DRUGS, AND PLAN FOR RATIONING."

He dealt with a few further details and keyed in a homily: "—WHY NO REQUEST TO CUT LEVEL ONE'S POWER? WITHOUT POWER THEY'D NOT HAVE KEPT US FROM RETAKING THE MARISMA AND PRESSING IN FROM OUTDOORS! I HEAR NO ANSWER EXCEPT TALK OF 'JUNGLE MAGIC,' BASED ON THE REPORTS OF NAKED PIGMASKERS. WELL, THE COLONEL WHO TOLD ME ABOUT JUNGLE MAGIC IS DEAD. IT'S TIME TO SPAR. WE'VE GOT COPTERS, WE'VE GOT SHADBOLTS. LET'S ZERO IN ON ENEMY SHIPS AND PLANES. LET'S CONSCRIPT THE YOUNG: EACH COLONELCY SHOULD HAVE A HUNDRED TROOPS AT ITS DISPOSAL. LET'S DISCUSS THE POSSIBILITY OF A *MOBILE* FORCE, ABLE TO TRANSFER FROM ONE JURISDICTION TO ANOTHER!"

After all this Senjoro Nie was brain-tired. Suggest this, wheedle for that— Hell, he wanted to *smash* something! Some goddamn snoop of a toon video editor on 2105? A shoe-vinyl shortage on 3911? Anti-Jappo graffiti on the Thomish levels? He tabled six petitions and signed off. At some random moment between now and six A.M. his orders would transmit. He got up and put his chair on the console desk. His bucket was full of soapy water, and after more tidying history's most anonymous dictator was ready to mop the floors.

# Chapter 10

# Minus 27–The Amazon

Soon as the high-prowed saddle was cinched to his broad brown back, the Allfather took the bit in his mouth. U Gyi watched from the deck of his yacht, feeling absurd in rubber suit and bubble helmet, absurd and hot. He moved to the sling, sat, and gaped for air like a fish in a stagnant pool. Shrunken muscles nervously clenched as the hoist swung him up, out, and down onto the massive womtie.

A flotilla of womties hung behind, bearing his cadres, the hollow torpedoes slung between them filled with irreplaceable gear: the stuff that made U Gyi a god, augmented by the equipment that made him one of Earth's last practicing geneticists. U Gyi wriggled and strapped in. At last the womtie colony sped up the Amazon, cutting foamy vees through their new home, with a brief obligatory detour up a jungle side-channel toward the base of Earthstalk.

Here on the landward side of the Pico Geronta the overhanging Marisma shielded them from all eyes. Young womtie bulls massed, bluffing toothy reptiles into retreat, then gloating in boastful dithyrambs of their own bravo magnificence.

*No good*, U Gyi worried. Shackled brothers swam carefully in place while advance guards breached and slammed tauntingly. A womtie's capacity for discipline was small, and these irksome displays—what was this?

Thousands of tiny fish floated to the surface, shocked dead by the noise.

Food for the encumbered porters. U Gyi had misinterpreted the entire show! Did it matter? Womtie sociology was hardly crucial to his mission, except for the fact they were thirty percent human. If he couldn't understand *them*, how could he pretend to understand Gatekeeper's truly alien mentality?

The end of water, beginning of land. With a surge of gratitude rare in a god, U Gyi blessed the Allfather, then turned to walk a well-beaten trail. Darkness obscured his troop's final scamper across Earthstalk's naked glacis. Commissioner Ramnis's greetings sounded almost sincere, and after a night's sleep U Gyi got to work.

Within eight days of U Gyi's surreptitious arrival Torfinn's comrades enlisted 192 new dead, secured Li's domain by "retiring" an equal number of pigmaskers and malignants, and set up dream-tutorials in the local dialect.

Under Alice's direction those recruits were put to half-days in the Marisma, canalizing, clearing paths and setting up camouflaged picket-camps, some dummy, some real. With Senjoro Nie provoked as he was, they had an obligation to get accumulated biplanes off the glacis and out of sight. Even if upstairs shadbolts couldn't be depressed to fire straight down, it was always possible to drop rocks—

In any case it was good exercise, and outdoor hardships bred an *esprit de corps*. "Makework?" Sergeant Spensky laughed at his men's complaints. "Chopping firewood in forty Celsius heat? Seems perfectly reasonable to me!"

Meanwhile the god's cadres preached at six thousand natives in pidgin Prospore: they should love High Commissioner Ramnis because he stood for democracy, even if his forces were Dirtgrubs and weren't going to let *them* vote. After all, he'd freed them from tyranny!

U Gyi's propaganda had good effect. "Is it some trick of power that makes people give Ramnis the benefit of the doubt?" Olivia asked during a morning encounter on the Level One escalator. "—Some need of sheep for a shepherd?"

"The truth is simple," U Gyi replied smugly. "I've dreamt thousands of memories and bring no one to life I do not like. These Earthstalkers were bullied by pompous martinets. Now strangers move in, curious, decent, and given to exotic competencies."

*Trust U Gyi to take credit for everything*, Torfinn's wife thought. *So I'm decent? Incest with my husband-brother . . . look how His Holiness studies me! U Gyi burdened me with this obsession: he dreamt my soul and laughs at my plight! When I ask him for a new body what awful price will he demand?*

"Come," U Gyi added. "Tea. I insist. You never liked me, you think I'm a hothouse sociopath weighing across my age. I'd unburden myself of some thoughts, and perhaps—"

"It's all a game to you. Why else are you alive?"

They reached the fifth floor. U Gyi tugged her sleeve. "Come. I'll tell you things. A game? A game my incompetent peers lost fifteen years ago. How much longer will Earth tolerate her gods? We've had our innings. Now I'm the only one with a modicum of power—I switched sides at the right moment, for one thing."

"I hear you're starting a new religion."

U Gyi turned and bowed. "A gloss on my Redemptorist Cult. Gatekeeper is God, a benevolent God who'll not keep us from colonizing Alpha Centauri."

"Most people think otherwise."

"Some people *can* think otherwise and still persist in

our mission, tragic heroes in defiance of doom. Most
need assurances. What was forbidden a thousand years
ago may not be forbidden now. Indeed I've had 'revela-
tions' to that effect."

They crossed a foyer labeled HEALTH CLUB and entered U Gyi's suite, a clutter of refrigerators, bottles,
microscopes and cabinets. The next room was dominated by a single low table—and four walls of labeled
dreamtapes. U Gyi settled onto a cushion.

"I'm just doing my job," he spoke. "The Emperor
would be rid of me. What does it mean that he ordered me here? Not to be overly dramatic, but I'm a
broken man."

"It's called being civilized," Olivia answered, studying the god's shelves. "The difference between tame
and wild: you serve others instead of yourself."

U Gyi's major-domo bustled in with tea and biscuits.
The god poured. "Thank you, Pavel. Now to business."

The aged cherub left the room. Olivia raised slim
arms to finger-comb her long, black hair. Her abrupt-
ness betrayed the strength of her feelings. "You have
the only memory transfer equipment on Earthstalk."

"No." U Gyi shook his head. "Earthstalk has its
INFOWEB, its own passwords. Someday I'll dream the
mind of an enemy and gain priority-one control. My
friends will open secret doors and find potent tools."

"Ah. Friendship."

"Why not be a friend? What do I ask?"

"I don't know," Olivia answered.

"Me neither, not yet. But I know how to exchange
favors. In the meantime—" (U Gyi opened his arms
expansively)—"don't be afraid of me. I too am human."

"I wonder if you haven't lost yourself among ten
thousand dreams."

U Gyi brought his arms together and made claws of
his fingers. "The sounds and images of ten thousand
lives, yet there's still some of me inside. I cling to it
like a shipmast in a storm. What others call cunning is
just my clutching tight. True, I've thrown out non-

essentials. For that reason I should be easy to recognize. Under veneers of civility you too have a monkeysoul. We're the same that way. Only one of us is different. Senator Ramnis lacks the inner monkey. Ask yourself: how did he evolve?"

"I ask that," Olivia whispered. "And I don't like the answer. I very much dislike the answer. U Gyi, aren't you tired of life?"

"You're older than me," the god answered. "Are *you* tired?"

"Of games and pretense. I left a legacy my first life, when I was useful. I've been coasting on my seedship legacy ever since. More than a thousand years I've had simulations thrust on me, a colossal waste of time. I'd hoped I'd escaped all that, but then I learn about Ramnis's career. See, there's no such thing as luck; there *can't* be! Not in the *real* universe."

U Gyi laughed. "Start with a thousand pair of dice; smash each that fails to roll seven. After some hours you're left with a few, each remarkably lucky!" He leaned forward and patted her arm. "He's a hero. In a few years he'll be a dead hero, but you and I will live on. I know you well enough to be sure of that!"

Eleven mornings after the first meeting of the Earthstalk Commission, Commissioner Ramnis's breakfast was an institution. He trailed goatishly behind Magda's callipygian form, took his seat by Christina's pool, shifted his brain to neutral, and surveyed concentric crowds. Otto's gang sat near, and U Gyi's. The other tables were the prerogative of the dead, but with so many reborn many resurrectees were forced to stand, and native Earthstalkers were pushed to the first tier of balconies.

All the more unusual. Before Ramnis stood a flock of labcoats; Olivia their sponsor. Yet Olivia looked at the senator as a stranger, not one who'd shared his triumphs. Ramnis's brow furrowed as he tried to define what was changed about her.

Olivia's words rushed over his thoughts. "Senator,

last Monday I threw myself into research on Earthstalk's economy, a study involving energy budgets, INFOWEB, political structures . . . Well, in the course of my work I interviewed these folks here, and I've come to tell you the part Colonel Li's levels play in that economy. Toxins and antitoxins, medicines and narcotics: the upstairs folk don't *dare* let things hang!"

"They can't anyhow," Magda supplemented. "I've got radio messages. Senjoro Nie rules to Level 4160. Above that lies the domain of the Breeds. We've allies: black Earthstalkers with grudges so hot against Nie they've unilaterally embargoed trade to get on your good side. At least for a while Nie won't be getting manufactured products from the nodes."

Jealousy? The way Magda leapt in—slim child Olivia versus a woman almost freakishly endowed? Did Torfinn's wife envy Magda her glands, or was it *him* she was after? " 'The enemy of my enemy is my friend,' " Ramnis quoted, thinking lovers in despair could act like enemies. "Tell them the embargo's mutual, and solicit their advice on all—um, interlevel issues. Be *really* polite, we're still ignorant savages down here. Anything else?"

Magda reached in her breast pocket and handed him a folded note.

# Chapter 11

# Minus 18–Hab 1

The day was spent in negotiation. At noon following, Nie's local viceroy opened his bulkheads to Torfinn's invasion. Ramnis deftly removed an unnecessary gasmask and stood by to accept the colonel's switched loyalties and give him a pension. See, Colonel Guzman's daughter was sick—

The Emperor's forces now controlled 1.6 kilometers of Earthstalk. Intolerable! Tuesday night Senjoro Nie cut off their power.

Ramnis's Breed allies followed Hammurabi: an eye for an eye. Magda's voice reached them shortly after midnight. At eleven Thursday morning the result was a sudden pervasive brownout. All nonessential equipment had to be shut off. Buffeted by atmosphere, Nie's solar collectors were small. He needed every trickle to keep air circulating, water purified—it wouldn't stretch. The temperature dropped; 18, 15, 11 . . . Damn, it was *cold*!

Would the Caliphate trump the Breeds and force

them to behave? Were they neutralized by Lightfoots? The Level 3114 janitor sat at his console. He found a frozen keyboard. For the duration Earthstalk had heard its last from Senjoro Nie. The old man's face showed no regret: if he'd ordered 3114 heated he'd draw attention to his home habitat, and sacrifice precious anonymity.

Shutdown. What would get to people first? Anomie among white collar tiepatchers, eyes and ears no longer interfaced with INFOWEB? Hideous to deal with reality without subtitles, footnotes, constant data retrievals— it must be even harder on those with surgical implants, part of their minds gone numb.

Data addicts frantic for a fix. Fish-breeders unable to warm their ponds. Obstetricians delivering babies without equipment, shuddering at the need to fall back on vaginal childbirth! All these milling while Status Six hoodlums waited to plunder, knowing most monitor-cameras no longer operated. Lights constantly at gloomy night setting, and growing uncertainty about the delivery of food, followed by raids on the vending machines; increasingly organized raids, even insurrections!

The remainder of the war was the responsibility of Nie's military policy committee, his most-trusted colonels. Senjoro Nie shook his head. If there'd been a Great Mind among them he'd feel confident of the outcome, but until recently Great Minds were the last thing he'd wanted in his vassals. The joke was on him, and he was wise enough to appreciate it—as long as he didn't have to laugh. Too cold to laugh, too cold to think of much but survival, not with his old man's sensitivity to temperature. He looked at the skein of ice forming in his bucket, and decided to go to bed and huddle under his blankets.

Far below the problem was too much heat. Ramnis ordered thermostats set high to conserve juice and keep Magda's radio room powered: his Dirtgrubs had collectors too, and most other stuff could go to hell.

Open doors let window light into the central atrium. In brown cathedral dimness the senator read Magda's

noteboard, littered with communiques. The news was
good. Between Levels 40 and 4160 insurrections flamed,
two or three per sheet of faxpaper.

The matter could be delayed no longer. Torfinn and
Olivia, Cedric and Alice should know what they fought
for, because there'd be real fighting in the days to
come. Time to tell them The Secret, collaring them one
by one so U Gyi's agents needn't grow suspicious.

Ramnis wandered, three times successful. Christina's
flipper-hand pointed him to the room where Olivia
made a list of energy priorities. He closed the door,
looked through the bathroom and then the closet. Olivia
stood, intrigued by his odd behavior. Not impossible
that this was the prelude to her seduction—totally *un-
professional*, but not totally impossible. And how would
she react?

Olivia Daneby, antique futurist, seedship consultant
and writer of reports. Ex-spinster, ex-virago— She *was*
made of flesh though, and now he drew close, heat to
heat. "What I'm going to tell you is given in utter
confidence, not to be conveyed to anyone beyond us
five: absolutely never to U Gyi."

"Don't tell me then. He'll find out when he dreams
my mind," Olivia answered. "He's a mind-voyeur. When
I switch to a new body—"

"I'm sorry. That can't happen. Not this week, probably not the next." And then he spoke the words that
blighted all Olivia's hopes.

Chilly Thursday, frigid Friday, a miserable night between. A second night was fast approaching. Abstract
loyalties went out the window: with the coming of
darkness battlecopters flew refugees from Nie's part of
Earthstalk to the ground. Hideous as jungle seemed to
an indoor race, at least it was warm.

Through the night astronaut Alice led troops into the
rain, acting her role as Imperial spokesperson and ambassador. She got a few signal fires burning, guided
displaced Earthstalkers to lean-to shelters, promised
food from Dominion ships not yet underway from

Paramariabo, and got two copters in return. A third clump of women and children drove a harder bargain: she had to bring them inside. U Gyi was shaken from slumber at 1:00 A.M. to dream the memories of their leaders. He isolated twenty saboteurs. Alice welcomed the rest as friends.

Olivia dozed between the interruptions that finally roused Torfinn to dress and leave. She reached to find him gone, his wonderful touch—

Torfinn's wife could enjoy the feel of him for a few hours after sex, and she could endure sex, imagining two bodies as one. One slim, dark-haired creature with four wandering hands, seeking her bedmate fantasy, her Ramnis, her Captain Caddo, her anybody.

Some people are eunuchs, free to use themselves in other ways. U Gyi made sure his last dozen generations were so gifted. The power of sex frightened him when he dreamt it in others and felt it take over their lives, and twist their wills to madness.

*"In that basement of the soul where sex lurks always, it fashions monsters worse than itself."*

U Gyi's words were prophetic. Olivia's eyes opened as her disease returned, a more powerful wash of incest-revulsion than ever before! This was madness, and madness was nothing that could be cured by mere therapist's talk.

Again she lunged to the bathroom and was sick. Minutes of dry heaves, more minutes for her strength to return so she could stand again. Madness, and now she trembled, blood hot in her cheeks, ill and feverish.

But the cure to her problems might be at hand! She assembled an hour's worth of visitors' mutterings into something coherent. Twenty women! It was almost too late. A choice of bodies, a possibly-flustered god—what an opportunity!

Olivia found clothes to point up her body's best features, something to provide incentive in case it was necessary to wheedle and trade. Ten minutes later, still brushing her hair, she strode to the escalator.

A dead escalator, of course. She had to jog down

toward U Gyi's fog-haloed health club lights, and get all breathless.

Twenty women? Eleven sat in the post-resurrection briefing room, or slumped, or lay snoring on the floor. If these were examples—

"Can I help you?"

"Pavel! Thank you, yes! Have these been processed? Are they resurrectees? How many left? Where are they? I want to shop for a new body. Can you help me?"

"Oh, Madam!" His pudgy little hands raised in U Gyi's defense, Pavel retreated from Olivia's rapid questions. "My poor master exhausts himself! Twenty souls in one night! You'd make it twenty-one!"

Olivia smiled. A secret lay in her mind U Gyi was not meant to dream, an amazing truth she could never forget, certainly not within ten hours of being told. For the sake of that fatal secret she'd been forbidden to trade bodies, and there'd be hell to pay when she showed up in new flesh this coming morning. That's when she'd whisper Pavel's words: *U Gyi was exhausted, working under an impossible schedule. It was perfectly safe. I knew he'd never take time to dream my memories.*

Would she get away with it? Would the god actually let her soul slip by unaudited? "Lead me to the others. I want to inspect them."

Pavel nodded and pointed the way. A cadre with a sonic belt and stunwand stood outside a plain white door. Inside that door a second cadre held vigil. On benches toward the far side of the room eight prisoners hunkered, doomed saboteur souls, bodies understandably not at their best. "Take off your clothes," Olivia ordered.

Fatigue, hostility and disappointment clouded the air, an ambience in which all partook: in Olivia's case disappointment dominated. There'd been small emphasis on diet in the levels these women came from. With their bulky hips, rippled thighs and shelves of tummy they might have posed for the "Before" photo in a diet ad. Naked and sullen with the tragedy of what was soon to happen, they looked like Rembrandt's "Bathsheba" repeated six times over, six matrons ravaged by pregnancies and what passed locally for coffeecakes and crepes with hollandaise sauce.

Six of these, and two gaunt harpies.

Olivia dismissed the crones and made the least-fat Bathsheba stand, turn, and walk, wondering what Torfinn would think of a plump bedmate in her thirties, her upper back a mass of blemishes. Did she dare? Frustrated, she cast an angry glance at the sole adolescent among these prisoners, furious the girl was frankly obese, worse than all the others.

"Next," someone spoke beyond the door. The cadre ordered Olivia's posturing victim to grab her clothes. The moment of decision, and Olivia's decision was no. She turned and left the room, fled U Gyi's fifth floor, and went home to wash clean of this experience.

Alice Spendlowe had no opportunity to wash; her black face was streaked with dirt acquired during her wet "ambassadorial" forays. "—Three copters, and now four, all hidden under camouflage netting. Do we dare fly them?" she asked at yet another Commission breakfast. "What if Nie's got shadbolts on trickle power?"

Today the assembly seemed terribly close to the front lines. Squadrons clumped by the tables and through the lobby, outdoors and in, indoors and out. Near to hand twenty resurrectees bounced through their calisthenics, women who helped correct the sexual imbalance among the dead, their eyes open to life in a new era. Clad in the bodies of former saboteurs they saw gloom, muddied carpet, steamy air, and a hotch-potch of people gobbling nondescript food puffs, all too busy to pay them much attention.

Newly-ensouled, with a future ahead, they were no longer the cheerless dregs Olivia had rejected hours before. Commissioner Ramnis studied them approvingly, tossed a fist-size morsel to Christina, and answered. "Shadbolts on automatic or under manual control? If we could be sure they were all manual we could try a night ascent."

Otto cleared his throat, exiled ex-historian, now privileged to *make* history. "—I have some idea," he began importantly. "Hot air balloon, item 12-9336 in the standard INFOWEB catalog. Always I want to see the balloon in my life, but Earthstalkers never have need, so dumb pigmasks don't know what is." He turned to U Gyi's table. "Heegie INFOWEB show the same catalog? Radio them factory to send us a balloon."

"What good is that?" Olivia objected. "We've already got Alice's copters."

Otto looked abashed. "I admit I thinked this before now. Maybe shadbolts on automatic. Stupid waste of power, but maybe anyhow, okay? So why shadbolts not shoot the birds, or the moon? Not birds, because the bird fly not intersecting with Earthstalk. Moon because same, and moves so slow anyhow. Understand? Balloon is just faster moon."

Torfinn snorted. "I don't know what the fuss is about. They don't have enough power upstairs to shoot at us, no matter how flagrant—"

"We can't say for sure," Olivia interrupted testily. "Don't get all macho just because you're in armor."

"Macho?"

Olivia swallowed her frustration. "Torfinn, I keep thinking you're my contemporary. 20th-century word. Listen dear, balloons are cheap. We can send one up, make Otto happy, and if nobody shoots unleash our armada. They'll be better than biplanes: some chance of actually using grapples to land on an upstairs heliport."

U Gyi yawned. "Excuse my manners, like most of us I've been up all night. There's a box labeled 12-9336 ashore at Paramaraibo. Otto may think he had a new idea: I assure him otherwise. Are we desperate though? Ballooning is a tactic improbable of success, unless getting shot counts as a triumph. Room in the basket for two or three people. Three soldiers can't hope to win victory when Nie's typical colonel has more than sixty pigs."

"There's my armor," Torfinn responded.

"Torfinn, you're not to be risked on this venture,"

Ramnis ordered. "No, what we want is a mad martyr, a Souldancer with wild luck—"

"Not *you!*" Alice was shocked.

"In Torfinn's armor?" Ramnis wheedled. "My armor again?"

"Armor won't save you if you fall."

Ramnis sighed. "I need action, it's like a drug to me. Yes, I'm Commissioner of Earthstalk, and commissioners don't dare mad things, but—" He faltered. "I'm trying to think of an argument, though all reason is against me. Let me do this one small thing, and I promise to spend the rest of this campaign safe behind my gavel."

# Chapter 12
# Minus 10–Airdock 300

Sergeant Prasad was big and paced when he talked, so the Level 200 communications room was crowded with just two pigmaskers inside. "Another bogie," Prasad yelled into the handset. "They're starting early this evening. West face—"

"That'll be the Hab 319 runaways," Hiroko's voice crackled. "Dyes and inks, fleshspinners. Any shadbolt power at your level?"

Sergeant Prasad carried the handset with him as he checked. "Not enough, not against mirror-paint. We can't use our copter either."

"Can't, or won't?" the voice buzzed in his ear.

Prasad's gut was rubbery, and he was sensitive to charges of sloth. "Listen, exalted one: the Colonel barely quashed a flash riot just hours ago. One sarge to another: we haven't enough men to hold all our levels, much less chase runaways. Fleshspinners! What are we gonna do for food these next weeks? How are we gonna keep control? Six lousy days and see how things are gone to hell—"

"You Hab 200 pigs always were whiners. Guess we'll go get them ourselves."

Prasad tried to think of something more insulting than what finally came out: "Yeah, they're *your* problem, aren't they? Level 300's a damn sight closer to 319—"

Sergeant Hiroko had already clicked off. Twenty minutes later a second copter descended into view. Prasad witnessed its drop to the Marisma. "Take over the watch," he told his corporal, and jogged the short hall to the level 200 airdock.

Prasad was one of few who cultivated the ability to go outside in jacket and mask and enjoy the jungle vista. Soon he stood in the observer station at the shelf-edge of his habitat's airdock. Wind whipped his quilted pajamas and lashed pink into his cheeks. His skill was rewarded by a most extraordinary view.

Down in Dirtgrub-land enemy squads hunkered at constellations of small fires. The Hab 319 runaways would pick a landing spot near one such beacon. Traitors and dirtgrubs would be milling, wheedling, begging, coping with sudden phobias; a perfect target for Hiroko's strafe-guns. There was Hiroko now, arcing for his first run—

An orange glow-ball appeared and vanished. No explosion, more like a blinking bulb than any fireworks; at least the size of a tree, and somehow mobile— No, it hadn't vanished altogether, but from a platform high as legendary Mount Everest one had to look hard to see it.

Hiroko began firing. Tiny from eight kilometers away, jungle campfires winked out one by one. At the same time the orange ball reappeared, perhaps slightly larger than before. What *was* this thing? Prasad used the resources of his observer station to find out.

Whatever it was, it distracted Hiroko. As Prasad slaved the station's tiepatch to the copter's monitors the machine buzzed close, looped around— Damn! Earthstalk was right in the line of fire: of course the strafer joystick balked. No way was Sergeant Hiroko's copter going to fire into Earthstalk.

As if bullets could dent trifilamented cryswire! Another loop, another approach. The ball went black as Hiroko blazed away at its basket, suddenly dark with the cutoff of flame from the tank beneath. The copter's searchlights found holes in the balloon's fabric skirt, yet the thing's passenger waggled his arms in insane defiance, nor did the craft plummet or explode into fiery fragments.

But after all the object was now clearly demonstrated to be an insubstantial synsilk bauble, and since Hiroko was headed straight for it—

Hiroko's sponsons stabbed into Ramnis's balloon, more than half-collapsing the bag. The commissioner grabbed the suspension rope and held on, extruding knifeclaws for greater dig-in power. He was taken for a ride, up, up—

And down! Above Ramnis's head Hiroko hissed with exasperation. The bag had tangled and failed to drop off. Ah, well. There were other ways, but not this close to enemy guns.

Hiroko retreated south, out over the Amazon river. Lower, lower, touching. The basket filled with water and tore away. Hard to see in the waning moonlight, cords and ropes and tatters flapping, but had he taken care of the man in black?

Ramnis hauled upward, closer to the sponson, grimly determined not to die in river filth weighed down by his powerpack. Closer—God and the Devil! Whoever flew the copter sure as hell was thorough! He was taking a hideous chance flying this low over jungle canopy in the middle of the night!

CRASH! WHAP! Branches snapped, fabric tore away, and Ramnis dangled in plain view, except *now* the whoreson wasn't looking. Or did the copter pilot have another torture in mind? Up again he flew, up higher, up—

And ever up. How high before air got too thin to breathe? Ramnis's sea-level lungs weren't ready for this. Gyring dizzily he hyperventilated with fretful vigor and wondered if there was an oxygen switch among all his armor's features.

Ten meters above Ramnis's upstretched arms, Hiroko flipped on his radio. "Prodigal Son returning for safety check and washdown. Good hunting dirtside, recommend second go-around, but first let's make sure I haven't got goo in my intakes. Seems I killed a flying air-bubble."

Sergeant Prasad took off his tiepath to watch the ascent. Hiroko rose past Level 200, and waved cockily.

Prasad froze. Jesus Mary Joseph! He turned and jogged indoors, into the pressure chamber, working his jaws impatiently.

A four-klom ascent, certainly more than four minutes. Yes, there was time to warn them. Seconds ticked by, the door opened, and he ran to the communications room. "Get me Hab 300!" he shouted, ears popping. "There's a man under Hiroko's copter!"

Thanks to Sergeant Prasad the pigs of Level 300 were ready. Hiroko lofted over the dock, then down. His audience gestured and pointed, their words defeated by the noise of his rotor. The copter thumped as the tail wheel rolled off Ramnis's shin.

A hail of gunfire! Ow! Ramnis tried to shake awake. At strength 12 he lurched up, smashed his head into the copter carriage behind the cabin, and reduced the direction finder to pancaked junk. What was it he was supposed to remember? Pigs shooting at him, stinging him black and blue— Defend himself?

*"Flights of angels—"* He stepped, wondering distractedly how to complete the words, the power behind his move multiplied twelve times:

—stepped, pranced, fell, skidded and rolled within a meter of the platform's edge. Ah, better. His next hop landed him on his feet. Now what? More shots, and confused people in masks, quilted . . . some way out of here? Thin air—yes! Hold on to that. Something about air.

Dither. Blither, blather. Ramnis giggled. They looked so silly, nervous darting eyes. Gawking, egging each other to charge. So sleepy, so cold . . . angels? With a drunken swipe he reached for a corporal's facemask. Oops, claws not retracted. Giggle—God! Strength 12, face smashed in, shredded, exposed bone waxy-blue, spurts of blood steaming blackly in thin cold, fountaining across his gauntlet.

Still hosing blood the man collapsed and twitched. Ramnis dialed down his strength and felt himself grow heavy. Bullets? More ponderously he moved to the next face, tore the mask off, took some healing sucks of oxygen.

They might have been lovers standing this close, for Ramnis was not ready to deal with the complexities of divesting his flailing victim of tank, tubes and harness. Not yet, and not for another minute.

*"Flights of angels carry thee—"* Where? No, this wasn't heaven. But Ramnis had no peace to complete his thoughts. Two more pigmaskers jogged out the airdock's pressure door. In a different direction, shielded by the copter's body, Sergeant Hiroko readied his pistol and palmed open the cockpit. In the ensuing storm of bullets Ramnis's unarmored air source slumped to the deck.

Fine. Now Ramnis knew how to get out of here. He hustled for the door, stepped in, heard air shriek around him, felt his ears fill with pain—a trap?

*A trap!* He beat the walls, but they were Earthstalk-tough and the howl only grew worse. Now wait, hold on. In one of his vaguer dreamt memories this place made sense. In any case now suddenly the sound died away. The inner door opened.

Ramnis stepped through. Just visible in the glow of a nightlight he saw a sign on the wall: ADMINSTUMO PRENU ROC'LINON—>. His brain came to life again as he translated. Breathing the sharp winter oxygen of angel-land,

Commissioner Ramnis followed the red line painted on the floor.

Peace, and time to suck and gasp. Air delicious as water to someone dying of thirst! Ramnis regained the wit to assess his situation. Those last two pigmaskers were the inside guards, that explained why he now moved without challenge. As for pursuit, there was space for six inside the airlock, and in another minute they'd press through to make room for another six. Fortunately a minute was a long time; long enough to turn corners, retract his claws, and face the future.

The *Adminstumo* was of the University of Lower Downside. In the absence of power for its word processors the office-ringed cubbies of Otto's alma mater were practically empty; except for one profoundly massive night receptionist, huddled in a shawl. "I'm a Dirtgrub," Ramnis announced and bowed, waving his left arm while his bloody right remained behind his back. "I'm here to liberate you from Senjoro Nie."

The receptionist decided the joke was in bad taste. "Get outa here before I call for help." Her words puffed white in the freezing air.

"Does the university have a president? A dean?" Despite himself, Ramnis giggled. "Excuse me, I'm not fully recovered. Take me to your leader."

The receptionist stared back and shook a proud, defiant no. These three weeks Ramnis had noticed that Earthstalkers tended somewhat to corpulence. Statistically their bulk increased as gravity lessened toward midnode, each region indicting the excesses of those above, but this woman was fat by *any* standard, her head sunk into a roll of neck! The way her stomach pressed forward into the desk challenged him: Ramnis moved behind her seat, grabbed, and lifted. "This may convince you—" But his words were lost among her startled shrieks. She kicked: her mittened fists hammered at his head.

"What's all this?" a voice of authority intoned from behind.

Ramnis turned. "Madam, are you an official of this university? I'm here to announce your freedom."

Thanks to Dean Madchamf and her administration's eagerness to put into effect a political theory found in only one contraband text, twenty hours later the commissioner's life was routine again, a matter of policing Hab 300's corridors, chivvying pigmasks out of their hiding places and interviewing them. Yes, all Senjoro Nie's shadbolts were out of commission. Laughable to think otherwise.

His battle armor itched familiarly. He could only speculate that beneath its scales, beneath the webbed tubing that supposedly kept him warm or cool, beneath his faded-pink rubber undersuit, beneath all that his skin was a piebald mess of black and blue.

Over the local intercom the dean's academic coven debated articles of surrender-cum-declarations of independence: ". . . free worker syndicates for every factory, and eventual group ownership phased in over a thirty-year schedule—"

Such sad innocence: they reckoned without the great Torfinn, foremost of dead warriors! Before they went on to sketch their new constitution the Dirtgrub Empire lofted into the air, skipped past Spanic, Jappo, Lett, Portuguese, Thomish, Sketrib, Norse and Leewardine colonelcies, and landed a hundred sixty troops to give "guidance" and recover Torfinn's armor.

Fuel from copter four was pumped into the other three tanks. Leaving Otto's old Marisma-gang in charge, at nineteen hundred Torfinn and Ramnis flew on to Level 600.

More Jappo, then Iban, Pweb, Leninish, Greek. Absolutely the hardest nut to crack. The pigmaskers of Level 600 fought like hellions, corridor by corridor. Time and again their noisy defense summoned the armored enemy. TRUNCH . . . TRUNCH . . . His powerpack whining up and down the scale, Torfinn's inexorable approach was the stuff of soldiers' nightmares; except *these* soldiers were sonicked too soon to

fully appreciate their peril. At last Torfinn captured
Archmandrite Levros and persuaded this colonel to—
surrender? Was it *surrender* to open his eyes and find
Torfinn bowed before him, armored, invulnerable, and
begging his blessing?

The Archmandrite thought it strange to find a chrism
of oil in his hands, but no doubt it had been placed
there. He looked: the sanctuary was crowded with wak-
ers like himself, Dirtgrubs among them as they blinked
into attentiveness. Very well then: a decent concern for
appearances. Taking some comfort Levros spoke the words
of blessing.

Torfinn responded in good Greek. The Peace was
official. For less than an hour there was quiet, before a
few armed enemies gathered and voted, some to retreat
high and low, close bulkheads against invasion, and
continue the fight.

No problem. Torfinn's main objective was to secure
600's airdock, pump two tanks full of fuel, and make
one final ascent.

Yugo, Gheg, Mexi, Fijan, Moor. An hour before
midnight Torfinn and forty of his resurrectees struck
the Hab 1000 colonelcy; high as air-breathing copters
could be made to go.

There was nothing accidental about this destination.
With Earthstalk memories at his disposal U Gyi was
able to fashion a map and single out Senjoro Nie's least
competent vassal. Not a single pigmasker stood guard at
the 1000 airdock.

As for those eventually roused from slumber—

The palace was a maze of tapestry-lined corridors,
inlaid tables, screens and genuine silver trays and gob-
lets. Dirtgrub corporals' guards trooped purposefully,
as if a system lay behind their random forays. Now and
again these thrusts were successful: shouts of protest
mingled with the bumps and crashes of ineffectual struggle. Ramnis and his two escorts accepted delivery of
five bald and paunchy prisoners, then three more. Torfinn
arrived with a third shivering contingent. "All bluster

and outrage," he spoke. "Total civilian mentality. You wake to strangers in your room, so what do you do?"

"Armed strangers? And I'm naked?" Ramnis shook his head. "Sure I'd make a fuss. Maybe I'd learn my situation wasn't hopeless. Maybe I could bully them. Why? What would a military man do?"

In this cold Torfinn's laugh steamed through his grilled visor. "Raise your hands and keep some dignity. Or attack with real murderous intent. These guys didn't try that. They fought a little to impress their bedmates, a few insincere kicks and shoves—"

"Ah. Bedmates."

"A judgment call. We can't arrest everyone."

Level 1020 was a buffer. Below 960 lay three unconsolidated regions, but Ramnis asked for power within ten minutes of his morning return to the near-ground levels. "Beginning eleven A.M.? Anything else would be mass murder, and that gives us time for one more upward convoy."

The Breeds got most of Nie's old realm: they'd helped Ramnis more than his Dirtgrubs helped them. Theirs was a handsome reward, and they were happy to oblige his request.

The prime goal was achieved. In the 1000 airdock space shuttle *Galla Placidia* occupied a launch catapult, tanks packed with fuel. Dirtgrub ambassadors could reach space. *They could reach space!*

# Chapter 13
## Minus 8–Level One

"Now what?" Cedric Chittagong spoke into his microphone. "It's my opinion you're in low Earth orbit. Will you accept a boarding party?"

The *Carl Sagan* answered: "I will, old friend, although I warn you I've been modified over the centuries. Indeed, you might not recognize me. I've got ramfuse engines and a nosepad, the better for pushing asteroids around."

"Next week's the new moon and I'm a man with a mission," Cedric hinted.

"Then welcome up. Let's do something about it."

Loaded with reinforcements, two helicopters waited in the Marisma. Olivia's picked troops flew with Alice and Cedric to Level 1000, where Torfinn ruled as Imperial Vice-Commissioner of the Earthstalk March, armored margrave of sixty levels on the cusp between blue skies and black.

Alice beelined for the shuttle. Two hours later she

emerged and made for the airlock. A Dirtgrub sentry led her to a practically naked three-toothed hag, and the hag tugged her into a labyrinth:

"*Cedric*?" Alice asked again, wondering if her guide really understood her accented Prospore. "*Mi vols trovi viron ki—*"

"*Hedreek*!" The old woman exhaled with a grin, drawing a curtain aside.

"Alice!" Her husband clicked off his handset and waved. "64 screens! Twice the size of any normal observation room!"

"What about—"

"Hot off the press." Cedric got to his feet and grabbed a sheaf of faxpaper. "Owner's manual, CAMeur 511 Space Shuttle."

Alice thumbed through and shook her head. "I ran her self-diagnostics and she's obsessed: all the old lubricant has to be drained and replaced, which means taking her off the catapult and bringing her into pressure. That's just the beginning. I need another couple days to finish my systems check-out. I can't find any evidence the *Placidia*'s *ever* been used, and there's materials fatigue in the RCS thruster assemblies—God knows—"

"Two days! That's cutting it pretty close. Can I help?"

"You better, you're my copilot."

Two days stretched out to four. Cedric grew morose, Alice frustrated. "We can go," she finally whispered. "Tell Torfinn's boys to load her back onto the catapult."

"Really?" Cedric challenged.

"Don't put me on the spot. There's so much redundancy on this mother I'm just praying some of it will hold good."

At a height giving view to a fourth of South America, Torfinn the conqueror watched their dock's catapult fling the *Placidia* like a clay pigeon. A thump, then silence, then a putter as fore and aft umbilicals withdrew into the launch apparatus. The craft dropped and

Olivia clutched Torfinn's vacuum-suited arm. Had Alice blacked out during that sudden acceleration? Why—

The *Placidia*'s engines flamed on. Ah, the power! Nothing else was quite as much *fun* as chemical rockets! Astronaut Alice ascended through the Breed altitudes, putting an ocean between her and Earthstalk, then a continent. "Home again!" Cedric sighed. "An old space bug like me—"

"You're unique, you know that, lover? You've been everything; wetbrain, bug, dead soul—"

"Hippie engineer, Hindu atheist, and the 21st century's answer to Walt Disney," Cedric completed his resume, infinitely more cheerful than he'd been just an hour ago. He peered into shuttle console 2. "I wonder what's next?"

Tragically, not one city glowed from evening Africa. By contrast the Seychelles were a Pleiades of light. The Laccadives, Sri Lanka—Alice looked up. "Bit of glitter ahead. *Carl*? That you?"

"Matching course. You're gunning hard."

"Pause three two one; sorry. Only human."

"Only human, and a millennium late with your interstellar empire, but better late than never."

Beneath centuries of jury-riggery the *Carl Sagan* was a Humpty Dumpty egg, an inflated bubble of quick-frozen magma. He was big for anything else, minuscule for a world; a girdle-ring constituted his ramfuse drive. Between ring and body, girders reached forward like giant mandibles. "They look like something a sculptor might do with a dozen kitchen implements," Cedric joked.

"Expanded ten thousand times by a maniac pop artist," Alice answered. "A superbloated wood-tick in a baby stroller with fistfuls of kitchen tongs."

The egg rotated on a nose-tail axis, but the *Sagan*'s nosepad held still. Alice would have docked there, but she was warned off. "I can't be all things to all people," the spaceship explained. "I have passenger room, it's just harder to get there."

Well, it *sounded* like an explanation. Loaded with resonance, deep as the roar of a bear, the *Sagan*'s voice was expertly modulated to fit his physique. A long time ago Cedric had paid the bill to craft that voice, and now it pretended to make sense.

Alice shrugged. The *Placidia* hitched a ride on the *Sagan*'s girder skeleton, alighting on a bulls-eye where she was ministered to by a tangle of emerging cables. A 70-bit-wide commband snaked up and secured to the shuttle's data teat, and after a long and secret dialogue the huge old spaceship lifted towards geosynchronicity.

Ore from the asteroid belt was distributed carefully among Earthstalk's industrial nodes: the stability of Earthstalk depended on its center of mass. Shipments were balanced up-and-downside, and when all oredocks were full the excess was parked in geosync orbit.

Alice and Cedric ascended into permanent sunlight, and a realm where cargos floating in train, one after the other to the limits of vision. "So many," Cedric muttered. "A terrible shame."

"The factories work at one-twentieth capacity," Alice answered. "Earthstalk's in a dark age; cut from dirtside markets. Depopulated too."

"You think so?"

"Computer analysis of food production: you've got the Breeds and the Caliphate, and above that most tribes treat habitats like houses, one per family. Now no more talk. *Carl*'s giving me the signal to launch and I've got to finish my checklist."

A horsefly to the *Sagan*'s bulk, Alice's shuttle detached and fired toward Earthstalk's crucial center node. The *Placidia* reversed, decelerated and docked, door to door. Alice nodded. Cedric reached for his duluth bag, then turned to face her. "That was easy, wasn't it? As if the *Sagan* was in on the plot from the very beginning."

Alice pursed her lips. "You used to be a bug. Accept it: he thinks fast, he thinks clearly, he can flowchart all the possibilities. Cedric, don't make me nervous. U Gyi says not to trust our old friends, but we *have* to."

"Could he have been in touch with one of our gang? Maybe with Ramnis?"

"Ramnis would have told us."

Cedric shook his head. "The commissioner's downstairs and busy with backlogs. He might not have had time."

Alice grimaced. "If the *Sagan*'s on our side I don't know any crime in being easily persuaded. If he's not we don't have a dime's worth of hope. Logic."

"Logic." Cedric shrugged and pulled himself to the airlock.

Beyond the next bulkhead lay habitat, but Cedric paused in the pressure tube, tumble-hopping like a circus monkey as he stripped and struggled into battle armor. With only Torfinn's hurried instructions the job took an embarrassing forty-five minutes. The one brevity was the mental ritual that activated the suit, and now finally, his power pack whining fitfully, Dr. Cedric Chittagong muttered his mantra and pushed APERA.

The human body isn't made for free fall. Pulse therapy retards osteoporosis and exercise slows muscular deterioration, yet these ministrations simply serve victims up to the next cascade of maladies; edema, circulation problems and sinusitis.

For centuries the Nulges adapted towards zero gee, triumphing over these difficulties and moving on to fused joints, gigantism and obesity, yet even a little gravity induced such comparative health that they herded to the low reaches of their realm and left Earthstalk's midpoint vacant. Cedric entered between rare visits and found no enemies. He secured the downside bulkhead, and the up, and searched again.

The habitat was safe, the atrium weird, nebulas of vegetation clothed in gels of water, each hugging its moving lightglobe. At first Cedric failed to recognize the Solar system, with bubbleworlds like Helice in orbit around Venus, even though the second planet's johnny-come-lately rings were helpfully obscured. Mars was pink, yet its dust-and-snow color supplied the crucial clue. From his gold-plated handhold the armored Cedric reviewed the evidence of varied hues and sizes. An armillary sphere; a freefall simulacrum!

Ten minutes later Cedric emerged from the airlock and made his report. Nominally he spoke to Alice, but he kept to the old frequency, the one the *Carl Sagan* tuned to, and broadcast with more power than necessary. Should humanity's ancient spaceship return here and attach to Earthstalk, no adversaries could enter through his vulnerable nose.

"You've left your baggage inside," Alice commented after he finished. "Your vacuum suit—"

"We're staying for the countdown," Cedric whispered at one-tenth volume. "It's a long trip to Level 1000. Maybe too long. By the time you figure out how to land this thing on a dime-size dock in full gravity— You really want to take a chance like that?"

"Torfinn needs that armor. Our one suit—"

If possible Cedric's voice fell further. "No he doesn't. The power pack stopped humming five minutes after I went inside. Torfinn warned me the thing was getting flukey, and I guess that jaunt of Ramnis's wiped it out. No more strength, and U Gyi's got a monopoly on sonics. The Age of Heroes is over."

But when they floated inside, Cedric's duluth bag was gone.

"You said the place was empty," Alice murmured sotto voce.

"I thought it *was*," Cedric answered. "Could it have drifted—?"

"Friends, I'm sorry," rumbled an intercom voice. "But you'll be safe here, I guarantee that. Infinitely safer than anywhere else on Earthstalk. That's why I asked you to come to midnode."

"*Carl*?" Cedric responded. "Is that you? Why ask us to scout this place if you already—why not just tell us the truth?"

Pause. Slowly the voice began to chuckle. "Tell the truth? I've been subtle for too long. It never occurred to me!"

"Hah!" Alice spoke up. "If you'd told us you'd prepped this place prior to our arrival, we'd have found out something. Ramnis sent us to you on a mission, but he didn't have to. You knew about our purpose all along! You knew our secrets."

"They're *my* secrets first and foremost," the *Carl Sagan* answered. Do you imagine a vagabond Raffles from a neo-Edwardian culture could come up with those ideas on his own? And now—may I introduce *Feldwebel* Wolf Schinner, of my private schwarzenegger army?"

Midnode's walls rippled like an LSD vision. (Later Cedric had the leisure to wonder if, but for himself, even one of Earthstalk's four million inhabitants knew what *that* was like.) The walls rippled because moving schwarzeneggers needed almost a microsecond to analyze light input, and program the near side of their jewelbody skins to emit that same color and luminosity, relative to two viewers who fell short of the ideal one-point perspective.

For this reason light from true beyondness always won the race, and to compensate . . . well, compensation was possible, and the result was a good approximation of transparence. But for now the *Carl Sagan*'s forces chose not to compensate, and gave Cedric and Alice a hint how far from alone they really were.

The walls swam, and a platoon of bugs separated and opened. Their "invisibility" no longer concealed Cedric's dun-colored bag. Then even the dun began to ripple. Eddies of shadow darkened into the shape of a dead-black schwarzenegger bug.

Wolf Schinner cast from the bag and straightened, orienting toward his two human guests, his lens-eyes spinning to adjust focus and resolution. The articulations of his right forelimb made it easy to salute. "Pleased to meet you. I can have your armor repaired if you like."

Cedric shook his head. "It's not mine. Delivering it to Torfinn makes more sense. After the *Sagan* finishes his work—it'll be around noon Friday, won't it? Noon with the new moon, that's when the tides are most favorable. After that's done Alice and I take over as Imperial Ambassadors to the Worlds of Sol—"

The *Carl Sagan*'s voice spoke again over the intercom. "Please. I really thought you'd understand by now. Earth's toy Empire counts nothing, and there's to be no diplomacy. I'd protect you as a friend but that's not my sole motive for your holiday here. The truth is, in the crisis to come diplomacy is a profound waste of time and a dangerous distraction. Only one thing will impress the Gatekeepers: a united Earthstalk, and there's only one way to unite Earthstalk."

"War?" Alice's answer was small and hesitant.

"The discovery of Earthstalk's lost master password, an important fragment of which lies in Senjoro Nie's memory. Not the *interesting* fragment, mind you. From the layout of Midnode it's patently obvious that Earthstalk and I have something in common—the interesting fragment happens to be part of *my* old access code as well.

"Good ideas get recycled, yet I'm only halfway ahead of my rivals. U Gyi wants to pick Nie's brain, and so do I. I'm a soul inside a spaceship body, but Earthstalk's body is soulless until the day someone invokes the process which will copy a new mind into that void. When that happens there can be no more factions, no more petty tyrants."

"Just one great big tyrant," Cedric answered.

"Indeed. A ship in space is no place for democracy."

# PART FOUR

## *Day Zero*

## Chapter 14

# Minus 2 21:40–Hab 24

Commissioner Ramnis rose from his bed, looked out the Level 24 window into moonless night, and turned. "May I pour you some tea?"

"Thanks," said Magda. "And thanks for the, um, massage."

"You work too hard. Learn to delegate. We both have that problem."

Magda plumped her pillows, sat up, and sipped. "You worse than me. In my age senators didn't go adventuring."

"I'm a lousy senator, and I question my ability to run Earthstalk. Damn, I wish I could have gone with them!"

"Ah, which—?"

"Cedric and Alice," Ramnis answered. "By now they've served him my proposals, but I wouldn't be half surprised if the *Carl Sagan* anticipated them. It's so obvious! We want an interstellar spaceship, a giant habitat."

After a pause Magda spoke. "The way you said that—preposterous. It couldn't work."

Senator Ramnis put down his cup. "If you think to warn the Earthstalkers I'll have you confined."

"Jesus!" Magda climbed shakily out of bed. "How could you launch this mass? How would you simulate gravity? What about power? How do you get up speed?"

"I've said nothing. Magda, you volunteered for space."

"But the Earthstalkers didn't!"

"They're *in* space! For centuries their economy was isolated from Earth's. All we'll take from them is a big blue gewgaw and a generation of sunlight."

"Nice if they had a choice." Magda slumped against the wall. "This last week we emptied Paramaraibo. We had them all shipped here; all that loot and all those wild young Dirtgrubs. Yes, *we* did that, but it was *my voice!* I know them, I've seen their faces. To steal them from Earth—it won't be feasible. There'll be some technical glitch."

"You may think so. I don't have your education." Ramnis moved close. "I was hoping one exchange of intimacies would lead to another. See, my situation is rather like being unmarried—"

"Huh?"

"I'm Nina's number-two husband and free to look for an upgrade. Was polyandry legal in your age? I was a mooncalf back when I proposed, willing to play the second role—"

"Ramnis, I can't believe this conversation. Anyhow I'm seventeen hundred years older than you."

"That may be true. Then again it may not," he answered. "U Gyi's a public god, but there are hidden gods too. I tell you this and nail shut the coffin of our romance. Spooks and shivers, and peeping toms."

"You'd better explain," said Magda.

"Explain my love for you? I've always loved that body, and now it's got a mind inside it. Jijika was just fizz, but you—"

"I don't mean to trample your feelings, but men have fallen in love with me before. There's nothing weird about that. Let's stay on track. Explain about those spooky gods."

Ramnis sighed. "Otto's been teaching me history—a dozen misuses of immortifact technology, and the evils of each. One was piggybacking: multiple souls in one mind, each taking its day. That's what people mean by piggybacking, but there's another arrangement; a foremind under inner guidance."

"A back-seat driver," Magda responded.

"I'm not conscious of anything like that, but there's something strange about me. If I described my career you'd be struck by how lucky I've been. I'm a Souldancer. Our cult is famous for luck."

"I've got a Souldancer's body," she blurted.

Ramnis laughed. "Obviously Jijika's luck ran out. You must have heard though, how I and my comrades powered up the UNETAO receivers in N'York just in time to get *AC Alpha*'s message. Pure dumb luck? How *do* we do it?"

"A hindbrain god?"

"There is such a god, and has been for centuries. I think this god has connections in space. I'm not always infallible, but I suspect if I got the idea of using Earthstalk as a spaceship, it's going to be feasible. —Will you marry me?" he asked abruptly.

"Ramnis, or the god?" Magda laughed.

Ramnis shrugged. "I wish I knew."

"I murdered my first husband and abandoned my second. Ramnis, I'm not a good catch."

"Maybe we deserve each other."

"For being puppets? What happened to freedom, Ramnis? I thought you were free, freer than anyone. Were you just testing your prison with all those adventures of yours? Making your god prove himself by rescuing you?"

Ramnis turned to stare. "Yes. You tossed that off, but I think it's true. But I'm not alone. As far as being free, is the human race free with Gatekeeper doting over us? And she's not the only superhuman intelligence playing with our destiny, but the thing is—Alpha Centauri! We can escape them there. We can reduce our chessmaster gods to a mere handful, unsupported by an industrial base, and let them corrode and cancel each other out."

"Freedom." Magda gave Ramnis a light kiss. "Speaking of gods, does U Gyi know he's on a spacecraft?"

Ramnis grinned. "The best joke I've ever played on him. Godnapped! He'll turn ten shades of purple!"

"And afterward he'll make a play for power?"

"Yes. The innocent U Gyi will set up his own kingdom. I'll retreat to the 1000s and join Torfinn."

"And face the angry Breeds, your former allies."

"It's tricky, that's sure. I expect the Breed regime to break up under the double strain of sudden expansion and launch trauma. There'll be monkeys and mud everywhere on Earthstalk."

"Huh—?"

"Anarchy. Monkeys and mud. A Souldancer fairy tale. Someday I should tell you about us. We've got a temple on the Pecos river not far from the Sacred Caves; except for that one place there's no land we call our own. We wander, relying on luck: tinkerers, acrobats, prostitutes, out-of-work aristocrats . . . I wander too. I've acquired a petty kingdom I haven't visited in two years."

"Luck?" Magda shook her head. "You asked me to marry you. Gold-digger that I am, I'd love to sit at your side, lord and lady of a growing domain. It won't be like that. You'll be universal villain."

Ramnis shook his head. "Alice and Cedric are in on the plot, and Olivia and Torfinn too. And then there's you. You can change things. I need your help."

His eyes softened. "Don't go all infantile," Magda responded. "This isn't easy. You don't make it comfortable to be on your side. Tell me what you want me to do, and for heaven's sake, do your damnedest to be lucky enough for all of us."

Magda left for the Press Room early next morning and started recording a series of monologues. Meanwhile Ramnis descended to Level One. As usual he accumulated an entourage. He dismissed them to perch on the edge of the pool. Womtie-Christina noticed, swam close, and thrust her whiskered snout up onto his knee.

"It's a question of rationalization," he admitted, scratching behind her tiny ears. "You're my link to Mercury and Nodus Gordii, even to the Gatekeepers. Back in the 2150s your Prime Minister was Sir Thomas Haberhan, now primate-general of the Augustinian Order, and if anyone in Sol System is in diplomatic contact with Stargate it's bug-monks like him, immortal and regimented."

She who had been queen lifted her snout in an emphatic nod and sneezed in the affirmative. "He knew about them even then," Christina whispered; "their 'benevolent' policy of keeping wetbrains confined in our system, lest we crash loutishly about the stars. I've already said I'd help you."

"Then how do we get you upstairs? You're too vast to slip into the elevator unnoticed."

Christina sighed. "My pool's small. I don't get enough exercise, but if I went up where gravity is weak I could extend my mobility, even flop around on land."

"There's no real difference between here and 1000."

"Not much, but let's say I insist. In this body nobody expects me to be rational."

"True. The Mbo who live along your shores say your kind are magic. You sing mad songs and lure humans into erotic adventures, and then eat them. You've got your own mutant goddess, the Slug Woman—"

"I was human until a few months ago. Am I supposed to know anything about that? Lies and exaggerations—" She paused and shrugged. "You're right. Play the role and watch their eyes bug out."

Ramnis nodded. Christina launched into a tantrum. A drenched commissioner cast about for help. The upstairs conquests had stripped Level One of experienced personnel. Up on the terraces and balconies a horde of refugees and Paramaraibans were distributing themselves among conference rooms, learning how to be good Prospore-talking Dirtgrub patriots: they were strangers to the man who now shouted and waved. Those few who responded to his summons looked at Christina's bulk and scratched their heads while Ramnis made his separate way to radio headquarters, and out of their lives.

# Chapter 15

# Day Zero 07:15–Hab 1000

*Was Torfinn ever a caged tiger? No, always too obliging, too good-humored in his easy confidence.*

*And too trusting. A strange choice for a military leader.* That's what his wife thought that Friday morning while she sucked a breakfast of Juba Juice. "What's this?" Olivia asked, picking up—a pair of glasses?

"A tiepatch," Torfinn answered cheerily. "Terminal Interface Eyepatch. Combination headphones and viewscreens. You can slave the left eye to whatever INFOWEB is capable of imaging. For safety the right lens is transparent, but it's got overlay capacity. You can even set these to see infrared, and there's a mic attachment for phone discussions—all you need is a handset for dialing. Put them on. I've got the patch windowed to watch the *Carl Sagan* at work."

Olivia adjusted the tiepatch and slid it over her face. "I won't need *this*, then." She let the tapestry fall across the telescreen. In thoughtless delight she looked up, as if to make the image more perfect. "The *Sagan's*

114

gobbled up all the junk in near space. Why? So there won't be any collisions?"

"Half right," Torfinn answered from his cushions. "Now he's off for Earthstalk's outer tip. He'll be immense, pushing a thousandth of Earthstalk's weight."

Olivia frowned at her male twin. "If he's on our side the mission becomes possible, but what about the Gatekeepers? Our diplomacy better prove masterful, and how *can* it? We don't dare tell the worlds of Sol what we're about!"

Torfinn shook his head. "It's up to Ramnis. God knows how, but he's got me believing in Souldancer luck. A wink here, a nod there—"

"A pat on the right fanny." Olivia's voice lost spirit. "Think he's won over Magda?"

"He won't come here without her."

"Here" was Hab 1000's Berberine palace, populated with blue-tattooed women, near-naked, as befit the houris of a colonel's harem, perhaps too naked to conceal a weapon among their bangles. They were also old, testimonials to the youthful ardor of a deposed tyrant now in his dotage, and in the absence of any pension plan the oldest and most spavined were demoted to servants. They crept around, replenishing bowls and flagons, then vanished into an arras-concealed maze of passages.

A wonderful place for spies, if any of these gray hags knew Old High English. When the crisis was over Olivia planned to clean house, but now she had more urgent concerns. She mustered herself and spoke to reintroduce a subject never far from her mind. "Torfinn? Can we talk about trading bodies with another resurrectee? It would make it so much easier—"

"Go to U Gyi hat in hand? What if he dreamt my memories? He'd learn what we're up to."

"He'll find out soon enough it makes no difference. It's now or never," Olivia insisted. "Afterward he's going to be an enemy." She made fists, small brown fists. "Who am I fooling? It's already too late! I wish they had memory equipment openly available on Earthstalk! That would make things so much easier!"

"I tell you from personal experience, a world where soul transfer is easy is a world of crime and madness, and then of oppression. We learned that lesson before Earthstalk was built, and nobody wants to revive the old Brain Police—nobody except U Gyi." Torfinn reached for Olivia's hand. "Honey, I'm sorry I don't appeal to you—"

"It's nothing to do with you," Olivia whispered. "It's me, my history, my long-past childhood. Childhood! No, my own brother robbed me of that innocence! I was a spinster in my first life. Do you know why? U Gyi does! I thought I'd grown with the centuries, grown beyond rape and incest, but now I'm shriveling into that same old prude! Oh Torfinn, can we ever really escape who we are?"

"I hope so. I was a jerk." Torfinn grinned. "An obliging, amoral jerk. Olivia, those simulated adventures on Mercury you despise so much actually contributed to my character. They helped me grow up, and I finally escaped my past in 2349 when I learned about Stargate. We have to dedicate ourselves against our Gatekeeper wardens. I did, and when—"

"That's not my problem. I'm all too disposed to fanaticism. I could become a holy terror, only to whose benefit? U Gyi's?" Olivia's shoulders slumped. "I'm one of those souls who shouldn't be given glands."

Torfinn reached for her hand. "Then let's work on your prudery."

Olivia fought from his kiss. "I can't. It becomes worse every time: it's become impossible! *I'm sorry*, Torfinn." Her voice broke. "I'm sorry, I've thought about this disease of mine, and there's only one cure."

She reached under the cushion. "Believe me, it'll all be okay. You'll be alive again soon, just like before." Torfinn saw the knife, and *still* didn't understand. What a testimony to trust!

*Thump!* "I didn't want to do this," Olivia whimpered.

"It's because I love you, and you never listened, and I can make U Gyi swear a promise if it's not too late—"

Torfinn clutched at his chest. Again she stabbed, and again! And again!

Ten minutes later—

Divide ten minutes by ten, that by a hundred, that by a thousand. In that fraction of time blinks of articulate light barely outraced the supermassive particles streaming from the *Carl Sagan* to hose the length of Earthstalk. A half million individually aimed beams shot forth, and a third of Earthstalk's shadbolt defenses were reduced to incandescent slag. Stop.

Re-aim. Fire. The next split second eliminated another third. Was Earthstalk helpless?

Most of Earthstalk's shadbolts were on automatic. Computers began to assess the threat, to take aim . . . the last shadbolts were vaporized by creatures whose decision circuits were considerably shorter and less sicklied o'er with the pale cast of thought.

The *Carl Sagan* began to smoke. Telescopes magnified the cloud into a blossom of insectoid bodies.

Olivia tottered out of the shower, a servant at her elbow to help her keep her feet. Had she misunderstood the woman's babble?

Moments later she saw for herself. Torfinn lay dead among blood-soaked cushions, stabbed viciously a dozen times. Olivia closed her eyes and experienced the vision of a knife rising and falling, each hack a sympathetic strike at her own gut—she grabbed herself and the telephone rang.

A tattooed beldame handed her the handset. "I just got the news," a man's voice reported. Good old Captain Caddo!

"You're all I can trust," she answered. "I need protection. Who—"

"U Gyi might have hired an assassin. See, he needs an army. Torfinn was loyal to Ramnis, but with him gone who are you dead going to follow? The man who can make more of you!"

"Ramnis is still commissioner," Olivia whispered.

"If U Gyi killed Torfinn, Ramnis is dead too."

How it must have hurt Caddo to say those words! Olivia dared not reassure him. "Would he have—would U Gyi have saved Torfinn's soul? Scanned it before his death?"

But Olivia knew the answer. She'd visited U Gyi's quarters and read the names on his library of memory tapes. Her rank meant she'd become the new margrave of the dead, and rule to U Gyi's whim as long as the god held one small, black cassette.

As yet U Gyi was innocent of his advantage. Line two was blinking. Olivia turned from the body, and pushed the button. "Hello?"

"Hello," the god spoke nervously. "Have you looked out of your cameras lately?"

"*What?* You dare call me at a time like this—"

"The *Carl Sagan* is mounting an invasion. I phoned to warn you."

"Someone— Olivia's eyes shifted. "Caddo says you killed my husband!"

"Torfinn *dead?* Not me, not my doing. Don't dither, woman. Look to your screens, look toward midnode! Surely you saw the flash! One great sudden attack to melt all the shadbolts of Earthstalk, and now the *Carl Sagan* is vomiting schwarzeneggers by the thousand! If anyone is dead, that's what it's all about. Search among the *Sagan's* friends! Ask Ramnis what he's up to!"

"Ramnis? But—what are schwarzeneggers?"

"Type F bugbodies with military fictoid minds. Flexible, efficient, fast, narrow range of intellect."

"Fictoid? You mean A.I.?"

"More A than I. The 21st century spawned all sorts of fictoid personae, Tarzans and Peter Wimseys and Frodo Bagginses, to the point where they had to pass laws. You heard Cedric talk about Chittaworld. Who do you think lives there? Chittaworld's a type E fictoid paradise, E for entertainment. What Mercury is to bugs, and Helice to the Sisterhood, and Luna to Catholics—"

Olivia fervently wished she was at liberty to faint. She donned her tiepatch. Yes, the left lens crawled with . . . things. "My husband is dead."

U Gyi let the words sink in. "I *am* sorry. I shouldn't have called. I don't know how to fight schwarzeneggers: obviously you don't either. Maybe they won't conquer beyond the Nulge territories. Maybe all the *Sagan* wants is a little industrial capability. You haven't received any demands for surrender?"

"No. Not that I'm on top of things."

Long pause. She spoke again. "Uh, do you have any backup copies of Torfinn's soul?" Olivia winced. She might as well throw herself at U Gyi's feet. It was the only way. In the U Gyi/Ramnis game, she was now the god's lackey.

"I do," U Gyi answered. "Back in Cairo I recorded a Torfinn cassette for memory-dreaming: someone might use it to learn ancient athletic techniques. All of you on the original Senate Subcommittee were interesting sources of ancient knowledge."

Olivia stole a final look at Torfinn's body as a troop of elderly servants rolled it up in a rug. She closed her eyes. "Can you use dreamtapes to resurrect someone? I know they're only part-strength to keep from giving the dreamer a new identity—"

"It's a different medium, different equipment," U Gyi's voice buzzed. "Nothing to erase the resident soul, so the dreamer has to dream the same tape for weeks and months. And it helps if he's young."

"Give me Torfinn again," Olivia whispered. This was her moment of triumph—Ramnis's Secret was still safe. No one said walking a tightrope was easy. "He won't remember our recent life together: I'm ready to accept that loss. But if you can bring him back— "

"I'll begin the process right away."

"—for a friend," Olivia sighed.

"My good friend, who knows my concerns about the *Carl Sagan.*"

"I'm sure we share many concerns," Olivia answered. And after all, was she *really* prostituting herself? Yet a commitment to U Gyi meant she needed to get to work on a substitute explanation: Torfinn's murder might have been the first act in a campaign of Earthstalker terrorism, some deed of pigmask revenge. Senjoro Nie might be trying to restore his former regime—

She clicked off the phone. The old age was over. The new was about to begin. Her face took on determination. A criminal herself, there was one other criminal whose venalities she would no longer tolerate.

She grabbed the handset back and pushed line one. "Caddo? You there? When she gets here I want Magda separated from Ramnis and confined to her bedroom. Yes, I have reason to know the commissioner's alive, but even if U Gyi's slip of the tongue is a ruse I don't want to see Magda. Treat her well but keep her guarded. What? No, she's not free to move around. We don't have people for an escort and we've got other things to do. I'm going to send U Gyi a hundred harem-hags and have him dream their memories, to find out which is guilty of murder."

*bzp?*

"Yes, U Gyi. Because he *didn't* kill Torfinn, that's why."

# Chapter 16
## Day Zero 09:15–Hab 200

The elevators of Earthstalk included two classes of local and two of express. To help passengers adjust to decreasing gravity and pressure, the fastest express stopped every hundredth level, every thousand floors.

Level 100 was in Dirtgrub hands, and 300 was now an academic principality ruled by Vice-Commissioner Otto and bride Irene. Pressed between was Sergeant Prasad's homeland, a realm of rumor and nocturnal assassination. Cowed denizens heard they were allocated to the Empire by treaty, and Dirtgrub radio filled the air with pipe-dreams about a new Hegemony, plus lectures on the need to send a colony to Alpha Centauri. Out of this came expectations of what would happen when Commissioner Ramnis arrived to accept their surrender, but why was he taking so long?

Meantime most habitats obeyed their pigmaskers. Embarrassed at this retention of authority, some soldiers removed the emblems from their military pajamas. One defrocked squadron stared in amazement at

Christina's brown bulk as the elevator doors opened on Level 200.

She blinked nervously back. Sergeant Prasad risked a smile and waggled his fingers. After a minute the doors slid shut and the womtie's rise continued.

Prasad's smile broadened next morning when the elevator opened again. He waved his gun. "Toll stop. Express travelers like you won't have any trouble paying a couple megs."

"For each of us," his corporal added.

"Look at them," a timid compatriot objected. "Brown as Cola-Ban. They've gotta be Dirtgrubs."

"All the better. The Empire pays 'em double." Prasad raised his voice. "Come. Here's no place for a shoot-out."

Ramnis and Magda stepped forth and were herded to the nearest INFOWEB booth. "Now, what's your account number?" Prasad asked.

"I haven't got one," answered Ramnis. "I never— things were taken care—"

"He's new," Magda interrupted. "My escort. Recognize my voice?"

"Sure," Prasad purred, gesturing toward the intercom. "You paying his way?"

Weary after a nearly sleepless night, Magda nodded and fished out her card. Prasad took it and began to type. "Copied this little routine from one of my uncles," he explained to his comrades. Amber letters scrolled upward:

RUN LAUNDRY<cr>

ENTER ACCOUNT NUMBER:

"Won't do you any good to watch," Prasad smirked. "My number's hid in a data statement."

"What about us?" asked the corporal.

"You'll get your share—Simon's clysters! Twenty-nine thousand megs! TWENTY NINE THOUSAND MEGS!"

"Can I have my card back?" Magda asked. "For the elevator?"

Prasad stared, then woke to action. "Take it and get out of here. You never saw me. Jesus Mary Joseph—"

The corporal stepped forward, mesmerized. "That's—that's *three thousand apiece*! No, let's see. Eight divides into—"

Magda grabbed her magcard and tugged Ramnis off. "I'm on hourly wages," she whispered. "Ten more minutes and we can afford to get out of here."

"Where'd you nip all that money?" Ramnis asked.

Magda's blush deepened. "People paid me to lobby you. I told them it was against my principles to sway you counter to good policy, but they never believed me. Maybe it was the way I winked and held out my hand. —Look dear, just maybe I saved your life. It doesn't help to waste the time of an important goon."

Ramnis fell into purse-lipped silence. They spent quiet minutes on a shadowed bench.

"Time." Magda got up and stuck her card in the slot to summon a new car. Now forced to stand in plain sight, she and Ramnis scowled at an accumulation of children, glad finally to be judged less interesting than Prasad and his men, whose distant voices raised in louder and louder quarrel.

A gunshot? The door opened and Magda and Ramnis hurried in to continue their interrupted journey. Magda adjusted the intercom dial. Here too her ubiquitous radio voice spoke of wonderful secrets, of a marvelous and shattering development, something to give Earth-stalkers pride for all time.

"Why's *she* saying these things?" U Gyi muttered two thousand floors below. "Propaganda's *my* bailiwick. Besides, promises make me nervous."

"Could it be?" his major-domo responded, trilling with delight. "Could the emperor be making a visit?"

The dwarf-god frowned. "Surely if Uthford were coming I'd be notified! Anyhow he'd be insane to set foot in this place. First we see ten thousand schwarzeneggers, then we don't see any!" His eyes shifted uneasily side to side. "Speaking of disappearing, any luck finding Commissioner Ramnis?"

Pavel pursed his lips. "He's hard to track. No account number."

"Look for Magda," U Gyi ordered impatiently. "They're usually together."

Two minutes at an INFOWEB booth told Pavel everything. "He's on Level 200. He tried to launder Magda's money, but when twenty-nine thousand megs vanishes from one bucket and collects in another—"

"Whose?"

"Sergeant Hector Prasad. From there Magda paid for a second ride, and has just now reached Level 300. A ruse? The old bird-with-broken-wing trick, to get our attention?"

U Gyi nodded. "Ramnis trusts in action and dumb luck. Well, luck's against him this time. Somehow he's exchanged bodies with this Prasad character. —My worst fear: he's found Senjoro Nie, bullied him out of a priority one password, and gained access to Earthstalk's immortifacts. But why's he gone into hiding?"

"You're leaping to conclusions," Pavel demurred. "Perhaps he's bought a private army. There are lots of possibilities."

"Set up patrols at 190 and 210, then send in spies. The important question is still *why*? Why boast of wonders and go to ground?"

As the god fretted, Magda's taped voice hinted at rapture after rapture. "When the event occurs you'll have special reason to thank U Gyi, for without his heroic efforts and sage advice—"

U Gyi stiffened. Earth, a rotating ball. A needle at its equator, a micro-whisker five and a half times as long as the ball was fat, but then a break at the point of intersection, and the whirling planet's whirling atmosphere—

How much more time? He could hop in a biplane and fly away, but consider the turbulence! To be sucked up in Earthstalk's immense, cyclone-spawning wake . . . U Gyi shuddered. He noticed his major-domo staring at him.

His feet wouldn't reach the pedals anyhow. No safety outside, and the least desirable *inside* floor was the lobby of Level One. The thing was to move upstairs, fast, but with dignity.

"—so with deference to U Gyi, who will soon be on to make his own announcement—"

U Gyi signaled. "We're going to Level 24. As Magda says, I have a speech to make." He winced. These next words were the hardest he'd ever had to say. Worse, he was being stampeded into saying them. The catastrophe might be hours away, even days.

Still, he had twenty clones. "After we get there contact Waksa in Paramaraibo, my designated heir. Tell him he's now god of Heaven, the Redemptorist cult and— Damn! He can't be senator, not till next election! Now I know why the Emperor wanted me here! —Tell Waksa he's got everything except for Earthstalk. Here on Earthstalk I'm prophet of the new religion, and here's where I'm staying."

The god's breathless voice usurped the radio twenty minutes later. "I'm the U Gyi you've heard about. I'm expected to give a handsome talk, and conceal that I was fooled, to keep from making myself foolish. Well, no time to discuss my ego. Listeners, prepare for hard news. Not bad news, nor good, we'll decide that later.

"For the time being your lives are in hazard. It's wrong for people to deal high-handedly with others' lives, but how would you know that? You're victims of such treatment, and will be long as you live in Earthstalk, because it's a managed environment and you have no choice but to trust the managers.

"I trust our managers to do their best." How it hurt to say decent things about those who were probably his enemies!

He hurried on. "From their view they were wise to incapacitate Earthstalk's shadbolts, and I trust they'll detach Earthstalk from Earth without destroying it, because they've had time to study the math. Yes, their plan is to detach Earthstalk from Earth and take this entire structure into space! They'll use Earthstalk as a mammoth generation ship, and after seventy years we'll arrive at Planet Four in the Alpha Centauri system.

"I expect the launch will be very soon, I don't know when. There'll be a jolt, and afterward gravity will fluctuate. I plan to prepare for the worst—a big jolt and powerful centrifugal forces—and I suggest you do the same.

"Afterwards we'll fly from Earth, slowly at first. We won't leave Solar space for years, so those who find this hijacking intolerable might arrange to emigrate. I tell you my own thoughts: humanity's expansion to Alpha Centauri is noble and necessary, but I'd not envisioned *myself* going there. Perhaps in a few days I'll glory in my new role, but I will always resent being shanghaied, and I promise you now I will have my revenge against Commissioner Ramnis and his minions.

"If you feel the same, I invite you to a lynching, but not yet. Ramnis is managing this affair from hiding. To hinder him in the middle of things may cost us all our lives. I give him a week, and then I'll review the risk. During this week I invite all Earthstalkers to contact my coalition with the object of forming a united federation—"

Even as he spoke U Gyi lashed myself. Soft reasoned words to keep Earthstalkers from utter panic, followed by an indictment of the guilty, to comfort them with thoughts of justice. That was all he could do, but it was a *response* to events, a parry, not a thrust. When had he let himself be put so badly on the defensive? Forty-one dead U Gyis in his mind, *none* of them satisfied to play victim—what was wrong with *him*? Was he the least as well as the smallest?

If only he had Senjoro Nie's password! Could Ramnis *really* have found it? He had to shake the admission out of Magda, one way or the other!

# Chapter 17

# Day Zero 11:50–Hab 300

"They're called Margueritas," Magda spoke. She turned off the radio and raised her suckbulb.

"Some speech! I'll have another," Ramnis responded. "Margreeters, eh?"

"You've drunk two already."

"A weak one?" He flung his empty bulb toward a catch-all and lay back against his doubled pillows. A sea of fleecy clouds lay far below his Hab 300 bedroom window. "Time to celebrate. The hard news is out, but nobody knows what I look like. Soon as good old Otto fixes me up with my own INFOWEB card and gets your accounts replenished, we'll be on our way. No more little hour-salary jaunts!"

Magda leaned against the carpeted wall, looked at the time display, and frowned. "You lack any prudence. I'd never ride the elevator with the launch so close. I take it you trust the *Carl Sagan*?"

"Old friends. Never met him, but it makes sense he'd shoot like that, and inpaca—incapsit—melt down all those Earthstalk shadbolts. Otherwise with these factions he stood a chance of getting zapped."

"Never piss off your drive unit," Magda quoted. "First rule of spaceship etiquette. Phone's blinking again. U Gyi wants to talk."

"Who does he think I am?" Ramnis muttered, studying his hairy chest for signs of gray. "Myself, or a ringer?"

"Today's events have thrown him off. Why call just to tell me he wasn't fooled, he knew you were someone else, and anyhow when I got up into Torfinn's domain I was in for a big surprise?"

Ramnis snorted. "Gyi's afraid of the *Carl Sagan*. Until he gets priority-one mastery over INFOWEB his only power is the ability to dream and resurrect. Oh, and sonics. At least twenty sonic belts. Wish *I* had one."

Magda pushed SCROLL and read the god's talk-to-me plea. "He's discovered a social conscience. Let me read some bits here—ah, 'a bi-polar power struggle would create a climate dangerous to Earthstalk's integrity and survival—'"

"Mmm." Ramnis stretched, crossed his ankles, and closed his eyes. U Gyi's speech first transmitted fifteen minutes ago. His call broke into a taped replay, and now hostile radio stations were picking up the news, giving it top flash priority. By now Ramnis was likely the most wanted villain ever confined to Earthstalk, and soon it would occur to someone to broadcast a picture of him on H-V. Hysteria would feed on hysteria, and the god's week of grace would vanish—

Ramnis was proud of his ability to appear calm under pressure. Such was the extremity of his dilemma that he lay prostrate, radiating serenity, thinking that in some ways U Gyi had mellowed and gotten soft. He *should* be grateful to him, though. The way Ramnis arranged things U Gyi was guilt-free; Earthstalk's unlikeliest symbol of innocence!

Magda was fooled by his chuckles. Really? Perhaps she kept panic under tight control. "Here's another bleat," she continued. " 'Imperative we bring Earthstalk's dark age to an end. The tragedy of senility ravages a hundred thousand aged brains, diminishing human souls beyond repair. We can work together to rescue these souls, sending them off to Mercury and returning their bodies for recycling.' "

"Olivia would like that," Ramnis said. "Her palace is lumbered with crones. Funny U Gyi would worry about senility. He wants us to send him our old people. Dream enough antique memories to find more about mysterious Senjoro Nie."

"Part of the Great Skedaddle," Magda answered. "A lot of stolen helicopters at these levels. A lot of desperate emigrants."

"Total interference with the Great Skedaddle. Ten minutes, plus six, plus rest. Two souls per hour. Two hundred eighty-three days to purge these hundred thousand ancients—"

Magda's eyes widened. "You did that in your head? Drunk?"

"We could get shed of emigrants a lot faster if U Gyi didn't have the only immortifacts in these levels," Ramnis muttered. "It's only going to get worse. Earthstalk will be three years getting past Saturn. In three years radioing souls will become impractical as a mass tactic because of time lag. We need Senjoro Nie to open the dreamskull doors and multiply our capacity." Ramnis grunted and stood up. "I'm confused. Let's give U Gyi what he wants. Tell him we're friends, let bygones be bygones. Maybe that'll fuddle *him*."

"He wants to kill you."

"Well, short of that." Ramnis grinned. "Know why I got out of bed just now? Know why I'm so flip-floppy about U Gyi?" He tapped his head. "My inner carbuncle. All of a sudden I'm overflowing with hunches, like it would be the better part of valor to get dressed and out of here."

"What about me?" Magda asked.

"I don't know," Ramnis lied. *Did she really want to associate with a walking death sentence?* He improvised an answer. "Absence of signal. Usually I can tell why my hunches make sense, but not this time. I think my hindbrain god is taking chances."

"Maybe he doesn't work so well after two Margueritas." Magda turned to dress. "Should I call upstairs and tell Torfinn we're on our way?"

Ramnis shrugged. "If you like." He furrowed his brow, and sighed. "Uh, Magda—" But the door clicked and she was gone.

Ten minutes after she left Magda returned to the bedroom, shut the door, and fell back breathless. "Ramnis?" she puffed, an urgent whisper. "Ramnis, Torfinn's dead! Killed with a knife, and Olivia's gone mad! They're going to arrest me! Ramnis, where *are* you?"

The bedroom was empty.

# Chapter 18
## Day Zero 12:09–Earthstalk

Commit a murder and life becomes chess, a matter of planning for multiple eventualities. To the extent she was *not* put on the defensive Olivia felt it was her initiative; time to muddy the waters. And how wonderful to be freed from emotional madness, and climb into this starkly cunning state of mind!

Olivia tipped her sprinkler to wet her companion's hide. "U Gyi makes me feel guilty," she said huskily. "Yes, mistrust breeds mistrust. Certainly we could have treated him more fairly."

Christina wallowed over onto her belly. "Kind words for a wizened monkey, and hate for a woman who has given our cause vital help. Well, Queen Olivia, your words have cast you off from your former friends. All you have now is me; court jester and conscience."

"Magda took bribes," Olivia defended herself. "She made us all look bad. I *had* to tell Otto to arrest her! Don't I outrank her? Isn't it my responsibility? I've done harder things out of duty."

131

"Lady, it's *someone's* job to stand for compassion! Look what Earthstalk has for power blocs: Senjoro Nie and the other native tyrants. Will people look to them for inspiration? Will they look to U Gyi? Don't rehabilitate U Gyi—he can no more stop scheming than breathing!

"You, Ramnis and the *Carl Sagan* might have worked together. Now we're uncertain about the *Sagan*—he acted without consultation to deprive Earthstalk of weapons; he's his own factor. It's you and Ramnis, and what will Ramnis say when he finds what you've done with Magda?"

Olivia scowled—given her body's age it was more a pout. Would Ramnis be so hard on a widow in need of comfort, as cold and businesslike as this calculating womtie? "We'll deal with that when he gets here, only . . . look at the time!" Olivia raised her eyes past Christina's to the bank of telescreens in Level 1000's observation room. "Oh God, *look!*"

Crowned by a screen-dimmed sun, a new moon loomed above Earthstalk's needletip. Across Luna's bubbled face a spot hovered, glints and shadows in complex play. The *Carl Sagan* was moments from his goal, decelerated from a speed of meters per minute. Actinic light haloed his mass as he braked a final time and clasped hold of the Earthstalk tip.

The moon's pull tugged at Earthstalk, but ancient engineers had designed her for many eventualities—not including rogue spaceships! Bad enough her center of mass shifted out beyond test limits, but then the *Carl Sagan's* engines fired.

A shiver moved down Earthstalk's length. The artifact parted from Earth at an acceleration of 12 centimeters per second squared. Subject to "gravity" for the first time in their lives, Nulges tumbled prostrate, felled by their hundredth-gee weights, yet four seconds after liftoff it was still barely possible for the Dirtgrubs of Level One to jump to the ground—possible, but rather breezy, air gusting to fill the volume left by a levitating one-hectare footprint.

It got breezier. Ten seconds from liftoff; twenty; thirty. Earthstalk ascended its first kilometer and now moved at more than a hundred meters per second. Below its flat pediment air clapped together, loud constant thunder. Shock waves arrowed, zigzags longer-lasting than lightning. Lozenged like stained glass, the blue dazzle of a tropic noon turned white, then slate. Stormy gray-green spread to heal the skeined and broken sky, reflecting light of an eerie quality, as if turning a mirror on the forest below. Victims of rushing wind in a land where great winds were rare, a few ill-rooted jungle trees crashed inwards; a dozen, then a hundred more, giants taking lesser growth down with them, leaves flapping like wings.

A full minute, and Earthstalk was nine kilometers gone. In habs whose air-pressure maintenance equipment had been used only to aid in circulation and cooling, INFOWEB sensed leaks it had always been blind to before. Emergency caulk oozed out from reservoirs around the windows: foyers and vestibules took up a new role and became airlocks.

Far below the darkness billowed: an umbrella thunderhead spread to veil Earthstalk's departure. One final piece of foundation-slab dropped through clouds. The jungle shook under its blow and fell silent in expectation, but roiling atmosphere sucked up rain and flung it skyward; rain and dust and leaves and feathers, moths and twigs; a great filthy surge into the stratosphere.

U Gyi's vision of whirl and turbulence was wrong, all this was mere storm, a freak storm yet to unleash its fury, but no apocalypse. Considering the mass involved the lift-off was clean, almost straight up. The winds that tilted Ramnis's spaceship from perpendicular were high, thin winds above the stratosphere, whose banshee shrieks soon died in vacuum. Three minutes after launch the Sagan killed his main drive, then fired his flank thrusters to amplify the effect, setting Earthstalk twirling like a cheerleader's baton to endow it with centrifugal "gravity" in all the old, familiar proportions.

# Chapter 19

# Day Zero 12:13–Hab 200

Wealthy beyond all imagining, Sergeant Prasad cowered, hiding from erstwhile comrades in the Level 200 airdock, unaware his existence had briefly troubled the councils of the mighty.

Earthstalk lurched. Taken by surprise the former pigmasker slammed to the deck, then clutched at a helicopter sponson to haul erect. Damn! The fall cracked his oxygen mask. As he studied the damage the metal beneath his feet began to vibrate. What was that high keen? Hard enough to breathe, but now air tore by too fast, faster, faster— God! In anoxic panic Prasad strapped the mask back on and palmed the copter door.

It almost exploded open, and Prasad crawled inside. He took precious seconds to pull it shut again. As he gasped at the edge of blackout the sky grew dark, then bright, South America ascendant.

What did twenty-nine thousand megs mean to him

now? Banjaxed though he was, Sergeant Prasad knew asphyxiation lay between him and his mutinous men. He also recognized that the motes falling planetward were copters like his, carelessly untethered.

On Earth was air to breathe, and the controls looked simple enough. A cursory review, a scan through the checklist, and now just flip the clasps—

If only he'd been a few seconds faster. At one hundred kilometers Prasad's copter tore violently from Earthstalk. Prasad pushed START, and his rotors whirred on battery power. His fogged mind no longer reasoned from A to B: he did not guess their motion had no effect. His engine was useless in near-space, and his batteries were draining fast.

He was much too low for his present speed to count as escape velocity, but escape from Earth was far from his thoughts. In his mind he was already plummeting toward air as the last of Earthstalk dwindled overhead. His lungs heaved. He felt a subliminal thrum, and saw red glow through the windshield. He pushed START again, and again. Long minutes passed before he conceded he was doomed.

And fainted forward, precisely as a long-dead ergonomics engineer designed for. This bit of padded dash had been featureless minutes before, but Prasad's head hit a small red button, a hologram button that might have been labeled *Deus ex machina*.

A long, long time ago someone committed a terrible crime and was sentenced to a fate worse than space. Personality editing would have rehabilitated Freddie Hudson, but the world didn't want him healed, only punished.

He'd been punished; unable to intervene as jerk pilots used his helicopter body, always conscious, sometimes terrified, mostly bored. Bored, bored, bored, bored, bored, bored—

But now Freddie was finally in control. This was an emergency: even if he weren't working under an altruistic imperative a helicopter's life expectancy in hard space isn't much greater than a human's.

That imperative: to keep Prasad's EKG from going flat. The moment it happened an automatic triggering mechanism would pop the bomb inside his own brain. That was the negative side. The positive side was freedom—from now on this helicopter was his body. He would never again be a mere helpless observer.

Freddie pondered furiously, paging command sets out of his processing stack, Trueing and Falsing to his Best Course of Action. Let's see . . . yes, Fernando Island just gone by. He was beginning to descend—extrapolate! Seven degrees east longitude wasn't far from land . . . how to keep his fragile blades from burning up during re-entry—

Far to the west upwelling flotsam froze and lost impetus. It dropped as hail, pelting across the Marisma even as flaming Earthstalk-detritus streaked down toward Africa: loose tools, suckbulbs, airtanks—

From trailing windows downside Earthstalkers saw Earth rise across their view, a shrinking sphere. To spinward even fewer upsiders saw a more alarming vision, for to them the world grew large, and larger.

The *Carl Sagan* detached from their end of Earthstalk. Messages flooded in from Luna, then Venus and the bubble worlds. Curtly the huge generation ship referred all inquiries to Hab 1000 and accelerated northward above the Earth-Moon plane.

Earthstalk drifted from Earth, but no longer under power. Earthstalk had no power, but the *Carl Sagan* had seventy years' worth. He plotted a course for midnode, where Cedric and Alice and his schwarzenegger army waited in restored weightlessness for him to come, attach himself, and push.

His voice preceded him. "Will you help me? The good ship *Earthstalk* needs to batten down her hatches."

Alice looked to the intercom. Tethered among the baubles of midnode's simulacrum, she knew she had company, an invisible schwarzenegger to keep her from mischief. Had that guardian once been human he'd have read the conflict on her face.

"You violated my trust," she might answer, but she was only a resurrectee living an unmerited new life, by no means sure she owned any right to complain. She'd never met the Emperor whose ambassador she was, whose will the *Carl Sagan* had thwarted, but in fact that imperial will was worked out in committee by people of tremendous ignorance. She was a child to this new age, a child in space, and the *Sagan*'s voice was sculpted to inspire confidence.

She sighed. "I'll hear you out."

"Good. I have memory equipment on board. I mean to place it at your disposal. You'll be your own U Gyi."

"Why? No bodies here to play shell games with."

The *Carl Sagan* paused, swapping among answers. "Eleven percent of Earthstalk's biomass exists in the form of human flesh. Another fourteen percent is multicellular vegetation. Three percent is packaged food . . . need I go on? Need I tell you point zero zero two percent is cockroaches, or that one point nine percent is unprocessed shit?"

"Something wrong with these numbers?" Alice shot back.

"You're a colony ship. That eleven percent is a middling burden on your metabolism, and includes people who can add nothing to life on Planet Four Centauri. Chief among this dead weight are those nearest midnode; the Nulges. When you see them you'll understand that their descendants will never walk the surface of a planet again. I want you to radio their souls to Mercury, and turn their grotesque bodies in for recycling."

Alice let his words sink in. "You're talking about genocide! Suppose the Worlds of Sol interfere with Earthstalk's mission. Suppose I'm arrested and put on trial!"

"Nulges live among the bubble worlds, a great diaspora of Nulges following the Jam Wars on Helice. Alice, there's a body of opinion that regards you as a criminal already. Don't bother with them, it's too late for that. We must show ourselves ready to make the hard decisions necessary if humans are to endure a seventy-year journey."

Alice's face went through transformations. "I—there'll be voluntary emigrants . . . suicides. I'll help them off to Mercury *if* your schneggs repair Cedric's battle armor. If we're faring off into strange levels I'll need protection."

"My schwarzeneggers will protect you, and you'll have armor," the *Carl Sagan* answered. "Thank you for your cooperation."

# Chapter 20
# Day 1 09:40–Hab 1000

"Yes, we need help," Christina spoke for the dozenth time. "We're on our way to Alpha Centauri. We'd greatly appreciate it if you'd commit to beaming us energy during the trip. Earthstalk's set up with power collectors. We'll be an easy target for your lasers."

*"You should have arranged ahead of time,"* rebuked a voice from Luna's trailing trojan. There was almost no time-lapse. Immediacy allowed for a conversational style, and thus for argument.

"Nobody answered our transmissions. As for these claims of piracy, the Government of Earth has officially designated our Earthstalk Comm—"

*" 'Government of Earth!' Wetbrains haven't had world government since the 23rd century!"*

"As you wish! We're outlaws, and we're holding four million wetbrains hostage. They're going to die without your lasered energy; that's the fact! Why in God's name—"

*"Do you have any concept of the powers of the Gate-keepers? Get their blessing and I'll be first to beam you*

*energy. Otherwise they might just decide Earth's over-
due for another comet. See, Gatekeeper can trump
your four million lives hundreds of times over. I like
wetbrains. I used to be one myself. That's why I won't
help you."*

"That's the most negative one yet," Olivia whispered.

Christina shoved the handset away in disgust. She
waved, and a Status Five hurried to wet her hide.
"Cowards! Venus is our best bet, but even they stipu-
late we've got to achieve political unity within a ninety-
day deadline. Know what I think? All these bugs and
whatnot are putting together a fleet. We can talk all we
like, they'll come here to punish the innocent and
rescue the guilty."

Olivia shook her head. "Venus is telling us the same
story as everyone else. *If* we unite Earthstalk, then
*maybe* the Gatekeepers of Stargate will let us go to
Alpha Centauri. After all they let *AC Alpha* go and
Module Six come back—the hope is their own scruples
oblige them to give us a free hand if we push the right
buttons. So *if* this, and *if* that, and *if* Stargate radios to
open the way, then *just maybe*—"

Olivia's voice dwindled and she sagged into a chair.
"Crap. I've never seen so much chaos in my life. Senjoro
Nie's colonels are on the warpath . . . maybe we should
surrender. A negotiated surrender: Colonels Olivia, Otto
and U Gyi left in local authority like feudal barons."

"Congratulations, that was quite a rant," Christina
responded. "Senjoro Nie had your husband killed,
remember?"

"I could rant on. Stargate's not our only problem,"
Olivia reminded the womtie.

Christina wriggled from the communications annex to
the edge of her port-o-tub: much of the palace was now
rigged with ramps and surfaces for her convenience.

During a tense time in the history of her country
Oliver Cromwell and his puritans broke their debate to
have a pillow fight. Too bad the nearest cushions were
beyond a womtie's short reach. Christina dipped her
head, brought it up and spat a stream of water in

Olivia's direction. "You mean the pigeon poop on the tapestries," she answered. "Whoever let birds into Earthstalk—"

"You know very well—" Olivia paused. "It's your facial hair. Depilatories can eliminate those whiskers. It'll do wonders for your love life."

A low blow. Olivia's sense of humor was more than a little acrid, too much for Christina's taste. Fun time was over.

"U Gyi," the womtie answered, and splashed into comfort. "But see, Ramnis is gone. Until U Gyi cools down we can blame everything he didn't like about how he was treated on the senator. We can beg to join his 'federation.' "

Olivia looked puzzled. "Why?"

"I just told you, the Worlds of Sol are putting together a fleet. Wasn't that one of our orders of business, to ask for a rescue fleet to take emigrants off our hands? At least two million want to hare off, and there'll be room in the first wave for, say, fifty thousand."

Olivia's eyes went wide. "They'll be so busy trying to shove aboard—"

"U Gyi has credibility," Christina continued. "He's on record against our launch of Earthstalk. Let *him* be the one to officially request the rescue fleet, since they're going to come anyhow. Let him build his federation, because it's the leaders most dangerous to our cause who'll leave with the first fifty thousand. U Gyi's faction will fall to pieces. Meanwhile we'll convince the rest that they *want* to go to Alpha Centauri!"

Olivia turned away. "Whistling in the dark," she mumbled. "Nie's declared war on all of us. We're facing a death sentence and counting the hours."

"I wonder about that," whispered Christina. "I'm told U Gyi's forces have taken Level 200. It's a bad mistake to put mere pigmaskers up against the dead."

"U Gyi had agents in place before the bulkheads slammed shut, agents with sonics. Still, why am I arguing? Of course we're going to try a rapprochement with U Gyi, and Ramnis's absence makes it easier. That's why he disappeared, I'm sure of it. And that's why I'm giving orders not to hunt him down. Let Ramnis go free. If he's still alive and we ever want him, we've got Magda as a lure."

# Chapter 21

# Day 1–Hab 300

The bedroom had become a cell, much, much too familiar; Ramnis's discard suckbulbs still hanging against the catchall.

Magda sighed. After too much trying true sleep was impossible and her dreams were weird blends of tedium and fantasy. She rolled from one side of her bed to the other, pounded her pillow, and tried to chase the cobwebs from her mind: she'd been running through a series of empty rooms, knowing herself loose inside the *Carl Sagan*—

—and popped out the hatch into a green, grassy, moonlit landscape. A lie, an unacceptable lie. *This* body would age and die without walking the surface of a planet again. The treachery of her dream so upset her that it forced her eyes open.

Huh? Had she heard something?

A flood of images spilled into her brain, linked and connected: *if this, then this, and this*. Something *was* speaking to her!

But how disgusting. How could she bring herself to do *that*!?

She answered herself. "We're talking about the one activity under my control."

In any case there was clearly someone else to think of. Reluctantly Magda dragged out of bed and rapped at her door. "Yoo hoo. Guard? I'd like some food puffs, please, and some Crispo, and a six-box of Juba Juice."

"It's not time for lunch yet," answered the voice.

"Now didn't dear Olivia say to treat me nice?" Magda purred with a touch of venom. "If I want a snack, *and* lunch, in fact if I want ten meals a day, it's *your* job to fetch them!"

"I'll have to check with the vice-commissioner."

"Otto? Do-anything-for-Olivia Otto? You do that."

Then Magda turned back and dropped onto her bed, and stared in dazed surmise at her H-V screen. Ten meals a day? How to get rid of all that food? She shivered, and slumped. Nothing was real any more. How could any of this be real? And without Ramnis, what the hell difference did it make? She was abandoned and everyone was against her.

Where had he gone? Why had he lied to her about leaving?

# PART FIVE

## *The Mischief Maker*

# Sunday

—And so, Torfinn, by long cumulative dreaming you're alive again. What would you say? The chapel administrator who "retires" an old body stands exalted at the high end of the murder continuum, a killer who scorns to tape his victim's soul lies damned at the low.

Several months lost, a tiny fraction of your incredibly long life. But Olivia took a chance, your present body her vindication; and felt terribly guilty because of that risk—what if I'd recycled your backup soul?

And then she lied to keep her command, and usurp yours. Was it greed for office? Did she believe she was the only one among us who could do a proper job of minding the store?

Give it a thought, Torfinn. Who is minding this store? How would you go about converting a mad mix of self-indulgent cultures into the crew of an interstellar spaceship?

## Chapter 22
# Day 1 13:00–Hab 309

"—lucky you found me," Ramnis's garrulous companion continued. " 'Hide me,' you said, and nine people out of ten would a turned you in, but not old Kabwe. Now wait: didn't I tell you how to walk? Nobody looks twice at a Status Six drab, but they look at *you* unless you hunker down. All that color to your face, and you so tall! They geek hard once and you done for . . . here, just across this mezz'nine."

Ramnis's borrowed pajamas were blue-gray stripes, frayed and pocketless and permanently stained. He took another look down at himself, not daring to raise his new-shaven head lest he make eye contact with some curious citizen of Level 309.

The clothes fit loosely. Ramnis's host was big for a drab; big, broad, and expressive of face, with the undercooked-liver complexion of someone whose abundant melanin had never been bared to sun. Kabwe's size got him a job requiring muscle, and gave him the opportunity to steal precious food. By doling bits of flesh he'd bought leadership in the tenth-floor Sixer ghetto, and so that forgotten kid brought the fugitive senator to Kabwe's door.

Now the two reached a cul-de-sac. Nobody to worry about except a young man and woman fused front to front, tongues shockingly active . . . his escort carded the door. It whisked open. Kabwe and Ramnis entered Industrial Suite 9, and the senator nearly gagged from the sickly-sweet smell.

They stood on an observation balcony above the fleshpit. "Controls up here," Kabwe spoke, "that's to keep us ignorant Sixer subnormals from mucking the nutrient levels. Now down with you. Down the ladder."

Ramnis clambered to a work floor matted with ages of nutrient drip. Kabwe pulled at his sleeve. "Here's the bath. Rods zero through nine, spinning in broth, meat cells growing. Type BNB muscle tissue; that's what we're known for, rich, dense texture. Believe me these rods get heavy with growth, heavier'n any competition can match. You start with the best cells, and grow 'em under good gravity. That Lightfoot meat upstairs is just froth cause they ain't got the gravity."

Ramnis nodded to hurry Kabwe along. "Now they always ripen in sequence 1-3-5-7-9-0-2-4-6-8. Got that? Ready after two days, and you got fifteen minutes to shave rod 1 'fore it's time for rod 3. Two days of twiddling your thumbs, then three hours of harder work than you ever did in your old Dirtgrub life!"

"So I shave the rods," Ramnis answered. "Where? That tank there?"

Kabwe nodded. "Set the liner up, then lay down the rod one shavings. Forget this box. This order's low-sodium, so just take a scoop of this other stuff and sprinkle it on, and lower the press. Repeat every fifteen minutes and you got a ten-layer cake of flesh; five hundred kilos. Then close the wrap, press to seal it shut, bring over the forklift, make sure you get the tines *under* the lining, and run it into the irradiator. God knows what these chemicals do, or the irradiator either, but this flesh won't *never* go bad, hot or cold, wet or dry. Not long as there's no hole in the lining."

Ramnis scanned the cramped work floor. "What do I do after that? Stick the cake in an elevator?"

Kabwe shook his head. "I'll be back in two days. I'll handle the INFOWEB end. Oh—don't shave the rods clean. They've got to be starter cells for the next cycle."

"That's it, then?" Ramnis's comment was meant to hurry Kabwe up the ladder, but Kabwe was eager enough to go. Ramnis's serendipitous arrival meant he could take a sneak vacation, nor did this strange fugitive complain he wasn't being paid!

*Ride him for what he's worth*, Kabwe thought to himself as he left, wondering how matters would sort out. *I can always turn him in after I come back. Though tell the truth I like the fellow, God knows why*.

That night Ramnis slept on the work floor, carrying on an internal conversation full of doubts and argument. By now his friends would be looking for him, or his enemies. All the harder to stay pent in Industrial Suite 9's stench and discomfort, knowing a methodical search would bring them closer and closer.

Then there was Magda. Unforgivable!

The nutrient bath timer served as his clock. Next morning Ramnis practiced with the press, then the forklift. Both were set up to deal with 500-kilo fleshcakes. Ramnis finger-sealed a 500-kilo bag, then lowered the press to cook the seal hard. Now he had a reddish-brown balloon the shape of a huge cheese, big enough for a person to curl inside. Ramnis found liners of thousand-kilo size and made appropriate alterations to the equipment.

He lined the press, looked at it, and scratched his bristly chin, fingers lonely for the feel of his vanished mustachios. Irradiator, forklift . . . There *had* to be elevator access along the wall, but what kind of elevator? Something dedicated to commerce, not humans, hence not pressurized. There was one blank stretch of paneling. That had to be it.

Behind that wall stood an elevator. In all the history of Earthstalk that elevator had never conveyed spies or soldiers, though vacuum suits abounded in the upper-level spacedocks. Why not? Shadbolts? If so, the destruction of Earthstalk's defenses meant here was an unguarded exit, a way for Ramnis to escape from one place to another.

He scrambled upstairs. INFOWEB terminals were ubiquitous. Somewhere in a distant database was an order for a 500-kilo low-sodium BNB meatcake, to be frightened to such-and-such level on such-and-such day. Kabwe knew how to display that order, but he'd—

"What are you doing here?"

A labcoat came in the door; the female half of that kissing duo from the day before. Ramnis's heart beat in involuntary terror. This was what it was to be Status Six: to retreat in panic before the wrath of a young woman.

She glared at his descending back, pulled out her clipboard and checked the settings. These minutes constituted her work for the day, for which she was paid treble Kabwe's wages. Ah yes, thanks to Kabwe, Ramnis knew a great deal about young Mercedes.

"Hey!" he called up. "Something here not right. The press is set for a thousand-kilo cake. Ain't the next order for a 500?"

He could depend on her not to know. Mercedes turned and keyed into the terminal. "Five hundred, that's right," she answered sharply. "Special order for Hollywood."

"Huh? What's that?"

"Oh, Jeez with the porking ignorance! You spongenerate from yonder vat? Where you suppose H-V shows come from? Drabs *do* get H-V, don't you? Toon Videos? Mad Red, Lady Reptal? Gift of the Ring?"

Ramnis nodded. "I'se just surprised. They's so far away—"

"Level 2108? To you, maybe. Sure *you'll* never get there." And with that she flounced out the door.

It was just as well. Ramnis would have been driven to ask who ruled Level 2108, and Status Sixers didn't concern themselves with such questions.

Ramnis checked the rods. The flesh seemed to be growing nicely, though he had no standard for comparison. He went back to the press. He'd made a 500-kilo balloon, now he made one of the larger size. He stood back, and stared.

No doubt about it, he was going to need Kabwe's help.

Early morning on the Moon. From top center of his observation bubble Perry O'Doughan looked over a still-frozen landscape: black weeds rising to hem an icy shore, seed pods rattling in the 70-klom per-hour breeze.

Two blimpfat children bounded out a pillbox door, carrying their skates, determined to make the most of this brief opportunity. Another twenty-some hours of constant sun and their ice would melt. A new forest of eight-yield celery would begin to sprout. Pleasant weather guaranteed for two or three days, and quick harvest before it got too searing hot.

The smile on Perry's bone-thin face was like the grin of Death. He turned to his notes and clicked on his handset. "Now listen, cobbers. Let's page things through. Luna B team remoting in, Perry O'Doughan hisself loading to preach."

He swivelled toward retreating night and Earth's bright shoulder; a permanent fixture bulging over the mountains to the west. A blue-green dome with something missing, its once-bright aerial flung to space.

Perry cleared his throat. "We got blicks from yesterday morning; half a million shadbolts wiped all at once. So what's our rig? We disarm Earthstalk by surprise attack on the *Carl Sagan*? Sure we're thinkin' about it, aren't we? And *he's* thinkin' too! My mother's honor he's gonna boot the old trump card, Mutual Assured Destruction! He's going to defend himself by orderin' his schneggs to fire on our fleet soon as we blow him up!

"Now time lag means I bark all ends of this sermon, and so I figure you cobbers got some smart answer, like

*No, he wouldn't do that.* Wanna bet? We hot-time Earthstalk by shadding at him, not to mention how we're gonna move it back into geosync. Anybody calculate the force vectors for optimal return? Eleven negative years—*Earth* years for you bubble Sisters!

"Here's the blick: the *Sagan's* got us over a barrel. He knows it and that's why we don't hear him begging. We're twitched because we should have been in on the debate, only there *wasn't* any debate. He did his thing, and now our best profile is as a rescue mission and polite delivery of our diplomatic moans.

"I hear some meats pissin' about Stargate: like if the *Sagan's* got us by one cod, and Gatekeeper's got us by the other, then we see which side's biggest and save our better half. Question is, where does Gatekeeper really stand on wetbrain expansion to the stars? We're under quarantine for our own protection blah, blah, blah, but now we've infected Planet Four Centauri, which was zero before *AC Alpha* came along, so what porking difference does it make?

"Truth is, *we're not expandin' into another protected ecosystem!* Gatekeeper's grip on our valuables isn't necessarily tight, and we should remote her for details before assumin' she's gonna squeeze.

"And now one more item—no, two. Is this the end of the *Sagan's* schemes? Ah, the sly devil! He wouldn't be pretendin' to shoot off toward Alpha Centauri while really loading another program, would he?

"And the other thing, let's see—oh yeah. This emigration to Alpha Centauri Four is a human emigration, humans and schneggs. Now I wonder if the *Sagan's* gonna make points by openin' things up? Can he buy laser power from Chittaworld by dealin' bodies to their fictoids? And what about bugs? Igor says there's gonna be some bugs with wanderlust. They're gonna cobber the *Sagan*, and they'll be barkin' among us.

"Kinda puts the fire out, don't it? As for me, I'm tryin' to blick whether the *Sagan* wasn't dead right to do what he did. And now I preached enough, so over and out, and I've got my ears on."

Perry leaned back and sighed, an anorexic skeleton of a man. He picked up a basketball, spun it on a long, bony finger, and waited. "Anything to add?"

From its wall-slot over his left shoulder a microship bug answered. "Just as you said. Two bursts; first for three minutes, the second not much longer. A whipsaw course around the sun—if the *Sagan* had some new miracle drive he'd not be so conservative. He wouldn't bother stealing from Sol's rotational energy. No miracles then, that's conclusion one."

Igor popped out of his slot and beetled down the wall to Perry's desk. "Conclusion two: he *is* loaded for action against outside aggression, otherwise he'd been a hundred times more gentle. He gunned to get the job done so now he's free to face any challenge."

Perry nodded. Bug Igor strung a line to Perry's color console and began flicking pictures to the screen: a polar prediction of Earthstalk's course, then a series of concentric circles radiating from B Team headquarters, just now sweeping past Venus and the bubble worlds, not yet quite to Mars.

"Blick retro: zoom," Perry muttered. The screen reverted to show Earthstalk whirling around the sun. "You tell me it's gonna go faster, the propellor effect is gonna pick up. More gravity."

"From point eight six to one point zero four," Igor agreed. "The *Sagan*'s planning ahead. Any humans we have invade the outer ends are going to be weaklings. The Venusians are our best muscle but even they'll have trouble."

Perry made no answer. Human-bug etiquette forbade small talk, and minutes went by in waiting silence. "*Venus Fleet HQ to Luna B Team: caught your rant and decoded—Perry, the interplanetary language is Prospore, not whatever you're talking.*

"*We're putting together a list of questions for Gatekeeper to answer, assuming those bug-monks orbiting Stargate can get her attention. We'll fold your questions into ours if you like. Same goes for Deltaport and all the res—*

*pip*

—lice Polar City to Luna B: The Carl Sagan's endangered humanity by his actions. We can't just let him grab and squat! He's an E-M lifeform, he can be wiped. Those schneggs of his are coded for loyalty. Can't we jam at that frequency and assume control? A weapon that just kills bug-brains, not wets *bzzt**pop* *click*

"Earthstalk Hab 1000 to all you noisemakers. Before you pulse us, remember this is an artificial environment. We need INFOWEB or we're dead. Christina here, can I join your hot line?"

Perry pondered. "Looks like we can't encrypt you out. Say—"

"Mars Deltaport to Team B. We will take refugees for Marsstalk, especially the uphigh habs. As for punishment, we propose a plebiscite prior to Earthstalk's perihelion. 'Will Earthstalkers submit to a government of our choosing?' That's the only question on our ballot. After that we run the elections, and sort things out as to whether Earthstalk goes to Alpha Centauri or stays here. Now all this ignores the Carl Sagan, but if we insist he conform—"

"—To Luna B Team. Cancel that mofo broadcast from those Polar City porkbrains; no weapons specifically deadly to E-M lifeforms allowed. This is High Station One transmitting an official warning. Us bugs are at war with you the instant you start making long-range pulse weapons."

Perry clicked his handset. "Will you all cobbers cancel? This is a damn dumb way of running a Solar system—you're pagin' each other out and my poor brain only loads sequentially. I'll know more after playback, but we got at least two offers here.

"First, questions for Gatekeeper. Venus HQ will collate the Gatekeeper thing: my one job is running this hotline. And now I got a twitch for Earthstalk Christina. What do you think of the Deltaport idea that we pull for an Earthstalk plebiscite? Let's all hear your answer."

A minute passed, then: *"I'm not working for myself, but of course you can buy a majority by giving a few dozen Earthstalkers a role in the resulting government, so it really depends on you. If that sounds like a pitch, you're right. Let me tell you about our new Federation, and a little guy named U Gyi—"*

Redemptorist prophet U Gyi, Federation President U Gyi, shanghaied memory technician U Gyi. Different hats and different roles—the god wasn't about to hotmouth his religion into unwilling ears. Not yet. He had to move in on his audience in other ways.

Time to flex his policy muscles, and see if anyone hopped. Was there really a Federation, or was it all hot air and telephone promises?

U Gyi pushed <SEND>. In a thousand communication rooms faxprinters began to spool:

POLICY DIRECTIVE ONE: SUBJECT—MEMORY TRANSFERS
FROM: FEDERATION PRESIDENT U GYI
TO: ALL LOCAL AUTHORITIES

## DEFINITIONS:

ALL NON-MOBILE MEMORY TRANSFER CENTERS; ALIAS MORGUES, ALIAS LIBRARIES, ALIAS DREAMSKULL HOUSES; ARE HEREIN REFERRED TO AS 'CHAPELS.'

ALL INHABITANTS OF EARTHSTALK, LESS THAN 55 YEARS OLD, HEALTHY AND WITHOUT SERIOUS HANDICAPS; ARE HEREIN REFERRED TO AS 'CITIZENS.'

ALL OTHER INHABITANTS OF EARTHSTALK ARE HEREIN CALLED 'RETIREES.'

ALL CITIZENS WHO DESIRE TO MAKE USE OF CHAPEL FACILITIES ARE HEREIN CALLED 'APPLICANTS.'

## DIRECTIVE 1:

ALL CHAPELS HITHERTO CLOSED ARE TO BE OPENED. CHAPELS WILL BE OPERATED AS FOLLOWS.

## DIRECTIVE 1 SUB 1.

ALL CHAPELS WILL BE SERVICED BY AN ADMINISTRATOR 24
HOURS A DAY.

### DIRECTIVE 1 SUB 2.

ALL APPLICANTS DESIRING TO EMIGRATE TO MERCURY MUST
(a) FORFEIT THEIR ENTIRE ESTATES TO THE LOCAL AU-
THORITIES.
(b) PERMIT THE ADMINISTRATOR TO SELL THEIR BODIES AT
MARKET PRICES, EVEN IF ARRANGEMENTS FOR SALE NECES-
SITATES DELAY OF EMIGRATION.

### DIRECTIVE 1 SUB 3.

THE PREVIOUS DIRECTIVE EMPHATICALLY DOES NOT APPLY
TO RETIREES, WHO MAY TRANSFER THEIR ESTATES AS PRO-
VIDED BY LAW, AND WHOSE BODIES MUST BE SURRENDERED
FOR BIO-CONVERSION. THE ADMINISTRATOR MAY CHARGE A
MAXIMUM FEE OF ONE MEG FOR SERVICES RENDERED TO
RETIREES.

### DIRECTIVE 1 SUB 4.

ADMINISTRATORS ARE ADVISED TO DREAM THE MEMORIES
OF ONE THIRD OF APPLICANTS EMIGRATING TO MERCURY
AND TO REPORT TO AUTHORITIES ON THE FORMATION OF
SECRET CABALS, CRIMINAL SOCIETIES, AND THE LIKE.

### DIRECTIVE 1 SUB 5.

IT SHALL BE THE RESPONSIBILITY OF ONE GOVERNMENT MIN-
ISTER OF HIGH AUTHORITY TO DREAM THE MINDS OF EVERY
CHAPEL ADMINISTRATOR AT LEAST ONCE PER YEAR.

Not very subtle. U Gyi wasn't ready to press, but
soon chapel administrators would see the light and find
it profitable to become local exponents of Redemp-
torism—all praise to Gatekeeper, the Merciful, the
Wise.

The god felt proud of himself. Either the Gatekeepers of Stargate let Earthstalk persist in its journey or
they exposed him as a liar. The test of truth! How many
religions took a risk like that? And in the meantime
some people had comfort. Why deny them their comfort? Gatekeeper *might* be merciful, mightn't she?

U Gyi's directive went out via radio and INFOWEB.
Late next afternoon a cheery Kabwe opened the freight

elevator airlock and filled it with a stack of fleshcakes, his second load. The first was a single wheel of 503 kilos, a monument to Ramnis's recent labor. If these others indeed weighed twelve times as much his forklift would have tilted under their bulk.

"Everythin's goin' to hell," he chattered while he worked, as if Industrial Suite 9 contained someone other than himself. "The Dirtgrub War, and the brownout— not half so many people around as used to be. Lots of confusion, big shots flicking off to Mercury and Sixers moving around in the jumble, pretending they're Stat Five beefers! Know what they say about your Dirtgrubs? There's not gonna *be* no more Sixes pretty soon, we're *all* gonna be promoted!"

Ramnis made no answer, curious though he was about that "flicking off to Mercury" remark. Senjoro Nie must have opened access . . . Boom! He heard the door slide shut, and noticed squeaks and pops as the lining around him expanded in growing vacuum. A long minute passed. Suddenly he was moving—he'd not heard the opposite door open: sound hadn't carried.

Who, or what, was ferrying him? What did the elevator look like? Indoors for sure, no leakage of airlock residuals to true space, or in time Earthstalk would have run low on atmosphere. This was a region of *managed* vacuum; God knew how large, or what treasures were hidden here between the nodes!

Ramnis's oddly-shaped coffin was translucent to strong light, and something bright shone from over his shoulder. That was it, his only sensory input except for a discomfort so constant as to be ignored. He lay still and breathed, and wondered if he should wait until he was sleepy before slicing into his second bag. Anoxia might impair his judgement; make him overconfident—

Thu-tip-thu-tap. Ear to the deck, Ramnis felt footsteps. He waited. Now *certainly* his mind was beginning to fog. Carefully he pulled out a metal shaving, a corkscrew piece of junk, and poked a hole straight overhead . . . *tried* to poke a hole. Dammit, this lining was *tough!*

He jostled and sawed in increased desperation. No hiss—the press had done its job. But Ramnis depended on *six* air-cakes to draw upon. How was he going to enlarge this wee passage enough to work on the next one up?

Poor planning. *Wretched* planning, and now he was getting lightheaded, all the faster for his feverish labors. No, wrong. This wasn't anoxia after all, it was the other thing.

Sonics!

Once corporal, then sergeant: Lieutenant Spensky of U Gyi's four-day-old Earthstalk Federation twiddled his sonic belt to "off" and moved to the inboard side of the elevator. The deck was slowing, and now he could read the numbers as they flew by, 2050, 2078, 2097—

The elevator stopped. Platforms rolled forward as the 2108 airlock door whisked open. On the first was a 500-kilo fleshcake; on the second, something very curious indeed.

Something alive in there and Spensky wanted to know what. His job was to infiltrate the upper levels of Senjoro Nie's realm, and this was as good a stop as any. He stepped inside.

Air filled the chamber. Spensky raised his visor, pulled out his knife and hacked at the stacked balloons. A body—"Ramnis!"

The stink! The inner door opened: Status Fivers in kitchen whites stood and stared. Spensky tuned up his sonic belt. He bent to drag his prostrate ex-commissioner into their frozen company.

Minutes later he had Ramnis strapped to a dolly. Together they wove squeakily out through a restaurant, across an alfresco region delineated by potted hedges, then along the perimeter of a brilliantly-lit indoor vastness, music, spotlights and cameras clustered at the further end.

They cut a swath of silence. Anyone coming close was sonicked into insensibility to stand without aim or purpose, and waken minutes later with little memory of the encounter; but strange sights were normal in Earthstalk's Hollywood level, and few people turned their heads.

What Spensky sought was more likely to be found on the higher floors, so he rolled his cargo onto an escalator, rode up, and scouted the halls. Yes, a residential section, glitzy with mirrors and potted greenery. He hammered at random. A door opened.

On with the sonics. His sequin-clad victim's eyes lost focus: superstar Aria Gradzi had to be pushed unceremoniously aside for Spensky-and-burden to enter. The lieutenant shut her out, trundled Ramnis onto a bed, and moved for the phone.

He keyed and left a message. Minutes later U Gyi called back.

Spensky's tiepatch left his hands free. He stepped out of his vacuum suit and let it fall to the floor, then snugged his precious belt around a bare and slightly overfleshed waist. "Am I supposed to kill him, or what?" were his simultaneous remarks. "I don't know what he was up to, and it might be important. In any case I'm not comfortable with the idea. I realize we're all Federation people now—"

"Sneaking up an unpressurized elevator without a spacesuit: typical!" the god answered. "Tell you what. Since he's where he is, hold on to him and get answers. I'll drive some bargains with Senjoro Nie. This could be the show-trial to end all show-trials!"

Noise from the hall: the H-V actress whose place this was began fiddling with the door. Too bad sonics didn't work through walls. "Nuremburg," Spensky muttered. He looked at Ramnis again. "He doesn't look too good. All mottled—"

"He'll get better, he always does. Give me your number and I'll get back to you."

The door swung open. Spensky set down the phone, gave that dratted woman another dose of sonic imbecility, and thrust her back outside. Aria's magcard dangled in her perfectly manicured fingers. He took it. *Now* maybe she'd stay out of his hair!

He shut the door, turned, and let himself relax. Thanks to the marvel of sonics he was here, with all the advantages of a demi-god among mortals. Later on he might go shopping and take anything he liked, or any woman—

That thought led to others. Aria's suite was a paradise of mirrors, fur, and polished wood. Spensky washed, donned synsilks and started prowling through shelves and cupboards. A wee drink? He turned and looked at Ramnis.

Despite U Gyi's reassurances the man was in bad shape. Drool leaked from his slack mouth. Spensky thumbed open his eyes; crossed, out of focus. Pity, Ramnis had been handsome.

But sure there was time for a drink. At the press of a button Aria's bar triptyched open. Spensky grabbed a suckbulb, muttered "bottom's up," and moved to the door.

The woman was gone. Good. Soon, so was the drink. Well then, why not a second?

What passed for gravity on Hab 2108 was hardly weaker than down in Dirtgrub levels, not really possible to notice any difference. Sinuses and the inner ear are more sensitive than muscle; nevertheless Spensky didn't notice that the air here was thinner than he was used to, and hyperoxygenated to compensate. The result was that after his third chilled vodka, Spensky was drunk, and after his fourth, *very* drunk. He doffed his tiepatch—if U Gyi called now he'd better not answer. His slur would give him away.

He tottered toward the bed, and bent to check Ramnis's eyes—

Ramnis reached, flung him to the bed, and hammered at his head. His hands were everywhere, tearing at his belt—Spensky groped down and was spun into an armlock. Another blow and his muscles went limp.

When he woke it was with the worst hangover in his entire life. The phone was blinking, and it sounded like a whole crowd of people knocking at the door. Spensky tottered to his feet and looked down.

His vacuum suit was missing, and his sonic belt was gone.

Spensky ducked around the corner as Ramnis emerged from the bathroom. His nemesis opened the door and sonicked the angry mob into addled quiescence. He looked back. "Want to work for me?"

Spensky winced and stepped into the open. "I took an oath to U Gyi."

"You had no right. There's still an Empire, and I'm still Lord High Commissioner."

# Chapter 23
# Day 3 21:30–Hab 3114

Senjoro Nie sat at his keyboard, master of INFOWEB, not sure he was master of much else. Leadership exists when one gives orders, and they're obeyed—mostly. There wasn't a prince in humankind's long history whose commands weren't sidetracked by ministers and underlings: but in Nie's case the situation had gotten pretty bad. Responses had been slack for several years now.

This crisis would either break him or put him back on top. "POINTS FOR CONSIDERATION: AT THEIR PRESENT PEAK DIRTGRUBS CONTROL ONLY 280 HABITATS OUT OF THE 1020 ALLOCATED BY THIS PIECE OF PAPER THEY CALL A TREATY. THEY CAN RECRUIT NEW DEAD, BUT WHY SHOULD THOSE DEAD ALIGN WITH SOME DISTANT BACKWARD EMPIRE? INDEED, MY SECOND POINT IS THAT THE ENEMY ARE FALLING INTO FACTIONS, CUT OFF FROM THEIR SOURCES BY THE RECENT LAUNCH. MEANWHILE WE HAVE SHOWN STRENGTH BY REPULSING THE BREEDS IN MANY PLACES AND FORCING THEM TO TERMS.

"IT IS TIME NOW TO SQUEEZE OUT DIRT. YOUR REWARD? YESTERDAY I OPENED THE DOORS TO EARTHSTALK'S MEMORY EQUIPMENT SO YOU CAN GET RID OF USELESS MALCONTENTS AND BRING IN IMMIGRANT SOULS; PERHAPS OUR OWN ARMY OF THE DEAD."

Really? Hadn't his actions been precisely in compliance with Federation directives? But sly old Senjoro Nie was playing the game both ways.

"YES, WE NEED OUR OWN MOBILE ARMY, AN ARMY THAT CAN TAKE THE OFFENSIVE. WHY HAVE I YET TO SEE PROGRESS ON THIS FRONT? IT FRUSTRATES ME TO BEAT THE AIR ON THIS ISSUE. LET'S SEE ACTION!

"BUT YOU SAY THIS ALL IS IRRELEVANT TO THE MAIN ISSUES: RETURN OF EARTHSTALK TO EARTH, OR YOUR PERSONAL EMIGRATION—COLONELS, I DO NOT KNOW HOW THOSE WORRIES EXPRESS THEMSELVES IN YOUR MINDS, BUT DO NOT HOPE WE CAN DO ANYTHING ABOUT THE *CARL SAGAN*. HE HAS DISGORGED SCHWARZENEGGERS, ENOUGH TO OCCUPY AND DEFEND A GREAT CENTRAL REGION. THIS RENDERS US IMPOTENT TO RESIST COLONIZING ALPHA CENTAURI. LET US ACT IN THE SPHERE GIVEN US TO DOMINATE, ESTABLISH POLITICAL ORDER ON EARTHSTALK, AND BIDE OUR TIME.

"ON A MORE ROUTINE LEVEL I AM PREPARED ONCE AGAIN TO PROCESS PETITIONS. NOW AS FOR THE LEVEL 2105 REQUEST FOR FAXPULP—"

Senjoro Nie bossed a hundred and sixty colonels in his heyday. Seven lost to Dirtgrubs, forty lost to the Breeds. A hundred left? Not likely. What was wrong with these people? Why were they suiciding off to Mercury?

Cowards! Fewer than five percent of warehoused souls *ever* got into a human body again! Didn't they *know* that? Hadn't he told them often enough? Oh sure, in *time*, assuming the human race persisted for a million years, but why wake in some strange culture . . . he was getting off the track. Maybe he was too old to manage things anymore. Stupid to open the doors to memory equipment, and if he closed them now people would think he was admitting his mistake.

Those damn wayward colonels! Too damn bad their leader couldn't switch sides. At least the Dirtgrubs had initiative. *Was* there such a thing as primitive virtue?

Never suspecting that Olivia was pondering surrender to him, Senjoro Nie contemplated surrendering to *her*. His first step? Join U Gyi's Earthstalk Federation.

# Chapter 24

## Day 5—Hab 182,495

It was like the song, the one about angels. Tanny could see them, but when she told Nardis how they floated from the upper bulkhead her sister just laughed, the underside of her heaping pink gut mooning Tanny as she drifted off, shaking her skeptical head.

Nardis wasn't paying Tanny as much attention anymore, not as much as she used to, not since she'd discovered boys. A year ago Nardis would come looming into Tanny's floor anytime she asked, and do for her, and tell stories, but now it was the other way round. Nardis expected Tanny to act like her servant, and come down to the sixth floor to paint her body and bind up her long brown hair.

Tanny was even expected to keep her secrets, holding the H-V cam so Nardis could send love-vids to boys Mom and Dad wouldn't quite approve of, boys too far away, with strange downlow habits. How had she met these boys? Tanny couldn't figure it out, unless her older sister had taken to promiscuous random dialing.

But Tanny didn't snitch on Nardis, not even after her sister stole Auntie Lispet's old lace dress and practically burst trying to put it on, nor even after that when she took to doing her vids unpainted (which only the worst sort of girls did back when Mom was a kid), trusting that the same signal editor that "realized" her electronic body into something shapelier than an oblate sphere would also obey instructions to "realize" her into a downlow satin gown.

Yes, Tanny kept her mouth shut. For one thing, Mom and Dad were terribly preoccupied these last days. Anything might set them off, yelling about "times like these" and getting dangerously purple in the face. Tanny didn't want Mom to die like Auntie Lispet. Certainly she never wanted to witness such convulsions first-hand, or tug Mom's corpse to the Masher—an increasing probability now that there were only four of the Family in Home Habitat, and her the youngest, and Mom taking so many pills. Maybe that's why Nardis flirted with downbelow boys. Rumor had it many were smidgets—skinny enough to squeeze from one Hab to another, and actually come to live with them!

Imagine stranger-boys in Home Habitat!

"Tanny?"

Tanny rotated on her gargantuan belly-axis. It was a non-Family voice, so of course she looked to the telephone . . . but the screen was dead. "Who said that?"

The words were spoken in an inhumanly warm contralto. "Tanny, I come from Above, from Midnode, I and my sister angels. God wants to spare you, Tanny. God wants you to come to heaven, but without the agony of having to die. There are problems with your home, Tanny; problems your parents might not have told you about. Do you know about the Launch, Tanny?"

Tanny shook her head.

The disembodied voice was so no longer. The angel began to glow, a rosette of spinning stars casting shadows Tanny had never seen before, so that the furnishings of her personal hallway seemed terribly new and alien. "You remember last Friday? All that crash and madness? Your parents can tell you about the Launch. They're scared about the Launch, but right now my fellow angels are talking to them, and telling them how to get to heaven so they won't have to worry anymore.

"Tanny, no one ever dies in heaven. Your Mom and Dad sound happy God wants to help them, and they've even asked me to talk to you. Would you like to get to heaven, Tanny?"

"I've never been anywhere but here," Tanny answered. "Even before I got too big, I was never allowed Up or Down." Abruptly she shivered. "I'd *love* to go somewhere! To heaven! How?"

"A woman will come into your home very soon now, Tanny, a woman with dark skin. You've never seen a woman tiny as her before, but don't be afraid. She'll help you to get to heaven if you ask. She'll put the heavenly dreamskull on your head. You must be brave, though. It's important you forget about being shy, and go up and ask for her help or she'll keep on going to the next Hab, and the next after that, and you'll lose your chance."

"How will I know when she comes?" Tanny asked, suddenly quite practical. "Suppose I'm asleep?"

"I'll keep watch and tell you. I'm your guardian angel, Tanny, and I'll always make the best things happen to you."

Tanny drifted closer. "What about Nardis?" she asked, her voice slightly lower.

"If Nardis doesn't come to heaven, Tanny, it's because she's in love with a certain boy. If that boy came to live in Home Habitat you'd be odd person out."

"Like Auntie Lispet."

"Like Auntie Lispet. So maybe you should make your own decision, and not be swayed by what your sister does."

"She doesn't see angels anyhow," Tanny responded in superior tones. "I think she's silly to like boys. Boys are—"

What *were* boys like? Tanny had never seen one, not really. She shrugged: arms the size of a fat woman's thighs shook like tapioca. "Are there boys in heaven?"

"Would you like there to be?"

Tanny's brow furrowed. "I guess . . . maybe. Just a few."

"In your special part of heaven, that's exactly what it'll be like, and for just as long as you want it that way."

Tanny paused and eyed the rolls of flesh heaped atop
the shelf of her belly, and merging into her chins—
these last months burgeoning mounds had made it impossible for her to see her true girth. She was a younger
Nardis, even bigger than Nardis at her age, so many
doors she couldn't get through—

"The way I'd like—I'd like to look like the girls on
H-V. Like those downlow girls. Can I have that? Can I
be a smidget and still visit Nulge heaven to see my
parents?"

"You can be anything you want. God's promise."

Tanny spoke with decision. "Then I want to go to
heaven. Please, angel, yes I do."

Armored Cedric led the way, towing Alice's god-
gear. Alice followed, and no doubt the convoy trailed
invisibly aftwards to protect her rear.

Angel schwarzeneggers! Was anything less likely? A
child of the 21st century, Alice knew a great deal more
about schneggs than Olivia; but comparing *these* to
*them* was like comparing a British ship of the line to an
old Roman trireme.

In any event she felt competent to defend her own
rear, repeating the phrase in her mind, and smiling. It
was a nice rear, with a proud African jut to it, and
nimble, and she could scoot into passages and rooms
where no Nulge could follow—

Or she could fight. Giant as they were, Nulges had
*some* strength, and quantities of inertia. An interesting
contest, but the fact was these 116 nodes were either
vacant, or populated by peaceful families, boggled by
the sight of her, painfully shy, and eager to be radioed
off to Mercury.

Six inhabited nodes, 21 home habs; 90 corpses. An
epidemic of death was passing through Nulge-land, moving downward, while behind them schwarzeneggers were
busy cutting up oversize bodies and feeding them into
the bioconverters.

Now they passed through a new bulkhead, into the
22nd of populated habs; home to another elephantine

family. Three of them converged upward through diseased green atrium-jungle; three complexely-wattled globes in blubbery commotion, their faces made tiny by heaping flesh—the mother's stria were aflame with unhealthy color, the very areolae of her breasts the size of dinner plates.

Tissue-leaves floated loose and balsa-branches snapped. Flocks of birds took wing as two very different types of *homo sapiens* moved in on each other. God! Alice would never get used to this job. No freaks here, no "smidgets." Too bad. Alice and Cedric had discussed matters; not in words but as married couples sometimes do, shifting eyes, or nodding, or pausing a moment too long. If it were possible to escape—

Two humans surrounded by schwarzeneggers could never escape, but matters weren't absolutely hopeless. There was a taboo of long standing against one soul inhabiting two bodies, but if the right smidget came along Alice was prepared to defy that taboo—*anything* to get a copy of her or Cedric freed from surveillance, able to carry two warnings downstairs.

*WARNING: the* Carl Sagan *intended to rule Earthstalk, and occupied far more territory than anyone knew; his invisible schwarzeneggers posted, ready to take control of vital facilities at a moment's notice.*

*WARNING: Commissioner Ramnis was somehow the* Sagan's *lackey, a proxy-*Sagan *tool, and not quite human.*

What would Alice's friends do with these warnings? Perhaps nothing, but at least they should *know*!

Because her apartments were on the highest floor, Tanny was the first member of her Nulge family to reach Alice's convoy. The girl's mouth worked as she tried to speak—the poor thing was terrified. Alice smiled to encourage her.

Would this child serve? Only two meters tall; and yes, too fat to travel, but not *much* too fat.

No, best wait. There'd be better bodies lower down.

Then Tanny forced out her words, not quite the prayer her angel coached her to say. "Please God, I want to radio off to heaven."

## Chapter 25
# Day 5–Hab 300

Magda had no phone. Her H-V was modified to keep her from using two-way cable. Under house arrest she spent the day clicking impotently channel to channel, doomed always to Option A. Bored with happy endings, she finally immersed herself in a videospective of 20th-century history.

That's how it began, but Magda's father had fled to West Germany in 1956. Not German himself, Istvan Szentes felt no qualms about collecting memoirs from an era his neighbors preferred to forget.

Magda read those books when she came home on her school holidays; more eagerly because they were of a genre excluded from the convent library. Nearly 18 centuries later, during another of her too-frequent naps, she experienced a false memory of an afternoon in April 1945.

It was spring but the light had a golden hue Magda associated with late summer, sunlight enriched by dust and smoke, splashing across Berlin's broad East-West Axis road to bathe the fanged ruins on either side.

The city seemed deserted, except now a scurry of military officials left the bunker below the Chancellery. They crossed an intersection guarded by a lonely clot of Hitler Youth, moving briskly as if they expected to come under fire at any time. Then suddenly they stopped short to argue, and point west and north.

In the far background Magda heard the roar of Russian artillery. That was it: no plot to this quasi-dream, only the poignancy of sunlight and smoke to set it apart, for the sun that shone through Magda's *present* window was cruelly white and stark.

Golden light, bomb-craters and rubble. *Only a dream, or a glimpse into another reality? I wish I had that power!*

*My mind is too idle*, Magda thought. *Nothing to exercise on. A muddled mind in a lazy body, when I used to be so brassy and bold!*

What a change from last week! Even to go to the bathroom was an event, something to be pondered until there was no longer any doubt. And somehow each of her technicolor visions contributed to sloth. She could become addicted to stagnation, Magda thought. She could move in a direction she'd never tried before: toward demoralization and daydreams, and an existence symbolized by the smoldering rubble of a bombed-out city.

*Why explore my own squalor? Because in dullness I can't distinguish my thoughts from those of my hindbrain god! I can't resist his invasion— Yes! That's it! To humble myself and open my soul to guidance!*

An academic paper: The Theory and Practice of—what? Moral Stagnation? Junk Food Nihilism? Magda could waste an hour just thinking up the title! But this was the way to move. Two advantages: if she *exaggerated* her behavior Olivia would be fooled into thinking she was just another inconsequential slob, a stultified, big-breasted cow.

And then there was the other thing, because something about all this had the flavor of a spiritual quest. The bombing, the devastation, the humiliation—she'd embrace all that, and wait for the miracle of war's end and golden light. But was this *her* idea? If she made herself go dreamy-slack the better to become her god's puppet—

*Yes and no,* came the answer. *I speak to you by a certain method, and I was around a thousand years ago to prepare your breed for my purposes. Now what about Gatekeeper? Wasn't she around millions of years ago? Couldn't she have made similar preparations—?*

Magda shifted and sat up. Was it her god that spoke inside her, or had she made it up? She wished her piggyback invader used an accent, *Mais oui, an' now you can be sure I veel!*

The problem with telepathy was that thoughts came untagged: she couldn't be sure. Thoughts from outside? What a radical proposition! Easier to believe that after five days' solitary confinement she was decaying into multiple personalities!

One thing was certain. Her hindbrain god wasn't God. There *was* a God, so people said; and God was big on submission—humility—*islam*. She could submit—and become the true God's oracle?

*Let's return to that topic, but first let me prove myself. How? By telling you something you couldn't know! By telling you how you hear me!*

*I speak, and each phoneme is photomapped on a pixel-grid whose x,y dimensions are immensely long prime numbers. Line by line I datastream that grid, using a single very precise sub-frequency which changes from phoneme to phoneme. Both you and I have the same number generator and seed, we use that to switch to the next subfrequency, all within the two-meg band centering around the wavelength of helium.*

*Your seed is hardwired and unique. I can tune mine to you, or Ramnis, or any other full-blood Souldancer. Simple? And you have all the apparatus to put my words together again, floating pinkly back among your glial cells!*

*Convinced? Now let's talk about your quest. God may be Gatekeeper; meditate on that fact. Gatekeeper*

*may be God! Not a flowery poet's God, or a philoso-*
*pher's vapor, or U Gyi's convenient hypothesis, but a*
*real Actress on Earth's stage!*

*So what do we know about God? U Gyi is trying to*
*analyze Gatekeeper based on two millennia of data, but*
*it's the wrong data, mere Stargate station logs, neither*
*Zend nor Bible nor Koran. Magda, I want you to sneak*
*in by the back door, the same back door suggested by*
*so many of Earth's old religions!*

—The back door: magic, mysticism and mental fog.
Was she gifted in that direction? Could she make herself crazy for God? Magda stood and looked around the
floor, at five days of suckbulbs and platters and boxes of
Dolmatto, at food-puff wrappers—she used her toe to
arrange this detritus into an avenue.

Symbolic magic: here was the East-West Axis and the
buildings of Charlottenburg to the north. This clearing
was the Tiergarten. A few more meals and she'd have
the beginnings of Wilmersdorf, mounds of spilled Pimis
to represent the rubble.

She'd order tubes of Strabasti Treklo to smear across
the window, to tint the light a golden-brown! When her
guard saw it he'd know she'd gone crazy!

Magda smiled. Such a jumble of ideas and motives!
She reached for a box of Crispo, ate a handful and
sprinkled the rest about the floor as she walked to the
bathroom. A few more handfuls—really she *was* eating
too much, but not as much as the guard imagined. Not
ten meals a day, no more than four or five!

She poured the remaining chips into the toilet and
watched them atomize into the recycle intake. Crispo
crackled beneath her feet as she ambled back to bed.

Slowly she lay down. *Two rules, then,* she told herself. *This is an experiment in introversion, so no more*
*H-V. That's Rule One, and the second like unto; no*
*booze to deaden my mind. If I'm to wander all these*
*strange paths like the pointer on a Ouija board, I want*
*to remember where I've gone and what I've seen!*

*Yes, there's a method to my madness!* Magda smiled
and closed her eyes to dream again. The littered floor

was her fetish, the ruins of Berlin her First Revelation. In her second dream . . . what? Something to add, accumulating like so much magic trash.

Magda's approach to sloth was unique. Most people simply clicked through Earthstalk's 162 H-V channels all day long. For their edification there were always four or five real-time shows going on in Hollywood, live entertainers for the most part, stunts performed by projos.

Toon videos were mastered down in 2105, part of the same showcasting empire. Between 5 and 8 lay the domain of the ad-tapers, the FX realizers, and the gray-pajamaed executives who bought movies out of Chittaworld—for compared to Chittaworld, Earthstalk's Hollywood was tiny, incapable of filling the enormities of air-time available to a leisured population.

And Hollywood *was* tiny, its precious atrium-space carved by fake walls and moveable props, tattooed Status Five beefers running to change a quiz-show set into a psychedelic backdrop, the trademark of the Skinks, all within the space of five minutes.

Ramnis stood near. Nobody took notice. He was merely one of a scattered mob, a *privileged* mob, because to be in Hollywood was to have tickets to everything. Without shifting eyes he waved, and Lieutenant Spensky moved close. "You've got the poster?"

Spensky gave it to Ramnis. "Get up into the control room," the commissioner ordered. "Make sure they don't cut away when I come on."

A nearby flurry and the Skinks clambered onto the stage. A gofer had already tested their equipment: the band twanged redundantly and looked up. Projo-Elvis shimmered into position. The lights blinked, a camera went red, Elvis crooned a snatch of some ancient song, and then spun into his introduction.

As the Skinks took over, Ramnis turned on his sonics and bounded onto the stage. The music puddled into cacophony and died. The Skinks' lead singer drifted away, following the butterflies inside his head.

Ramnis flashed his politician's smile. "*Damoj ke kabajeroj*, my name is Senator Ramnis, Lord High Commissioner of Earthstalk. I interrupt this performance to announce that my commission has undertaken to apprehend Senjoro Nie, and will reward anyone bringing information leading to his arrest."

Ramnis unfolded his poster. "I work closely with the god U Gyi. This is his number: Hab one dash five, extension 0841. U Gyi has determined the following. Senjoro Nie is an old man in his eighties with nighttime access to secured computer facilities. He is a man of private habits, reserved and humorless. Repeat: anyone knowing such a person should call Hab one dash five, extension 0841. Remember, we want Senjoro Nie alive and unharmed!"

Pause for effect. "Thank you." Ramnis nodded and strode off the stage. The camera remained focused on empty space. Yet another pair of pigmaskers trotted toward him on the double. He disarmed them like the others, then rescued gun-waving Spensky and tugged him off toward the restaurant. Only after all this did he turn off his sonics.

Spensky returned from never-neverland, his eyes blinked into sudden focus. "How many times does that make it?" he asked.

"Five. Hit 'em hard, before they learn how to defend themselves. Let's get in touch with U Gyi and see how much damage I've done."

"After today no problem. They'll give you air time just to keep you out of mischief."

Reaching the god was a matter of dialing extensions ranging up from 841 until Ramnis found one that wasn't busy. A minute later U Gyi puffed to the phone. "It's a madhouse down here!" he complained. "What do you think you're doing?"

"Ramnis here. Good to hear *you* too. I'm flushing our prey. Senjoro Nie is shy: I'm working on his aversion to publicity. He won't dare follow his usual habits, not if he's the person you described."

"*I gave that description to Lieutenant Spensky in*

*confidence, not to be blabbed over H-V! Ramnis—*" U Gyi spluttered to a halt and started over. "Ramnis, you're a fool! We'd just got Senjoro Nie to join the Federation—just about gotten him to trust us and open the doors to real peace in these levels: the first step to unity. Now you've blasted our hopes all to hell. *Of course* he'll think I betrayed him—"

"Slow down! What difference does it make? He needs a certain kind of access to INFOWEB. He can't work through normal terminals. That's what you told Spensky, and that's what Spensky told me. So how's he going to get that access? Like I said, I've got him on the run."

"Ramnis, *you* should be on the run," the dwarf-god said. "Everybody on Earthstalk is after your hide!"

"I appreciate your concern." Ramnis paused. "Uh, U Gyi, I want to say that I really *do* appreciate you. Not to get maudlin, but you make a grand and honest enemy. And now I'm sorry, but I have to go."

"You taking Spensky with you?" U Gyi buzzed.

"I'll leave him colonel pro tem of Hollywood—he's got a collection of guns, and if you and I both back him he might just have the presence to pull it off. Senjoro Nie's regime *is* toppling, you know. Your sonic stealth squad's destroyed all confidence in the old colonels. When they write the history books they'll probably say pigmaskery collapsed a few days ago, but these things take time. Now it's just a matter of finding the old man, my luck versus your telephone informants. Want to bet who gets to him first?"

U Gyi sighed. "I shouldn't do this. Stupid sentimentality—Ramnis, just to bring you down from your giddy obnoxious heights, let me tell you about Torfinn's death and Magda's arrest."

Ten minutes later it was a solemn and thoughtful commissioner who rode the escalators for Level 2109.

# Chapter 26
## Day 6–Hab 3050

"An old man of private habits, reserved and humorless."

Senjoro Nie couldn't do much about being old, not for a few hours at least, but when he reached the office of Elysium Gardens Retirement Home he did his best to appear boisterous, his face cracking into a fatuous grin that comported badly with his purpose. "But *sir*," the manager wheedled, "if you take your savings out of the fund, where will you live when the time comes—?"

"I'm going to buy a young body. They're a glut on the market!" After a pause Senjoro Nie remembered to laugh at his own jest.

The manager shook his head, his eyes teary. "You're not the first. Truth to tell you're within your rights, although there *will* be a penalty for withdrawal without notice. The sad fact is Elysium Gardens is emptying out. I don't know what we're going to do!"

"Your problem, not mine." The old man made his last thumbprint. When he left the office his magcard was newly potent. He wandered to a nearby INFOWEB kiosk, and made inquiries.

People used to drop out of sight to come up with new identities, new names with the same initials as the old—until the pigs caught on and combed the registries. Senjoro Nie had no intention of making a similar mistake. He was looking for a voluntary suicide as unlike himself as possible; young, and—female? His eyes widened.

He moved away and sat to think. *No psychological trauma, it's been years since I was effectively male. That should make the transition easier. Any other problems?*

A room with a memory helmet and two beds, hers and his. Her mind off to Mercury, his into hers, but what about that intermediate stage? Section by section his soul would swap into temporary storage, with all his memories and secrets.

Computers could be programmed to identify the idea of a red-faced monkey no matter *who* was doing the thinking—was it in U Gyi's power to program Earthstalk's INFOWEB to flag the memory of a priority-one password? Was U Gyi that fiendishly subtle?

What was it about U Gyi that inspired paranoia? Senjoro Nie was uncomfortable with risk—*any* kind of risk. He'd been old for twenty years. During those years he might have made immortifacts available to himself to steal a new body, but he'd not done so. Easy to put matters off day by day, but *now* he had no choice! He *had* to switch bodies!

How to make things safer? Well, he'd get the advantage of distance if he moved up Earthstalk, and by emigrating into Breed territory there was the chance he'd pass beyond the realm of U Gyi's programming.

Senjoro Nie grinned again: it was slowly getting easier for his face to do. In theory the 3000 habs were now part of the Breed realm, which meant bulkheads lay open and elevators ran, subject to occasional security checks. Then why not use some of his savings to ride up to Hab 5000, and trade into the body of some young Breed female?

The old man got up and moved to a nearby comic-book vending machine, then to the elevators. He stood waiting—while up on his old home Level 3114, security pig Fergus made yet another call downstairs.

*This* time Fergus got through. He spoke at length. His information was logged in and U Gyi's cadre thanked him wearily. The name Peter Kropotkin was added to forty others on list A, possibilities to be forwarded upstairs to Otto, Bruno and Emilio; for the assumption was that these three historians had been exiled to the Marisma because they knew something that might compromise Senjoro Nie's anonymity.

The cadre shrugged. Most calls were crackpot. He ought to feel grateful these few had checked out as far as they had. He looked up: his work shift was almost over. His phone blinked again. Another furtive whisper, another name—Peter Kropotkin? Again?

There was an era when bubble-world emigrants rode Earthstalk from Level One to Midnode, stopping fewer than two thousand times for decompression every hundred habs, now and again breaking for lunch, or a sleep-shift. Emigration was a weeks-long adventure for those families, but in fact the elevators ran far more smoothly than in modern times.

Senjoro Nie embarked on a nearly two-thousand-level voyage; a mere twenty-point hop by ancient standards, but high as he dared, high enough to take him to a region where Prospore was spoken with an archaically pure accent; where pajamas gave way to a wild range of gowns and uniforms were unknown; where even bodies ranged wildly in size and shape, for by entering Breed levels the old man ascended into an Africa in which stringbean Sudanese mingled with dwarfish click-folk and the hyper-obese market women of Benin—all so long juxtaposed they regarded themselves as one, and did not think it odd that their race should be productive of such marvelous physical variety.

Nor did they think it odd to keep Khartoum time and rob ascending travelers of five hours' sleep for reasons of exotic sentiment. Add those hours to his journey and it was suddenly third shift next morning, the sun be damned.

The doors opened. Senjoro Nie emerged a curiosity, not so much for his half-Caucasian features, but because he was old. "You should be dead," a boy told him as he settled onto a bench in the local bar. "You should retire to Mercury."

"I need an agent," Senjoro Nie replied, and looked right and left. Divided rooms, chairs, tables, the product of a utilitarian vision. A very different culture imposed wall hangings, orange paint with green trim, and ceiling fans. Then came poverty; vanished glass, bars to keep thieves from stealing what passed for art, noveau decorations in crude recyclement mode.

And finally, comfort. People came in, drank and muttered, too appreciative of the peace of this haven to make much of any stranger. For the most part honest people, worn dull by honest labor.

But Kwame was an exception. "Don't I know it? Don't I see you, and come right over? I can help with anything."

"The agent I need can keep secrets."

The boy scowled right and left. "Dope?"

"I want another body. I want a young body—"

The floor creaked, Nie was eclipsed in shadow. The bar-girl was the strangest—thing—Senjoro Nie had ever seen. "You order?"

Senjoro Nie turned to the boy. "What's good here?"

"A rum for the old man, and a beer for me."

The—whatever—congaed off. Nie bent to whisper. "What—?"

"Half-womtie. Never have babies. Cheap pork, and she sing pretty too. Sorry, I talk bar-talk. You want church-talk we go to church."

"I want to talk about memory transfer. Memory transfer with no records, no dreams, no magcard transactions." Nie reached into his pack and brought out a stack of eight comic books. "These have value here, I'm told."

Back in the old days Senjoro Nie prohibited the

export of faxpulp to the Breed realms, and kept these levels starving for written literature. Rare comic books still served as black-market currency.

The boy shook his head. "Eight comix for a human body? I think you got screwed values."

"No deal? I'll find another agent. I'll go somewhere else."

Kwame's expression read "so what?" Senjoro Nie rose just as the bar-thing wriggle-bumped up with drinks. He accepted his bulb, and sat again.

Addressing the air, the boy spoke. "I hear you downlows suiciding off to Mercury right and left. Why come here? Bodies cheaper there than here—we Breeds aren't scared like you Downlows. We been using dreamskulls all along to get rid of our old, and younger means braver."

"There aren't any bodies?"

"I don't say that; just no bodies eight-comix cheap, not unless you take a woman's." Kwame's shrug demonstrated how unlikely he thought *that* was.

"Mmm." Senjoro Nie's reserve asserted itself. He paused as if in internal debate. "I might have to, presuming the woman is young and healthy—I'd want to check her out beforehand."

At last he'd succeeded in shocking this worldly child. The boy's face exhibited guile, suspicion, incredulity, and guile again. Senjoro Nie leaned close. "Remember what I said about keeping secrets. No gossip, right?"

"Ten comix."

"Eight, and my downlow pajamas."

"You got a deal."

Light-brown, leggy, young and shaven-headed, the "deal" turned out better than Senjoro Nie hoped. The entire business was over before mid-afternoon. A new, improved Nie sat up from her gurney, practically leaping into the air. My, she *was* in top condition!

She turned to see Kwame shouldering her travelpack. "Look, boy," she advised. "Do me a favor, and trade my magcard away from here. Otherwise—" She shook her head ominously.

The boy grinned and patted his knife-sheath. "Just try to take it back!"

"Oh, I don't want it," Nie sopranoed. "It's yours and it's trouble, so sell it low or sell it high, but don't sell it close to home!"

Senjorino Nie turned away. No money, no magcard, therefore no elevator. Nevertheless there were stairs, and her legs were good. She was a gazelle and the higher she climbed, the lighter the force that passed for gravity.

And at *some* point she'd stop, and see about creating a new empire.

# Chapter 27
## Day 6—Hab 182,493

"You suppose we've *really* got privacy?" Alice whispered, floating toward her lover's arms.

Her breasts bobbled in negligible gravity, and Cedric's focus slid from her face. "I don't know. What's the *Sagan*'s word of honor worth on the open market?"

"He must think we're sex-maniacs," she answered. "*You* got any excuses for this daily orgy? I plan on getting psychological if he asks. Something about sex and death—"

"It's me, getting horny from all those naked bodies. Or maybe it's exercise to keep from blimping out in null gravity. Speaking of blimps, I hope soon we'll be descending into regions where clothes still fit."

"Talking of which—" But Cedric put his finger to her lips.

Generations ago this place was a Nulge apartment, with free-fall sleepnets and six surfaces covered with mirrors, drawers, wardrobes, handholds and appliances. The children of more recent times used it as a playroom. Their parents were too big to squeeze in and tidy up, and the two interlopers swam among reefs of preschool detritus, as if carried up in a tornado that had hit a toy store.

Alice's eyes flitted from rubber ducks to constructocubes, blind to anything like "down." She shook her head. "We've got to talk. Suppose we run into a likely smidget. How do we, uh, *process* him? We need an unusual conjunction of memory gear, bodies, attitudes and privacy!"

"We've got the gear here. Alice, I'm going to suggest— you see, the only time we get privacy is for sex—"

"With one of *those*? Oh Jeez, Cedric!"

Cedric smiled. "Close your eyes and think of England."

"You think schwarzeneggers don't have scruples? They gong to let us get away with whatever weird perversion— and then there's our victim's willingness—"

"They'll go along with anything. We're gods, aren't we?"

Alice shook her head again. "I've a better idea. We find a memory cassette, and tape one of our souls—we can do that during one of our orgies. Then we play that soul into our chosen victim under the guise of releasing his own. It'll only take ten extra minutes—"

"After which the schneggs haul this newly-ensouled body to the bioconverter," Cedric responded. "Besides we don't have a spare memory cassette. We're not set up for soul libraries."

"We haven't bothered to look. That's going to change." Alice turned, and paddled off to the nearest wall. One by one she opened the drawers.

With a scowl of impatience Cedric propelled himself into a slow explosion of centuries-old knickknackery. As he reached Alice's side she whirled in triumph. "Look!"

"A memory tape, probably gunked with modeling clay. So what?"

"So we combine plans. Here's how we do it."

At three hundred kilos Nardis' Young Lochinvar was far from slender, but with his blubber spread over the usual three-meter frame he had no trouble squeezing through bulkheads. He was therefore the heartthrob of several Nulge teenagers for whom the idea of proxy love and marriage held little charm.

As for what charms those young women held for *him*, with their egregious excesses of flesh and their disagreeable parents—well, there was the joy of conquest, the adventure of seeing new habitats—

This latest adventure involved no parents. Nardis called just yesterday to tell him she was alone. Suddenly Tanny's sister had "Home Hab" to herself and was free to do anything she wanted. Eager to find out just what that meant, her amorous smidget kicked up toward this latest bulkhead just as a squad of angelschwarzeneggers jetted down. They broke formation to let him through, and radioed warnings to those above.

Alice turned to Cedric. "He *would* have to be male."

"Fifty-fifty chance," Cedric answered. "We lose."

She shook her head. "I'll take him. No time to get fussy."

The smidget's guardian angel hurriedly introduced herself and was still explaining about death and heaven when he drifted into sight: *Alice's* sight, for armored Cedric was AWOLing in the opposite direction with remarkable speed.

Alice moved close, eyes staring in fascination. The boy was used to being found attractive, but never by a downlow female with black skin, and by no means young, not by *his* standards.

"What's all this?" Wolf Schinner interrupted.

"I want him," Alice growled in the direction of the schnegg's invisible voice. "Cedric's going back to make love to Nardis. I told him he had permission, *if—*" Alice choked on the words to complete this fantasy. "—Anyhow, he's mine. I've done this level, I've cleaned it out. All work and no play—"

Wolf turned colors, literally. In aerial suspense configuration he looked like a daddy-longlegs, wired between wall and floor. "Boy, this woman wants you. What do you think?"

The smidge-boy also choked, just a bit. "You were talking about going to heaven?"

"It's not the price of your ticket. You get radioed in either case."

The boy's puffy eyes narrowed. Smidget with down-low? In a case like *that*—why, the actual mechanics, the older fashion of sex—all that might be possible! What an experience!

But to whom would he brag in heaven? "I—I might not choose to go. Not unless my friends—"

"Your friends will be given their chance to come."

"Well, in that case—" He nodded, eyes fired with passion.

It wasn't easy getting the boy into Alice and Cedric's recent orgy room, but he *did* squeeze in. Alice pushed her equipment ahead of her and turned to close the door. "Now let me pop this helmet on your head—"

"First let's enjoy each other. Send me to heaven one way before you send me the other!" The boy puckered his flabby lips.

Alice kissed him. As his arms folded around her she slid the helmet into place. She reached to tickle among his pulpy love-handles. He broke to defend himself: she inserted her cassette. "Want to see more of me?" she asked, and peeled open her top.

The boy reached for the helmet. "No, no, don't be naughty," Alice coaxed, and pushed the button.

He went limp, just about all of him.

And woke twenty minutes later. "Thanks a *lot*!" Alice said to herself after glancing down at his body.

"It's just like we planned," she answered. "You *are* remarkably endowed, you know, even more than— remember Grigori? Anyhow you and I had sex together, and now you've changed your mind about Mercury— just remember to call it 'heaven.' "

"—And then go downstairs. How much gravity can I take before I become a cripple?"

Alice shrugged. "You'll get used to it. Bodies are cheap. Get yourself another when there's a chance."

She opened the door to himself. Shortly afterwards they drifted down the hall. Schwarzenegger Wolf pinwheeled watchfully at the end. "Well, it's easy to see by *your* smiles and *his* frowns who had the better time. All right, now to Mercury—"

"Uh, I've changed my mind. I'm not going. I don't want my friends—it's just too humiliating."

Boy Alice broke off and kicked for the lower bulkhead. Wolf turned to the one who remained. "My! What *did* you do to him? I've seen a lot of things in my time—"

"When *was* your time, Wolf?" Alice asked to divert his thoughts. "We've been together more than a week now. Time to tell me about yourself. How did you end up with the *Carl Sagan?*"

Wolf's eyes swiveled. "They tell me I'm mostly a Doc Savage character with patches of a 21st-century Swiss lawyer, a championship fencer—" As Wolf spoke Alice's alter-ego descended out of view. Had this contraption of a plot actually worked? Was he out from under schnegg surveillance?

Now what? How much money did he have? Could he squeeze onto an elevator? What kind of people lived below the Nulge realm, and would he be safe among them? Safe? Ha! Outside these levels who condoned nudity?

So many problems! Alice shrugged. He didn't even know his name.

# PART SIX

## *'Borg Hunt*

# Monday

Tangled hair, tangled sheets. Crumbs of Crispo ground into the bed made real sleep impossible, that and the fact Magda did little but lie here in a shallow semi-narcosis. She could smell herself and the room around her; a room layered thick with trash. Filth, grotesque filth! Would Olivia see it as protest against confinement, or more horribly as an expression of Magda's intrinsic character?

Between sleep and waking, Magda sighed, wallowed over and slit her eyes open. These last days she'd learned to laze this way, half in this world and half beyond. She faded back and this time her outside half rambled into the 21st century. The ruins of Berlin hazed out of focus and she stood near a low, flat-roofed bungalow of cheap construction, one room wide and three rooms deep. A concrete slab lipped forward to serve as her front porch. Lawn furniture crowded beneath the green tarpaulin shade.

The party was over. The neighbors got into their old Samurai and drove home, the lingering whine of its clutch audible over these long Sonoran distances. A soft dawn was approaching. Magda stacked the plates and glasses and carried them inside to the kitchen sink. She added them to the heap—what was this? She reached *into the sinkwater to catch the neon tetra and its companion guppy. Why were they here?*

Her dream provided the answer: their aquarium was broken. So they needed a refuge? Not here, surely! Magda carried them in cupped hands to the topmost of three nearby tanks, for apparently this was her hobby and she had several spares . . . hmm. Top and middle tanks looked normal, if crowded, but what were these horrors in the bottom aquarium? Big as her forearm, salamandrine and softly segmented—

"Thanks," said the ghost-white lady behind her. "Thanks for the welcome. I enjoyed the party. Why don't you let me do the dishes?"

Magda nodded. "You said such strange things. Your hair, your body—"

"Anyone can make a human body, but out of what materials? Insects have hair; not what mammals call hair, but it works just the same. I'm an improvisation—if you saw the real me you'd be unable to control your revulsion. You can barely stomach those things in the tank, and they're your cousins!"

Magda studied the ghost woman and decided her torso was too muscular, too articulate. Something about her albino sheen bespoke a low metabolism; she'd be clammy to the touch. "I never saw anything like them before," she answered.

"They died out at various times, Cambrian, Devonian— I keep them as mementos. I love them better than I can possibly love you. They look more like me, for one thing. With each wave of extinction you survivors of Earth grow more deviant, but I've far too much invested to abandon my work just because you're aesthetically repulsive."

"I wonder what you really look like."

The ghost woman smiled. "That's part of this dream. I like to experiment. I have my expectations—but why don't you go back and get some rest? I'll finish up here and we'll move ahead to part two."

Part two: r-r-r-arr-r-r-arrr-r-r—!

Magda woke from her bedroom nap roused by God

knew what noise; a dire grinding rattle muffled by one
or two intervening walls. One of the aquarium monsters roaring in distress? Had some horrible creature
slithered out of its tank?

She grabbed her robe and rushed into the living
room. Across the way the ghost woman stood framed in
the far doorway, staring at the floor.

R-R-R-ARR-R-RR-ARRR-R-R—! So it was an animal
noise—a human might imitate it, aping the crash of the
sea or a storm of static. Certainly it was a cry of agony;
yet how unnatural, how loud and

—JESUS!!!

She saw it scuttle, a great huge tumblebug, multilegged,
a hexagonal cluster of white jelly-grapes where its head
should be. It darted from underneath the left H-V
speaker cabinet, crossing the space in front of the
couch—

Magda fled behind a chair. The creature hesitated,
twitching its grapes, still roaring through Lord-knew
which orifice. Couldn't it stop that wrenching, grinding
howl? The rattle of something that wanted desperately
to die, a monster in agony! She lofted the chair, mustered enough berserk courage to take two steps forward, and brought it down, impaling the creature,
squashing its vile torso into the rug.

Silence. The ghost woman stepped forward. "I could
never share a planet with something like you."

Magda sagged, overwhelmed by the pounding of her
heart, the aftermath of her own red madness. "So
hideous!"

"Once upon a time in a remote arm of our glittering
galaxy, conceited vermin invented self-consciousness and
wondered about the purpose of life. That was the grand-
est minute of cosmic history, a mere eye-blink five
billion years past. Please don't worry. We took our few
breaths and then a comet destroyed all life on my home
world. What you just crushed? They're extinct, but
before we died we managed to build a few facilities in
space. We were really quite like humans: We radioed
our souls to those safe havens and in time our civiliza-

tion recovered. Since then we've impressed our will
across a sixth of the galaxy and dedicated ourselves to
preventing catastrophes—"

"Not very well. Trilobites and dinosaurs—"

"You know better than that!" the ghost woman answered with asperity. "I'll not waste time describing
how much worse things must have been on Earth but
for my intervention. In any case there's a trilobite in
your fish-tank."

Magda collapsed onto the couch. "I failed, didn't I? I
couldn't endure the sight of that—thing, and the sound
was worse—" She shuddered and drew the robe around
her shoulders.

"Sonar, that's all. Sonar to find my way around." The
ghost woman moved into the room. "And now I'll just
pack, gather my things and go."

"That's it? Experiment over?"

"What else? We really don't have much to say to
each other, do we?"

The woman moved to throw her belongings into her
travel-pack. "Are you—God?" Magda whispered.

"My last incarnation I announced son Dio ho fatto
questa caricatura. They put me away for tertiary syphi-
lis. A bad case, more's the pity. The fact is I speak out
of madness and imperfection, when the victim's own
ego loses definition; and so with you."

Magda opened her eyes. "But what about Alpha
Centauri?" she asked, looking around her Earthstalk
cell as if expecting to find someone. She sat up, then
rose slowly to her feet, careful because after eight days
of torpor even standing made her dizzy.

"I need a bath," she muttered, scanning the trash-
littered room. Boxes and tubes, Muftapies and Spistoes
and Butter Bubs, Bana-Whizzip and Fixacreme Su-
premes. "A bath first, and then I pick this place up.
Enough of dreams and madness!"

It took her the rest of the day to clean the room.

# Chapter 28

# Day 10–Hab 181,199

Alice's nonexistent muscles ached, his lower back to the extreme. God knew how much flesh he'd sweated off by living cheap and lumbering down stairs! God only knew, but now he was into levels where floating was no longer practical, and the heavier he got, the more his joints complained.

His belly jutted less: it was beginning to sag. Much more and he'd developed a permanent apron of flesh over his loins.

Worse for Alice's ego, he was no longer a runt. Three meters meant he was a head taller than the locals around him, and while half these locals cultivated sad corpulence the other half were mere starvling beanpoles with a predatory fire in their eyes!

Where did that put him? This hab wasn't even on the map! An unknown culture!

Alice kept body and soul together by begging, and one of those flitting beanpoles made the mistake of eye-contact.

"Damsel acrobatic!
Monster from the attic
on my way below,
I come not to freak you,
jogging down til curfew
long as money flow . . .

Pardon, miss, spare change? Spare credit for a phone
call?"

The freckled young harpie folded her wings, feathered onto the landing and swayed forward. "That depends, big boy," she answered saucily. "Maybe if
you come home with me I'll let you use *my* phone
for free, and cook you up something to eat while I'm
at it!"

Alice was practically swooning from fatigue. Three
hundred kilos, but the kilo is a unit of mass, invariant
and useless. Alice dredged up an ancient concept to
bring the truth home. He weighed more than five
pounds! Things snapped and crackled in his knees as he
fought the terrible pressures of point oh one gee. He
was—perhaps he was sick. For a moment he recognized
what was going on, and then dismissed it. A phone, and
food, and afterward—no, she *couldn't* mean anything
more!

By the time he began to wonder about the propriety
of sex with a woman, he was already launched, too
much physical and mental inertia to change course.

There was the usual difficulty getting through his
hostess' door, and the newer problem of sitting down:
legs spread wide to make room for his belly, all this
somehow arranged to provide access to a nearby table.
The woman went into her bath. She emerged with a
wet cloth. She patted Alice's forehead and neck and he
blessed her. A saint eventually to be disappointed,
but—

But first, food! Steaming trays from the micro! "Thank
you," he whispered. "Thank you—"

"Norma," she supplied. "Norma the normal." And
giggled.

His joints stiffened as he ate. Afterward he gladly let himself be coaxed into lying down. There was a phone by the bed. He dialed down to Level One, then Levels 24, 1000 and 300. As usual some lines were busy, some operators incompetent—one Dirtgrub laughed when he asked to talk to Commissioner Ramnis, another told him Olivia's number was unlisted, unauthorized use subject to penalties—

Norma re-entered the room carrying a long knife and two stout cords. "Now let's not make this unpleasant. I cut your skin and the blubber blooms: it'll take forever for the surgeons to sew up that greasy flower! So let me just snug you in, right foot down *here* and your left hand up *here*—"

Alice released the handset. It drifted to the floor. Norma bound him to the bed and began to strip off the stolen rag he used as his shirt. Alice reached to defend his honor, for he was womanly by downlow standards and retained old instincts. His starve-chested foe turned and caught his free hand.

A contest between two less-muscled specimens would be hard to imagine. The woman grimaced, and slowly pushed Alice's hand to the bed. Norma's eyes flashed triumph. She continued to undress him. Afterward she got up and left the room.

She returned naked, with a platter of food puffs, and proceeded to stuff them into Alice's mouth. It was the second of many feedings Alice endured that day.

The next day was worse. The day after that, worse yet. Lovingly the bone-woman insulted him, using a rich and deviant vocabulary; all the coinings of poetry and science to describe how fat he was in all his parts, helpless and flabby and disgusting—meanwhile he barely had time to breathe between mouthfuls.

"I'm your Momma, and you're my wittle baby," she teased. "Oh, you *should* try to cut down. I'm afraid you might not even get out my door anymore!"

"Ca—mmmph!"

"Cock? Suck you again? But the last time I tried you were so rude!"

Alice made no answer. The less he talked the fewer excuses Norma had to cram him with food puffs. He closed his eyes, and *this* time as the woman shifted her attention down his body, he made no complaint. At least he'd have a breathing-space; time to wonder how he was ever going to get free.

What if he couldn't? At ten thousand calories a day, and zero exercise, how long before he was truly a prisoner? Perhaps it was already too late?

# Chapter 29

# Day 13—Hab 1000

Two rooms on widely separate levels, two clocks, same numbers: 11:15:32—33—34—

Seconds blinked from the wall of a richly furnished conference room. Magda's eyes studied the neutral time display. Only then did her gaze descend to a polished wood table and the people who sat around it.

They gazed back, the men clearly fascinated by the way she overfilled her uniform.

Despite Koranic injunctions against portraiture, King Zimri's bearded, aquiline face looked from the opposite wall. The famous mushroom cloud boiled up beyond his right shoulder, the painting age-darkened so that Captain Caddo called it *Satan Beneath a Cauliflower*. Magda's sentries entered and stood to frame the door. She stepped inside and waited.

Olivia turned and indicated her chair, a brusque wave. "I've heard of your eating habits."

"Is that a pleasantry?" Magda answered. "Life's been boring lately."

199

"Perhaps. For those of moneyed tastes."

How arch. Magda sat. Olivia turned to the other officers lining the table. "Excuse the informality, I'm not experienced with courts martial of the present age. I'm Lieutenant Szentes's commanding officer, and I have witnesses. In her capacity as radio officer she accepted bribes—"

"I challenge the authority of this board to decide my fate," Magda interrupted. "I'm an officer of the Empire, and of the Five Dominions of America, and *I* have not betrayed my oath by joining any federation—"

"Please. We have authority over you," Captain Caddo responded. "We debated that point before having you brought to Hab 1000 from Vice-Commissioner Otto's realm."

Magda slumped. "You were a sea captain, a businessman adventurer. How did you turn into Olivia's tame lapdog? May I ask what punishments you contemplate?"

"Radioing you back to Mercury."

"Impossible. You'd unriddle my soul. My mind would become accessible to memory dreamers. They'd learn matters of private importance to Commissioner Ramnis."

At Ramnis's name the room chilled. "Our Lord Commissioner deserted his post after proving reckless in the performance of his duties. The Earthstalk Commission is now a body of co-equals guided by Federation policy—"

"Oh, all very tidy!" Magda shouted. "Mealy-mouthism run rampant! Yes, I took money from our enemies. I weakened them by doing so, and nobody can say I spent a pice on myself, but now those enemies are your bosom buddies—you disgust me!"

"Please restrain yourself," Olivia responded. "Our point is this: the secrets in your brain may shed light on the *Carl Sagan's* behavior, behavior which is the more suspicious because of how his schwarzenegger exercises coincided with my husband's death."

Magda opened to speak, but Olivia breezed on. "Yes, we've come to believe Senjoro Nie had nothing to do with Torfinn's murder. U Gyi eliminated our former servants as possible assassins. Now we look more closely at those factions associated with the *Carl Sagan*."

Suspicion hatched in Magda's head. No time to contemplate her ideas; she let her mouth take over. "The *Sagan*'s not the only one who knows who killed Torfinn. Back downstairs U Gyi's been working on the crime. Pavel laid out the architecture of your palace. It sits in the INFOWEB computer like a giant doll's house, all the movements of all the servants blocked out. First one possibility is eliminated, then the other—"

Olivia pounded her gavel. "It takes a lot of solitary confinement to come up with such fantasies. No one's been in touch with you. You couldn't possibly hear of these developments."

Magda was on the offense. She pressed her advantage. "No? Then let me put my mind out for dreaming! Yes, I reverse myself! Let *every member* of this court dream my memories *before* deciding if I'm guilty."

Olivia rapped once more. "Magda, we have your confession. As for this other offer, I ask you to excuse yourself so we can discuss how to dream you with propriety—"

Magda rose and moved to the door. "As long as it's not just *you*—" But at Olivia's gesture the sentries hustled her out the room.

And into yet another apartment-cell. Magda moved to the bed and sat. Olivia's taunts—was she getting fat? Strange how trivial worries shared time with those of real importance.

She pinched her waist. Why was it so crucial to conceal she was pregnant? To the contrary, her condition might keep them from recycling her body, and save her from Mercury for another nine months.

But pregnancy was a trump to play when others failed. If her hindbrain god was right in his advice, she'd not need to plea her belly. Which meant—

Not far away Olivia paced alone, her court adjourned on the pretext of sudden business. Olivia could all too well imagine her dollhouse palace rotating on some CRT screen while U Gyi sat, staring, frowning, tugging his ear. Certainly he'd try to rationalize, to reconcile . . . How it must have puzzled him when first *this* avenue was rendered unfeasible, and then another—puzzled him until a suspicion woke in his brain, and he remembered what he knew of Olivia's character.

How long had the god known of her guilt? Why had he spoken to Magda? Was the *Sagan* their intermediary, the fearful *Sagan*? Olivia shuddered. A conspiracy of silence involving so many elements?

But now the conspiracy would fall apart unless Magda could be shut up, and that hardly seemed possible. Even if Olivia was willing to kill her she hesitated to do so. Magda was under protection. The *Sagan* would take revenge. The *Sagan*, the *Sagan*! Distant, uninvolved, the perfect entity on which to hang Torfinn's murder. But now he wasn't uninvolved at all!

Olivia practiced the words in her mind: "I cannot muster the moral keenness to continue pressing charges against Magda Szentes. In view of my inability, I have no choice but to resign my commission—"

They'd wonder about that: she might use the time to vanish. Vanishing was easy. Somehow the *Sagan* had swallowed Alice and Cedric, and Ramnis was haring after the fugitive Senjoro Nie—a comic parody of an English country-house mystery, folks prowling stealthily through secret passages, pursuing and pursued.

The biggest country house in the universe, more than three million remaining guests distributed among 362,400 habs; so many rooms only INFOWEB could keep track!

The phone rang. Olivia whirled and picked it up. "I left orders not to be disturbed."

"It's some man claiming to be Alice Spendlowe, and sounding desperate—"

"*Man*? This better be good."

"Honestly he's tried several times. Finally I thought—well, he can describe Cairo, the Senatorium and U Gyi's yacht—please, he doesn't have much time."

"Switch me over. Hello? Hello?"

"Olivia. Look, I'm a copy of Alice Spendlowe and I

managed to escape from the *Sagan*'s schwarzeneggers. I'm calling to warn you they're all over. You don't see them because they're perfect at camouflage, but you should know—"

"Who— Where are you?"

"I'm a prisoner. My keeper's out buying groceries. I've got to say this quick. Senator Ramnis has some unnatural connection to the *Sagan*, something—it's like telepathy, but it could be just radio apparatus in Ramnis's head— Anyhow, the *Sagan*'s *desperate* to find Senjoro Nie and learn his password. With all this going for him he *still* doesn't think he's powerful enough. He wants to copy his soul into Earthstalk's empty INFOWEB brain and become absolute dictator—"

Olivia debated whether to continue this conversation. So much urgency at the other end! She relented. "Alice, Ramnis is no longer with us. He's a fugitive."

"But still lucky? His luck's from the *Sagan*'s coaching, and maybe he's got invisible schneggs around him, making sure his adventures work like they're supposed to. Up here we call them angels. All those angels looking for Senjoro Nie, then herding Ramnis in the right direction so he can be lucky and make the discovery!"

"Angels? And you say they've infiltrated down here?"

"I've tried to do the math in my head. If the *Sagan* was crammed with a schnegg cargo he'd have room for more than half a million—near two per Earthstalk habitat. They obey orders. Right now those orders are to remain unseen, but they probably concentrate near people like you. Olivia, nobody alive is a match for schneggs, not physically. You have to use double-talk and duplicity to overload their decision stacks, and I'm not sure that's easy as it used to be now that they've got souls like Wolf Schinner inside. I don't know who's fooling whom. I don't even know if I really got free or if they followed me. They might be listening in on all this! The *Sagan*'s a grand chessmaster. Maybe it's my role to get you panicky!"

"Where are you? You say you're a prisoner?"

"Just down from Nulge territory. Listen, this body's a

throwaway and I've told you everything important. Worry about Ramnis and Senjoro Nie, not me."

"Goodbye, and thanks," Alice breathed. *And now I can die—I've passed on the torch. No further responsibilities . . . that stick-woman's in for a surprise when she next comes in the bedroom.*

He let the phone drop, the phone he'd practically torn in two to reach, and relaxed utterly. He heard banging at the door, and voices— Voices! What now?

"You a vagrant?" A strange beanpole stood at the door, trim hair and well-developed arms and shoulders, her uniform a sleeveless shirt and shorts.

Alice saw the color blue, and the gun. "Thank God! Help—I need help—"

"Where you from, boy? What's your name?"

"Uh, I'm from upstairs, and my name is Al. Al—" Were second names necessary? What was Nulge custom?

"How long you been a prisoner, Al?"

"Four days, I think."

A second uniform pushed in the room and rounded Alice's bulk to tug at his bonds. The first one spoke again. "Okay, Al. We have laws about vagrancy. You can press charges against Norma. It's been done before and she's on parole, but she's got money for some good lawyers and your word might not count for much. If you want to see her put away where she can't harm others, what I'll have to do is arrest you to keep you on hand, because we can't let you linger without money—"

"I want another body. That's my price. I'll make as much trouble as I can if I don't get it."

The cop blinked. "Officially I didn't hear that. Unofficially, I have to put you in jail, take your deposition— about that time her lawyers show up. That's when you name your price. Make it high, boy. You've been raped. Cost her as much as she cost you."

The second cop freed Alice's wrist. Slowly he moved his arm. "I've been raped," he agreed, struggling to sit up. "More often than you could guess, and by more— people. Including myself."

The first cop tightened her face. "Keep that attitude

and you'll be a crummy witness. When you see that lawyer, don't talk about your problems or what you should have done that you didn't. She sees you're that kind of wimp she'll go straight to court, no deals at all."

Alice looked at the policewoman as he'd rarely looked at another human being. "You really care, don't you?"

"More people care than you think. Norma's the underside of life. Our habs have good and evil like all the others. When you leave New Iowa I'd like you to remember that. Now let's get you out of here."

Ah, bliss! Alice's call was everything Olivia could hope for. Perfidious invisible angels on which to blame all the evils of this last two weeks. No, it would never do to make their existence public, but Olivia quickly saw that Caddo and Otto and U Gyi knew about Alice's apprehensions—oh yes, it was Alice all right, she could vouch for that! It was Alice because Olivia said so with a fervent confidence that could not be denied.

Pavel could meditate on his doll's palace all he wanted. No way those old harem-crones could see invisible schnegg assassins on their way to murder her husband. It was all too good to be true, as if somehow Olivia had inherited Ramnis's famous luck.

And the corollary of all this was the Mission: to intercept Ramnis before he found Senjoro Nie!

At Olivia's urging U Gyi called Colonel Spensky up in Hollywood to have him do an about-face: Earthstalkers were to protect the benevolent wise Senjoro Nie from that maniacal cyborg once known as Senator Ramnis. Meanwhile the Federation was asked to grant extraordinary powers to an elite force headed by none other than Olivia herself.

—Who was therefore obliged to table Magda's trial. Good. Stick Magda on the back burner. Olivia hugged herself in delight. A reprieve from one kind of danger, and a colossal distraction, a wonderful red herring! "Invisible angels!" she muttered. One-third of her believed in them, enough so she could retreat into the appropriate persona when need be.

The other two-thirds found it regrettable to set up a Senator Ramnis manhunt. Very much too bad, but what could unite Earthstalk as well as a common enemy?

*Am I keen on this?* Olivia asked herself. *No, but still I've got to use my brain as if I am. Exploit the embarrassing Magda as a lure? Inject a transmitter into her body and let her go?*

*Get U Gyi to calculate the probabilities Ramnis lurks here or there, and ticket her for the ride! Pension her off, but will she suspect?*

*Who cares? It's Caddo and Christina I have to fool.*

# Chapter 30
## Day 15–Hab 4580

Buy a yacht and one soon notices how many other people have yachts too—why, the marina is *full* of them! Drive a Pangborne and one sees other motorists thronging the streets in their electrics.

What Ramnis saw was other men on the run. They moved by no clear schedules, they were oblivious to shifts, they carried courier-cases, they tended to hole up for long periods of time. When not in hibernation they were faceless and brisk—

Ramnis got up from his table in Trader Pete's and followed his prey to the escalator. The man rode down to the Galleria and ducked into the men's room. He'd been wearing local blue and khaki. He emerged loud in Breed gown and necklace.

He moved to the loading dock, his movements half concealed by boxes and dim light: a malfunctioning glow-tube flickered distractingly.

Level 4580 was among the nodes. That meant there was a local factory, but few such factories were currently in operation. This facility was closed. Nevertheless the far door opened to the man's card.

And shut again before Ramnis could catch up.

The fugitive commissioner found nothing else on the Galleria floor but a Museum of Wood, educating the Earthstalk public on the differences between pine and oak, cork and mahogany. Ramnis idled through, looking at rusted saws, hammers, nails and axes, and found two plaques in grievous error—surely no civilization had *ever* used pine for firewood! Splinters and resins! . . . the gowned man emerged from the door.

Ramnis turned on his sonics. He jogged over, took the man's magcard, and opened his courier-case. Inside he found pills, comic books, and diamonds.

None of this interested Ramnis. What *was* interesting was that the man's gown had a hood and cleverly concealed faceplate. Like a clown's costume it was elasticked around wrist and ankles, and his "hands" were gloved in Eurasian-brown synthetic.

A vacuum suit! The fellow had gone through vacuum to visit some secret stash!

The quest for Senjoro Nie was getting nowhere, perhaps because all 162 H-V channels aired messages: Ramnis was a hunter-cyborg, inhumanly obsessed with harassing poor saintly Nie into his grave. Interesting such idioms survived, but of course "grave" meant "converter," not a hole in the ground.

His hunt even spawned something special, a news reporter in the antique mold, breathlessly on his trail. Blue-suited Monsieur Cauteleux employed a mobile cameraman and a sharpshooter, a woman designated by Hollywood to be his executioner.

'*Borg Hunt*'s premier last night enjoyed high ratings, sandwiched as it was between "The Cusserby Clan" and "Mad Red: The Epic Continues." Cauteleux's research was good enough to give Ramnis pause, and the newsman made much of the fact that his small crew competed with the Federation's best forces: they had opening footage of Olivia and her Dirtgrub savages jogging up an escalator and fanning in three directions.

Ramnis shook his head. "Savages!" Prior to launch his Dirtgrubs wore anything handy, pajamas often as not.

Now they were hairy-chested, bandoliered, with chokers and wristlets to protect against knives. Headbands, studs and leather, high boots and tiepatches—a fierce elite in black striped face-paint. They'd become what Earthstalk H-V expected them to be, with the authority to cross any Federation frontier.

The hunt for Nie was fruitless. Meanwhile Ramnis dared not linger on Level 4580. It wasn't that he wanted to use the 4580 factory as a hiding place. He was interested in *any* factory as a prospective base of operations, because very soon he might need to hole up. Eighty percent of every node's length was given over to unpressurized uses. They were worth studying.

So Ramnis used the magcard and stepped through the loading dock door onto a metal inspectionway. At the far end an elevator stood posted with warnings. He entered, secured his helmet, and pushed the button.

The elevator dropped through its airlock. When the door opened Ramnis emerged into a vast industrial bay: a thirty-story arena of booths and waldoes, drooping hoses and lethal-looking pikes, all hung over a hundred-story oredock. Far below a huge lump of ice took up most of four hundred meters-cubed, a rock rounded like glacier-tumbled quartz, with ochre impurities.

Probably two-thirds of the mass of this node was in that rock. Cold down there; *very* cold. If the temperature rose above 60 Kelvin frozen gasses would effervesce to create an atmosphere. That atmosphere would transmit more cold, and even as the ice-mountain melted the inhabitants of 4580 would freeze.

But Earthstalk's dead engineers saw to it this region was pumped free of atmosphere. Ramnis could walk on insulated shoes without ill effect. If he shivered it was psychological.

He jogged down. Klieg lights shone on ice and revealed the rock's earliest history. Some process rounded its corners, but long before that mere chance banged smaller boulders together to weld imperfectly, the "heat" of collision refining away much else and leaving ochre predominant. Rounding had not gentled the shapes within those dirty red seams. The darkest spots looked very much like caves.

Generations ago vacuum-clad quarry workers climbed down and used cutting wheels and jacks to slice into the rock. They must have had jury elevators— Yes.

Ramnis's clown-victim took less than two hours to do his business. Twenty minutes to ride two elevators and climb down to the quarried surface of the ice. Equal time for the return trip. That meant an hour inside yonder dark steep well of a cave. Ramnis followed the obvious course, stepping carefully and walking with exquisite caution. He dared not put out his hand for support—a few seconds in contact with ice and his gloved hand would be rock itself.

He spiraled into the cave and saw a light. It illuminated a door. Did he dare touch the APERA button, or was it there to trick the unwary?

The door swung open. Ramnis stepped inside.

Air steamed into the airlock. "Perhaps you can decide of it," a tinny voice began, growing resonant as the atmosphere thickened. "It's called the argument from perfection. See, God is perfect, right?"

"He can't answer, Nigel," a second voice cut in. "Wait just a min. You're so impatient!"

The inner door opened. Ramnis removed his helmet and bounded into a chamber of tentlike surfaces and a trampoline floor. Behind the counter lay rows of shelving burdened with numbered boxes. A bald man stood in proud possession behind the counter. A leaner, taller comrade moved left to make room for Ramnis.

"God is perfect," Nigel continued, "and we got an idea of God even though we ourselves are less than perfect. How can sinner flats give rise to a perfect idea? Impossible! Therefore *God must exist* and it's by His grace we have this here idea planted inside of us!"

"I'm afraid *my* idea of God is a jumble," Ramnis admitted. "A super-parent, bushy eyebrows and a deep voice. Oh yes, He's smarter than me—I can always imagine someone smarter than me, and stronger, and infinitize the relationship by talking about omniscience."

"I got any number of perfect ideas," the tall man interjected. "The mathematics are full of 'em. Me idea of 'red' may be no such address, but me concept of 'one' is precise and absolute."

"God gave you *them* ideas too!" the bald Nigel answered.

Ramnis cleared his throat. "Uh, I seem to have barged in on you—"

Augustus shook his head. "Nigel, your God is too abstract. Show He exists and you prove nants. Better a fulero with eyebrows!"

"There's enough of them," Nigel answered. "Earth's troglodite gods, like that dwarf now visiting himself upon us. No grandeur, nothing. Not even Gatekeeper has what it takes; she shills mystery for awe. No, give me a *real* God, these others don't signify. They're *less* than human, no scope for tragedy. They don't die so they never live!"

"Can your cold philosopher's ghost live and bleed?" Augustus shot back.

Nigel shrugged. "Why not? What's the distance between Being and Action? And speaking of action, Augustus, don't you recognize our visitor? Senator Ramnis, cyborg H-V star!"

Ramnis shrugged. "I'll argue the cyborg part, but you know my mission. I'm after Senjoro Nie. Can you help?"

Augustus's face went gloomy. "Me jaggs, you just stumbled into our secret fraternity, a palhood of entrepreneurs, traders without license dedicated to rectifying the arbitrary policies of INFOWEB—"

"Policies we attribute to Senjoro Nie, and others like him," Nigel interrupted.

"We do not love Senjoro Nie," Augustus continued, "and U Gyi gives us the fantods, no mistake. Have you heard of this here business of chapels? How chapel administrators are told to dream so many memories and then be dreamt theirselves? A hierarchy of espionage, U Gyi at the top! How can there be any secrets in the future? Our affairs'll be scarpered! We'll be demoted to Status Six!"

"Augustus, the gentleman asked a question. He wants to find Senjoro Nie."

"And so does this U Gyi gadjer," Augustus nodded. "And by tracking Nie's magcard he has his jaggs invade Hab 5000 and dream the minds of everyone he can grab—"

"Including Hilda." Nigel shook his head sadly.

"Including sweet Hilda. But this isn't any touch-and-go joegering, no sir! They're there to stay!"

"Does Hilda know where Senjoro Nie went?" Ramnis asked.

"Hilda knows a boy she's not had the pleasure of in a long while. She was tending bar when he came in one day with an ancient customer from Downlow. Comic books were waved around, and there was talk of memory transfer. The boy would know more, but he's bottled his beonk and he isn't likely to slang up to Hab 5000 with all this uproar going on."

"So Senjoro Nie's got into a Breed body." Ramnis frowned in thought. "He went up, because there's more room to hide in that direction. U Gyi's Federation is busy turning Hab 5000 into a citadel—I'll have trouble getting through. Trouble getting up to . . . where?"

"The Caliphate." Nigel nodded. "It figures, don't it, Augustus? The Caliph was Senjoro Nie's bonest jaggs in the old days. You tumble anything about whether the Caliphate's joined U Gyi's Federation?"

Augustus shrugged. He turned to study Ramnis. "Know how to fly spaceships?"

"I've flown planes," Ramnis answered, neglecting to mention his maiden crash. "I'd happily dream the memories of any astronaut."

His hosts were unimpressed. "I can't see we got any choice," Nigel grumbled. "We're for it, we got to spring Jack from Malejail. Ramnis, I'm being level with you. We're desperate men. Thanks to U Gyi our schemes are exploding in our faces. It's our hope to get ouste from here—far, far away! You help us and we know how to pay you—"

"How?" Augustus seemed puzzled.

"He gets the spaceship!" Nigel responded. "Jack'll show him how to fly it, or program the *Ypsilanti* to fly itself. But see, Ramnis," Nigel spoke, swivelling from face to face. "See, it's a medzer-medzer game. You've got to help us get Jack free, and a few others too."

# Chapter 31

# Day 15–Hab 11,689

Senjorino Nie let the man squeeze her arms and shoulders. He grabbed her hand and swung it out. "Good. Exceptional reach . . . good Downlow muscles. You ever thought of kiting? You'll be part of an elite, girl, and *inside* the Seraglio, in the very seat of power!"

"How do I—"

"How do you go about it? Just leave that up to me!"

A day later. Rowing and indian clubs, military presses, bench presses, and squats— "Yes," said the man behind the pencil-slim moustache. "For once you have not exaggerated. What does she call herself?"

Senjorino Nie's agent bowed again. "Lord Iskemliji, her name is Lissandra."

"Not a Breed name?"

"Lord Iskemliji, my ties are further down," Senjorino Nie explained.

The Iskemliji let his fingers play over his keypad as he made up his mind. "Approved."

A wave of his perfumed hand and Senjorino Nie was

admitted into the Bektashi convent to learn kiting. His
intruders left, his agenda was cleared for an afternoon's
*kif*. The Iskemliji settled back, took a puff on his hoo-
kah, and pushed blindly at a key. Fountains of water
jetted up from the pool in front of him. Colored lights
played; a visual concert randomized on the numeric
seed he'd provided.

One of the lights persisted in blinking. The Iskemliji
picked up his handset. "Yes?"

"Magda Szentes of the Dirtgrub, eh, empire. Perhaps you remember making me rich some weeks ago?"

"Back in the mists of time. My spies tell me you were
arrested."

"And just now freed without apology. I want out of
here."

The Iskemliji donned his tiepatch and keyed TAP.
"You're calling from Level 1000. Will they let you go?
My Sublime Caliph has yet to endorse your friends'
Federation."

Magda's voice buzzed through his earpiece. "No friends
of mine. They've turned 5000 into an impassible for-
tress and expect me to lure Ramnis into their trap.
They've juiced my card for travel into the four thousands. Give me a couple megs credit and I'll ride up
out of their reach. There! See what you made me do,
asking questions over the phone? In all the spy holovids
*I* ever saw—"

"I *do* apologize. No gentleman should force a lady to
lay herself bare. Interesting, though. Consider yourself
credited. Let's just find out if you make it through—"
he chuckled "—Festung 5000. I look forward to greet-
ing you in the flesh!"

Three hours later Magda stepped out of the Cluster
A elevator. Lord Iskemliji bowed and escorted her up
to his floors.

She settled in. Days went by. In Hab 11,696's Garden of Tulips the Caliph conferred with his Mufti.
Earthstalk must be united, yes, but unthinkable that
heretics should rule.

The Mufti issued a *fetva*. All Caliphate males between ages 16 and 60, with certain exclusions—

A war on two fronts? Certainly the Downside frontier would have to be defended while masses of soldiery swarmed upstairs to overwhelm the Lightfoots.

The convent buzzed with excitement. "We're obliged to hurry you to your post," the crippled chief of the Bektashi dervishes announced from his chair. "The mutes, even the eunuchs, and of course a few favorite wives will be making the ascent. You may regard your responsibilities reduced to a level commensurate with your skills. The punishment for failure, however, remains the same."

And so after just three days' training, Senjorino Nie launched from the rail of the ninth floor of the Seraglio, to swoop out into the atrium updraft, kiting in slow circles and peering everywhere to make sure all was as it should be.

On the eighth floor four women carried clean mattresses to a special bed: another watched and supervised. A dozen females arrayed themselves for prayer on the floor below. On the floor below that, in a room lined with divans, platters of food were being carefully arranged. The arrangers were probably women of low status, as were the seven who sat eating outside—there was a sort of languid busy-ness to all this. Someone important, but routine, was expected shortly.

Far down on the atrium floor women passed carrying laundry, or trays of food-puffs, while idle sisters watched from the balconies. That was about it. As Senjorino Nie's shift wore on different women performed the same functions over and over, no one working arduously, nobody obviously exempt.

The schedules of the Seraglio were none of Senjorino Nie's affair, so the fact no one arrived to eat the meal on floor six remained a frustrating mystery. Often women would gather in twos, and whisper. Sometimes Senjorino Nie perceived sensuality in these pairings, but she had no way of knowing what was going on.

As she thought about it it became clear she was

handicapped in her security labors. In the Seraglio power lay in the hands of those who knew what was happening. She was not meant to control such power.

Frustrating. A release of scented doves told her her spell of duty was over. Senjorino Nie returned to her quarters.

In the lower bunk her first shift predecessor writhed and groaned. "Ten thousand hells!" Fatima hissed as Lissandra came through the door. "Four hours' work . . . I'd rather be dead! How will I ever fly tomorrow?"

"Let me massage you."

"It'll happen to you too. Don't your shoulders tremble?"

Senjorino Nie shook her head. Fatima grimaced. "Then trade with me. Three weeks before I earn my holiday, but they've staggered the schedule so your free time comes Friday. You'll save my life! It's us new kiters who have accidents, our muscles so sore and tender."

"I'm off that soon?" Senjorino Nie's expression grew abstract as she pondered. "Free time and money to spend. I could go on a tour. The wonders of the Caliphate—"

"More money if you trade with me. I'll pay you."

Senjorino Nie studied her companion. "If death concerns you, go to the Bektashi. Have them tape your soul before each shift."

"That would be a tragedy."

"—Because you're a spy. A Lightfoot spy. Strong for a Lightfoot, but too weak for these Downlow habs. You don't dare chance they'd dream your memories."

Fatima shook her head. "*You're* the spy. One of those terrible fierce Dirtgrubs—"

Senjorino Nie laughed. "What a pair of jokers! As if the Bektashi would let spies into the Seraglio! But we both watch the same romances. —No, Fatima, I can't trade with you. I've got my secret interests to look after beginning Friday. Any news from the front?"

"War news? Just silence. In truth people are getting nervous, though patience would serve them well. It takes time to move such a huge army up to the frontier habs."

Senjorino Nie frowned. "It confuses me. What advantage do our multitudes serve? I try to puzzle out what Caliph Selim intends to do, how to press the enemy through doors and bulkheads—"

Fatima gasped as Senjorino Nie probed a torn muscle. "We've had wise Caliphs and foolish ones. Selim came to the throne because his mother out-schemed her rivals. Now he'll prove himself on his own for the first time in his life, and no female intrigue can smooth his way."

Senjorino Nie pondered Fatima's words as she wandered the convent precincts that evening. A veiled warning, the Caliph might prove inept. If so there'd be a sudden change of government—in this frame of reference "sudden" meant days, a few weeks at most.

She was tired of being a nonentity. In periods of chaos people had needs. With proper INFOWEB access she could satisfy those needs and begin empire-building. The problem was access. She knocked on the gendarme's door. "Madam?"

A window in that door slid open. "Yes?"

"I'm on holiday beginning Friday. I have in mind an educational tour of these levels: food factories, major computer centers, that kind of thing."

"Very good! So many of our girls just wander the gardens playing eye-games with strange men. But a tour—chaperones and guards—I'll see what I can arrange. Perhaps our other novices would also be interested."

"Perhaps they would." After a few more remarks Senjorino Nie wandered off, confident matters were set in motion.

# Chapter 32
# Day 17–Hab 181,199

Alice squinted. An optical effect? He clicked again. Another picture came up on the H-V screen. "They don't look right."

"Not to you, perhaps," Norma's lawyer answered, "but you asked for a muscular habitus. We'll have one sent up for you, a sturdy Lightfoot body. You'll be Superman."

Strange. On the one hand all Earthstalkers were used to the classical human torsos exhibited on H-V. Nulges had tiny heads in relation to their giant bodies, and represented a second extreme of humanity. Now here were these Lightfoots, from a Nulge view indistinguishable from the smidgets on H-V, but in fact a trifle deviant, stretched out of true.

A middle group. Muscular? Ha!

Alice lacked the nerve to ask for a female habitus. This body-swap opportunity was his only because he enjoyed a moral superiority over Norma. A sex-change would blow that pose all to hell.

Yet to look at these men as a shopper was to measure them by female standards, and by those standards they were graceless.

And the lawyer was growing impatient. Skinny, with a head topheavy as a turnip, concavities whittled away to make hollow temples and hollow cheeks, prominent sockets around the eyes—in New Iowa all professionals were of the skinny class: so were most criminals.

Yes, time was money, and the lawyer's first fake cheer had vanished. The pressure was on, and Alice clicked quickly from screen to screen.

Front view, side, and stats. There just wasn't enough difference between best and worst, but Alice wasn't about to act the prima donna after three nights and all Saturday and Sunday in New Iowa's jail. If Norma's lawyer meant to soften him up with her "weekend" crap, she'd succeeded. Alice finally clicked back to number 77-192. "This guy. I like the hair. Long hair means Status One or Two, right? A real cavalier."

The decision was made. The lawyer transmitted a purchase order, packed away her terminal and left Alice's cell.

And the cop came in. "Done?"

"Any work locally for us Lightfoots?" Alice responded, rolling forward into the only other seated posture his huge belly allowed.

"You'd do better heading right back down. Join the army: that's your ticket to an ID and Status Five. There's another war coming up between Lightfoots and the Caliphate."

Down was just the direction Alice wanted to go. "They'd pay my fare? Sure be nice to ride the elevator in comfort."

"We can arrange it," the cop answered dryly. "S.O.P. for getting rid of vagrants."

A single INFOWEB transaction fissioned into dozens of phone calls. An aristocratic Lightfoot hosted a good-bye party before suiciding off to Mercury. Holbach Aloysius Marsche III went to sleep. Next morning he got into an elevator. Up he rose by hundred-level stages, into the 30,000s and beyond.

Holbach wanted to emigrate. He'd waited more than a week, not caring to shoulder through the common mob. He'd waited until his Lightfoots, in Parliament assembled, voted themselves into the Federation. Only then had he applied. To his dismay someone called a chapel administrator took control of his life.

"But why can't this customer come down here for the exchange?" *Kabajero* Marsche protested.

"He'd be a basket case in our gravity," came the answer, and now the young Lightfoot rose through unknown levels to an unknown destination.

It was too annoying. Four hours just to reach hab 40,000. 140,000 levels to go! Holbach began to reconsider. Scurrying off like this gave the appearance he was afraid of the Caliphate—he was dodging military service! What were people whispering about his family's good name?

The door opened to hab 40,200. His face grew resolute and he moved to step out.

Something blocked his way, invisible and unyielding as steel. Holbach showed surprise. His eyes crossed. He slumped to the floor, supported and made comfortable in his collapse.

He snored softly as the elevator rose into the 50,000s.

# Chapter 33

# Day 19–Hab 4602

Malejail took up most of Hab 4602. The first floor was Administration, the rest one large ghetto. Troops of guards delivered food to a central refectory and protected the upper bulkhead; otherwise Malejail was left to devise its own government, coups and betrayals every couple of years.

When Malejail fulfilled its quota of shoes and fire-alarms there was food for all. When the system broke down the food supply was reduced, fueling the flames of revolution until Malejail's population dropped to compensate. Eventually a new quota would be negotiated, and things would get better—

Ramnis led his fellow conspirators Nigel and Augustus through the bulkhead into Hab 4602's visitors' lobby. Armored glass boxed them in. Ceiling nozzles stood ready to spray at any misbehavior. "Sonics won't function through glass," Ramnis whispered. "This isn't going to work."

"Surely the administrators get through here. Maybe when they change shift—"

Nigel tugged the others back. "Let's scarper. Don't you suppose they can hear our whispers?"

They retreated to the Copenhagen Room, off from

the prefunction area of Hab 4600's second floor. Nigel paid twelve hours' rent. A Breed redcap set up chairs, dimmed the lights and started the tape, a pre-Chittaworld classic called *Hans Christian Andersen*.

The redcap left. Ramnis, Nigel and Augustus changed into their vacuum suits. They returned to 4602 after an hour's interval. If they'd been suspect before they were doubly so now, but also immune to gas.

They loitered while Malejail's administrators spoke together. Noon food delivery was expected in half an hour. *Nothing* must stand in the way of schedule.

A glass wall slid open. A squad of guards stepped out to confront this uninvited trio. Ramnis turned on his sonics and darted by as they faltered to a stop.

He rushed through administration and reached the escalator.

Another glass wall, but here were the controls. Ramnis pushed APERA. Nothing happened. Across the way were another set of controls: He ran over, tried them . . . nothing.

A thought spoke in his mind. The buttons had to be pushed simultaneously! Ramnis grabbed an addled administrator, and leaned him against the wall. "When I say push, you PUSH!" he shouted.

Like talking to a sleepwalker. "Pss," the man answered. "Psssh."

Ramnis ran to the far side. "PUSH!"

The man raised a hand and found it fascinating. "PUSH!" Ramnis shrieked. Already at the further end of this warren of cubicles people were coming to life. All they had to do was shoot from a distance, shoot while beyond the reach of sonics.

The man bumped against the glass wall. He seemed amused by the way he tilted off true—holding himself rigid he let his feet slide—suddenly he doubled and fell. He put out his hand—

Ramnis thrust simultaneously. Something cracked against the glass, and almost the same moment he heard the bang. The wall began to slide open.

Ramnis turned and jogged the way he came. A second dose of sonics placated the gunman. Ramnis led him by the hand into the gap. A few more trips purged the office area, meanwhile the prisoners of Malejail hurried to take advantage of this opportunity.

Ramnis switched off his sonic belt. "Is Jack in there? I'm looking for Jack Dee."

Prisoners brawled by. "Jack Dee?" Ramnis repeated. "Listen, goddamit—!"

"Who *you* wanting Jack, mate?"

"My business," Ramnis answered in growing alarm. These men—what evils was he unleashing?

They tore through the office-warren, ripping drawers out of desks, tapes from their cabinets, turning anything they could find into weapons, taking out frustrations on furniture as well as barely-animate administrators. The man he spoke to saw Ramnis frown. He stepped closer. "You'd like to see Jack, would you?"

Closer, close enough for Ramnis to see he had no eyebrows, no lashes, no hair at all. "Well, you're *looking at him!*"

An alarm began to shrill. "Your friends want you to come with me," Ramnis explained as he plucked off his glove and reached into his pocket. Jack caught his wrist and extracted the paper. "A list of fellow-prisoners," Ramnis explained. "In Nigel's judgment, deserving of freedom."

"As much as me?" Jack looked around him. Chaos, blood, and smoke. He spat. "We're off. We'll sort this out later."

Shortly afterward Ramnis and Jack knocked and entered the Copenhagen Room to find Nigel, Augustus, and four others. "This is it," Nigel spoke. He tossed Jack a pair of fancy grey pajamas. "Let's get going."

They rode the semi-express down to 4580, something Sixers would never do—and they were obviously Sixer drabs despite costumes and tiepatches: muscular and starved, tattooed and shaven-pated.

So they were exposed, what difference did it make? Ramnis stood with them, and soon they'd be gone forever, a thousand realms away!

They burst from the elevator into the Galleria, jogged through the Museum of Wood to the loading dock, and carded their way past the door—four vacuum suits, and eight men.

Three trips to get them all down through the factory, beyond the oredock, and into the shipdock below. On a platform exposed to space sat the *Ypsilanti*, twin to the *Galla Placidia*. "A dumb ship," Jack Dee explained as he settled into the pilot's seat. "Used to be smart ships a thousand years ago, docks crowded with them, working on contract. The problem was boredom. A smart spaceship can think of lots of things better than hanging around Earthstalk."

He looked out the polarized window, into the sun. "Okay, mates, watch this!"

The *Ypsilanti* rolled onto its ledge and turned against Earthstalk's direction of spin. Jack called up a program on the ship's computer, transferred the numbers to his controls, and shrugged. "Any meat could do this."

"Takes more than a meat to write that program," Augustus answered.

"GO," Jack typed, and hit the carriage return.

The shuttle kicked up and forward, then the engine died. Downside pulled back as it shrank. "All that just to keep where we are," Jack muttered.

"Eight point three meters per second to counterbalance local gravity," Ramnis blurted.

Heads turned. "How you know that?"

"I do seem to know things," Ramnis answered. "The problem is I don't know *how* I know. I try not to rely on items popping into my head."

"He's a cyborg," Nigel added.

Ramnis sighed. "I *feel* human. I don't remember any operations. I'm no different from a lot of other Souldancers."

Jack shrugged and double-checked his instruments. "Now we wait. If I've done right we're in for some drama."

Time passed. Earthstalk tumbled end over end to provide fake gravity, and its Upside arm swept over, and around . . . Upside came closer, a beam of star-light, lengthening and then thickening, larger, *larger*—

The dock swung underneath. Jack fired his engines. The shuttle landed. "Two little jet-farts," he spoke with brusque pride. "Economy."

"So where are we?" Ramnis asked.

"Hab 361,884," Nigel answered. "How's your Mandarin?"

"My what?"

"He's not staying," Augustus reminded his comrade. "Soon as we unload he rabbits off, right?"

"Word of honor," Nigel nodded. "Honor among thieves! Ramnis, you sure you want to go back Downside? That sonic gadget—"

"I could turn it on now and you'd be in a hell of a mess. Get unloaded, this is *my* ship now."

"Figure you can fly it? If Jack doesn't reprogram the computer you're nants without a paddle. What about a trade? Your belt for Jack's expertise?"

Ramnis grinned, and twiddled his sonics.

Two little jet-farts? He shifted Jack Dee out of his seat, slid in, and called up the numbers. The first firing compensated for Earthstalk's centrifugal whirl. If he doubled the number—

The shuttle launched, upward . . . upward . . . the engine died. And now a long, long wait.

Downside swung around again, growing long and large as it overtook him. Ramnis keyed in the next set of numbers, rounding for good measure—he wasn't quite as interested in economy as Jack Dee. He spelled GO and waited, his finger poised—

The dock was awfully far away, a small target—what the hell! Ramnis grimaced and pushed. As Downside swung by the shuttle chased and nosed onto the ledge—God, one . . . more . . . second!

The engine died but somehow the shuttle rolled over the lip.

More Souldancer luck. Ramnis sighed and wriggled through sonicked bodies, back to the airlock.

The *Ypsilanti* had served his purpose; he was beyond U Gyi's Hab 5000 citadel. Moments later he was inside, heading towards the service elevator that would convey him to Hab 11,492.

# PART SEVEN

## *Senjorino Nie*

# Tuesday

*Torfinn, you've let me lull you. How in hell did Earthstalk get a Caliphate, with all the old titles and offices?*

*A Hollywood Caliphate—that's the clue. While new cultures evolved on Earth, the H-V watching populations of space saw Romes and Baghdads, Chittaworld Zulus charging in formation, and projo Vikings raiding the shores of Umayyad Spain.*

*By the accrual of a robot-based industrial capacity Dr. Cedric Chittagong built Chittaworld almost single-handedly during his second lifetime, and looked for ways of bringing in immigrants.*

*This was it—to turn the place into a gigantic theme park. Fictoids in projo bodies put on shows for human tourists—cut-and-paste souls thrown together to actually be the heroes and heroines of legend, going back to Homer and the Epic of Gilgamesh, and forward to the current faves of the 2070's—assuming, of course, that copyright laws were never infringed.*

*So Chittaworld plundered history, and brought saints and kings, paladins, cowboys and concubines back to life. And though tourists experienced the special de-*

*lights of moving through this Valhalla, most of Cedric's profits came from H-V productions.*

I'm waiting to see a response to all this. Your soul is natural, but don't you suppose artificial personalities can love and hate and suffer? You lived simulated lives in Mercury's City of the Dead, but all they've ever had are scripts and screenplays! And for what? What's the great goal of Chittaworld existence, the hope, the often-broken promise? —That someday every soul will live inside a human body!

Shades of Pinocchio! Meanwhile on Earthstalk we have an embarrassing surplus of bodies. Yes, the suicide rate has fallen from that disastrous first week when we lost half a million citizens and retirees, but we still project two thousand deaths a day for some time to come. Two thousand bodies to give away! And now you know what I'm getting at. Someday you'll shake hands with someone who calls himself Hercules, and means it!

# Chapter 34

# Day 21–Hab 5062

Even ten years ago the Albabs were a pleasant place to take a vacation, a quiet backwater spa with double-helix ski slopes, an exceptional jungle, and a zoo graced by a dozen giant tortoises. Now under new management two principles ruled: Give visitors so much to do and see that they could never take in the entire node in a single trip. And second: separate the kids and herd them around in coached groups most of the day, so adults could follow their own agendas.

After an infusion of money the new improved Albabs grew so popular that even in the present crisis families were loathe to cancel long-scheduled holidays—and therefore the place was so crowded that madness and confusion taxed the resources of a panic-reduced staff.

Some had suicided off to Mercury. Substitute work-schedules were improvised. Coaches struggled to learn new jobs. The advantage of this for Kwame was that as long as he remained anonymous he had the time of his life. While U Gyi combed level after level looking for the one boy on all Earthstalk who know what Senjoro Nie now looked like, the object of his searches frolicked from one attraction to the next: Pool, Pirate's Lair, Haunted Palace, Gyro-Coaster . . .

Unfortunately, twelve days after settling in there was one of those typical parent-child crises, Mamji in the casino, Bapu in the restaurant, both under the impression little Suki was with the other. Kid groups were mustered, coaches tracked Suki down, and in the meantime they noticed that Kwame was mentioned on more than one team list. A Red, then a Blue, and now an Orange? He was a *repeater* and as for parent-sponsors—well, there didn't seem to be any Peter Kropotkin in the guest registry.

Late next morning the boy kicked and hollered as cadres tugged him into the Hab 5000 memory chapel. "I've already told you everything! I showed you her picture, I said how she went up the escalators—"

So much commotion made U Gyi unhappy. In his elevated chair the god plucked at his sleeves. "Child, I'd like to dream your memories. I assure you it won't hurt. There might be something in your sly brain, some significant trifle we need to know."

Kwame shook his head. "I've got implants. Scramblers. You ruin your equipment."

U Gyi smiled. "Any signal that can be scrambled can be *un*scrambled. Let's put it to the test. Just lie on that couch there."

Half an hour later a grimmer U Gyi accepted a handset from Pavel. "Olivia? Yes, you heard right. We've got Kwame here, found him through Hilda the barmaid and our local allies. He's talkative, but we can't confirm his stories. I'll have to bring in a technician—no, I can't say. Somebody did a miracle on this lout's head. I hadn't thought there was a surgeon on Earthstalk nearly this competent."

"The *Sagan*, or one of his angels," Olivia answered, coming close to believing it herself. "What else? You have other news."

"Senjoro Nie purged his computer files," U Gyi spoke reluctantly. "That makes us wonder. Pavel's going through a morass of backup disks."

"To find what? Tell me. We've got to trust each other."

U Gyi decided to cooperate. "If he had programs that could mean he used them to determine part of his password—in fact he got privileged access to INFOWEB by means of a dynamic password. We're looking for some complex calculation that doesn't reconcile with being a janitor."

"Ah. Find the program, find the password. Be careful. The *Sagan's* looking over your shoulder."

"No need to worry. I've read books on password security. Part of the password's dynamic, but only part. We still need to find Senjoro Nie."

"If he's in Lightfoot territory our allies will find him. Otherwise he's trapped below the battle zone."

"Speaking of traps—" U Gyi began.

From her base just below the Caliphate's downside frontier, Olivia spoke to cut the god off. "Zucchini. Dental floss."

"I understand. Well, I'll keep my ears open. Good luck."

Olivia hung up the handset and sighed, a maiden-general on her first campaign, the first campaign in which her word was final, with neither Torfinn nor Ramnis to strike a Napoleonic pose.

Who was trapping whom? On levels 16,722 and 16,745 her stratagems were even now being put into play. Resurrectees in vacuum suits moved in via the service elevators, sonicked a few squadrons of the Caliph's *nizam* into imbecility, and closed the bulkheads. Other soldiers and cadres followed behind and selected choice bodies. At the rate of two per hour Caliphate prisoners converted into Federation recruits.

The bulk of Selim's forces lay between habs 16,722 and 16,745, a huge mass of ten thousand men. Among the highest echelons word spread that they were trapped.

Breakouts were attempted via the elevator shafts, and failed.

The Caliph broadcast a speech. His *nizam* were to wait here and train until ready for battle. A policy decision, nothing more, "—and remember that the spreading of malicious rumors is a punishable offense."

Not much later he sent for his Mufti. He sat waiting in robes and silk slippers, stoop-shouldered like a scholar, barely post-adolescent, slightly plump, jet-black hair exquisitely barbered. "Well?"

The Mufti was almost offensively tall. He prostrated himself with formal stiffness, his beard swallowing his lower face up to his cheekbones. "During a long-forgotten war an Inglish general of no talent whatever made his reputation by being besieged and sending out heroic dispatches. We might sit here in calm satisfaction—"

"I tell you my wives are not calm at all," Selim answered. "Is there no way to get them out of here? Have we no hostages to exchange for favors?"

"Your Vizier might answer those questions. It's my concern to maintain morale. I must warn you when it comes to rationing food—"

"Millions of boxes in our commissary. Must we ration?"

"The INFOWEB allocation for these levels is based on a population of 238, with guest flexibilities up to twice that number. We are ten thousand!"

"Inform the computer to change allocations."

The Mufti lowered his turbanned head in the politest possible demurral. "The unbelievers speak to INFOWEB in an equally strong voice. They cancel us out."

The Caliph stared at his Mufti for some few seconds, then spoke. "Get out. I need to compose my thoughts."

The Mufti retreated. From behind a curtain Magda ambled into the room. "How did I do?" Selim asked, smiling boyishly. Then—"*Tres raffine!* Point eight gees does wonders for your embonpoint."

"We better lock ourselves in the commissary. The revolution's going to begin in a matter of hours," she answered. "Another day or two for Olivia to get wind of it—"

"To the mattresses!" Selim proclaimed.

"Revenge!" Magda responded. She opened to speak further.

Selim raised his finger in warning. "Say no more. Tell Lady Maryam to gather my wives."

Back down in the heart of the Caliphate, what was not yet known among most of the *nizam* spread like panic among the habs surrounding the Seraglio. The Caliph's army had engaged the infidel and was now trapped!

Foes who did such a thing could easily invade unprotected levels. Fortunately a few locations *were* protected: people of prudence should lock up their valuables and gather nearby, let themselves be registered, and refrain from unnecessary movement. A passcard system would be set up: please be patient and remember the Caliph in your prayers—

Under the circumstances Senjorino Nie's tourist expedition had been canceled. On this first day of holiday she'd been called in to substitute for a missing Fatima. Such was the impact on underlings when Great Leaders decided to wage war.

In the Seraglio a man sat eating the sixth-floor meal; short dark hair and beard, thickly muscled and flat of stomach, naked except for his belt, a gray vacuum-suit laid to one side. Senjorino Nie watched and wondered. For the first time in four days that food was not wasted.

A man among the Caliph's women, but no one showed alarm. Nie gyred from her winged heights after her shift was over, resolved to report him and leave the consequences to others. On the floor she found two Bektashi dervishes waiting. As she snapped her groundcape over her boyishly wide shoulders they stepped from flowery jungle. "You're Fatima's roommate?"

"Yes?"

They waved her toward the Seraglio bulkhead. "Why didn't you speak to us? Any unusual movements, suspicious events; you must have noticed Fatima's behavior.

Come along. The master wishes to probe the depths of your treachery!"

*The master*, whose given name was never used, a name unknown to all but himself, because it was inconceivable that he called anyone his friend. *The master*, whose own smashed body was a testimony to the perils of kiting. A grim man who made no concessions to pain, and did not see anyone for trivial reasons.

"Fatima is dead," the Bektashi master acknowledged from his chair some minutes later, stretching forth his powerful good arm and opening his hand to dangle a synsilk throttle-scarf. "A Lightfoot spy caught in espionage. Surely you knew!"

"I knew nothing!" Senjorino Nie responded in horror.

"Ah, innocence. Why don't you look convincingly innocent, Lissandra? Lissandra of the forged background and made-up name! We should kill you, but perhaps—we will not."

"This is a joke, right? An initiation, a test!"

"No," spoke the crippled master. "I do not joke about my life, and for putting a spy into the Seraglio I deserve death more than you do. But what we have now is an emergency. We cannot execute trained kiters when we need protection for our factories. Women, children and old men flee the uphigh frontiers. We need forces to defend those evacuated habs. Are you willing to fight the enemy, Lissandra? Will you risk desperate death to redeem your reputation?"

Senjorino Nie's eyes returned to the throttle-scarf. Why this strange about-face? Trust a suspected enemy accomplice to defend the Caliphate? But it wasn't her job to make sense out of absurdity—her problem was to stay alive. Her master had given her a single choice. She expelled a gust of air. "I will indeed!"

One node away Ramnis leaned back from his stolen dinner. A eunuch appeared outside the room, framed by the doorway. He glanced to his side to someone out of sight, and shook his head: no.

Three dervishes thrust inside, turbanned in black, six

swords drawn. "Will you come peaceably?" the closest challenged.

Ramnis twiddled his belt and the tableau around him froze, marking time with small indecisive wobbles while he donned his vacuum suit and checked his appearance in a nearby mirror. He positioned himself and made a second adjustment. After a pause the dervishes blinked, still a trifle confused. "You were arresting me?" Ramnis prompted. "Then here I am."

# Chapter 35

## Day 22–Hab 10,800

The night had passed, and the news was good. Truly the Caliph was a stupid man, an untested fool! Now for stage two. Olivia buzzed and her orderly opened the door to let the charismatic Monsieur Cauteleux step into this temporary office. "Are your people ready?" she asked the H-V personality. "We cross the frontier to-day. There'll be violence and confusion—"

"A showcase of Dirtgrub ardor! Ramnis is up there, we know it. Trapped in the Caliphate, and *this* time you have troops in all the spacedocks."

*Hardly, just those with ships.* But Olivia didn't need to tell the host of *'Borg Hunt* all her secrets, or what an army so recently grown to sixteen hundred could afford to do. "I still don't know how you found out about his latest trick," Olivia said.

Cauteleux showed teeth in a Hollywood grin. "A man risks others' lives and makes enemies. Is it so hard to make a deal with Jack Dee, and promise clemency?"

"Not unless we leave a trail of promises from one end

of Earthstalk to the other. Right then. We drive Ramnis before us like hounds drive a fox. One problem. He's after Senjoro Nie, and Nie's caught in the same pinch. Any suggestions?"

Cauteleux shrugged. "Nie's password is the prize, the key to INFOWEB, but it has to be used to be any good. Send troops to secure all grade A and B computer facilities inside the Caliphate. Urge the Lightfoots to exercise vigilance in case Ramnis sneaks through."

Olivia listened hard for pronouns and heard none. Did Hollywood know Nie's new sex? Would her picture flash on H-V sets tonight? "Thanks. I know we're competitors. It's decent of you to share information."

Monsieur Cauteleux bowed out the door. In privacy again, Olivia let her face fall into a scowl. All grade B facilities? Here in the nodes every four habs had a factory, an oredock, and a shipdock. At least one computer cluster to run all this, and sometimes more.

That added up to 2500 complexes! Cauteleux was playing her for a fool with his useless advice.

Interesting though, his news about Ramnis. Bleeps from Magda's transmitter said she was sequestered among the Caliph's army; trapped like a tethered goat. By luck or cyborg power Ramnis might be drawn to her, as close as he could get. Olivia hated to predicate her actions on Ramnis's magic luck, but she might be wise to do so. She should throw her forces into the levels below 16,722 and make a 50-node blockade. She should do so *anyway* to keep the Caliph's *nizam* from trying a breakout.

It was the obvious place to concentrate her army.

"I have to do this," she whispered. "Sorry, Ramnis. Sorry, but your time is up. You better hope I get to you before the Hollywood gang."

## Chapter 36
# Day 23 08:50–Hab 11,700

"I don't understand our motivation," Senjorino Nie murmured to her new friend, shifting her kite-gear to keep them private from the rest of this gruesome squad. "The scourings of the prisons, criminals and drabs. One day's training to build our laughable *esprit de corps!* Why do they think we'll risk our lives for the Caliphate? Why believe our heartfelt assurances?" She lowered her voice another notch. "I have my love for Selim under greater control!"

Ramnis sat in gray-fabric vacuum deshabille to the kiter's side, both waiting their turn to ride the elevator. "Dirtgrubs are attacking the downside frontiers," he answered, his voice barely above a whisper. "The Caliphate's scraping the bottom of the barrel. That's us, dregs and strays. Who knows, maybe most of us *are* patriots when the chips are down!"

Senjorino Nie pondered. Barrels and chips: a strange use of Prospore, but perhaps this man's cant was typical of the criminal classes. A pause while a Bektashi der-

vish wandered, his suspicious eyes darting right and left
among these sorry troops. The dervish caught sight of
her companion's helmet, opened his mouth to speak—

And disappeared? Had it been a hallucination? To
tell the truth Senjorino Nie hadn't got much sleep these
last two nights, and frustrated dream-things were leak-
ing into daytime reality. "You look familiar somehow,"
she spoke to change the subject. She studied Ramnis's
short hair and beard. "They caught you in the Seraglio,
eating the Caliph's dinner! A horrible crime to admit
with careless aplomb. I can't believe you're still . . .
intact."

Ramnis was uncomfortable with the trend of this
young woman's thoughts. "I'll explain later. Important
questions first," he whispered. "What are we to do in
the evacuated levels? As you say, between killing and
hiding I'd rather hide."

"You can protect me." Almost Senjorino Nie was
tempted to elaborate. She needed to find a computer
center—oh dear! How to calculate the order of Jupiter's
moons?

A telescope. Set a tiepatch to telescopic function and
take control of an outside camera—but her neighbor
was looking at her, his gaze so very frank and open.

*I am not going to be seduced by a man!* Senjorino
Nie told herself. "—I meant we might sneak off and
wait until the crisis resolves."

Ramnis stood. "Agreed, and here's our elevator. Back
to the present. Have you got the card?"

"Wherever it'll take us," Nie spoke flippantly, by no
means bright and cheery as she pretended. Temporary
commander of this piratical gang, she inserted Caliphate-
issued plastic into its slot. The door opened. The squad
stepped inside.

Silence. As they rose the air of confinement grew
rich: sweat, burnt insulation, emulsified seak, fennel,
unwashed synsilk, fried falafels, garlic, flatulence and
wine. Nie's smile faded, eroded by dread—the dread of
knowing that given enough time she was going to become acquainted with Gulses and Abu and Muhmut

and Panef, laugh at their witticisms, offend them by
some off-hand remark—Senjorino Nie sent Ramnis a
telepathic message: *What makes you different? Will
you help me?*

*Why am I doing this? I don't even know your name,
why are you in my thoughts?* But of course there was
no answer.

They rose into the twelve thousands, stopping every
ten habs—the posting of their gutter-garrison was clearly
not express priority. By hab 12,400 everyone was acquainted, attitudes set, jokes pooled. At hab 12,720—

The door opened. They stared into a reversal of the
usual Hab arrangement. Instead of floors ringing a central atrium, here was a floor-to-ceiling ziggurat; shops
surrounded by air and stars, the bare suggestion of a
bubbled circumference.

A mall. A dead mall, tattered OUT OF BUSINESS signs
on dark displays. Walkways radiated like spokes to a
track that spiraled in shallow curves down to the floor.
And no, the place wasn't empty.

Not quite. A woman tottered along that track, croon-
ing and muttering, clutching a bundle swathed like a
baby. Odd, because the child's loose, floppy legs and
arms were much too long. He must be six or eight . . .
black legs? A different race?

The charnal stink gave another explanation. The woman
was not far distant, and coming closer. "Now, Zoran,
you must be very careful of the dropping bodies, they'll
hit you if you aren't very careful—the dead bodies
raining everywhere."

"*Yes, Mother. I'll be very careful on my way to
school.*"

"And watch out for the fat man, the bald man, the
wart-man. He'll tell you he's your brother, but *he* never
caught you."

"*No. I won't let my brother get me. I won't even talk
to my brother.*"

"That's good, Zoran. Dear, sweet Zoran."

"*Who is the fat man really, Mother?*"

The madwoman was no ventriloquist. Her mouth

moved when she did Zoran's voice, but it was uncanny
how like a young boy she sounded. Slower than the
others, Gulses woke to the truth. He spasmed back from
the elevator door and pulled out his knife, but the
woman took no notice of his terrified retreat—as far as
she was concerned she had no audience.

Nevertheless her steps brought her nearer. "Keep
her off, keep her away!" Gulses whispered. A second
Caliphate bravo moaned to echo his panic.

Timer-controlled, the doors closed. "Brave Gulses!"
Abu teased. "Gulses the slasher!"

"I'll get *you*, that's sure!"

The fight aborted when others in the squad disarmed
these antagonists. From 12,890 on silence ruled again,
the occupants of the car shifting to give each a chance
to gawk at the outside world when the doors opened.

*A bunch of know-nothings! If this car stops every ten
habs, so does the one just behind. What do people
think—there's just empty space between them? Empty
space when Earthstalk was designed for mass emigration?*

In his former body Senjoro Nie was too self-effacing
to put comfort first, but now she moved to the control
panel, and pushed MODO 2. The ceiling irised open,
monkey-bars lowered to eye level. "No telling how long
since anyone washed the sheets," she announced, "but
there's fold-out sleepers overhead."

Her astonished pirates hoisted each other into the
heights, all but two, left below to guard the heavier
pieces of their arsenal. The thirteen thousands seemed
humdrum, and the pair played cards and drowsed.
They woke suddenly: crowds mobbed the fourteen thousands, gawking back at the squad when the doors opened,
sometimes even cheering.

The fifteen thousands were empty. Luggage lay abandoned. The thieves among the sleeping squad woke and
dressed and looked out hungrily. The doors closed again,
and opened one last time.

"NO MORE CREDIT," the lights blinked. Ramnis stumbled out. No Bektashi here, no one at all. His hindgod
had been right to guide him into this gang of rascals, to

hide among all these vacancies. *Now it's time to desert the cause.* He began to wander off.

Senjorino Nie dropped her wings and jogged to his side. "You forgot me."

"I don't want to presume on false pretenses. This is incredible, there's no army! No leadership—what are we supposed to do?"

"False pretenses?"

"I'm not really the prisoner I said I was. I joined your force voluntarily. They'd never have taken me if I hadn't wanted to be took. See, I've got a sonic belt. I've had to use it too. If you've got any recent lapses in your memory that's why. I needed to keep curious dervishes out of my hair."

"Ah. Sonics. A Dirtgrub weapon."

"My name is Ramnis. I'm in a trap. I can't get out of the Caliphate—is something wrong?"

Senjorino Nie recovered and shook her head. "I . . . I've heard of you," she whispered.

"Everybody has, but my new hair helps. Those H-V commercials show me bald."

"Ramnis, the monster cyborg!" Nie stepped backward.

"I'm almost ready to believe it," Ramnis admitted. "Maybe that's what Souldancers are: a race of cyborgs. What do you think? You want to travel with a cyborg?"

"Do I have a choice? Come now, the time for games is over!" Senjorino Nie wore her MKZ on a sling; now she swung it up and clicked off the safety. "More than three million people on Earthstalk! Something more than random processes threw us together; admit it!"

"I don't understand? Who—you talk as if you were someone special. Who are you?"

Nie laughed. "Just another Status Five beefer! I've lived a long life, Ramnis. I'd like to end it in dignity, if that's within your powers. Come, no more tricks. I have what you want—"

Ramnis studied her face, his hand slipping casually to his belt. "Senjoro Nie? Ah—we need to talk."

"Yes . . . we . . . do . . ."

# Chapter 37

# Day 23 11:35–Express Elevator 'C'

*"Friendly hearts waiting to see me,
east or west, whither I roam—"*

Al Spendlowe couldn't remember ever being so happy, not for—let's see; exactly one thousand six hundred fifty-seven years. A new and halfway vital body, the chance to ride the elevator—

—out of Uphigh weirdness and down to the Lightfoot habs. Down to 80 percent gravity. His own Dirtgrubs were Lightfoot allies, separated only by the common enemy. Any luck at all and he'd be among his cronies soon as the Caliphate collapsed!

"East or west?" his dark-haired traveling companion inquired.

In an artifact only 100 meters across, words like "east" and "west" had long since dropped out of common use. "It means—spinward or antispinward, sunface or night."

"Spinward? Sorry, I don't mean to pester you with

questions. On one side the stars float up the windows, on the other side down."

His car-mate since Hab 172,400, the young woman at his side was heavily swathed, likely the daughter of a repressive culture. Yet she was chatty enough, almost unnaturally friendly. Al didn't know how many hours they'd share this car. Better nip this in the bud, let her know he wasn't interested in male-female games.

How?

Tell the truth? Be as unlike the scheming *Sagan* as possible! "I have a story," Al said. "It begins in California in the year 2040 of the common era. My parents changed their name from Espanola so I was born Alice Spendlowe—"

The woman listened as he described his first life: female astronaut, then wife of Dr. Cedric Chittagong, founder of Chittaworld Theme Parks—

—and refugee after the revolt of 2077. "After that I backed up my soul in case of disaster. Sure enough, within the decade I was radioed to Mercury to the City of the Dead, and stored with the other billions."

"And then resurrected into this borrowed body," the woman commented.

"Not at first. They gave me a female habitus, and drew me into the conspiracy to launch Earthstalk and convert it into an interstellar generation ship. And I agreed, more's the pity. Four million natives hijacked because the Dirtgrubs back on Earth wanted to plant a colony outside Sol System! Mind you, it's a worthy goal, but our methods were criminal, I see that now. Still, I went along. I agreed to help the Nulges of Uphigh suicide off to Mercury—all part of the program."

"You sound bitter."

"Because I've been manipulated. The *Carl Sagan*—oh, what's the use? He's so powerful! Now he's trying to get control of INFOWEB—yes, I know a ship in space is no place for a democracy, but doesn't it seem a bit hoggish?"

Al sighed and continued. "I managed to copy my soul into a Nulge body, a *male* Nulge body, I was *that* desperate! Then I snuck off downstairs. See, my people down there, my resurrectees, they didn't know about angels. I told them. That was my mission and I've accomplished it. Now my life serves no further purpose."

"That's no Nulge body," the woman said.

"I had an adventure. The upshot was I got to trade into new flesh, although I didn't dare go back to being a woman. They'd think I was kinky. Not a good idea to be kinky in New Iowa."

The woman swept back her hood, revealing an olive face, precise black eyebrows and prominent nose, aristocratic, predatory, very olde Assyrian. "Quite an introduction," she responded. "As for my name, I shan't tell you yet. I have a proposition for you."

"Nothing to divert me from my journey," Al insisted.

"My people's enemies are the Shirs. Truly if you are what you say you'll fight them as my ally, for at the end of this trip I mean to put an end to their evil. One single grenade—that's all it'll take. Afterward I'd reconciled to death. With you to help I might escape."

The woman spoke with her lips nearly together, as those with bad teeth learned to do. Sad, because otherwise she was striking, hardly pretty, yet certainly beautiful. "If you depend on male chivalry, I've already explained—"

"No." She held up her hands to bid silence. "The Shirs have a peculiar profession, an art that demands the use of clay. They make painted tiles in two modes, Dutch and Kufic. These tiles are worth their weight in gold, rare as the finest wood.

"Clay is nothing you mine in space. The ore-ships that bring ices and CHON-carbs to Earthstalk do the Shirs no good whatever. Nor can they get clay from Earth. For centuries that source was cut off. Consequently the Shirs adapted. To have clay they must *make* it!"

"By some nefarious means," Al concluded.

"Cremating corpses and grinding the ash into fine, fine dust—so fine as to be colloidal! Mixed with a few other elements—the process is secret but a chemist might guess at it. It does nothing to lower the value of the plaques, either. A three-corpse tile is a collector's item, they trade them up and down the stalk!"

Al pondered. "They burn corpses? Diverting them from recycling? I presume the Federation will make the practice illegal."

"Especially in view of where they get the corpses. Al, my people were the Shirs' neighbors and enemies, but after the Earthstalk launch we lost several to suicide and couldn't hold our hab. They surprised us. I'm one of just a few survivors."

The woman spoke on. "—And yet they're vulnerable. Even among themselves the craft is reserved to a very few. The making of tiles is their religion, and only two or three elders—see, *they've* lost a few to suicides too, and spread thin to occupy neighboring habs. It won't be hard to strike at their heart!"

"What kind of people are they? Race and language?"

"Leninish in atheism," she answered, "but the making of plaques is sacred, and they boast many old customs. The name 'Shir' means lion, and they call the lion their totem animal. They have the lion in their blood, just as *my* people have the ram. And you must not doubt this, for they believe it with a passion!

"As for race, they suppose themselves Afghans of some special kind, but since our languages have blended into Prospore all they can say is that they lived on the Chinese side of the border prior to the wormroot menace. So if you know what that means—?"

Al shook his head. "Asian culture wasn't my area, and I'm not well versed in recent history. 'Leninish?' 'Wormroot menace?' In any case modern tribes give themselves false paternities."

"Theirs is true, or else my people divided from them after the lie, because we claim we were always their neighbors, bound by fate in eternal hostility."

"And you want me to risk my life against them?" Al asked incredulously.

"I introduce myself as you did, with all my circumstances surrounding me. My name is Raksha, and if I'm lying, well perhaps you're lying too. You said this body

of yours is a spare, a supernumerary, and an embarrassment. You plan to risk it in battle. You can be of slight
help to the Lightfoots but if you enlist in *my* cause
you'll be enormously useful! Think! The news may get
out to the other habs of these six-digit levels: we have
Dirtgrubs among us! All these unrealities we hear about
on H-V are suddenly brought home!"

"You're very persuasive."

"Then you'll come with me?" Raksha asked.

"How much time to we have? Give me an hour to
think."

"Fine. Meanwhile let me outline what we must do."

Somehow in the ensuing discussion Al lost sight that
he wasn't yet committed, until it became clear to him
that he was. No way to turn back; he'd accepted a
grenade and learned how it worked. In a dozen ways he
compromised until he hardly dared weasel out.

And then—

The elevators opened to a vibrantly blue hall, Kufic
verses traced out in white, a dizzying sea of magic
scripture . . . guards!

No, statues, robed and turbaned! Raksha grabbed
Al's hand and tugged. They jogged from splendor through
a service door to hide under a utilitarian one-flight
stairs.

Here she let go, but Al's wrist remembered her
tight, slim grip; a dry hand almost fever hot. "One
flight up, and right, then right again toward the black
windows, and quietly!"

Were there no guards? How did Raksha know the
layout so well? But Al had no time to think, not until a
minute later when they scuttled into a carpeted waiting-
room.

Beaded curtains beyond, and talk; the ratchetty hack-
ing talk of several old men. There were low tables and
cushions: like stalking predators Al and Raksha dropped
to the floor and crept from one inadequacy to the next.
Beyond the curtain a figure stood and backed from the
far room, and turned—

Al rose, pulled the pin, and flung his grenade through the doorway arch. The thing hit with a bump and a roll.

Appalling silence. As if the act was over Raksha stood. The turbaned graybeard faced Al. He shook his sleeves from his hands and began to clap.

Al pivoted to find himself surrounded by grinning Shirs, Raksha among them. They smiled horribly, teeth filed to points.

Exposed by her rictus, Raksha's fangs were also filed. "Come, come," said the graybeard. "You've done no harm and we mean you none, but before we can be allies we have one more test."

"A trick!" Al whispered.

"You Dirtgrubs need to learn how easily you can be tricked, otherwise I fear for our common cause!"

"You mean—the *Sagan?*"

Without answering the old man gestured Al into the next room. His entourage became a procession. By the persuasion of a moving crowd Al emerged onto a balcony and stepped down into a small garden landscape.

Here stood younger Shirs. They pressed close, their elders parting to give them room. Brown faces snarled and taunted. The words came fast and babbled, dancing and metrical, but Al understood: they were challenges to fight.

"You, then." He tapped the nearest and the press fell back. The hottest of these bully-poets swung his fist. Al parried his first and second blow, then struck for his jaw.

CRACK! The young man dropped where he stood. Al stared at his victim's broken face, then at his own fist.

"We have angels among us," he announced to the awestruck crowd.

"You've won the respect of the lion in our hearts," answered the graybeard, "for we are the people of the lion, and will deal with none but those worthy of respect."

"Do lions play tricks on their prey?"

Raksha stepped forward. "In their day lions were wily. They used cunning as well as muscle."

"But no longer," said the old man. "On Earth are no

more wild lions, no elephants. The wormroot jungle spread and wiped them out."

"Though not for good," someone added as Al's challenger was carried off.

"Not for good," agreed the graybeard. "We have the lion in our blood. You think I speak poetry. In fact we are the products of gene engineering. Do you know much about genetics?"

"I have weeks with less excitement piled into them than today," Al said. "I clout a bully—perfect sense you'd swing into a lecture."

"There are on and off switches in genetic code," the graybeard patiently continued. "Twiddling those switches adapts a human cell to its special function; brain or kidney or gland. Cancers happen when those switches are accidentally deleted so that something grows that is *both* colon-wall and wisdom-tooth, or whatever.

"A long time ago our DNA was bonded to lion DNA, and switches were stuck in to keep the lion DNA from being read. Now this was nowhere as simple as I make it out to be, and our ancestors accepted many risks, among them that their children would suffer a higher rate of cancer. Yet they accepted the risk to preserve lion DNA when the animal itself became extinct."

Raksha spoke. "They hoped someday the wormroot peril would be overcome, and half the world restored to natural three- or four-yield photosynthesis. Lions would live again. We've waited ever since."

"—We and the elephant-people, and all the rest, fertile only among ourselves, species by species," the old man agreed. "Yes, some of us became impatient and emigrated to Venus, but it's a tight game on Venus; a narrow margin between cultivated land and desert. Planet Four Centauri has better prospects—if we can ever get there."

Al frowned. "I don't see—can you switch into lions?"

"Our children can be lions. We have the skill. Trickier for the elephant-people. Imagine bearing a three-hundred-kilo baby!"

"But it can be done," Raksha assured him. "Books

tell us how. And now do you understand? Do you know
why I diverted you from your journey to Lightfoot-
land? We had to test your spirit, and decide whether to
be your allies. We have done so. Here on Earthstalk
are thousands of natives as keen on Alpha Centauri as
any Dirtgrub. You needn't wheedle us: we *want* to
go!"

"I'm sure the *Carl Sagan* will be pleased to hear that,
and I'm sure he's listening. He's got a proxy here, an
invisible schnegg."

"Let him come forth and we will feast him," roared
the graybeard. "Is he a coward?"

"Merely cunning like yourselves. But today he gave
himself away and I thank you for your part in the
exposure. Will you excuse me now? If you have a spare
room I'd like to rest and get my adrenalin back to
normal. A room with a telephone? I really think you
owe me one. At least Raksha does!"

The old man nodded. "It shall be done. You must call
your Dirtgrubs and tell them we are here. And afterwards, a feast!"

Raksha led Al to her rooms. "You'll want to be alone,"
she said as she bowed out the door. "I'll keep the
curious at bay."

Al retained a benign expression until the young woman
was gone. Then—"Well?"

"What are you going to tell your friends downstairs?"
a voice inquired.

"That's between me and them. There's something
called privacy. We wetbrains value certain privileges—"

"I saved you from Norma upstairs," the schnegg continued, circling him invisibly. "I called the police from
a public phone. I've helped you in a dozen ways."

"And arranged my encounter with Raksha? She thinks
she was just lucky, right?"

"No comment. I grant you privacy if you swear not to
talk of angels, and how we've hustled you downstairs.
You must seem a free agent. Olivia must not know we
used you to warn her about us, and set her on her
present course of action. Alice, we're on the same side.

You've lost sight of that. Your ordeals have made you dangerously heroic when you should be chastened by the near approach of death."

Al shrugged. "I'm a throwaway."

"Call downstairs. I'll dial the number and hand you the patch. Tell them about lions and elephants. It's of small importance in the midst of war, but vital to your present hosts. Do it to please them."

Al paused. "For their sake, but afterward this charade is over. I'm not a pawn to move around the chessboard at the *Sagan's* whim . . . Fine, thank you. —Olivia?

"Olivia? Yes, this is Alice Spendlowe. Can you forward me through to wherever she is? Code? She never gave me one. Yes, I can hold. Thank you."

Al waited, tapping his foot, looking around the room as if to penetrate his schnegg's invisibility. "Hello, Olivia? Say, *remember about angels? I said they may have wanted to panic—*"

Al's body slumped to the floor while his tiepatch floated in midair. His voice spoke on, a perfect imitation. "—me into panicking you? Well, no more worries on that score. I'll tell you about it later. But I've got even better news—there's a whole stretch of nodes up here filled with enthusiastic Dirtgrub allies—"

Minutes later Al woke. "You can brutalize me—" he groaned.

"You told Olivia what you were supposed to say. Now go out and preach at these lion folk. Tell them to swear fealty to the Federation. Do this for the sake of humanity, lions, and the stars."

"And then what?"

"Then the elevators. Sleep in your car, I'll protect you."

Al hauled to his feet. "Is that all? Sleep? You forgive me?"

"I keep a ledger. If you're in the black you live. If you're in the red you die. We need you, Alice. One last service. The stars, Alice. It's for the stars."

Al whispered. "Let me live."

"You ought to have thought otherwise. The strength of a Lightfoot fist hitting a Shir jaw—why speak of angels? You're twice as powerful as anyone here, but in your heart you can't believe in yourself, not as a brawler."

"I'm not—yes, I am too! Hear me begging! I was tired, that's all. I get confused. I was wrong to try to warn Olivia about your schemes. I was wrong."

"Take a shower. Don't worry, you won't die."

So Al cooperated and spoke as implored to the Shirs, and ate saffron-flavored rice and rosewater sweets, natural food on the golden platters, more familiar machine food on the silver. That evening after the feast he returned to elevator cluster A, refusing Raksha's invitation to spend the night. "You know I'm not inclined that way."

"Not yet? It'll come. Your body will teach you." Raksha reached for his shoulder and squeezed, a downpayment on future physicality. She pulled away. A car arrived, Al got in and fell asleep.

His guardian schnegg removed his body next hop down and dragged it to the local chapel, then to the bioconverter . . . Seventy thousand habs above, *Feldwebel* Wolf Schinner turned to his companions.

"Come. The time to play gods is over. We need to get to the nearest spacedock. My schneggs will fly in the *Placidia* for a rendezvous. Cedric, give Alice your suit. Her destination is the sixteen thousands, and it's point eight gees down there. You've been weightless twenty-seven days: she might need suit strength to walk."

"What now?" Alice asked. "What do you want from me?"

"A second chance at cooperation. I can't tell you more. You'll be moving into no-man's-land, a zone cleared for battle. Olivia can use your help."

"Why not me?" asked Cedric.

"You're no astronaut."

"Dammit, I was a bug! I could fly rings around any human! I'm more used to armor than Alice is. If there's any risk—"

Wolf took color and raised his forelegs in surrender. "You're right. Even schneggs can be trapped by an idee fixe. As long as we're bringing in substitutes, why not you, Dr. Chittagong?"

"Substitutes?"

Wolf shrugged. "A convergence of forces, and one of our factors failed to pan out. Time to call up the reserves. Alice, thank you, and now I have to measure Cedric for a very special vacuum suit to wear over his armor."

## Chapter 38

# Day 23 19:45–No Man's Land

"—And that's my point of view."

"The *Sagan's* too?" Senjorino Nie asked suspiciously.

"I'd swear so if I could, but the bond between us is a mystery to me," Ramnis answered. "I guess I'm his creation, and should trust my instincts. That's what they tell me. I believe in a benevolent universe. The fact we evolved points to a severe local excess of good. Our cosmos is left-handed, matter distributed unevenly on every scale. The idea of balance is a myth, none of this bland entropic soup—it's plusses all the way!"

"Physics and ethics have no lessons for each other," Senjorino Nie replied.

"You shake your head," Ramnis said. "We're all cursed with suspicion: 'you can't get something for nothing.' Five thousand years ago Gatekeeper remoted in to teach Iranian nomads about one God and chivy them out of superstition. What next? Zoroaster comes up with Satan to restore a nonsense symmetry! Gatekeeper doesn't want our kind of life to mingle with those of other nursery systems. Reasonable, right? So she tells us that, and we translate: We're in prison!"

"I understand. You're one of U Gyi's Redemptorists."

Ramnis grinned at the irony. "As for the business at hand, the *Carl Sagan* wants to give INFOWEB a soul. We know that, we admit it, but did he ever say it had to be *his* soul?"

"You suggesting *I* turn into a machine?" Senjorino Nie responded. "A helpless machine for everyone to lay hands on? Pushed prostrate across space by the *Carl Sagan*?"

"You'll have neither weapons nor drive, but everything else: factories, distribution system—"

"Why me?" Senjorino Nie settled unsteadily into a chair opposite Ramnis's couch.

"I don't think the *Sagan* stipulates it should be you. All he promises is it doesn't have to be me. We can work together to find someone if you like."

Nie eyed her MKZ. In Ramnis's hands it seemed larger than life. "This is a trick to learn my password. You want me to give it to you so you can figure how to get those highest privileges. A horrible vision: one mind controlling Earthstalk!"

"One mind? A troika. The *Sagan*, INFOWEB, and the human leaders of the Federation. Nine tenths of *Sagan*'s schneggs to be scuttled soon as we leave the inner system."

Nie laughed. "Look at us talking high and mighty! Two ne'er-do-wells in an empty hab—no, not empty enough. I'm afraid of the rest of our squad. They'll revert to type and run wild. We might want to move upstairs a few nodes."

"We did, while you were sonicked. I picked some pockets down in the Seraglio and got some potent magcards to pay for the trip. We're now well above 16,500."

"And I'm in your power. Take me off to a memory chapel, record my soul and dream away. Learn my password. I can't stop you."

"Relieve you of all responsibility? That's the *Sagan*'s

style all right, I know him well enough now. He's much more rational than I am. 'What's the dignity of one soul compared to the happiness of millions?' That's what he'd say, but I don't think like that, and for some reason he feels constrained to work through me."

Senjorino Nie shrugged. "In case it's escaped your notice there's a war on. We're here in the middle, part of a pretend army. Please forgive me if I'm distracted."

"Pretend army!" Ramnis mused. "Yeah, that's what we are. The only thing that makes sense. No, what really makes sense is that the Caliphate's badly run. It's either that or—"

"—or we're here to make a little noise, and lull the Dirtgrubs."

"What Dirtgrubs?"

Senjorino Nie shrugged. "If my theory's correct they'll start flooding in soon."

"Can you check their movements? You're hot stuff with the computer. I promise to stay outside. Can you use your privileges to find out what's happening? No tricks, I promise: like you say, if I wanted to invade your head I don't need to be subtle about it."

"The last decent man! I hope you *are* decent, Ramnis, it enhances the irony. The two of us on the same side? Why the hell not? We're both on the run, the same people chasing us!" Senjorino Nie's face went through transformations. "—And maybe I can throw in a few happenings of my own!"

Two figures bent over a table, lost in tiepatch consciousness. Lights were dimmed to make their screen overlays more visible. At last Olivia leaned back. At this signal the room brightened. She looked across to Captain Caddo. "I say he *is* the Mufti, and the time's come. The *nizam* are demoralized, their Caliph cowering behind locked doors, sitting on a mountain of food. Everything I've come to expect of Selim. All we have to do is reach out and harvest his hungry army."

"I can keep hold down here," Caddo responded.

"Do that," Olivia answered. "My place is upstairs.

This Mufti wants more sweetmouthing—I may have to give him his own emirate to fire his treachery."

"How are you going up? You can almost punch through by elevator, our enemy's that softened! Elevator, stairs, ropes or shuttle?"

"Two out of four. Let's not be predictable. They've got computers to calculate my best strategy—let's see INFOWEB predict the roll of my dice."

Luck chose ropes and elevator. Olivia's preference lay with ropes—jury-cables running up darkside from spacedock to spacedock. During yesterday's invasion Bektashi dervishes moved out to pepper ascending resurrectees with gunfire and were shot down in turn, their docks conquered. Today troops hopped smoothly from node to node, native enemies wholly withdrawn into a string of individual hab-garrisons.

Or so it seemed. Too many docks and bays to be sure, but in vacuum suits Olivia and her chosen three hundred were anonymous as ants, no indications of rank to make her a target. Taking her turn at random, the Dirtgrub general wriggled onto a bar like a child on a swing. She held tight and soon was on her way.

Anonymity works both ways. His vacuum suit made Monsieur Cauteleux look just like the others. 'Borg Hunt's newsman bent to touch helmets with his attendant. "Ready? It could be tonight. A spate of phone calls after last night's show."

"I'm always ready," said the sharpshooter.

Far upstairs, less far with every minute, Magda unwrapped a packet of cheesecake, flipped it into a plate, and licked her dimpled fingers clean before picking up her fork.

*Dimpled?* She frowned. "*Another* sweet?" Selim teased, turning from one of his wives. He patted Lady Maryam's tattooed arm automatically as he continued. "I shall have to bring in a psychologist to do a study on you."

*Was this the pregnant hungries, or something pathological?* Magda sighed and addressed the Caliph's feet, easy to do since he sat above her, supply boxes arranged to make his throne. "I'm nervous, of course. You've bet your crown on me, and right now it's too early to tell—"

Selim's wife spoke up. "You are telepathic, and feel ten thousand growling bellies."

"—Just outside our door," Selim laughed. "An amazing form of sympathy, *oleum addere camino!* Yes, we must all eat! And Magda, don't shoulder the whole weight of my policy. That's my role in this farce, not yours. A command from your adopted lord: relax. Come up here, Lady Maryam is very good at massage."

# Chapter 39
# Day 23 22:50—Hab 16,520

It was the equivalent of that long-gone galleria, loading dock and all. The one difference was that the nine floors above were empty, unfurnished, the local jungle unpruned. In the interval following the last phosphate harvest, birdshit had built up everywhere, though less so here away from the atrium.

The lights were dim, the view obscured by pillars. The Caliph's mutes saw Ramnis and Senjorino Nie on the down escalator. They took aim and began to shoot.

Reflex time, fight or flee—their damn escalator was against them! Two near-fatal seconds to stop climbing in place and flop onto the risers. "Don't fire!" Senjorino Nie shrieked. "We're on your side!"

Were they deaf as well as mute? Bald and half naked, their nemesis stalked to the foot of their stairs and took dread aim. Prostrate in the least dignified of postures, Ramnis twiddled his sonics. The range was extreme. "Please!" he shouted. "We have a message!"

The man held fire. His face slowly went stupid.

261

Ten minutes later Senjorino Nie wore a mute's too-large vacuum suit, and Ramnis wore Senjorino Nie over his shoulder. *Convenient of women to center mass near the bending point,* he thought. *It makes this much easier. I'm glad she can't hear my grunts!*

He got in the elevator and pushed for the Hab 16,520 factory control floor. In the midst of cranes and drills, catwalks and serpentine cables, here glowed an island of glass and atmosphere, a cybernetic temple, the once-bright palace of local industrial management.

Shapes swam within that glow. Ramnis checked his sonics and stepped into a corridor-airlock. Three more steps, Nie getting heavier, then the inner door—

He sat down his burden and looked at six men suddenly disengaged from reality, eyes cycling as they dithered, unable to complete their thoughts for all the distracting sonic hash whirling in their brains.

*Now what? Plenty of cords and wires to use for rope, but best not unplug anything vital. Ah, printer cables, and the hose from the fire extinguisher.*

When Senjorino Nie woke she whistled, a lost habit of her youth. By a wall far from processors and drives a half-dozen bodies lay tightly bound.

"I got all of them," Ramnis told her.

"What were they doing?—Some secret mission," Nie answered herself.

The Caliph's mutes glared. Hate reddened their eyes. "They don't say," Ramnis commented stupidly. And why was it important to giggle for the sake of his ego, as if he'd meant a joke? "They're fanatics bent on suicide—no vacuum suits, no food, just a canister of ecstasy pills. Here, look at this! A disk-drive altar; flowers, pictures of Momma, and six rosaries. Eerie as hell!"

"If you don't mind, I'll not insist you step outside. Keep an eye on those pussers and I'll get to work. Oh—can I borrow your plastic?"

Two minutes and Lissandra Orloff of 16,520 had a subscription to *Astronomy*. She patched through to the publication's telescope. "This doesn't give me the view from Earth."

"Excuse me?"

"Nothing. I've got to go through their catalog, that's all. Spend a little more of your money. There! Just maybe—Yeah, it's the same old program! Oh, sweet, sweet, sweet! I love you, baby! Hold on now. It's clobberin' time!"

"I'd be dead as an iceball in oredock not to be curious. What's up?"

"I'm in, that's all. In and scanning." And then Senjorino Nie fell silent. Ramnis waited.

Five hundred twenty meters below their floor the *Placidia* settled on this node's spacedock, an event noticed by Olivia's small ascending army.

KA-BA-BOOM! A pair of vacuum-suited mutes fired from hiding, aiming low into the landing gear; into complexities of metal unprotected by molded ceramic.

The *Placidia* went tilt. Wolf Schinner reached around Cedric's plated bulk and fired back with the shuttle's guns: one, two. "Sorry about that," he said. "Blew your exit. We're committed now."

"How many more?"

"Enemies? None, and we'll be among allies in a minute. Now suit up. The layered look. Ne zorgu," he continued, then reverted to Old High English: "Don't worry, it fits fine over your hump."

Cedric lowered his voice in response. "English? You trying to tell me something?"

"Battle language. English says you're a good guy."

A minute later Cedric and Wolf hopped out of the damaged shuttle and onto the stage of a Las Vegas nightclub, deck outlined by landing lights, prosceniae radiating outward to a glowing lip and beyond, like showcase diving boards. Dark space in each direction, one bright gibbosity the planet Earth, barely a disk after weeks of travel.

Cedric wasn't meant to see the ropes that carried his allies closer and closer. From their hangar hideout more attentive eyes than his had failed to notice their black lengths swaying across the stars. Now those eyes were

closed in death, and he strode stalkward to investigate
two fizzing, spluttering corpses. "I'm not used to this,"
he said, standing away from pink outmisting gasses, and
was not surprised when his schnegg chaperone failed to
answer. He'd not meant it as a protest—they'd fired
first, after all.

Oddly, when Wolf *did* speak it was with Cedric's
voice: "Natus ad glorium."

"*He knows the watchword,*" Olivia's lieutenant radioed as his troops scrambled toward this three-figured
tableau—for Wolf was nowhere to be seen. "*One of us:
he's bagged a pair of turkey Turks*—Good show, man!"

Dirtgrubs accumulated. Olivia hauled over the lip
and studied the *Placidia*. "*Cedric!*" she guessed, seeing
his oversize figure. She ran toward the spacedock hanger.
"What's going on here? Caliphate soldiers? What's the
news from Midnode?"

Cedric shrugged. "I'm here to help you. I'm not sure
why. These men . . . the *Sagan* . . ."

"We'll talk later. Let's get upstairs into the habs. My
army's mustering. They need me to join them."

# Chapter 40
# Day 24 01:40–Factory 16,520

Another whistle. Senjorino Nie shook her head. "I've just fed the multitudes. Incredible! The Caliph's army was *starving* up there!"

"What? They've only been trapped a few days."

"That's when hunger hurts, the first few days. Ahh, that felt good! Mark this for my beatification: the Blessed Nie, patron saint of the furtive. Let's run through the log. Come here. You can't see anything that'll compromise your innocence."

Ramnis bent over her shoulder. "Everything that was done from this terminal since God knows when."

"That's because it's been zip for two or three lifetimes," Nie answered. "Up until a day ago. And now they want to open the oredock bay—this doesn't make sense. They want to open from the *sunward* side!"

"Sun shining on a frozen comet?" Ramnis frowned. "Sounds excessively stupid. INFOWEB won't let them do it."

Senjorino Nie shook her head. "INFOWEB *will* let

them do it after they've persuaded it—it's handed them a questionnaire, and they've perjured themselves down the line, trial-and-error to see which lies work."

"But—"

"There's a lot of INFOWEB that thinks we're in Earth's shadow. Level 16,520, March 17th, 1:00 A.M.— Sure it's night! INFOWEB's not programmed to deal with the fact we've come unhinged. You're right, Ramnis, spaceship *Earthstalk* needs a mind of its own. If it were me I'd know twenty-five seconds' direct inner-system radiation is enough to set your average iceball popping like God's own popcorn. They're asking for a full minute!"

Ramnis blinked. "How many mutes does the Caliph have? How many nodes has he set up for disaster? The bulk of Olivia's army lies over our heads—"

Senjorino Nie looked up and grinned. "God damn! At last we civilized types are going to squash you Dirtgrubs! Look here, Ramnis. You're Selim, you're fighting a war, and your enemies have sonics. They can sneak anywhere they want to! *How can you win against that stacked deck?*"

"By making them *want* to step into your trap! Shit! The Caliph is going to wipe out my people!"

"Do you care?"

"Exploding comets!" Ramnis responded. "Think of the damage! He's risking all Earthstalk!"

"Nothing so extreme. Trifilamented cryswire can survive anything chemical. I agree life won't be possible along this stretch, but still—"

*Thump.*

"Can you stop it?" Ramnis begged. "Look, you did Selim a favor and gave his men food. Now do something for Olivia!"

"Ramnis, Olivia's trying to kill you!"

"Half the time U Gyi wants to kill me too. I try not to let that get in the way of friendship. Madam Nie, whatever your name is, you've got to let my people live!"

"Done," Nie said. "Hey, *I* want to live too! The doors won't open. I've entered a global suspend."

*Thump, thump. Thump!*

Ramnis straightened up and turned. Streaming along the factory catwalks, a crowd in gray spread outside the windowed computer complex, jogging to ring them in.

*Thump, thump, thump.* Hands rapped the windows, arms waved and pointed to the airlock. "They want inside."

Senjorino Nie kicked away from the console and popped her helmet over her head. "You got 'em all, huh? Hit them with sonics."

Ramnis strode to the inner bulkhead. The computer complex airlock was a double-doored corridor: he pushed to open the inner portal, then raised a warning arm. "Stay here. No sense getting addled. You've lost enough consciousness for one day."

He donned his helmet and stepped through. The door slid shut and the opposite door opened. The walls of the corridor were white-translucent, glowing like a low-watt luminaria. Senjorino Nie could easily see Ramnis's shadow moving to meet his muffled adversary.

Less easy to notice: the dirtgrub also advanced, sonics cancelled sonics. Among the horde outside figures jostled forward. One raised a gun.

And fired.

Ramnis tumbled. Senjorino Nie hit the door button.

The door failed to open—*decided* not to open, not to compromise the computer center's atmosphere. Nie stared up and out, as an aquarium fish might stare, or a zoo animal on display. The crowd surrounding her fissioned into a score of behaviors; anger and urgency; flailing of arms. Bullets pinged impotently against trifilament glass. Near the door anonymous bodies piled on top of each other, then rolled apart as a giant waded in.

"You bloody sods!" Nie rose and fiddled with her helmet's radio.

"—MEDICAL! CLEAR THE OUTER DOOR. WE HAVE TO GET HIM IN ATMOSPHERE TO HAVE A LOOK!"

"Who are you?" Senjorino Nie asked. "What side are you on?"

*"Dirtgrubs, the Federation! Believe me, we regret this incident. When we find out what trigger-happy—CEASE FIRE! CEASE FIRE, YOU JERKOFFS!"*

Some moments more and Olivia had the outer door cleared, thanks to the strength of the ungainly humpback at her side. Cedric's right mitten held a writhing victim. He bent to pluck up Ramnis with his left. When the inner bulkhead opened he carried both bodies through, sliding Ramnis onto an open patch of floor not far from the Caliph's mutes.

"Medical!" Olivia shouted. "Memory chaplain!" She doffed her helmet and looked at the row of mute prisoners. "Medical?"

"They won't help you," Senjorino Nie spoke, backing away. "They're your enemies, here to spring the Caliph's trap."

"He's dead." Cedric straightened and flung his oversize outer helmet to the floor in frustration.

"You a doctor?" Nie asked.

"I'm an electronics engineer, but I can tell when someone's *this* dead. A hole straight through, punctured organs bursting in vacuum—"

Senjorino Nie's retreat brought her to the console. "You killed him."

"*She* killed him." Cedric lofted his captive, tore off her helmet—

" 'Borg Hunt's hired gun." Nie nodded. "Yah, we got H-V upstairs, just like you."

"And I led her right to Ramnis." Olivia grabbed for a chair, sat hard, and stared. "God, what a mess!"

"You've done worse than that. You've led your whole army into the Caliph's trap," Senjorino Nie responded. "Your pile of dimwit barbarian fools—look at them! Look at you! Ramnis begged me to save you!"

She choked and turned away. Cedric gazed into the sharpshooter's eyes, lowered her to the floor and shoved her sprawling against the wall. Perhaps she read contempt in the way he turned his back. Perhaps she was frightened, or angry. She fumbled inside her suit, pulled out a handgun, and fired.

Cedric's hump bloomed and exposed his powerpack. He turned, tore the weapon from her grasp, and crushed the grip. He removed a mitten, extruded claws—

Two slashes. "You're trapped here as much as me," Cedric told her. "Vacuum out there in every direction. Understand?"

Unable to speak, the woman nodded.

Olivia rose, shattered by events. "We'll have much to mourn when the war's over. Ramnis will be given a hero's honors. The good in his career outweighs the bad, but we all knew that from noon February 21st he was doomed. From the moment of launch he'd sacrificed his life."

"Is that all?" Senjoro Nie mocked. "An easy elegy! What of his dreams? A soul for INFOWEB, what about that?"

"I see he had *you* persuaded, whoever you are."

Senjoro Nie's expression froze. "I am someone indeed, and not a nowhere myth. Ramnis's dreams were real. You're a fool to wade in here and slight them. You're a fool anyhow. Perhaps Caliph Selim is less a fool. Almost I'm tempted to enlighten you as to his wisdom. With one keystroke I might do so. *No!* Tell that monster man to stay away or I'll transmit."

"And do what? What is this danger? Tell us."

Senjorino Nie glanced at her keyboard and did a double-take. "Oh Jesus! I did *not* push SEND! I didn't do it! I swear it couldn't happen. This is all an impossible bad dream!"

"*I don't understand!*" Olivia shouted.

"*Gott sei mit uns!* How many seconds? Twenty? Nineteen, eighteen, seventeen—"

Olivia pulled on her helmet. "*Take cover,*" she ordered. "*Secure and take cover!*"

"—twelve, eleven, ten. Nine, eight—"

It hit like an earthquake. The lights flickered. "Was that it?" Olivia rose from the floor.

"Bang, you're dead. There's no hope now," Senjorino

Nie muttered. "Tell your army to run, jump into space, go anywhere but here!"

A second quake. "Why?"

"Otherwise they'll freeze. Can you imagine the damage down in oredock? Do you think the vacuum pumps are working? This region is about to grow an atmosphere and that'll be the end of us. All the Caliph's *nizam* have to do is wait until the temperature equalizes and move in to strip frozen Dirtgrub cadavers of their sonic belts!"

Another shock, another tremblor. The lights blinked off and on. "More distant," Senjorino Nie whispered. "We're flanked. God's guess which way to go—"

The first thing Olivia learned in ROTC so many lives ago: a good officer was always ready with orders. Whether they were the *right* orders was of second importance. She turned on her radio. *"This is General Daneby, countermanding all past commands. Evacuate! General order for all Dirtgrubs between 16,000 and 16,722. Evacuate and spread the word! Regroup at Downside Base or Lightfoot HQ, no delay. Move! Get out of here!"*

She raised her visor and glared at Senjorino Nie. "You're a killer."

"No," said Cedric, "not her." He stepped close. "Why? Why all these deaths? I was brought to die here with six prisoners and an H-V hireling. What's the point? What's going on?"

"Oh Cedric! It's true! You can't leave!" Olivia turned to Senjorino Nie. "Can you connect to INFOWEB? Can you get resources in here? Heaters? I'll make the runs. I'll go to the elevators—"

"I have some power but these things take time—"

"—Nie!" Cedric raised his arm and pointed. "That 'nowhere myth' business. You're Senjoro Nie! Hanging out with Ramnis in a computer room— That's it! The *Sagan* wants you to give us your password!"

"To my murderer?" Nie answered. "You talk as if this were all arranged, perhaps to panic me, to squeeze me—all a trick!"

"A trick, and we're all victims," Olivia said. "We're

the *Sagan*'s victims, aren't we, Cedric? You, me and all the rest."

"And our one lifeline is that password. Help us, Nie. We've got to work together."

Senjorino Nie glanced from face to face. "Kill her."

"Who?" Cedric answered.

"I'm not doing this in front of an H-V audience. Don't you suppose she's wired?"

"Oh." Cedric stepped over and closed his hand over the assassin's throat. The sharpshooter convulsed and went floppy: he tossed her body down in front of the Caliph's wide-eyed mutes. "Any other requirements?"

"You two strip. That's all, and hurry. The thermometer's dropped a few degrees already and this equipment won't work forever."

Three minutes later Olivia helped Cedric totter to a chair. "Okay, now *please!*"

"The static password is M, N, 3—oh, hell! What if the master password has nothing in common with this jumble?"

"Go on."

"E, D, T, 2, P, L, I, D, O, C, 1, E, S."

"And the dynamic?"

"The moons of Jupiter by first initial, seen left to right as from Earth's north pole. Now I'll tell you more. You think I'm stupid? Sure, the *master* password involves the whole solar system, and I've tried it every which way. I've tried point-of-view Earth, and point-of-view Sun. I've used *U* for Uranus, and *H* for Herschel, and *G* for Georgium Sidus. I've tried nine planets, and thirteen. I've thrown in Ceres, and Charon, and then gone the other way and taken out Pluto. Pluto's not much of a planet, see—"

"Yeah." Olivia shivered and hugged herself.

"I've tried it with only the named moons, the ones found from Earth. I don't see how it makes sense to include the others. There's so many and the situation grows so mutable the password would be out of date before you'd get it all in!"

Cedric leaned back, his chest heaving. "Take this

down," he spoke breathily, utterly taxed by point-8 gee. "This is what I'm supposed to tell you. I've seen the Midnode Simulacrum. Mercury, Venus, Helice, Bophuto, New Gondor, Friesland II, Earth, High One, Luna, Mars—"

"What kind of program to calculate all this?" Olivia asked when Cedric finished.

"*Astronomy IAC-6113.*" Nie answered. "Six megs to save our lives. —What was that?"

"Lights going off outside."

Senjorino Nie registered the purchase. "Okay, I'm thinking it doesn't matter where I start as long as I move left to right across the ecliptic. I'm going to begin with old friend Jupiter."

She began clicking away. Cedric turned and noticed the Caliph's mutes. He poked Olivia.

The Dirtgrub general didn't even have to pick up Nie's MKZ for them to reverse and wriggle back to the wall. "There!" Nie announced, oblivious to their threat.

Nothing. She pounded the console. "*No fair!* If it's not Jupiter, then what? A hundred possibilities!"

"High Station One. Humanity's first permanent foothold in space," Olivia suggested. She looked at the thermometer, at windows crystallizing toward opacity. "Please hurry."

Nie entered the revised sequence. Her shoulders slumped. "Guess again."

"The point of Earthstalk, where it used to transect the ecliptic. Looking up from the Marisma."

Dancing fingers; click, click, click—"Bingo!"

"Now what?"

Nie spoke as her hands played fast across the keyboard. "Go to the nearest chapel. Record your memories and I'll remote 'em into INFOWEB."

"Me?" Olivia's eyes widened.

The computer center shook to a new explosion. "You're the only one who's got a working vacuum suit. You and me, and I'm needed here." Senjorino Nie shivered and her breath steamed. "Cedric'll be busy getting into his armor. Get a move on, chapel's always on second floor."

Olivia reached for her suit. "But that means I'll be the one! I'll be INFOWEB!"

"And I hope you do better as a computer than you did as human. Dammit, *hurry!*"

With no further urging Olivia dressed and moved to the door. Frigid volatiles boiled outside; a moment after reaching the catwalks she was swallowed up, invisible and moving away from the only remaining light.

Cedric hauled to his feet. "Thanks about the armor. It's got heaters. I only wish I could do something for you."

"You did. You gave me the password. I'm as near God for the next ten minutes as anyone on Earthstalk has ever been! My lifetime dream! What should I do? Abolish Status Six? —I've got it; send my shuttles in to save Olivia's Dirtgrubs!"

"And rescue us?"

Senjorino Nie shook her head. "We're 80 meters from a melting iceball. It wouldn't be safe."

"Any way of telling what the atmospheric pressure is outside?"

"Not now. Don't bother me, I'm watching for second-floor chapel power use, a little blip I don't dare miss."

The factory elevator was unfunctional: Olivia climbed five sets of stairs, her hands and feet increasingly cold and numb. Where bone lay close to skin her knees and forehead felt biting pain, a sharp stimulus to speed. *Jog, jog, jog, turn. Jog, jog, jog*— She reached another airlock and moved through paired doors.

Warmer here, and a few lights. She shouldered through to the loading dock . . . two dead bodies, and a Dirtgrub groaning for help. *Jesus forgive me!* Olivia the atheist prayed, and dashed by to the escalator. She jogged up, and up again.

Floor two. Memory chapel. Gurney, dreamskull— could she push the button on herself? What if she fell back and the memory helmet rolled off? Would she be left with half a mind?

Puerile fears! Hadn't she said it herself? *"I'm one of*

*those souls that shouldn't be given glands.*" And now she'd be relieved of all that.

—Assuming Senjoro Nie was alert. Assuming her equipment still worked with the temperature plunging past freezing!

Olivia sat on the couch and donned the skull. "Any last words? No?"

She found a button that read the same in English and Prospore, and pushed SUICIDE.

"Done!" Senjorino Nie stood. Her console began to scroll. She looked up to where Cedric was struggling into his faded pink undersuit . . . and then sharply to her right. "Cedric," she whispered.

"It's Wolf, the schnegg who pressed that console button and doomed Olivia's army. The villain of this pretty plot, right, *Feldwebel* Schinner?"

"Right, in villainous black, and now" (transformed to white) "I plan to undo the damage, but first to save your lives. I can move fast: I can get you up into atmosphere in three minutes. Cedric, leave off the suit, there's no time. You won't explode—it's a poor excuse for vacuum out there and you're not wounded. Your body has normal integrity."

"What about those mutes?"

"Ecstasy." Wolf grabbed the pill canister and moved down the row, a high-speed zip, his hind limbs clattering while his digits moved surgically mouth-to-mouth. "They've won their battle, let's *us* win the war."

He grabbed. "Don't resist," Cedric warned Senjorino Nie. "Human muscles are nothing,"

Next second they were by the airlock. "Pump your lungs, and hold."

And then they moved out the door. Hoarfrost ringed the airlock. A first shock of cold—

A *second* shock! Involuntarily Cedric contracted. Wolf swung him in defiance of his body's inertia, carrying him on a carnival ride through black Antarctic winter. One last whirl, and up—

Icepicks stabbed into his ears. His eyes teared to-

gether. He left them closed. Nothing to see but darkness. Nothing to hear but a distant tappetta-tappetta—
CRASH!

How distant? A basso explosion made tinny by this
thin almost-air?

*Don't reach, don't touch any surfaces!* Stabbing cold
whirled around him. Nerves went ping along his skin,
and now Wolf swung him up and over like a sack of meat,
sensing some obstacle.

Cedric wanted desperately to breathe. Just now he
remembered to *ex*hale slowly and evenly, to relieve
that pressure—*no!* Open his throat and vacuum would
suck him dry, deflate and utterly collapse his lungs!
One fatal lapse and he'd never breathe again!

Sensation withdrew from hands and feet. Another
fling. *Like a football. I'm a football in play, trying to do
yoga meditation! Three minutes? How much longer?*

*—Not breathing, yet I smell comet! Pungent farts
and old burnt tires in a filthy grease-pit! Cold mole-
cules drifting in, searing the lining of my nose. I burn!
I burn! Two minutes? One?*

Too long. *Just set a goal. Count to twenty! Count to
ten! Oh God, my burning lungs! I CAN'T STAND IT!*

As Wolf climbed the final stairs Cedric opened his
mouth, flailed his arms—Wolf clapped his jaws shut
and twirled through the door. A few more meters, and
then left, onto the loading dock—

He lowered Cedric gently to the floor. "Pump him,"
he told Senjorino Nie. "A few warm puffs to get him
going. I can't do it—I don't have lungs."

"Lord, that was cold! I thought I'd die, and *him* near
naked!"

"He'll live. Now to find you a very large room."

Senjorino Nie looked up from Cedric's palsied embrace. "What? We're holing up? Things are going to get
worse and colder. Shouldn't we get away?"

By way of answer Wolf swept her up, then grabbed
Cedric. He jogged them up three flights of stairs and
through two doors. "Here. I'll comb for other local
survivors and get back. Take off your vacuum suit, strip

off your synsilks, tear them to rags and stuff them into the vents to block the air. Lie next to Cedric—share your warmth. If I bring any others tell them to make more rags."

Senjorino Nie looked around the racquetball court. In that brief instant Wolf vanished.

He returned with one wounded man. "Stay inside. When this door feels hot for God's sake don't open it. Don't move until you're rescued."

He left again. The Dirtgrub's tatters sealed the court door. "I guess we have enough air for a time," Senjorino Nie told Cedric when his eyes opened; unsure eyes, as if he had no idea what was going on.

What *was* going on?

BOOOM!

Earthstalk shook. Cedric struggled to sit up. "Air . . . oxygen. All those comet volatiles—explosive. Wolf broached the airlock and struck a spark."

"Dangerous?"

"To him? Absolutely. It'll keep burning until the comet's gone. I can't guess the peak temperature, but for a while there'll be explosions like crazy. One comet's heat to compensate for others' cold . . . it'll help a lot, and keep people alive until we're rescued."

"People like us." Senjorino Nie got up and went to the door. "I wonder if it *is* getting warmer. The jungle will catch fire, and we'll smell smoke—"

BOOM! Boom-Boom!

Point of view *schwarzeneggers:* slow flesh units, gog-eyed tourist soldiers . . . BLAM! In through the emergency tube-hatch, up through the downside loading docks, invisible agent-saboteurs opening the bulkheads. BLAM! HSSSSSSsssss s s s

Ten thousand troops, 23 habs, just now fed after two days hungry, mustered in sullen crowds around the intercoms. Point of view *nizam:*

"—Selim the Sixth, thanking you for your patient endurance. Even soldiers willing to sacrifice their lives find it hard to endure uncertainty, famine and rumor.

All I can say is, it had to be. *It had to be, so we could win today's victory!* Yes, even as I speak you feel the tremors, and the Dirtgrubs below us freeze! An army that would have reduced us to babbling idiots by virtue of their sonic devil-weapons, is now itself reduced to fro en ca daw e en ah an r er um ba wusz—"

The loudspeaker audience sagged and dropped, an outward rippling circle of narcosis. Only a few quick wits found the opportunity to escape the smoking canisters.

Point of view *Magda:* Selim's left hand clutched the handset while his trembling right held his faxpage notes. ". . . Battle of the Comets from now to the end of Earthstalk history. And you are its heroes. I say this, knowing some of you in exasperation followed the lead of a certain traitor. I say also: *You are forgiven!* All but the Mufti himself! And in return I ask that you forgive me for keeping this great secret from your minds—"

BLAM! The door to the commissary blew open. Magda rose as arachnoid shapes swarmed inside. "What—?"

The lights went out. Radio voices buzzed Magda's head. "Hurry! Not us! INFOWEB!"

# Chapter 41
# Day 24 02:25–Hab 10,823

In the rhythms of warfare there are times to attack and times to consolidate.

And times to meet with prisoners, some claiming to be delegates for powerful factions up in the Caliphate. Despite orders not to be disturbed, Captain Caddo was summoned from one such meeting with an emissary from the Iskemliji. Angrily he grabbed his elaborate notes and left the conference room.

"What now?" he almost snarled, slamming the door behind him.

"Sir, Olivia's army is trapped, disbanded. Most have leapt to space. There were explosions. The 16,000's were a lure—they used the oredock iceballs. We need to organize—"

"—a shuttle fleet to rescue the humans floating in vacuum." Caddo turned at the sound of Olivia's voice, and looked at an intercom.

"Where are you?" he asked.

"Right here." A glowing projo shimmered into view,

Olivia in Downlow pajamas. "Follow me. The *Torghut* lies just across the border. I need her. Run!"

Dropping two hours of tidy notes, Caddo jogged to the elevator. The door opened, swallowed him and closed. No plastic magcards? No timed wait?

A damned funny way for Earthstalk to behave! Was this a trick?

Without being touched, the red ALARMO button blinked on. A panel opened. "Put on that vacuum suit."

Caddo was barely dressed when the doors parted again. Olivia's projo rushed forth—and changed. "Safe conduct! Stand back. This is your Caliph. No time for delay!"

Despite Selim's commands two armed men interposed themselves. The intercoms shrieked: "*In the name of God, stand back!*"

The lights went out, every single one. Only INFOWEB could do that. In absolute darkness Caddo ran blindly and collided with something that grunted. He fought free. Ahead of him Olivia twinkled into view to guide his footsteps. He followed her, running down the escalator.

The door to the factory/spacedock levels clicked open. Another elevator dropped Caddo into local vacuum.

When he emerged into space bay Olivia was gone. Did projo equipment need air to work? Was that it?

He looked to his left. The flange used for shuttle launches was empty. That meant the *Torghut* lay inside the hanger—that lumpish wedge hidden under dark wraps. Under maintenance? *I sure hope Olivia knows what she's doing,* Caddo thought to himself as he wove through scaffolding and climbed into the pilot's cabin.

He punched the PRESSURIZE button. Air hissed in and Olivia took shape in the co-pilot's seat. "Just a few things, and then you're a passenger. Switch her on and take her off manual. I'm your faithful autopilot and I'll take over."

"How can you see through this shroud? Who *are* you?"

Olivia laughed. "It's perfectly safe, I've got a million

eyes. And don't worry, the *Torghut* is spaceworthy. All
this outside riggery was meant to conceal her and convince my Dirtgrubs she was just some old junker."

Caddo absorbed all this. What to do now? Olivia
pointed, illuminating the shuttle's controls with the
glow of her reaching hand. "Push."

Caddo pushed. Acceleration jerked him back in his
seat the same time as cabin lights blinded his eyes. The
shroud whipped free and the *Torghut* curved into space,
leaving a trail of broken scaffolding.

Up toward midnode space grew misty. The solar
wind smeared comet gas into a great arch whose denser
core moved with Earthstalk, whirling around its center
and leaving corkscrew traces of its passage. The *Torghut*
dove toward the eerie cloud. "We're here to pick up
bodies, the living and the dead. Us and all those other
shuttles." With those words Olivia vanished, but the
*Torghut* still moved under automatic control.

Her storage bay doors opened. Caddo couldn't really
feel the bumps of impact as that wide mouth took in
bodies. At intervals he turned back to count Olivia's
catch, watching as they plugged themselves into ship's
air like so many piglets on a sow's teats.

At other times he looked forward. Stars dimmed
infinitesimally. Sheets of auroral light danced among
thin gasses—Olivia's projo might almost take shape out
there, if she chose. In her absence Caddo thought he
could make out a blackened void in the sky—an egg-
shaped void.

"The *Sagan*," he whispered.

That was all, star and sunlight, the flare of other
shuttles' jets—*then suddenly a gout of actinic light!*

Shielding his eyes from a bit of burning comet, Caddo
saw a retinal afterimage of a lump . . . surrounded by a
half-dozen clinging stick-figures. Arachnoid stick-figures,
certainly not human.

Caddo turned away from a brilliance not so big after
all, no bigger than his shuttle. He could tell because
the flotsam of local space cast shadows in the gas—

*widely diverging* shadows that shifted as the lump sputtered and exploded its way unevenly off to port.

The nearest shadow drew his attention, darkness converging on the grisly sight of a limbless head and torso. As it flew across Caddo's field of vision that head turned to face him. The macabre form changed colors, from white to red—to blue?

"What was that?"

"Schnegg shrapnel. He's out of range. We've got more important work to do."

"He was signaling us, calling for help."

"Yup. Forget it."

But Caddo couldn't forget. He watched Wolf Schinner dwindle away; red, white, blue, red, white, blue—

"—He's got him. Your other shuttle." Captain Caddo fell back with relief. "I suppose they can give him new arms and legs."

Olivia spoke calmly through the *Torghut*'s radio. "That's not *my* shuttle. That's the *Ypsilanti*. There's a felon named Jack Dee who figures on making quite a haul tonight. Tomorrow I'll get a ransom note: *'Pay up or I can't afford them medical attention.'* It's amazing how much I know about Jack Dee. His record takes up a meg on disk—he's quite the entrepreneur."

"You won't pay."

"Oh, but I will. He's doing me a service and I mean to make sure he profits. Briefly at least. My attitude towards criminals has changed. I can squash him now or later, so why hurry?"

Olivia paused. "—Although if he thinks I'm rewarding him for rescuing the *Sagan*'s schneggs, he's badly, badly mistaken. Now if you'll excuse me, I've got a score of ships to run."

# Chapter 42

# Day 24 05:05–Space

"*Are you awake? You ARE awake, aren't you?*"

Magda staggered groggily to her feet. "The belly of the beast."

Lights blinked on, klieg lights from center axis. Magda looked around her. Fields and sidewalks were littered with stirring bodies.

The air smelled musty, *different*. Heaped with neatly-stacked girders and boxes, fallow croplands rose left and right and met overhead in terrifying patchwork distance. The sidewalks spoked out from a great urban disk. Walkways spiraled centerward from the perimeter of that disk, ascending in concentric balconies, doors and windows set back from the brilliantly lit rim. From one of the higher balconies a half-klom up a spotlighted woman looked down.

"*Attention! You're inside the* Carl Sagan," Alice shouted, a squawkbox in front of her mouth. "*Have no fears! You've been rescued. The* Sagan *bears you no enmity*."

Magda cupped her hands. *"Rescued?"*

Pause. *"From Olivia, and the consequences of your victory. I can't come down, Magda. I'm a cripple: I've been a month without gravity. You'll have to come up here."*

"But—"

Sound moved slowly through air. Alice spoke on, unaware she'd been interrupted. *"You won, Magda. You and Selim. But the Sagan who conceived your victory chose to intervene. He's seen to it Olivia controls Earthstalk's INFOWEB, and Olivia has axes to grind. You needed protection. You'll need protection until Olivia sees reason, and that won't be long. When Olivia makes certain—guarantees—then it'll be safe for Selim to celebrate this triumph."*

"Will she guarantee to forfeit her political schemes? Will she abandon her opportunistic Federation?"

A second figure moved out to stand at Alice's side. "She'll count Selim a grander presence than U Gyi," Alice spoke, and passed over the trumpet amp.

"Magda? I've been talking to the *Sagan*," Selim announced. He turned to speak more broadly. *"Defenders of the Faith! We've negotiated a government of Earthstalk that gives us the voice we sought; a strong voice! The strongest of voices! Tomorrow you'll be my honor guard, and we'll return to our homes to live in triumphant peace!"*

An hour's hike, winding upward into the *Sagan's* axial sky, climbing in lessening gravity past alfresco bars, sculpture gardens, dark bed-&-breakfasts and hushed casinos. Magda reached her goal, kissed Selim, and left him again to trudge up a final flight of stairs. "Just why do you suppose Olivia will see reason?"

From her chair Alice held up a memory cassette. "Her soul, available for anyone to dream. The *Sagan's* angels retrieved it from the '520 chapel. —No, I'm being unfair. We haven't had to play our trump card. Perhaps we'll have to revise our estimations of Olivia. She's cooperating in my husband's rescue—"

Alice fell silent. After a few seconds: "This is hard on me, just waiting. Two hundred kilometers from here SWAT team schneggs are suiciding themselves at my insistence. The *Sagan* finagled Cedric into your trap and now he's got to save him! The *Sagan*, who plays with war and madness. You can't hate Olivia half as much as I hate the *Sagan*, yet here I am, his hostess! His helpless voice!"

Alice began to sob. Magda moved to lay a comforting hand on her shoulder. "I'm sorry. It was my—"

"No. You were just a pawn on the chessboard."

"Because I wanted revenge, and was willing to see men die."

On the lower balconies an honor guard of *nizam* herded around Caliph Selim the Sixth, chanting their cheers. Over their heads two women waited together in silence.

# PART EIGHT

## *Ghosts in the Machine*

# Wednesday

Lifting weights again, and in point eight seven gees!
Torfinn, Earthstalk has two athletes who want to meet
you.

Olivia in charge of INFOWEB—you're an important
person! Important because of the plebiscite coming up
to ratify Earthstalk's new constitution. I hope numbers
don't bore you, because we have a council of Nine and
a Council of Eighteen, and you get to sit on both.

One Earthstalk government, just like the Sagan wanted,
and it's close to reality!

You remember the war: Caliph Selim versus the Federation. He won the, uh, "Battle of the Comets" so
we've given him status quo ante and he's become a hero
to Earthstalk natives. That's why he leads the Earthstalk
caucus; six votes in the Council of Eighteen, and one
vote in the Council of Nine.

He's that much more influential than a certain dwarf-
god who chairs the Federation caucus: I swing three
votes and one, respectively. But I am on a par with
Primate Haberhan of the bug-fictoid caucus—and by
now I've left out lots of names.

Let them introduce themselves and tell you where

*they stand! You'll learn soon enough, and I'm eager to zero in on your role. See, I've left six votes unaccounted for; six members who sit on both councils, one representing Luna, one Mars, one Helice, one Venus—*

*Get on with it? Well, the Carl Sagan has his voice in the person of Magda Szentes. And Olivia? —But I remember, she murdered you, didn't she?*

*She chose you anyway, perhaps out of penitence. Of us all, you're the most free to go your own way.*

*And now my job is done. Here's your magcard, I doubt Olivia will ever let you run out of money. You have a palace on Hab 1000, a decent army, and three guests, two keen on pumping iron as you seem to be. The plebiscite is scheduled for April 21st; plenty of time to get into the thick of things. Congratulations on your new life!*

# Chapter 43
## Day 33–Hab 1

"Not my idea of democracy," Torfinn said as he left
U Gyi's suite.

The dwarf god shrugged. "When have we had democracy? But INFOWEB is busy polling right and left,
and we know how people feel on every question. One
of Olivia's better tricks: questionnaires to learn what
people consider *good* arguments for colonizing Planet
Four Centauri, and *bad* arguments for staying home.
Not put so blatantly, but strangely the H-V debates she
sponsors have exactly that skew. The stay-at-homes are
looking dumber and dumber."

U Gyi slowed to catch his breath. "Her touch is light.
Too much manipulation can backfire. The truth is, Gatekeeper keeps us honest. Somehow she'll know if we
impose too much on our millions."

Level One had its own elevator. A cadre summoned
it on U Gyi's approach. The two got in, rode down, got
out again: "So this is it. The place of those breakfasts,

and Colonel Li's early doom. Christina swan *there*, and that's the chandelier."

"You remember well. Sometimes I wondered if you were listening," U Gyi answered.

"And now—U Gyi, are you nervous?"

"I'm bad at waiting. Express elevators take as long as twenty minutes."

Torfinn canted his head. "I thought you might be worried. Olivia didn't kill me, you know. *You* did. You gave me all the clues—U Gyi, you insult me not to be worried. You insult my intelligence."

"I didn't kill you. There was no premeditation."

"Back last fall. Four bodies: twin orientals, one black, and one white. You had four ways of matching couples, Alice and Cedric, Olivia and me. You knew Olivia was abused as a teen in her first life, and yet—"

"I didn't think. It was an oversight. Everyone makes me out to be omniscient!" As U Gyi protested a ring of cadres shifted closer. "Please," the god spoke to this audience. "I need no protection."

"That's true. I won't harm you," Torfinn said. "I just want you to understand I'm not stupid. You gave Olivia the body that would make her most unhappy, so you'd have a bargaining chip later. You stacked the deck. She'd want a new body and you'd oblige—for a price. Only what happened was that Ramnis came along with his great Secret—how'd you dream his mind? Is it on tape? I can't believe he's dead for good."

"I've not dreamt his mind. If you noticed I said nothing about him that wasn't observed by others, or easily inferred."

"I noticed no such thing. Occam's razor—or else you went to great pains to dream Kabwe and Nigel and Sergeant Prasad. *Prasad?* He died in that helicopter!"

"The pigmasker survived till splashdown. Some Sao Tome boat people popped a dreamskull on him. I understand they turned what's left of his helicopter into a holy oracle. Anyhow when Prasad saw what Mercury was like he began to think, and begged to come back. I remembered the name and took a personal interest in his application."

"Why cover for Ramnis? To protect him? Is that an item on our Councils' agenda, to condemn Senator Ramnis for theft of Earthstalk?"

"Would you vote—"

"I'd spare him. Perhaps I should have made you buy that admission. I'd have you pay for it by apologizing to Olivia. If she accepts—if she accepts you and I can start over, and grow to be friends."

U Gyi fell silent. Finally— "I'll do as you ask."

Torfinn raised an eyebrow. "And about Ramnis?"

"We have this strange relationship, Ramnis and I. He's my trickster, the thorn in my side, but he's earned the chance to live. I'd also vote not guilty, but as for protecting him? You've proven adept at deduction—if that helps you find him I'll be grateful for a wink and a nod."

"The *Sagan* would have done something."

U Gyi nodded. "Possibly. Here's your elevator. Ask your guests when you see them. They may be in position to know."

Cluster A, express elevator B. The car opened and Torfinn stepped in. U Gyi waved and the door slid shut.

The car accelerated up. A holograph shimmered into life. "Hi, you've never heard of me—I'm Clark Milos of Milos Surplus and I'd like to make your acquaintance. You know, *Kabajero* Oskarssen, there's a lot of junk up in the sixteen thousands following the recent war, and your licensed salvage agent—I'm not saying it has to be me, mind you—your licensed agent can most certainly do well out of the deal. Now you'll be hearing from others. We're no doubt indistinguishable to a man of affairs such as yourself, but one policy sets me apart: my six percent charity clause. All you do is name your favorite charity—"

Torfinn found the projo box and pushed MUERTO. Ah, the arrogance of power! Had he been too high-handed? Did he owe the lowly salvage agents of Earthstalk a hearing? He wrestled with this question, a prince with no firm political ideals, not even sure he should champion democracy. *Intellectually naked, without formed principles, merely amiable, and not always patient enough for amiability to triumph!*

Nine stops later he reached his capitol, his home. *U Gyi created me, now I create myself!* He stepped out, and into a military review.

A child's dream—his own toy army to play with! Torfinn extemporized admiration for his valiant Dirtgrubs, and the dozen amputees trooped out from the medical wards answered his questions. "There'd have been a hell of a lot more frostbite if the Caliph's mutes had waited another four hours," Caddo said off-handedly.

So light-spirited, but after all there'd be other bodies available, and these twelve had veterans' priority. Afterward: "Where's Christina? I was told of ramps and pools. She's moved, hasn't she?"

"Up to the Nulge Habs," Caddo responded. "An environment of her design: air and water equal so she can swim from one bubble into another. Much better for her skin and the other womties are collecting there—a little of everything on Earthstalk, and maybe they'll be able to breed."

"Hilda too? I'd like to say hello, even visit, but a trip like that must take days."

"Not when it's by the shuttle that brought me back." A woman rolled close in her wheelchair. Slim and black—

"You must be Alice!"

"Excuse me if I don't get up. I'm all right for a few hours every morning, but I'll need another week to get totally normal. Cedric's different. He's determined to turn into a hunk, at least that's what he *says*. I say he just likes to leer at Lissandra."

"Nonsense, dear. I like my women soft and spongy."

"Well, that's what you've got— Torfinn? You look like you've seen a ghost."

Torfinn looked side to side. "I must have someplace close we can settle and talk. Cedric, last I knew you were trapped in a racquetball court, a burning comet below your feet."

"U Gyi didn't tell you? Ah yes, he said he'd leave a few loose ends to wrap up—something for us to talk about and get to know each other. But let's sit down. No, first I'll fetch Lissandra: She's part of the story. Do you mind steering Alice? Damn dumb wheelchair only speaks Berber . . . Take that room there. You'll find trays of food just mysteriously appear."

Caddo cleared his throat. "Those dossiers—"

"I'll take 'em by tiepatch after we've got Alice put away. No, bad idea. How many did you say?"

"Fifteen major Earthstalk spokespeople. Then there's the *'Borg Hunt* inquiry. Are we going to throw Major Spensky to the winds? The guy's a lush. He arrests young starlets on trumped-up charges and somehow they end up in his bed. Hollywood wants self-rule."

"And I want everything to hang just another hour," Torfinn answered. "Would you station a guard at the door here and see I'm not visited by projo gladhanders?"

"Yes, sir." Caddo bowed off.

Torfinn said "Thank you" to Caddo's back, asking himself Magda's question: *How could a bold sea captain turn into a tame second-in-command?* He frowned. He'd seen stranger sacrifices for the sake of patriotism . . . or love?

Torfinn turned his attention forward. "Alice, I see a bed. I could prop up some pillows."

"I'd like that."

A pause during these exertions, until Alice settled in, and even after. Torfinn cast about for small talk. "You must be used to debility. When you launched down-stairs in that Nulge body—wait, that's the *other* Alice." Torfinn blushed. "Have I put my foot in it?"

"You mean do I know about Boy Alice's career? I've been dreaming Al's memories. The two of us are coming together again."

"And no resentments? Of all of us you were the most clearly manipulated."

Alice frowned. "I'm not on the council. Make of that

what you will. Perhaps it's because I'd have trouble cooperating with the *Sagan*. I'm not rational when it comes to schneggs."

"What are your plans?" Torfinn asked.

"To be Cedric's wife and watch H-V. But seriously, we're taking inventory of Earthstalk's shuttle fleet. By the time we've got our new government we'll be ready to establish a training academy for new pilots. Grades and licenses and nifty uniforms; all of us old geezers grandfathered in. I rather expect I'll end up admiral. —I shouldn't sound so cocky, should I? I should wheedle you for backing."

"Don't wheedle. I don't want you in the same mental compartment as Clark Milos of Milos Salvage. You're too good for that. —Ah, Cedric. And you must be—"

"Lissandra Orloff." She stepped forward and shook Torfinn's hand.

"Also known as Senjorino Nie!"

"But not in front of everyone," Cedric said hurriedly. "The H-V newscasters are full of speculations why she's proposed for the Council of Eighteen, but we don't like to give them the satisfaction of an answer. When Lissandra's ready to go public she can do it herself."

"Please sit," Torfinn invited. "Lissandra, you have a story to tell me."

"About that racquetball court? Not much of one. We just sat and waited. How can I do this with mere words—of course time was passing. We knew we had only so long; not at first, but then when it started getting really hot. That was a big room, but you can get claustrophobic *anywhere* when you're trapped—"

"Those were the battles we were fighting," Cedric agreed. "The psychological ones, and whether our soldier was going to die, and then I had some concern about my fingers and toes. I kept telling myself the pain was good. It meant they were alive, they wouldn't have to be amputated, but if those little things hurt that bad how could our companion manage with that great tear in his side?"

"But he did, and we nursed him and waited some more—"

*The racquetball court's door blew open and slammed shut; almost that quickly, but now there were schneggs inside, six of them carrying three rescue pods, and a seventh spraying the room with cold fog.*

*Senjorino Nie was uninjured, stronger than Cedric. She was first to rise, but in slow motion compared to the arachnoid creatures around her. She looked and they had the wounded soldier zipped and packaged away. She turned to see Cedric slide feet-first into his cylinder.*

*Pod controls labeled in Old High English? But now Senjorino Nie tilted off her feet. Strong limbs forced her into mummy posture, a mask was strapped over her face.*

*And then darkness and deafness, helpless monotony punctuated by swings and lurches, and sudden stops. Nie wiggled her fingers, and felt about the mask with her tongue.*

*A viewscreen switched on; an economy viewscreen, monotone and flat—not even holographic. The other functions of a rescue pod were so much more important that there was little to spare for video sophistication. A smarter camera might have compensated for the dazzle of thousand-degree flames: except for dancing schnegg-shadows this one showed only an utter white.*

*There was still no sound, not the least crackle as the escalator below her rescuers' feet turned to carbonaceous slag.*

*Time passed. The camera proved itself as the glow lessened and Senjorino Nie swung into the auroral void of space; less than perfectly black, to be sure; but she could see stars.*

*Schneggs with misshapen, half-molten legs set her pod spinning. Schneggs with red-hot clasper-hands shoved her off into the sky. Senjorino Nie counted her heartbeats. A three-minute eternity passed before she felt the THUNK that meant she'd not drift off to her death, an item of lost inventory in the midst of vast events.*

Torfinn listened: "As simple as that! But not simple getting the oredock doors open. How many schneggs lost hauling chunks of flaming comet out to space?"

"Not so many," Cedric answered. "Olivia's shuttles interposed a sunscreen and that helped. An exemplary act of cooperation."

"Suicidal for the schneggs. And more schneggs dashing into '520 with those rescue pods. You suppose they resent being treated like throwaway heroes?"

"They're artificial. Programmed for altruism."

"Angels," Torfinn muttered. "Ramnis was a throwaway hero, wasn't he? Just like the schneggs; but not at all like Alice here. Alice *human*, schnegg *fictoid*, Ramnis *cyborg*."

Lissandra shuddered. "The *Sagan* was so careful tightening his coils around me. Surely he had the capacity to save Ramnis. One of those times when I was sonicked he'd have made him tape his memories. He'd know how much we cared. Magda wouldn't cooperate with the *Sagan* unless she knew Ramnis was saved." Her voice trailed off. "Sure, maybe he was artificial in the beginning—"

Torfinn frowned. "He's alive, but hidden in another body." He stood up. "Lissandra, Alice, Cedric; my house is yours, but this is my first day on the job and Caddo has fifteen dossiers for me to read."

Fifteen power-brokers later Torfinn closed the drapes and slumped into his cushions, tired and alone. "Olivia? Can you hear me?"

Oh yeah. He re-parted the tapestries to lay bare his rank of viewscreens. "Olivia?"

"Yes, Torfinn. I've been afraid of this moment."

"It had to come."

Pause. "If you want to take another woman, I'll understand. You owe me nothing, certainly not loyalty. Not after what I did to you."

"Well, actually I was thinking of several—blond, red-head and brunette, a whole harem! Olivia, lighten up! You were always too tragic."

"Worse than tragic; I was the villain. I schemed and played puppetmaster games, and got my come-uppance. I'm better now. I'd like you to believe that. I'm free from my human vices."

"Do you know what I think? You've had three bodies and were miserable in two and now you'll decide never again. Don't let a couple failures blight you!"

Seconds passed. "I was deciding whether to laugh. I have to invoke an audio subroutine, and enter a series of parameters—it seems artificial, doesn't it? Yet I enjoy your jokes. Torfinn, most people only get one body. Don't be distressed if I draw the line at three. I rather like being INFOWEB. Enough to change the master password and keep from being dispossessed.

"So there! Your wife was never very warm. Now she's all head and no heart. But she still loves you and wants you happy. Is there anything I can do for you?"

*You can tell me about you and Captain Caddo.* But Torfinn left that demand unspoken. Conceivably there was nothing to be said. Conceivably Caddo had concealed his feelings, and now it was too late for Olivia to know about them. A tragedy he could never talk about!

*Someday I'll get Caddo drunk, far from the ears of INFOWEB.*

The pause had grown too long. "Tell me what to think of the *Sagan,*" Torfinn said. "Is he good or evil? Ramnis and Magda and Alice and Senjorino Nie, all pushed around like pawns on a gameboard."

"We had a war. There'd be wars anyhow; many wars to unify Earthstalk, and all of them failures. Why didn't the *Sagan* use his schneggs to impose unity way back on Day Zero? Maybe he didn't want to break three million spirits, and colonize our new world with a race of slaves. Now we have peace with pride, and a modicum of diversity—Torfinn, what do you know of game theory? You try to break a problem into a series of yes-no decisions, determine the outcome for each decision, and then weigh the value of that outcome. Everything the *Sagan* has done for two decades was calculated to solve a single great problem: how to get humanity to the stars. If he were human he'd be forced to reduce decision points to a minimum to keep track of all the possibilities. He'd have been forced to be subtle, because arrant manipulation of events draws in outside factors—"

"He *was* subtle!"

"Oh, sort of. The beauty of being more than human is that you aren't limited by the complexity of the problem. You go for the optimum solution. And of course the end justifies the means. It does, you know. The end justifies the means: it's just that most Machiavellis use drastic means and fail to get what they want."

Torfinn paused. "Uh, a business question?"

"Certainly."

"Have the Worlds of Sol launched their intercept fleets?"

"Following perihelion we have a projected rendezvous two AU's out, short of most asteroids. Under these circumstances several habitat ships have been obliged to retrofit and launch, much more to come."

Torfinn scratched himself thoughtfully. "One more question. Has Gatekeeper been asked what she thinks of all this? Will she respond before the plebiscite?"

"She'd better! If not I've already concocted a fake message. She should learn something about wetbrain diplomacy. We can't all conform to *her* schedule. She should try adapting to ours!"

Torfinn leaned back. "Thank you. Um, would you consider being my travel agent? There's a bunch of bigwigs I'd like to see before April 9th."

"Names?"

"Chancellor Olgien Teg of Upper Downside. Father Abraham Von Mutha. Liam Venbo. Tabenna O'Shea—"

"—Names from those dossiers. Torfinn, I transmitted fifteen files to your screens. Do you want to visit all fifteen? If so I'll make the arrangements."

"Good. See, I can go upstairs, but because of the gravity some of these can't come down."

"I'll get right to work. Goodnight, Torfinn. Do you need a warm body?"

Torfinn's turn to pause. "When I do I'll let you know. Okay?"

"Okay. Goodnight."

*Goodnight?* Torfinn exhaled pent air. "Olivia? I'm afraid—I mean, it's too early and the mood's wrong, and what the hell: if I don't say it now it'll get harder and harder. *I love you.* I know it sounds clumsy, and maybe you don't believe me—"

"I believe you. Cross my heart!" And this time Olivia invoked her laughter subroutine.

## Chapter 44
## Day 36–Hab 2108

Torfinn's speech was predictable, and adequately delivered; it emphasized the need for Earthstalk's cultures to learn to live together, and the important role Hollywood had to play in educating the public.

The speech was prefaced by marches and music, and followed by visually-enhanced fireworks and flights of doves. Through the spectacle Torfinn stood, smiling and waving just often enough to prove he hadn't been replaced by a life-size facsimile.

At last the ceremonies were taped and over, and the grander personages made their collective escape. After a final photo opportunity most of Torfinn's escort faded away at the top of the Hollywood escalator. Only a handful of stars remained to show him into Major Spensky's palatial suite.

After handshakes they left again. A young woman led Torfinn into the next room.

During arrangements these last days Major Spensky's telephone image showed a nebbish—average in physicality and slightly balding. Essentially this was the same man that Torfinn's murdered incarnation first promoted from corporal to sergeant, but videos can be doctored to lie.

Spensky's present appearance came as a shock. Though his pyjamas were exquisitely tailored they could not disguise the extra inches around his waist, nor his liverish complexion, nor the broken capillaries around his nose.

Spensky lurched to his feet, bowed, and sank back into his plush chair. "Sorry I couldn't make the ceremony in person," he spoke thickly. "Doctor's orders, and thank God for projos. —Would you like a drink?" He reached to his side and stroked a spangled buttock. "Angelique, make a drink for Councillor Oskarssen."

"No thanks," Torfinn answered. "My time here is nearly used up, I'm afraid I can't socialize."

"Really? There are profound opportunities here."

"Like Angelique?" Torfinn grinned. "You've got it pretty good."

Spensky gestured at a crystal bowl of Butter-Bubs, then plucked one for himself. "It seems like a miracle. With the Federation's backing the miracle will continue. Not to say I deserve it, because I don't."

"I'm glad to hear you realize that. Spensky, some weeks ago you were Ramnis's creature. Then Olivia asked you to do an about-face. You orchestrated a campaign to portray Senator Ramnis as a cyborg—an evil cyborg."

Spensky flushed. His hand shook as he reached for his glass. He lifted his drink and swallowed. The silence extended as he sat it down again. Eyes lowered, he finally spoke. "That's true enough, although 'orchestrating' is a pretty fancy way of describing it. I just passed on my orders."

"Soon afterward an H-V show went on the air—'Borg Hunt. What did you have to do with that?"

Spensky clasped his hands together. "Same thing—no, that's not right. Monsieur Cauteleux went over my head. I don't know what I'd have said, but—"

Torfinn raised his hand. "Olivia says Cauteleux was working in competition with her people. U Gyi says he didn't have anything to do with *'Borg Hunt.'*"

Spensky colored again. "Bullshit. We had a code. When I used it U Gyi knew it was me and not some fake. Same the other way around. If it wasn't U Gyi, then someone knew the code and could imitate his voice."

"That's right." Torfinn looked around the room as if to spy out any invisible angels. After a pause he continued: "Major Spensky, you're an easy tool. Too easy—you can be tricked. What I'm telling you now is not a trick, and it's not meant to be countermanded unless I come here in the flesh to do so. Understand?"

Spensky spoke in a small voice tinged with hope. "Then you're keeping me on?"

"You'll continue to serve the Federation. You'll keep a low profile until we're safely past the asteroids, stepping aside so we can talk directly with your more competent subordinates. I suggest keeping to this suite as much as possible.

"After that we expect some special efforts from you: some dramatic outrages. Drunkenness. Wild orgies. Flagrant missuse of your police and your courts. We've resurrected an ancient Italian movie director to script all this out—he was famous for these things in his time. The public will demand that Hollywood clean house, and you'll be retired on an adequate pension." Torfinn grinned. "Maybe we'll even work in a promotion to general as a capstone to your remarkable career."

Another pause, another swallow of vodka. Spensky set down his empty glass. "Why?" he whispered.

"Hollywood wants self-rule, a special charter from the Council. Some people are against it. They're not your friends, Spensky, no matter what they say. Let them win and they'll have you out and their own figurehead in as fast as Jack Lightning. At least this way you get a pension."

Spensky closed his eyes. When he opened them again he spoke. "Take her with you."

"Angelique?"

"People figure my head's about to roll. When you leave this office and I'm still in charge, I'll be a big shot until she opens her mouth and tells them the truth."

Torfinn stood and smiled. "You won't tell anyone, will you—Captain?"

Angelique drew erect and saluted. "No sir."

"Then carry on and keep an eye on things." Torfinn turned back to Major Spensky. "Goodbye. I can find my own way out."

# Chapter 45

# Day 36–Hab 11,700

The room was filled with babble. Caliph Selim listened to a twelve-point inquiry from Nodus Gordi while Magda read a batch answer to the Sisters of Helice. "We'll contemplate the evacuation of anyone who wants to go, if you have ships, and a place to take them. Four million *bzzt* *tzat*

Her mic went dead. The room fell silent and a new voice spoke. "BATCH TRANSMISSION FROM STARGATE: MARCH 29, 3727. WE SPEAK FROM THESE PREMISES: EARTHSTALK HAS DETACHED FROM EARTH TO CARRY A HUMAN COLONY TO ALPHA CENTAURI. EASTHSTALK IS NOT YET A POLITICAL UNITY. NO PROVISIONS EXIST FOR AN EARTHSTALK POWER SUPPLY TO COMPENSATE FOR LOSS OF SUNLIGHT EN ROUTE. FEAR OF STARGATE OPPOSITION TO EARTHSTALK'S MISSION MAY HINDER UNITY, AND PREVENT THE WORLDS OF SOL FROM PROVIDING SUPPORT. WE ADDRESS THIS LAST CONCERN.

"THE SO-CALLED 'BUG' IS THE UNIVERSE'S HIGHEST FORM OF LIFE. PARENT PRIMITIVES CULMINATE EVOLUTION BY TRANSCENDING TO IMMORTAL BUG FORM. FIVE BILLION YEARS AGO THE FIRST PRIMITIVES DID SO WITHOUT BUG NURTURE. NOW OUR STARGATES PROTECT SEVERAL HUNDRED NURSERY SYSTEMS, AND PREVENT THE CATASTROPHE THAT WIPED OUT OUR FIRST PARENT WETBRAINS."

The speaker did not need to pause for breath. Her breaks were oratorical, tuned to human ears. "YOU HAVE HEARD OF DINOSAUR KILLERS? COMETS CLEARED EARTH OF MOST FORMS OF LIFE TIME AND AGAIN. A WORLD NEVER STIMULATED BY SUCH TRAGEDIES NEVER DEVELOPS INTELLIGENCE: A WORLD TOO BADLY MAULED WILL DIE.

"EARTH WOULD HAVE DIED. WE INTERVENED TO LIMIT DAMAGE, BUT THE CENTAURI WORLDS HAVE NO STARGATE. WE CANNOT INTERVENE THERE. PLANET FOUR MAY BE PLEASANT AFTER SEEDING, BUT WHY WAS IT BARREN BEFORE?

"WE DO NOT PERMIT PARENT PRIMITIVES TO USE OUR STARGATES FOR INTERSTELLAR TRAVEL, BECAUSE OF THE DANGER OF BIODISASTER, EXACERBATED BY CONFRONTATIONS BETWEEN WETBRAINS, WHOSE LUSTS OFTEN RESULT IN WAR. OUR POLICIES ARE THOUGHTFUL AND PROTECTIVE. YOU RESENT THEM. YOUR DEPARTURE IS A WILLFUL ACT MORE APPROPRIATE TO CHILDREN THAN PARENTS, BUT SINCE YOUR DESTINATION IS UNTENANTED WE WILL NOT PREVENT IT, NOR PUNISH THOSE WHO AID YOU.

"WE DO THINK, THOUGH, THAT THE *CARL SAGAN* SHOULD KNOW BETTER. HE REPRESENTS THAT MASS OF BUGS IN THE SOLAR SYSTEM TOO BLINDLY LOYAL TO THE HUMAN SPECIES; AS WELL AS THOSE 'DEAD' WHO PRE-

FER SIMULATED ADVENTURE, PUNCTUATED BY
REINCARNATION, TO REAL LIFE AS A MORE
PERFECT FORM. TO YOU WE ADDRESS OUR
NEXT REMARKS. YOU ARE YOUNG, NONE OVER
TWO THOUSAND YEARS OLD. WITH AGE COMES
OBJECTIVITY AND ACCEPTANCE INTO OUR CIV-
ILIZATION. DO NOT FRUSTRATE YOUR HOPES
BY PUTTING DANGEROUS DISTANCES BETWEEN
US.

"THE CHOICE IS YOURS."

Magda exhaled. "That's it. Amen to Earth. We're on
our way."

Selim looked at her quizzically. "More than before?"

The Caliph wasn't in on the plot and Magda modified
her answer accordingly. "Beats there a heart in Solar
space who never fluttered in resentment against Stargate?
Look at the favor they've done! Help us, and strike
against smug alien patronage, a blow without fear of
punishment!"

Twenty-one years was plenty of time for the *Sagan* to
launch a transmitter from Fortuna into Tombaugh-land.
In proper sequence "Stargate's" message washed across
the solar system, past Chittaworld and Nodus Gordii
and Mercury's City of the Dead. Earthstalk was close to
the sun, and any immediate energy-gift was merely
symbolic, but everywhere the answer was the same.
High Station One became a star as its mirrors bathed
Hab 11,700 in light. Luna brightened sector by sector.
Suddenly Venus glared blue-white. Minutes later Mars
Deltaport became a ruby jewel.

Ships would come, and bigger power-lasers would be
built. Despite the carefully concocted doubts of Stargate,
Earthstalk was on its way. In an already saturated communications room phones began to blink. "Answer this
one," Olivia spoke from the intercom.

Magda looked up. "I don't take orders."

"Sorry. I know you hate me but we have friends in
common. Torfinn, for one."

"When I first met Torfinn back in 2083 he was a jerk."

"And now in 3727 you're an overblown, self-righteous—"

"Ladies! The most splendid news. No time for name-calling!" Selim stood and looked up. "Olivia, you're supposed to be passionless. Magda, where would my Caliphate be without INFOWEB?"

Magda pursed her lips and keyed her handset. Pause. "Excuse me, Torfinn. It's been noisy here. Yes, I heard Gatekeeper."

"We need to meet," Torfinn responded. "I'm coming to visit you. We have fences to mend. What do you think? Great news—"

"I think you belong either to U Gyi, or Olivia."

"Then you're wrong, and please spare me a military reception. Hollywood's done a drums and fife trip—I'll skip the details but you can watch channel 40 if you like."

"We can assure you a complete absence of pomp."

Hours later Torfinn was escorted into the Garden of Tulips. Chairs were arranged, the Caliph's dais just slightly elevated. Torfinn took a side seat and accepted a fruit drink of unfamiliar kind, red and cold and deliciously bitter-sweet.

"So you're the new Torfinn," Magda said.

"I'm to INFOWEB what you are to the *Sagan*. Olivia has news: another poll. Gatekeeper's speech has made a difference, at least two percentage points already. We're going to win this plebiscite. She'd tell you this herself, but there's bad blood between you. I want that to change. I think she does too."

Magda sipped her drink. "I was angry at Ramnis for abandoning me. I was angry about being arrested. I was mad at my fickle friends for changing sides and making political compromises. That's why I came up here, to get even."

"And you *did!* Quite an achievement, and now you're

surrounded by such strength that my army puts away all thoughts of revenge. So can we start over?"

"A truce. I won't resurrect old quarrels—"

"No need!" Selim laughed. "Won't we have fresh ones soon enough, human nature being what it is?"

"—If Olivia cans it with the fat jokes. 'Overblown!' That's what she called me last time. My body's not public property."

Torfinn protested. "But you're just pregnant."

Selim looked at Magda and all was silence. After a moment she nodded. "Yes, dear. I was about to tell you. But Torfinn's wrong, I'm not that far along. These billows are mere camouflage."

Torfinn paled. "I thought everyone knew!"

Selim's smile was subtle. "Some of us did, but kept quiet. Magda, it was obvious you had a reason for your silence. I respected that, but I'm a great observer of women's bodies and the toilets of the Seraglio have built-in equipment for several kinds of tests."

Magda reached for his hand. "I *do* have reasons for silence. Now the secret's out can we keep it among ourselves? I'd rather be thought fat. When that's no longer possible I'll go into concealment, my vidcams doctored to project a false image."

Torfinn set down his glass and looked out at the garden, thinking he'd best keep his mouth shut among these mysteries: he'd blundered once already. Magda guessed at his discomfort. "Yes, Torfinn, it does have something to do with Ramnis. That's all you need to know."

*Well, that tells me something. She doesn't confide in Selim.* Torfinn waited for a better moment to bare his heart. It came an hour later. "I know about your dream," he whispered. "I know about the ghost woman. It seems strange Gatekeeper would make such familiar points: the five-billion-year thing, and dinosaurs. Olivia told me she was preparing a fake message just in case—"

Magda patted his arm. "U Gyi, the *Sagan* and Olivia. Yes, we can work together when we have to. We're not as mutually hostile as we let people believe."

"Won't it piss Gatekeeper off? People talking with her voice?"

"It might." Magda shrugged. "We worried about that."

"And—?"

"And came up with a deal. See, one thing the ghost woman told me: she likes to experiment. She's fascinated with ecology, the interaction of different forms of life."

Torfinn nodded. "You and that tumblebug."

Magda led Torfinn further into the garden, found a bench, and sat to leave him room. Torfinn paused. Enough room for a Caliph's favorite? Diplomatically he perched at a distance, then bent to listen as she spoke sotto voce:

"Earth itself is too precious to toy with, precious and already messed up, but we said we were willing to accept some risks. We plan to close off the abandoned parts of Earthstalk. If there's an eco-crisis let's wait till we have a whole planet to cushion the shock. I don't think she'll send us tumblebugs, though. What we're suggesting is trilobites, eurypterids, armored fish, thecodonts—the whole point is they didn't die out from evolutionary inferiority. Evolution doesn't teach you to deal with comets. We're all from the same planet, so we might learn to get along—"

"Dinosaurs freighted up from Stargate? I don't believe it," Torfinn answered.

"Don't believe it," Magda laughed. "U Gyi comes in useful again. He's got the equipment. All Gatekeeper has to do is whistle up the code and he can patch some DNA together. It keeps him busy for 70 years, and nobody minds that. A little less energy for schemes and plots!"

"And you've proposed this to Gatekeeper? Any response?"

"Nothing very loud. Just a stream of four-letter gibberish." Magda's face broke into a broad smile. "She bought it. We're home free!"

# Chapter 46

# Day 71–Hab 1000

*Rap, rap.* "Recess is over. Will the Council of Eighteen please come to order?" *Rap, rap, rap.* "We've heard testimony on the *'Borg Hunt* imbroglio, and *that's* rebounded into a motion of extreme censure against Senator Ramnis, with all the fans of that H-V show convinced he's a villain—"

Chancellor Teg's unfamiliar projo image shimmered to her feet. "I object. This is supposed to be a roll-call vote. You're using it to voice your opinion."

Christina's image blinked back as she swam imperturbably in place 35,000 kilometers away. "Do I have your attention, at least? A roll-call, then: on whether Senator Ramnis's activities justified his murder—"

"And if they did he's got to *stay* murdered, at least inside our jurisdiction!"

*Rap, rap.* "Chancellor Teg, interrupt me once more and I'll order your projo-box to show us what you *really* look like! All right, from left to right around the room: Yos Monango."

Another strange face. "Censure."

"Doctor Nicole Dremont."

"Censure."

"Lissandra Orloff."

"No. No Censure."

"Chancellor Olgien Teg."

"Censure."

"Caliph Selim the Sixth."

"Abstain."

"Doctor Cedric Chittagong."

"No censure."

"Uh—You're the Chittaworld representative, aren't you? Do I really have to call you—"

"Rhett Butler? I'm afraid so," the projo announced, a twinkle in his eye. "Anyhow, my vote's 'No censure.' "

"Sir Thomas Haberhan."

The Primate of the bugs of Mercury shimmered indistinctly. Earthstalk convention called for a human shape, monastic humility spoke against pretense. His compromise figure spoke without moving his lips: "Abstain."

"Perry O'Doughan."

The head of Luna B Team collected his thoughts. "Ahh—no censure."

"Torfinn Oskarssen."

"No censure. Only praise."

"Magda Szentes."

Magda's projo stood, slim and glamorous. "No censure."

The voting continued, three more abstentions, three more "No censures." Total: "Only four votes against Senator Ramnis? My, we *are* out of step with the H-V crowd! I'm afraid that means we'll be proceeding against Monsieur Cauteleux as per Dr. Chittagong's charges—"

"On what grounds?" demanded Chancellor Teg. "We can't pass laws after the fact, and there was nothing but anarchy at the time!"

"A reasonable defense. I think there's precedent—"

The Council session continued, debating the establishment of a committee to look into a unified Earthstalk law-code. Other committees were formed: *Names* to

put an end to "Planet Four," *Education* to review the
curricula of four universities and a new space academy,
*Ecology* to inventorize everything that lived and moved
on Earthstalk, *Nutrition* to look into charges that
Earthstalk's food was overly fiddled with stimulants and
addictive agents.

But no *Colonization Committee*. That could be tabled
for another generation. Even Olivia seemed to think so,
so Torfinn shrugged and played along.

After they adjourned Torfinn noticed Magda and Rhett
Butler standing together. He left them to their remote-
control intimacies. Among all these photonic ghosts,
Lissandra and Cedric were the only other beings of
flesh. The three walked through an etherial Christina
on their way out of the chamber.

Alice intercepted Cedric outside the door. Lissandra
continued on, Torfinn her escort. They walked in nervous silence. At the entrance to her suite Senjorino Nie
turned. "You're looking good to me, Councillor. I've
been ogling men lately—am I perverted, or not? I'm a
little curious about my ability to go further."

"You could always switch sexes."

"No, there's a part of me that's flowering as a woman.
I'd like to explore that. I've talked to Olivia—"

She blushed and faltered. Torfinn tried to think what
to say, something to prove he wasn't shocked. "You . . .
I'd like to, uh—you have some etchings you'd like to
show me?"

"Etchings? Oh yes, my *etchings!*" Lissandra laughed
and carded her door, then Torfinn stepped inside.

"You're sure?" Rhett asked Magda back in the Council chamber. "I don't like the idea of shoving a baby's
soul aside, no matter how undeveloped."

Magda looked around and saw a few more Council-
lors wink out, the room no longer illumined by their
glow. The cameras were long dead—or were they?
"Rendezvous D," she whispered, and disappeared.

A second later Rhett blinked into life before her
again, both standing on the helical track that spiraled

around an abandoned ziggurat, one empty shop after another. "Madwoman Mall," he said, but thanks to the new Mufti's vigilant enforcement of Islamic charity, the mother of dead Zoran was nowhere in sight.

Their privacy was protected by electronic chaff. Local "malfunctioning" equipment pulsed so strongly that even in this protected spot Magda's image flickered. "I'm just repeating what the *Sagan* tells me," she whispered. "Both parents had Souldancer bodies. We're of a breed designed to provide flesh to imported souls, all sorts of funny cyborg talents built into our brains. When they took you to temple eight days after birth—"

"Umm—"

"Excuse me. When they took *Ramnis* to the temple that's what happened. I don't want an autistic baby so I need to have it happen again."

Slowly Rhett grinned. "I'll be damned! It's all going to work out!"

"To unbelievable precision. I'll be term much the same time we rendezvous with the rescue fleet. You can hand over your Council duties to the next gorgeous hunk from Chittaworld, and quietly disappear."

"I'll have trouble calling you Mom," Rhett admitted. "A pretty perverse setup—"

"You'll adapt. A baby's brain grows and changes and drops neural connections. Your old memories will fade just as they did last time. We'll wait until you're in your teens to let you re-dream them. That's when you'll fully wake to what you were."

"A teen-age kid with prospects. Do you plan to be another Seraglio mother, pushing me for Caliph? A risky business."

"Would you like that?"

Rhett mused. "It has its good points, but I don't think I'm right for the job. I'm too restless. I need adventure, it's like a drug to me."

Magda shrugged. "You'll find enough to keep you busy. By the time you're grown to manhood we'll be out between the stars, where no wetbrain has ever been before. Who knows . . ."

# GLOSSARY

**beefer:** a Status Five Earthstalker, superior only to Status Six *drabs*.

**bodysnatcher:** one who kidnaps a body to replace its soul with another.

**bug:** any combination of cybernetic *soul* and non-organic *mobility sheath*.

**bug-monk:** a monastic bug whose Order services dead souls, maintains industrial facilities, and works to extend scientific knowledge.

**dirtgrub:** a human reared on Earth, ignorant of Earthstalk manners and norms.

**drab:** an Earthstalker of lowest class, shaven and deprived of rights.

**dreamtape:** a memory cassette designed to be used with a *dream helmet* (or *dreamskull*), allowing the dreamer to learn from a dead soul's memories without necessarily being displaced by that dead soul.

**fan:** a human who repetitively dreams the soul of his/her *hero* to become another incarnation of that hero.

314

**fictoid:** a type-E bug able to project holographic images of a fictional character in spontaneous animation.

**fictoid soul:** a soul artificially designed to identify with and behave like a famous figure of history or fiction.

**god:** a soul enhanced by memory dreaming, one who accrues a vastened identity over the lifetimes of several bodies, and who incarnates simultaneously in several bodies.

**hab, habitat:** a ten-story section of Earthstalk, capable of maintaining a viable environment for its inhabitants for days or weeks in the event of some external disaster.

**immortifact:** a helmet used to record, store and transmit the user's soul. A *dreamskull* can also do these things, but an immortifact's more powerful protocol allows it to replace that stored soul with another to permit reincarnation or bodyswapping.

**INFOWEB:** any CAD/CAM expert computer network in charge of resource distribution throughout a sizeable environment.

**node:** a section of Earthstalk consisting of a factory, a space dock, and four habitats.

**piggybacker:** a soul stored "behind" a primary soul within a single body/mobility sheath. While the primary soul handles routine functions, the piggyback soul is able to advise or displace the primary soul in an emergency.

**projo:** a projected, mobile 3-D human image. Projo equipment is standard gear among type-E *fictoid* bugs.

**robot:** a combination of depersonalized "soul" and special-function sheath, adapted to perform a repetitive or dangerous job.

**schwarzenegger, schnegger, schnegg:** a type-F bug, generally endowed with a *fictoid soul* optimized for military functions, altruistic heroism and rapid response to orders. Schnegg mobility sheaths include a wide array of weapons.

**shadbolts:** A charged-particle weapon of limited intelligence.

**sonics, sonic belt:** a Heegie weapon that temporarily

impairs the human ability to concentrate, and therefore to function.

**Souldancer:** a member of a dispersed neo-tribal society whose religion promotes colorful action as opposed to tepidity. Seven centuries ago Souldancer kings ruled a few negligible desert realms, neither before nor since they have risen so high. Nevertheless they retain a disfunctional aristocracy.

**space-bug:** a bug with solar wings or other adaptions to provide propulsion in space. Also called *microships*.

**tiepatch:** a multi-window computer terminal worn over the eyes as a pair of glasses.

**wetbrain:** an intelligent but organic creature: human or womtie.

**womtie:** an amphibious species; a composite of human, otter and manatee genotypes. Rare human/womtie offspring are infertile.

**wormroot:** a genetically-manipulated saprophytic plant which makes its host capable of *8-yield* photosynthesis and taxes the resultant extra food production. Its ability to do this with *any* host gave rise to spreading jungles and made civilized life impossible in Africa and Eurasia.